Polite
Calamities

ALSO BY JENNIFER GOLD

Halfway to You

Keep Me Afloat

The Ingredients of Us

Polite Calamities

A Novel

JENNIFER GOLD

LAKE UNION
PUBLISHING

Published by Lake Union Publishing, Seattle

www.apub.com

Amazon, the Amazon logo, and Lake Union Publishing are trademarks of Amazon.com, Inc., or its affiliates.

ISBN-13: 9781662521089 (paperback)
ISBN-13: 9781662521096 (digital)

Cover design by Faceout Studio, Elisha Zepeda
Cover image: © RetroAtelier / Getty; © Marco Govel / Stocksy;
© Anan Kaewkhammul / Shutterstock

Printed in the United States of America

For Violet, who taught me that softness can be a strength.
And for all the women who lift me up: thank you.

AUTHOR'S NOTE

This book delves into the topics of infertility and chronic pain, specifically related to how they can affect a woman's sense of self-worth. My character June engages in harmful self-talk in relation to these conditions, and her thoughts might be hard for some readers. I offer this caution in case you have struggled with negative self-talk in relation to your body and are sensitive to these topics.

PROLOGUE

October 1966

The official report listed the cause of the fire at Mrs. Hurst's seaside mansion as "unknown."

The fire department cited the blown transformer. The gasoline can. But the wreckage was so thorough that they couldn't say for certain.

Partygoers made guesses about extension cords near the pool, lit cigarettes in close proximity to velvet drapery, the stove left on to keep the fondue hot.

Housewives in the neighborhood whispered mostly about the party's host: how she wasn't well liked even before her husband died; how, thereafter, she became volatile. To them, the logical explanation was that her carelessness had simply caught up to her.

Arson was not considered. Sometimes there's power in being underestimated.

1

Winifred Hurst wasn't good at fitting in, but she was great at throwing parties—and this was her best yet, if she did say so herself.

Three hundred people had come, mingling in all corners of the Seacastle, the Hursts' sprawling beach cottage. In the ballroom, a swing band's snare cracked and trumpets pealed. Ladies wearing expensive gowns sloshed martinis on the curved staircase. Glasses broke in the parlor and were promptly swept up by the staff. The chandelier in the foyer tinkled from the vibrations of footsteps, voices, music.

Winifred had developed her skill for hosting parties shortly after her mother left, when she was eleven and friendless. Her father had said, *If no one invites you to a party, throw one!* She'd taken that lesson into adulthood and into her new husband's old-money existence. Bruce wanted the families of his world—with their stratospheric legacies and exclusive proclivities—to welcome her.

But they did not care for Winifred.

Bruce had hoped the other wives would come around, but so far, exactly *none* of his tactics—gala tickets, tennis lessons, salon appointments—had worked, so Winifred insisted that they host an end-of-summer soiree before everyone vacated their summer homes and returned to New York and Boston.

The beauty of hosting was that it gave Winifred something to do or somewhere to be at all times—the perfect guarantee against tedious etiquette, loaded small talk, and self-consciousness. Winifred wasn't like the society housewives. Her father was a philosophy professor, and she'd practically grown up at NYU, eventually getting her own degree in art history. Beyond engaging in simple pleasantries, she often sensed that she came across as overly direct in her opinions or unrefined in her habits—but as host, she had the excuse to stay busy.

As she wove through her home with a bottle of champagne, flitting from clique to clique, topping off glasses, she was both a part of the crowds and apart from them. Everywhere she looked, people were red-faced and drunk and having the time of their lives. All because of *her*.

Winifred paused on the fringes, admiring her work. A hand grazed her hip, breath warmed her neck, and before she could think, Bruce was wrapping his arms around her middle. "Where've you been hiding?" he murmured into her hair.

"Everywhere," Winifred said, breathless. She turned to face him, and his arms relaxed, one hand lingering on her waist as she asked, "Where have *you* been?"

"My study." He didn't need to elaborate. Despite the season, business didn't cease; Bruce made deals like Winifred threw parties: expertly, and with pride.

"Do try to have *some* fun tonight, will you?" Winifred chided.

Bruce smiled, the late-night stubble on his tan face making the expression appear devilish. "Anything for you, dear."

She shoved his arm. There were times she still couldn't believe she'd found Bruce. The nice clothes and fancy mansions were mere accessories to the connection they shared. They both appreciated nature, philosophy, art. They both believed in feminism and ate way too much fondue. They both loved to tease and laugh. It didn't hurt that Bruce came with an entire community, a guarantee against the loneliness that'd plagued Winifred's life until that point.

Winifred didn't mind that Bruce couldn't have children—she didn't know how to be a mother, having had no real example. It didn't matter that Bruce worked all the time, either—when they came together, it was fireworks. Winifred had grown up with a certain independence that most men found tiresome—but not Bruce. As her beloved father liked to say, Winifred and Bruce were a team.

"Have you visited with the other ladies?" Bruce asked.

Winifred hefted the champagne bottle. "I've been a little busy."

"Freddie, what's the point of hosting this party if not to socialize?"

Winifred folded her arms, still clutching the neck of the bottle. "Isn't hosting obvious enough, without me badgering them?"

"*Befriending* them," Bruce amended.

"I don't want to appear desperate," Winifred said, though that yacht had already sailed. "Besides, I can befriend them at their precious charity auction next week."

The Society of Philanthropic Women was an organization that sought to recognize and assist the efforts of women supporting *other* charities. It was a glorified sorority for the ladies who summered here in Wave Watch—a self-indulgent hat on a hat—but all of Bruce's friends' wives were a part of it, and Winifred had promised him she'd try harder to fit in. She *wanted* to fit in.

But she still had her dignity.

Though she had joined the SPW's planning committee and was hosting the biggest party of the summer, none of the other wives had so much as said hello to her tonight.

Bruce tugged her close and kissed her temple. "I just want them—"

"To like me," Winifred finished.

Bruce wanted so badly for his social circle—one that went back for generations, like a linked chain—to welcome her. But Winifred didn't fit. She was academic rather than domestic, passionate rather than mild. She was *modern*, while many of these people were stuck in the past. Sometimes she wondered if becoming friends with them was even possible, when they so clearly shunned her as punishment for what had happened at her wedding. But she didn't voice her doubt now.

Winifred placed her fingers on her husband's sandpapery cheek. "What matters is that *you* like me."

His mouth softened. "I don't just *like* you, Freddie." He squeezed her hip.

She met his cool gray eyes and smiled.

It was a complete fluke that she'd met Bruce Hurst, head of an investment empire, at a fundraising event put on by NYU. Her father had brought her along as his favorite conversation piece: the charming daughter who could wipe the floor with the men who dared to challenge her.

Men at fancy functions were always trying to stoke their own egos by extinguishing her fire—or, at least, by attempting to. But Bruce hadn't. His family possessed enough wealth and importance for him to exist without ever having to prove himself. This gave him a friendly, approachable quality that other cerebral men lacked. He wasn't threatened by Winifred. Rather, he was stimulated.

When Bruce later proposed, Winifred worried she'd cause a social rift in his New England existence. She wasn't refined or conservative or traditional, but that's what he loved about her. He'd been a bachelor for so long that everyone was guaranteed to love Winifred, the woman who'd locked him down. That was the theory, at least.

The reality was people whispering behind her back, claiming she'd married Bruce for his money (which, in her opinion, was the least interesting thing about him). And now, over three years into their marriage, she still hadn't made any meaningful friendships. The only support system she had here was Bruce; she told herself she didn't need anyone else, but in truth, she craved the connection that only other women could offer. So she ignored the petty judgments, participated in all their social clubs, and tried to make nice, telling herself that one day, she'd succeed in winning them over.

"I see Maxwell," Bruce said, raising a hand to get the other man's attention. "Mind if I . . . ?"

She kissed his cheek. "Run along."

He smiled the crooked, boyish smile that was reserved only for her, a single dimple puckering his scruffy cheek. "You look stunning tonight, dear," he said. "Try to enjoy your party, too, hmm?"

She raised the champagne bottle. "I will," she drawled.

Bruce squeezed her hip again, and then he was parting the crowd with his broad shoulders, a bull cutting through a herd of cows. On the opposite side of the room, he clapped a man on the back and was greeted with a big grin and an animated handshake. She waited for Bruce to steal a glance at her, and when he did, she blew a kiss.

Winifred turned away, topping off more champagne glasses as she traveled down the hall. In the foyer, she flagged down a waiter carrying a tray of hors d'oeuvres and reached for a stuffie. The clam-and-stuffing balls might not've been the most refined choice, but she thought the Rhode Island delicacy would bring a whimsical, local flair to the rest of tonight's menu. She chewed—careful not to disturb her lipstick—and then placed her hand on the waiter's arm.

"It seems to be going well, doesn't it?" she asked, speaking low.

He flushed, nodded.

No one ever spoke to the waitstaff, but she found them the easiest to converse with. She might've paid for their politeness, but when she showed them the respect they deserved, the kindness was reciprocated. Unlike with the academics at NYU or the elite in Wave Watch, this was a social transaction that wouldn't be leveraged against her.

"How are you?" she pressed. "Do you need a break?"

His throat bobbed. "No, ma'am."

"All right. Well, will you go to the ballroom? The musicians are due for an intermission, and anyone who's been dancing will be ravenous." She swigged the last gulp of champagne, then pressed the empty bottle into his grasp. "And please take this back to the kitchen."

Another nod, this time to excuse himself.

Winifred rolled the bubbles over her tongue and made her rounds through quieter rooms, greeting guests and clearing used plates. In the first-floor sunroom, uppity old-money wives—the ones she was supposed to befriend—were poised on the rattan furniture, whispering and chittering like schoolgirls; Winifred hesitated outside the doorway.

Drained Gibson glasses littered their side tables. Winifred wanted to replace the women's drinks, but the last time she tried to socialize with them, it hadn't gone well. Their conversation had been barbed, censorious. She knew they thought she was a gold digger, a verdict predicated not on evidence but on willful cruelty. Never mind her previous faux pas—they disliked Winifred because Winifred wasn't like them. Winifred was a mutt among purebreds; she insulted their pedigree.

But none of them threw parties like hers.

At their parties, tired themes failed to inspire the stiff small talk, and dry hors d'oeuvres preceded expensive but predictable entrées. Winifred's cheerful menu and brand-new crystal glassware *must've* impressed them. The decorator had assured her that her maximalist taste—fun wallpapers, velvet drapery, and abundant room themes—was sure to impress, and redecorating with lush shapes and fabrics would prove her style. The makeover had cost more than her father made in a year, but Bruce loved what she'd done, and she was confident the decor would catch the other ladies' attention.

Tonight, they had holed themselves up in the sunroom—the most casual space among the home's thirteen thousand square feet—but their mussed hair and empty glasses proved they were at least having fun. Beyond the windows, howls were coming from the direction of the pool. The women's proximity to the scandalous behavior must've thrilled them; they were all blushing, giggling. To Winifred, their laughter was a victory.

What Winifred didn't know was that June Duxbury and the other ladies were enjoying themselves at her expense.

2

June was embarrassed to even enter such a tacky affair. Not to mention the insulting timing of Winifred's party, which was unnecessarily close to the Society of Philanthropic Women's fundraiser. This year's auction was especially important to June, because the head organizer, Deanna, was officially handing the reins to June and stepping down. It was an honor she'd been working toward her entire adult life; *of course* Winifred's soiree would infringe.

But the Duxburys and Hursts had been vacationing here together—along with her own family, the Clearmonts, and others—since the Gilded Age. They were all determined to keep the old traditions alive; this connection sadly meant they had to humor Bruce's new wife—despite what she'd said to June at the wedding. When June heard Winifred had hired an interior designer, she had hoped Winifred would finally adopt some refinement, but June should've known better. The house had turned out outrageously colorful and horrendously cluttered; she felt as if the splashy walls might stain her dress.

The sunroom was not exempt from the hideousness, but at least it wasn't overdressed, so that's where June and her friends had settled. Unfortunately, they couldn't escape the hubbub. Piercing shouts came from outside; how had all these miscreants gotten in? It seemed Winifred attracted them like flies.

The din and decor were not the worst parts of the night, however. As Victoria blathered on about her daughter—who had just starred in her summer camp play—an acute tearing sensation stretched through June's abdomen. She had the urge to visit the powder room again, but she'd already excused herself twice. It was a miracle she'd been able to leave the house; normally, menstruation left her bedridden and lying on a hot-water bottle. She was here only because her husband had insisted, and upright only because of the three Gibsons she'd drunk in quick succession.

But the pain lingered like the threat of lightning during a hard rain, a crackling electricity destined to strike again, and it was distracting. The other ladies laughed, and she laughed, not having heard the joke.

"At least the stuffies are good," Victoria interjected.

Barbara smirked. "If you like getting your fingers grimy."

"I think they're fun," Victoria said.

Sandra fanned her face. "I think they're greasy."

June clenched her teeth, and not just from the cramping. Winifred was blunt, opinionated, garish. June had spent her whole life striving to be a good homemaker, neighbor, and volunteer. Those were the legacies of the women who'd come before June and her friends; their circle was built on those ideals. Winifred was an affront to their efforts.

"The stuffies are cumbersome," June said. "Formal attire and street food are hardly an appropriate match. Does she not have any sense? I shouldn't have to wash my hands after every hors d'oeuvre."

Barbara waved dismissively. "Just wipe them on the cushions; it's not like a stain will make the fabric look any worse."

Sandra—who had little tolerance for gin—hiccuped, spilling a dribble of her Gibson on the seat of her chair. The liquid instantly bled into the floral pattern.

"See?" Barbara said. "You can hardly spot the dark splotch." She leaned toward Sandra and stage-whispered, "I think that's enough for you."

"I'm *fine*," Sandra said, checking for dampness along the side of her dress.

"Should we tell the staff?" Victoria asked.

A flash of pain radiated into June's right leg, and her head swam.

Barbara cut in. "It's just a Gibson; it won't stain."

"Yes, it will," Victoria countered.

"The fabric can't get any uglier," Barbara said.

Victoria frowned. "We should still tell someone."

"Tell someone what?" a clear voice inquired.

All four of them pivoted to see Winifred in the doorway.

"Is there something to tell?" Winifred prompted, approaching their circle of chairs.

Sandra gulped the last of her Gibson, and the onion wobbled in the bottom of her glass. Victoria twisted the gold bracelet on her wrist. Barbara simply lifted her eyebrows; she had a skill for looking down her nose, saying everything with a glance.

Apparently, they expected June to speak. She shifted her legs to the side and twisted, aligning her chin with her shoulder to look at Winifred looming behind her. The angle made June queasy in her already-fragile state, but she fixed Winifred with a glare. "It's not polite to eavesdrop."

Her comment appeared to knock Winifred off balance.

"I came to refill your drinks," Winifred said tightly.

"Don't you have staff to do that?" Barbara asked.

"We're fine, thanks," Victoria said.

"I could have another," Sandra said.

"I don't think that's such a good idea," Barbara said.

"She spilled on the cushion," Victoria admitted. "That's what we wanted to say."

The corner of Winifred's mouth twitched. "Oh."

June wished Winifred wouldn't hover over the back of her seat. Her position—back stiffened and neck craned—made her kidneys ache.

"The spot is already fading," Sandra said.

"I'm sure it'll come out," Victoria added.

"I don't know . . . ," Barbara said in a tone June knew was insincere, "you might have to throw out the whole set."

Everyone but Winifred laughed.

Winifred's face felt hot. She told herself it was the Gibsons making them cruel. They couldn't possibly mean what they'd said, could they? She'd spent weeks planning this party: meeting with caterers, auditioning bands, making sure the lawn was manicured just so. And still, it wasn't good enough. Why? She didn't get it.

"You know," Winifred began, placing her hands on the back of June's chair, "being a bully looks rather poorly on you." She glanced around the circle. "All of you." She straightened to her full height, towering over them. "In fact, it's tacky—and I would know. I'm the queen of tackiness. Isn't that what you said outside the yacht club last week?"

Before June could reply, a cascade of howls outside the window snagged everyone's attention. No one noticed June's wince as the lightning inside her abdomen spiderwebbed into her hips.

"You might want to get out there," June gritted out. "Your guests are becoming disorderly."

Winifred's mouth spread into an insincere smile. "Can I get you anything before I go?"

"Some appropriate food, please," Barbara said.

Winifred pressed her lips together. If it weren't for Bruce, she would've already laid into them, propriety be damned.

"Barbara," Victoria hissed. "That wasn't very nice, was it?"

"What?" Barbara said. "I was serious."

Unwilling to take any more abuse, Winifred stalked out of the room.

"You scared her off," Victoria said.

Barbara spread her arms. "You're welcome."

June untwisted her body and faced her friends again. She tried to breathe through the worst of the radiating cramps while Victoria and Barbara bickered.

"Do you think she's actually going to come back?" Sandra whined. "I wanted another drink."

Barbara guffawed. "You need *bread*, dear. Something to soak up all that gin."

Sandra folded her arms. "You know I'm watching my weight."

June glanced at her watch, wondering when Harry would arrive.

She and her husband had come separately: June from the cottage once the babysitter arrived, and Harry from the city; he'd been in Boston this week—something about a deal at the firm that couldn't be put off—and had said he'd return to Wave Watch this afternoon.

Ever since he'd inherited his father's advertising firm, Duxbury & Pierce, he always came home late, smelling like alcohol and perfume. Summer had once been a respite from such habits, a chance to reconnect, but this year Harry had spent half their vacation in Boston. June knew it wasn't work that made him linger, but she also knew her husband was under a lot of pressure and had to let off steam. When June was little, her mother had shared a similar sentiment about her father often missing dinner: *It's just the way of things.*

Except: June and Harry had once run into Winifred and Bruce at the Shore House restaurant. They'd been so affectionate: kissing each other's hands, murmuring in each other's ears, sharing bites of food. June had felt as if she were watching a movie, a fantasy. She wanted to rush to their table and tell Winifred it wouldn't last; it wasn't real. But that was over a year ago now, and they had only seemed to grow closer.

Then again, they hadn't had children.

After years of trying to get pregnant, June had a challenging labor and recovery. That's when Harry's late nights had started. Now, their daughter was four—many years behind June's friends' children, who had been conceived immediately and were all now in the double digits—and Bella was always needing something, always waking in the middle of the night, always screeching or interrupting. Some days, after the worst tantrums, June couldn't blame Harry for his absence.

Tonight, however, was the summer soiree. All their friends were here, at this bastardized version of their families' sacred summer tradition, and Harry had said he would arrive by eight o'clock. June resisted the urge to go looking for him. He was here already; he must be. Probably caught in a conversation about sailing with Victoria's husband, already making plans for next summer.

June settled against the back of her chair; it might be ugly, but it was soft enough to cushion another surge of pain.

3

Outside the sunroom, Winifred leaned against the wall, trying to blink away the wetness in her eyes. The furniture, the food, the party—she had been certain they would love it all. How could she have been so wrong?

Pressing her lips together, she hurried away, down the hall and around the corner and upstairs. Hosting was tiring. She needed to reapply her lipstick.

No matter how hard she tried, Winifred was never good enough for these women. They might attend all the same functions, play tennis on the same courts, donate to the same charities, but this was yet another reminder that she would never be one of them.

The worst part was not their rejection, though—it was the feeling of letting Bruce down. He wanted so badly for Winifred to fit in, to be a part of this community—in a way, he *was* his community, both a product of it and revered by it. And each time she misstepped—with the wrong sort of appetizer, or an inappropriate fabric for the occasion, or an overly honest comment—she was failing the man she loved.

She had failed her mother, too, somehow, and she'd never been able to figure out why. Social engagements like this brought on that same girlhood struggle, a sourness in her stomach that—no matter how hard she tried—she couldn't seem to fix.

Winifred rushed down the second-floor hallway and turned into her favorite bathroom of the house: a narrow space with a huge porcelain tub and a long row of windows overlooking the ocean. It was her place of tranquility, an escape. Here, the bustle of the party was muted through the tile floor.

But the room wasn't empty.

A woman stood with her back to the door, admiring the painting on the far wall, shocked that the hostess of this party would have an original Georgia O'Keeffe tucked in an upstairs bathroom—and not even the master bath. Marie Clarke was too swept up in the painting to notice Winifred appear in the doorway.

Marie recognized the piece as part of O'Keeffe's *Hawaii* collection. The flower was a narrow ribbon of pink, the delicate petals folded protectively about themselves. The textured, cloudlike grading of faint lavender and periwinkle in the background exhilarated Marie. She took a step closer, wondering if she had the oils at home to recreate the exact shade of morning purple on her own canvas.

She hadn't completed a painting in months. There was a common misconception that if you whip a racehorse harder, it will run faster. Marie always thought the opposite. If you wanted a horse to run faster, you had to convince the horse that *faster* was possible. Marie had been whipping herself for two years now, unable to convince herself that anything was possible anymore. The art world had all but put her out to pasture.

But the O'Keeffe . . . it awakened something in Marie, the soft inner voice that had once told her that painting was how she could see the world in a better light. Make it make sense. She could practically smell the oils, feel the weight of a hog-bristle brush in her hand. Suddenly, her hand felt empty without one.

Marie was mixing colors in her head when she heard heels on tile. She turned. A redheaded woman draped in a silk dress stood in the doorway, her eyes widened enough to reveal their raw umber hue. She must not have expected someone to be here.

"I'm sorry," Marie said. "I was admiring . . ."

"*Pink Ornamental Banana*," the woman said, walking up to Marie so they were side by side, facing the canvas. "Thrilling, isn't it?"

"Is this your house?" Marie asked.

The woman nodded, still staring at the painting. "I know this collection isn't considered O'Keeffe's best work, but I find it so lush."

"I agree." Marie watched the woman's profile. Her eyes were devouring the painting, flitting from one brushstroke to the next like a hummingbird searching for a place to land.

"I'm Winifred." Her gaze darted to Marie's and paused. "Winifred Hurst. Are you having fun at my party?"

"I'm afraid I'm a little overwhelmed by the crowd." Marie glanced down at her oxfords. They were her only pair of shoes that weren't splattered with paint, but now she spotted a speck of cerulean on the leather.

"This is a fine place to escape," Winifred said. "That's what I was doing." She chuckled lightly, but it rang false. "It's not easy hosting this many guests." She opened a drawer and retrieved a gold tube of lipstick, then turned toward the mirror and, with great care, applied the color: a deep, rich mauve.

After pressing her lips onto a tissue, Winifred faced Marie again. "Would you like a touch-up? I have other colors."

Marie gestured at her wrinkled blouse. "I'm afraid lipstick won't make me any less drab."

"Nonsense." Winifred's tone was surprisingly genuine when she added, "You look lovely." She dug around in the drawer again. "Here." She handed Marie a tube. "It's a classic red. I know nudes are on trend, but there's nothing like the right red to complement one's complexion."

Marie held the tube loosely, as if a noncommittal grasp would somehow release her from the responsibility of using it.

"Lipstick is about *confidence*." When Marie didn't move, Winifred retrieved the tube from Marie's reluctant fingers and pulled off the cap. "I'll help. Come, stand in the light."

Marie shifted toward the mirror, where a bright overhead light made the polished countertop shine. Winifred reached toward Marie's face and tucked a strand of hair behind her ear, then uncapped the tube and twisted the bottom until the waxy crimson stick appeared. It *was* a beautiful color. Winifred had great taste—in shades of lipstick *and* painters. Perhaps it was simply expensive taste.

Marie felt awkward tipping her chin up toward Winifred, but the other woman had an easy way about her that made Marie feel safe. Marie always wondered how other women could do that . . . just *exist*, with so little effort. As if they weren't self-conscious every moment of the day. The only time Marie felt like *herself* was when she was painting, and lately, even her easel lacked its usual solace.

Marie tried not to flinch as the other woman dabbed the lipstick onto her bottom lip with quick, efficient pressure. Winifred's eyes were fixated on Marie's mouth—on her task—giving Marie a chance to notice that her irises had flecks of burnt sienna around the pupils. Winifred's closeness was—oddly—a welcome discomfort. She made this seem like the most natural thing in the world. Like they fixed each other's makeup in the upstairs bathroom all the time.

"There." Winifred snapped the cap back on the tube and handed Marie a tissue.

Marie copied Winifred's earlier movements, closing her lips on the tissue once before allowing it to flutter into the wastebasket. The color felt like velvet on her mouth.

Winifred watched her with an exuberant, expectant expression: wide cheeks, raised brows, spread lips. "What do you think?"

Marie regarded herself in the ornate mirror, a little shocked by what she saw. The woman staring back at her was a new woman altogether. Winifred had been right about the shade—it perfectly complemented the warmth of Marie's brunette hair, the flush of her cheeks, and the cool undertones of her skin.

"I love it," Marie said, and this seemed to please Winifred, who clapped her hands and grinned at Marie's reflection. Inexplicably, Marie was glad to please her, as if Winifred shining more brightly would some-how light up Marie's world too.

"I believe it's time we return to the party, don't you?"

4

Harry Duxbury *had* arrived. June spotted him on her fourth trip to the powder room. He was standing just inside the ballroom, right on the fringes of the chaos—and he was not standing alone. His thumb grazed the hip of a brunette in a low-cut gown. It was not a cautious, flirtatious touch—no. It was slow, luxuriating. After tracing her spine, he clutched possessively at the fabric just above the swell of her backside.

The audacity of the display was like ice water to June's senses: a cold shock.

Harry and the woman were chatting with another man, whom June recognized from Harry's office. Could they tell what the other man was saying, over the brazen conversation they were having with their hands? Idly, *thoughtlessly*, the woman slid her claws around June's husband's forearm and squeezed.

As pain threatened to split June in two, she veered away from the restroom, plastered a big smile across her face, and approached the trio. As soon as Harry caught sight of her, he released the other woman and shoved his hand deep into the pocket of his perfectly creased slacks— the slacks June had ironed countless times.

"You're here," June said.

"June, dear, where have you been hiding?" As if he'd been looking for her.

"The sunroom," she said. "Are you going to introduce me?"

To his credit, Harry flushed. "Of course. June, you remember Maxwell from my office."

"Yes, of course," she said, allowing the other man to take her hand. He had a full head of hair, a square jawline, and glasses. Dark and sophisticated. The opposite of her husband, who was blond as a summer fling. If June were more like Harry, she might've allowed herself to appreciate Maxwell's handsomeness—but June believed in the sanctity of marriage.

When Maxwell released her, she turned to the brunette. "And you are?"

Harry coughed. "This is Evelyn. She's a consultant at our office"— another cough—"for the accounts that require a female perspective."

June didn't offer the woman a single meaningful gesture—she *wouldn't*.

Harry coughed again, and June asked, "Do you need another drink, dear?"

He frowned, and June looked to Maxwell. "Please excuse us."

Looping her arm through Harry's, she pretended to allow him to lead her toward the parlor. The doorway was located on the opposite end of the ballroom, far away from Evelyn-the-consultant. When they had bypassed the dancers and clusters of other conversations, June dropped her voice.

"What is she doing here?"

"Who?"

"You know who."

"What are you talking about?"

"Do you think I'm stupid, Harry?"

"Of course not, dear, I—"

"You're sleeping with her."

He at least had the decency to blanch, to appear surprised and hurt and angry at her accusation—but the expression was short lived. "Why are we having this conversation here?"

"Because you *brought her here*," she hissed.

"The whole Boston office was invited, *June*." The way he said her name—like a bad taste—it *hurt*.

"You're embarrassing me," June said, glancing away, hoping he wouldn't see the weakness in her eyes. "You couldn't stop touching her. Do you have no decency? For the sake of appearances—"

"To hell with appearances."

"What do you mean?"

"I mean to hell with them." His jaw ticked. "You see me with Evelyn, and all you can think about is appearances? Christ, June, I thought you loved me more than that."

June tried not to frown or raise her voice and make a scene even as her heart was fissuring. "Of course I love you."

"But you love appearances more."

June didn't know what to say. What was life without propriety? Family and community were crafted from it; you couldn't build a legacy without it. As a Clearmont, June had grown up with such pressures. And on her wedding day, June's mother-in-law had reminded her: *You're a Duxbury, now, and with that name comes a responsibility to not only serve Harry as a wife should but to also uphold the family's legacy of power and respect.* For June, there was no room for missteps.

Harry looked out at the happy party. "Evelyn wants to get married."

"To whom?"

"To me."

June blinked. She had weathered searing, aching, blooming, burning pain in her abdomen for years. Pain that would make other women faint. Pain that would make a man like Harry weep for his mother. Intense discomfort had plagued June since she became a woman, and she hadn't known different until one of her elder sisters told her so. It had only gotten worse as June got older, like the gnarly root of a tree, burrowing into her body, growing harder and knobbier and more terrible by the month.

But none of that pain compared to the way her heart shattered then.

It burst into a million sharp pieces, and she became paralyzed, afraid to move, because if she did, she was sure to cut herself on the shards.

"No," she whispered.

"No?" he asked.

"No," she repeated. "I won't let this happen. You have no grounds." If anyone had grounds for divorce, it was June, what with Harry's adultery. "I *won't*," she repeated.

"I will find a way."

She had poured all her energy into doing what was expected of her, doing everything right—how had it ended up so wrong?

"I'm sorry, June," Harry said, as if it were already done. As if he'd already disgraced her by leaving. "I'm going to get that drink now." And his hand—which had been resting on her arm, as if to hold her back, or steady her, or claim her—unceremoniously fell.

June could no longer distinguish the ache in her belly from the ache in her chest. She bit her lip, just to chase away the tears. She bit until she felt the pucker of a bruise, a pain she could control.

Had Harry not just broken her heart, June might've spotted Winifred and Marie descending the stairs into the mouth of the ballroom. While the party faded around June, Winifred and Marie found themselves overpowered by its sudden volume as it came into focus. The band was in full swing, unbelievably loud. The room was filled to the gills with giddy women in gorgeous dresses and jovial men in perfectly cut sport jackets. Waiters wove through the crowd carrying precarious trays of fun foods and cocktails in crystal.

Marie didn't belong with these people.

She had been invited by the Iris Gallery, which had first discovered her paintings nearly four years ago. They still distributed her funding from a patron foundation, her one remaining supporter after her sharp rise and fall in fame. She'd come all the way out here from New York with the hope that she could associate with other potential art patrons—their purse strings made looser from the lavishness of summer vacation—but as soon as she'd walked in, she hurried off to the quietest part of the house.

Now, as the crowd came into view, Marie's aspirations felt silly all over again; she considered darting back up the stairs.

Winifred must've sensed the urge. "Let's get you some champagne, shall we?" she said, pulling Marie along by the wrist. Her grip was rather firm.

They had almost reached the bottom of the stairs when a loud shriek sliced through the rest of the noise, bringing everyone—servers, guests, trumpeters—to a sudden hush.

A man had collapsed, though Marie couldn't see who, even from the stairs. People were crowding around him, men dirtying the knees of their trousers on the floor. A doctor announced himself and pushed his way through. Someone screeched at a waiter to call an ambulance.

"Bruce?" Winifred's voice quavered, watery and thin. She raised a shaking hand to her mouth, her cheeks reddening with emotion.

Because she was six inches taller than Marie, Winifred saw it all. The blurring bodies surrounding her husband, the way he lay on the floor, face up, expression pinched, a hand clutching his own breast pocket. Then a man was hunched over him, blocking his stricken face, and Winifred was both relieved and concerned that she could no longer see it.

She wanted to run to his side—and she should have—but she couldn't move. Her ankles wobbled in her heels, and she knew if she took a step, she'd collapse.

"Bruce," she whispered again. She sounded pitiful. She sounded like a child. She *felt* like a child, useless and helpless as the world charged forward without explanation.

"Is that your husband?" Marie asked her.

Winifred could only nod, the motion barely more than a shiver.

Marie squeezed Winifred's hand. "Come," she said firmly.

Marie led Winifred through the crowd, gritting her teeth against her own sense of horror. Marie knew what it was like to have someone she loved die behind a closed door, and she didn't wish the regret of absence on anyone—even a perfect stranger like Winifred. If this didn't end well, Winifred's immobility would haunt her forever. She had to go to him.

"Step aside, step aside," Marie said, practically shoving rubberneckers out of her way as she plowed across the ballroom floor.

Without Marie yanking her forward, Winifred wouldn't have been able to get through the crowd. Every step felt futile, as if her joints would buckle. But as long as the other woman's hand was gripping hers—Marie's calloused palm warm and strong around Winifred's manicured fingers—she could keep going.

When they made it to Bruce, his head was lolling in the lap of Dr. Kensington, a family friend of the Hursts. He told Winifred that Bruce was likely having a heart attack and the ambulance was already on the way. The sight of her lionhearted husband on the dirty hardwood floor, his face pale and his eyes closed, made her queasy. His family had a history of heart trouble, but he was still so youthful, so young. What would Winifred do without him?

Winifred crouched, placing her palms on his cheeks. His eyelids fluttered and cracked open, and he smiled when he saw her face. "Freddie." His right hand, which had been resting on his chest, reached up to cover her own on his cheek.

Hearing his pet name for her unraveled her thin thread of composure, like pulling one end of a bow and having it all come undone. His eyes closed again, and she stifled a gasp, trying furiously to blink back the tears that were now cutting through the makeup on her face. Everyone was watching this, watching her life fall apart, and somehow that made it so much worse. So many witnesses to this terrible moment of doubt, when all Winifred wanted was to be alone with Bruce in his peril so that he could preserve some dignity and she could abandon composure.

But that wasn't an option. Instead, she pressed a kiss against his clammy lips. "It'll be all right," she whispered, shaking. "It'll be all right."

The ambulance arrived; she could hear the siren ringing out front. Heavy, running footsteps found them, and suddenly Winifred was being ushered out of the way, making room for the emergency professionals who intended to save her husband's life.

Marie was beside her again—or maybe she was *still* beside her—rubbing Winifred's back and clutching her elbow as Bruce was transferred to a gurney. The commotion was too loud. People's voices, so many voices, filled Winifred's head, when all she wanted was to hear the whispers coming from Bruce's feebly moving lips. Everything was too fast, too slow, too terrible.

The clock in the parlor was clanging midnight when Winifred became a widow.

5

"Do you think that's enough gruyère?" Winifred asked.

The checkout clerk at Stop & Shop—a plump, kind-faced woman—picked up the second wedge of cheese and hit a button on the cash register. "Absolutely."

"Thank you, Irene. I take your advice very seriously."

Irene felt sorry for the young rich widow. She waved her hand. "Nonsense."

"Please, you're being modest. Your suggestion last week to put vodka in the dough? Genius. It was the flakiest quiche crust in all of Rhode Island."

Her delight seemed to cut through her instinct to be humble. "And the onions? Did you try browning the onions?"

"I did!" Winifred leaned closer. "*Please* tell me you've written a cookbook. You could be the next Julia Child."

Irene chuckled, genuinely delighted by the compliment. "I'm afraid quiche is my only specialty."

"A cookbook of a hundred quiches, then. I would buy it."

"You flatter me," she said, back to punching numbers into the register.

Winifred liked Irene—she planned her weekly grocery trips around the woman's schedule. Irene's husband had died, too, and that's why she worked at this Stop & Shop. "We're sorrow sisters," Irene had told Winifred when they first met.

After the funeral flowers had wilted and the attorneys stopped calling about Winifred's share of Bruce's wealth—his family retained the family business and estate in New York, while Winifred was left with all of Bruce's personal funds and the beach cottage in Wave Watch—the worst thing about her husband's absence was how empty life felt: the house, their bed, her heart.

But Stop & Shop was never empty. Stop & Shop had Irene, with her sweet face and fabulous cooking advice. And Fred, the bag boy who always blushed when Winifred looked his way. And twenty other employees to get to know.

Sometimes Winifred went to Stop & Shop simply to wander the aisles and make conversation. What else was there to do during the offseason but get to know the townspeople who lived here year round? Once, she'd gone all the way home with a young mother whose baby wouldn't stop crying; Winifred had spent the afternoon bouncing the babe on her knee so his mother could take a nap.

It was June now, and all the cottagers were back in town, filling Wave Watch with their haughty bustle. It was a different energy from the lonesome winter months, when sand blew down the empty streets under ominous skies; the summer season was like a fog lifting on Winifred's life. It felt familiar. It felt like Bruce.

On her way out of the store, Winifred considered making a detour to Maquette, her favorite local boutique. Today was Thursday, and new shipments always arrived on Thursdays. Opal, the young sales associate there, knew Winifred's taste to a tee. She would've set a few new pieces aside. But—no. Winifred had to get home. Bake the quiches.

After Bruce died, Winifred had remained on the Society of Philanthropic Women's planning committee. Though they only had two major fundraisers per year, they convened weekly, and Winifred—despite her better judgment—looked forward to the socialization. The other ladies remained cold, but their disdain had been tempered by pity. Winifred was determined to wear them down, to prove that Bruce hadn't been wrong when he said she belonged. After all—aside from their summer cottage—Bruce's community was all Winifred had left of him. It made her want to hold on, in spite of the other ladies' cruelty.

Throughout the winter, June Duxbury—the new head of the planning committee—had held the winter meetings in her Boston estate. Winifred had traveled back and forth from Wave Watch to Boston to keep up with the SPW's goings-on. But now that everyone had arrived in Wave Watch for the summer, the meetings were being held at members' cottages on a rotating schedule. This week, it was Winifred's turn to host. Hence the quiches.

When she arrived home, the foyer floor shone mirrorlike in the morning sunlight. She'd let the maid, Alma, go two months ago—it wasn't practical to have a maid for one person, even if she liked the company—and Winifred had taken to cleaning in the early mornings. She liked the sense of accomplishment it brought, but sometimes her home's spotlessness felt sterile. She missed the scuff marks of Bruce's shoes on the tile and his dirty dishes in the sink.

As Winifred shuffled in with her groceries, the grandfather clock in the parlor—a monstrous thing that had belonged to Bruce's grandfather—ticked ominously. The clangs always startled Winifred. They echoed off the high ceiling when she least expected—but she couldn't bring herself to do away with it. Bruce had once said it reminded him of simpler times.

She hurried to the kitchen. A southeastern wind was whooshing against the windows that overlooked the distant sea, kicking up sand enough to hiss against the glass. A shutter rattled, the loose hinge squeaking. Last summer, Winifred had offered to call the handyman, but Bruce had said he'd repair it himself. Like Winifred, he liked a sense of accomplishment. But he never got the chance to follow through.

Foyer, parlor, kitchen—Bruce was in every corner of this place, his absence loud. Winifred put on a Beatles record to drown out all the lonely sounds of their big, empty house. June and the other committee women would eliminate the silence in just two hours—she only had to last that long.

Winifred had made the quiche dough this morning; she removed it from the refrigerator to allow the butter to soften. Then she unpacked her groceries and arranged her ingredients on the counter. She donned an apron, tying the straps tightly around her waist. She greased three pie dishes, tapping her foot in time to the music. She sang along while she whisked the eggs, cooked the bacon, grated the cheese. She sang along so she wouldn't lose herself in thought. While she sang, she pretended the Beatles were there with her in the kitchen. She always thought Paul was handsome. Who didn't?

When the quiches were in the oven, Winifred climbed the stairs to change her dress and apply more makeup. She hadn't slept in the master bedroom in months—it smelled too much like Bruce's aftershave—so she'd claimed the south-facing guest room that opened into the bathroom with the O'Keeffe. It was still her favorite room in the house; the big windows and *Pink Ornamental Banana* soothed her.

Art was the only thing she felt she could still reach out and touch—something that had always been just hers and therefore had not succumbed to the blight of Bruce's death. Still, grief had taken its toll. She hadn't involved herself in the art scene all year. Before Bruce's death, he'd helped her set up a patron foundation, and she'd worked with galleries across New England to sponsor up-and-coming female artists. Nine months had passed since she'd checked in with the galleries and artists she supported. She met with Bruce's accountant—*her* accountant—once a month to confirm the payments, and that was that. She wondered if she ought to commission a new piece from one of her artists. D—her favorite beneficiary—was probably due for a creative nudge.

Winifred had just zipped herself into a fresh dress when the timer buzzed downstairs. She rushed to the kitchen and removed the quiches—perfectly golden, billowing delicious steam—and set them on trivets to cool. Then she made the table: a vase of fresh flowers, her best china, silverware arranged at perfect right angles. She prepared coffee milk (a local delicacy) and a pot of tea, unboxed a dozen almond tarts onto a gold tray, and swapped her Beatles record for instrumental piano. Then she waited, tapping her foot with a nervous anticipation.

Minutes passed, her excitement morphing into a niggling dread as the top of the hour neared. When one o'clock came with the clanging of the parlor clock, Winifred was so tightly wound that she jumped at the noise. June and the other committee ladies were always prompt; the clock ringing before the doorbell did not bode well. By fifteen after the hour, Winifred knew for a fact they weren't coming.

Today was Thursday, wasn't it? She checked her watch, checked her calendar, checked the notepad by the phone. Nothing was amiss, as far as she knew. Resignation bloomed in her chest; she blinked rapidly, resisting the sense of defeat.

She sank into a chair and served herself a big piece of quiche. Irene had been right about the extra gruyère. Chewing a flaky piece of crust, Winifred decided to have a drink at the Shore House restaurant, now that her afternoon was free. She liked to people watch there, and her favorite waiter, Lyle, worked on Thursdays.

Before Bruce died, Winifred's life had been close and full: crowded with charity events, parties, dinners, holidays. Her life still contained all those things, but lately, the hours in between felt hollow and stretched. She imagined herself as an astronaut launched into space—suddenly, the universe was so much bigger than it had once seemed, and therefore life on Earth that much smaller by comparison.

Bruce's death was like the moon—huge, looming, a reminder of the vastness surrounding her.

6

June paced the kitchen of her beach cottage as far as the corded phone would allow. Back and forth, back and forth, like a hound on a leash. Bella had just gone down for a nap, the kitchen was finally clean, and this was June's only opportunity to call Mr. Duxbury in Boston.

As she waited for him to pick up, she cataloged her next tasks. She still had to catch up on paperwork for the SPW and call the other committee ladies to change the meeting location. If she could help it, she'd never set foot in Winifred Hurst's cottage again. June could only imagine the lunch she'd prepare—probably that awful chowder with the tomatoes in it, or one of those terrible quiches, gloppy from too much cheese.

June needed a drink. Maybe the Shore House would suffice as an appropriate change for their meeting, so no one would have to throw together a last-minute lunch.

The ringing continued, and finally her husband answered. She was relieved to hear his voice; a part of her had feared that a woman would pick up—for all she knew, Evelyn was there with him.

"I'm calling to ask when you'll arrive," June said.

Harry launched into his usual run of excuses, from vague (*I don't know if it's such a good idea for me to come*) to irritating (*I still have a lot of work to do at the firm*). June stopped pacing and—because she didn't want to wake Bella—used a forceful whisper to remind Harry that he was still her husband, still Bella's father, still a man with responsibilities and a reputation to uphold.

This was how their past twenty conversations had gone. June, asking for little more than his presence; Harry, acting like June had demanded he buy her the moon. It had been an argumentative winter, but June was determined to get her life back on track, and summer was the perfect season for reconnection. She had a vision of her family of three on the beach, all of them laughing. Harry had loved June once—which meant maybe she could convince him to love her again.

"Bella misses you," June added. She couldn't bear the thought of their daughter growing up in a broken home. It would scar her forever. "She's been asking about a baby brother." A desperate lie. "I don't want Bella to be an only child." A heartsick truth.

"June, please." He sounded tired—exasperated, really. As if his family was an inconvenience.

June pressed on. "I want to have another baby. We always said we wanted two kids—one of each—remember? Just like you and your sister. I want to give you a son. I want to grow our family. Wouldn't that be a happy thing, Harry? A brand-new baby?"

Bella's arrival had been particularly hard. That's when the marital strain had occurred, like a snag in pantyhose leading to a spidery run that lengthened and spread with every stretch and pull and point of friction. But throughout June's pregnancy, Harry had been the perfect husband: he'd rubbed her feet, made her Jell-O—a nonstop craving—and was always complimenting June's glow.

Those happy times could be recreated. A new baby might bring Harry back to her. Remind him that they were husband and wife, and they were meant to be. Not just because of the vows they'd taken, but because Harry loved Jell-O-craving June.

"Just think about it, all right?" Before he could refuse, she hurriedly added, "Come soon. We miss you."

After she hung up, June pushed a stool up against the fridge and retrieved the bottle of vodka she'd stored in the otherwise unused cabinet above. She took a long two-gulp swig. The liquid scoured a trail between her breasts.

This was the worst time of day: that midday pause when she felt both tired *and* as if she hadn't yet accomplished anything of importance. It was a nameless, creeping sort of boredom—an excruciating stretch in time—like the moment between an inhale and an exhale, when her chest felt unusually tight.

The morning chores were done, the laundry machine was rumbling, and Bella was asleep. She had a full afternoon ahead, lots to manage and find purpose in—and yet this moment stood still.

She tried to suppress the dull dissatisfaction. This was the life she'd so carefully and strategically built for herself—to feel empty or incomplete within it was to feel dissatisfied with the very thing that made June who she was. Had Harry noticed this particular change in her? Had that unfeminine feeling bubbled up somehow and repelled him without her knowing?

No, she told herself. *No.*

She was fairly certain that this strange desperation was for another child, not another life.

Atop the stool, June took another swig of vodka. Her kitchen looked strange from this angle. There was a lot of dust up here; she would talk to the maid about it, but she didn't want her bottle to be discovered and placed in the ornate liquor cabinet that Harry tended to. She liked having something that was just hers.

Swallowing one last pull, June screwed the cap back on, replaced the bottle, climbed down from her perch, and reset the stool by the phone. Next, she dialed Barbara to alert her of the committee-meeting change; if they forgot to call Winifred, the SPW wouldn't suffer for it. Afterward, June poured herself a glass of lemonade and sank into a patio chair to watch the waves until the laundry finished.

June drew in a deep breath of ocean air, feeling her lungs grow taut. Every moment of every day that Harry chose not to come home, June felt as if she was failing at the one thing she'd always wanted: to be a wife and mother. She had never felt so much purpose and promise as she had when she was pregnant with Bella, and she longed to have that again. That sense of wonder, love, *meaning*.

For a polite woman like June, her family and her good social standing were the only ways she knew to assert her importance in the world.

~

Summer sunshine shimmered in heat waves above the beach, but seated in the breezy veranda of the Shore House, June and the other committee members were shaded from the worst of the sun. A second round of juleps and gin fizzes had just been delivered. The ladies had already enjoyed an appetizer of chilled cucumber soup.

Rosie, the youngest of the bunch, checked the diamond watch on her delicate wrist. "Is Winifred not coming?" she asked. "It's nearly two."

June and Barbara shared a knowing glance.

"You know, I must've forgotten to inform her of our change of plans," Barbara said. "Silly me."

The other ladies giggled.

Rosie frowned. "You didn't want her here?"

"Better to discuss the fundraiser without her." Deanna sipped her julep. "We're doing her a favor."

Deanna had stepped down from her role as head of the planning committee last summer, passing the sacred baton to June—but she still attended the occasional meeting. Some whispered that Deanna couldn't let go, that she didn't fully trust June to run the SPW. But June was grateful for the other woman's mentorship. It made for a more peaceful transition.

Besides, June admired Deanna. She wanted to *be* Deanna: a model housewife married to a powerful man who loved her to pieces, with well-adjusted and polite children. A respected voice in their community. Effortlessly polished and chic—today, in a belted, peach-hued A-line.

"But she seems nice enough," Rosie said, still not getting it.

"Winifred does her best," Bobbie, another committee girl, chimed in with a patronizing tone, "but she doesn't know how to act. She doesn't know how things work here. She's not *from* this society—Bruce was."

"She's been a bit pathetic since Bruce died, hasn't she?" Barbara commented.

Rosie shook her head, empathy creasing her pretty face. "I can't imagine losing Eugene that way—to just collapse at your own party."

Barbara tsked. "That party was out of hand."

Deanna smirked. "I'm glad I abstained."

"Good Gibsons, though," Barbara said with a flick of her wrist. "Nice and strong."

Bobbie gave Barbara a little shove. "You're *bad*."

June smiled. Her lips felt numb, but that didn't stop her from sipping more of her gin fizz.

"Without him, she won't last long in this community," Deanna said. "This has never been her home."

"Apparently it's her *only* home," Bobbie muttered, and the lot of them laughed.

They were all aware that Winifred, with no place left to go, had spent the winter in Wave Watch. Most of them found it funny in a disgraceful sort of way—but a faint, frightening whisper in the back of June's mind made her fear she'd suffer a similar fate if Harry actually left.

Then again, her parents would likely sequester her in one of their homes. June could hardly entertain such thoughts—the sickening humiliation—but at least she had the comfort of knowing she'd always be better off than Winifred.

"We're doing her a favor," June explained to Rosie. "Now she has the afternoon off."

"She told me she likes the committee—it keeps her busy," Rosie said.

Deanna scoffed. "The committee isn't a hobby just to stay busy; it's serious business."

"Speaking of business," June said, "should we discuss the fundraiser?"

The group's conversation pivoted into committee details. The end-of-summer silent auction and award ceremony—at which they granted one philanthropic woman one thousand dollars to donate to her cause of choice—was their biggest event of the season. Today, they needed to discuss the menu.

Two tables down from theirs, Winifred sat with her back to them. *Be angry,* she told herself; she couldn't stand feeling hurt. She plucked the cherry from her Tom Collins and sucked it off the stem. Then she waved at Lyle and pointed to her empty highball. His sun-kissed features pulled into a smile, and he hurried through the glass-paneled doors to retrieve her another refreshment.

As she watched him leave, her eyes stung behind her sunglasses.

7

Derivative.

That's what all the critics and galleries had said about Marie's latest artwork. And they were right. You could only use a motif for so long before it became *derivative*.

Marie stepped back from her canvas and tilted her head. She'd taken that same familiar image—her famous "girl" motif—and zoomed up on the face. Eye, cheek, nostril. Monochrome greens from forest to lime. At this angle, the ten-year-old girl Marie had been painting for the past eighteen years appeared almost abstract.

Some days, the girl seemed like the only thing Marie knew how to paint. The only thing that made sense.

Critics had loved the girl at first. They called her innocent but melancholy. Polite but clever. Brazen with wide-eyed wonder. Reviewers had posited that the girl was a metaphor representing "the contrasts of womanhood." This had made Marie somewhat of a feminist icon, at least when the collection was first exhibited. But Marie hadn't set out to work in metaphors. The girl was real.

Marie dabbed a line brush into a light shade of mint, twirled the bristles into a point, and stepped forward again. She traced the bridge of the girl's nose with the highlight, trying to bring the shape farther into the foreground.

Derivative.

The worst part was that she was being derivative of herself. Marie would rather be a bold plagiarist than be deemed stale and uninspired compared to her younger self. At least her younger self had done something new. The older Marie got, the more fearful and boxed in and boring she became.

With a huff of frustration, Marie set down her line brush and took up a two-inch flat brush. She dragged it through the remaining glop of forest green on her palette and swiped the dark color across the careful brushstrokes of the girl's eye. She ran the brush up and down, side to side, until the whole unoriginal disappointment was buried in the rich evergreen hue.

This was how it went: Marie, living in her own shadow. Painting and repainting until her fingers couldn't straighten from clutching a brush or palette knife for so long. Her tiny apartment filling up with the scent of paint thinner until she had to stick her head out the window just for a fresh breath. Wondering how long it would take for her to suffocate on fumes of her failure.

She walked over to the sink to fill a glass of water, then leaned against the counter and drank.

She hated this apartment. The daylight made it ugly. A huge tarp and easel were set up by the only window, which overlooked a dumpster-cluttered alley that reeked on warm June weekends like this one. Rows of canvases slanted against the neighboring wall, ten deep. A mattress on the floor was wedged into the darkest corner, flush against a doorless closet. The kitchen—a stove, sink, and pantry—barely spanned wider than Marie's outstretched arms. The only furniture—a sideboard cabinet and a stool—were covered in paint tubes and jars of brushes.

All her life's necessities—her clothing, her food, her bed—had been shoved into corners to allow space for her art. What did she have to show for it? Painting had once been a place of solace from grief. A way to turn scars into beauty. But now, even her scars were considered trite. All her support, her funding, her patrons—except for one—had dried up. Marie wouldn't be surprised if the last anonymous fund would bow out soon too. In fact, she was surprised they'd lasted this long. She hadn't created anything new in months. At this point, she wasn't an artist—she was a leech.

Marie turned the tap on the sink and washed the paint off her hands, scrubbing until her palms were pink. Then she studied the canvas, the girl's up close face peeking through the gaps of giant green-black strokes. It made for a solid underpainting, at least. All paintings were made richer by their layers; the mistakes and false starts gave a final piece character.

Marie tried desperately to believe that people were the same way, that a mistake was merely texture, something a person could redefine with a new tube of forest green. She wished she could paint over herself and start everything over again, fresh.

The phone rang, and she turned her back on the painting. "Hi, James," she answered.

Her brother still lived in Pennsylvania, where he had a family and a steady job. He was the only person who called.

"You sound tired."

"I've been painting."

"Have you eaten?"

"Is that why you called?"

Their parents had died shortly before Marie's *Girl* collection became famous. They'd been proud of her, anyhow—proud of the financial independence she'd earned by illustrating advertisements, proud of her skill and determination with more creative projects. Her mother had died of some unknown sickness, and her father had gone shortly thereafter—which was why James took it upon himself to check in.

"Actually, I have news," James said. "It's about the track."

Marie slumped against the kitchen counter as James explained what he'd heard from his old friend and veteran jockey Eddie Espinoza. Hurley Downs Racetrack—including the on-site groundskeeper house,

Marie and James's childhood home—was about to be put up for sale. At long last.

"You're serious?" Hope pulsed in Marie's chest like the light of a firefly, small but sure.

Hurley Downs had fallen into disrepair some seven years before. The owner—a real estate mogul named Dick Bishop—had clung to it, not willing to let go of the cash cow it'd once been. But now he was dead, and James had heard rumblings that Bishop's children intended to sell.

Marie had dreamed of purchasing the track for years. James didn't understand her interest. She didn't own Thoroughbreds and thought horse racing was cruel. But Hurley Downs wasn't a career dream. She'd lost everything to that godforsaken place—to own it would be to triumph over her life's greatest grief.

It was her version of painting over her past. Because once it was hers, Marie intended to tear it all down and bury her sorrows in the fallow ground—turn all that pain into a mere underpainting.

Marie knew her plan was illogical, but the way she saw it, leveling Hurley Downs was the only way she would be able to move on. Start fresh.

"How much?" Marie asked.

A long pause. "You'll need ten thousand dollars down," James said. "At least."

Marie swore. She'd been saving everything she could for the past five years, but she was still short.

"How long do I have?"

"Eddie's best guess? Six months." James sighed, and Marie knew what was coming. "I promised you I would call when I heard, and I know you're tired of the lectures—"

"Then save your breath," Marie suggested.

"It's a bad investment."

"James—"

"Buying Hurley Downs isn't going to change anything, Marie. The past is the past. Let it go."

"Thank you for calling," Marie said. "Please keep an eye on the situation, will you?"

"You need me to cosign. I could refuse."

"We both know you won't do that."

"Marie," he said, voice pillowy and patient.

But she wouldn't allow his sympathy to sway her. "Send my love to Katherine and the kids." She hung up.

Clutching her own elbows, Marie wandered over to the canvas, where the paint still shone wet in the fading afternoon light. Marie wasn't a fool. She knew buying Hurley Downs didn't make sense to James—but inside her own head, it felt like taking control of her grief. And that was worth every penny.

She glanced around the room. Her rent didn't cost much, but she didn't need this place. It was a dump, anyway. If she lived in her car, she could pour more money into savings. Use every last bit of her measly patron income. Maybe she could reach out to the advertising firm she used to work with. And she would keep painting, of course. Even a mediocre gallery collection could make more than advert jobs, so it was imperative that Marie continue creating—and *selling*—original works. Certainly not *all* her ideas were derivative, were they?

Marie lifted her canvas from the easel and flipped it around, revealing the wooden frame and glinting nails that held the fabric in place. Using a pencil, she did the math on the back. Six months. If she could live in her car, pick up a few advertising projects, and sell a painting or two—maybe she could finally paint over her past by bulldozing Hurley Downs.

8

Winifred hadn't thrown a party since last summer, but maybe it was time.

A week had come and gone since June Duxbury and the other SPW women excluded her from their meeting, and as of today, it seemed they'd done it a second time. Clearly, they didn't want her there, so to hell with them. Better to be recalcitrant than wallow in their rejection.

She strode into Stop & Shop with her party list in hand. Winifred was tired of trying for these women. Tired of sailboats and tennis and boozy lunches with uptight, unwelcoming reception. Winifred had wanted so badly to make Bruce happy, to fit neatly into his life, to prove—even after his death—that she belonged in his world. But Bruce wasn't here to worry about her anymore. Winifred no longer had to fit in.

She paced the aisles with a rush of freedom in her veins, filling her cart with everything that made her happy. She'd make more quiches, of course, because though they somehow didn't live up to the other ladies' standards, Winifred loved them. And fondue, which meant three types of cheese, plus accompaniments, like sourdough and apples and small russet potatoes. Salmon, for a salmon dip, plus crackers. Ingredients for meatballs, including the toothpicks for serving. Cocktail franks and shrimp cocktail. She would also bake a Black Forest cake—with extra cherries. And she couldn't forget piña coladas. Recipes that June Duxbury and the other ladies would probably question—recipes that Winifred thought were colorful, flavorful, and fun.

"Throwing a party?" Irene asked when Winifred pushed her cart toward the checkout counter.

"Yes, and you're invited!"

"Am I?" Irene didn't believe her at first, until she saw the sincerity in Winifred's eyes. The desperate sheen. "I'm guessing this isn't a party for your committee friends?"

Winifred flicked her wrist dismissively. "They aren't my friends."

"Who wouldn't be your friend?"

Winifred frowned quickly, almost imperceptibly, and Irene's heart pulsed with pity.

Irene smiled. "Didn't they try your quiches?"

Winifred cocked a shoulder in a halfhearted shrug.

Irene snorted. "They aren't worth your trouble, then."

Winifred's cheeks pulled tight once again. "Exactly."

"So, who *is* this party for?" Irene asked, though she knew it was for Winifred. She understood that kind of grief: the need to surround oneself with people to drown out the loneliness.

Winifred lifted her arms triumphantly, defiantly. "It's a party for everyone else."

"What day is this party?"

"Tomorrow."

"Isn't that lucky?" Irene said. "I happen to be available."

It wasn't luck; Winifred knew Irene didn't work Fridays. "There will be plenty of food," she continued, gesturing at her groceries. "Tell all your coworkers; bring your friends. The more the merrier."

"I'll do that," Irene said, and she meant it.

Outside, Winifred pushed her cart across the parking lot toward her Mercedes; the Pagoda had been a wedding gift from Bruce, and her heart always twisted like a lemon rind when she saw the cream enamel glinting. Winifred swallowed. She fished the keys from her purse, organizing the party menu in her head. She couldn't think about her husband; there was too much to do.

The weather was cool and breezy, the morning young, and the parking lot quiet, save for employee cars lined up along the edge and a few other early shoppers parked in the middle. Compared to New York, which was already humid with the threat of summer, Wave Watch was a pleasant escape from the hustle and bustle; it's why, with nowhere else to go, Marie had driven here. Like the rest of the summer vacationers, Marie had figured that the sea salt air would do her some good.

Standing among the middle-lot cars, Marie spotted Winifred as soon as Winifred exited the store. She was hard to miss: all legs and style, wearing a short dress and large dark sunglasses. Though they had only met once, Marie would recognize Winifred anywhere.

But Marie was not glad to see Winifred. In fact, Marie felt quite the opposite, namely dread and shame. She had just exited her old Plymouth Suburban and was headed into Stop & Shop to wash her face in the public restroom and buy herself a box of cereal. She'd been living in her wagon for only a week and hadn't yet worked out where to bathe. She couldn't face Winifred like this. Winifred would make a fuss.

Marie ducked her head and turned on her heel, stalking back to her car. With hunched shoulders and a tucked chin, she was certain she looked suspicious. But she was almost there, just another few steps, and maybe Winifred wouldn't recognize her, and—

"Marie?" Winifred's voice was high and clear as a chime.

Marie halted. She forced her chin up and turned around. "Winifred."

"Ah! I thought that was you. My, how long has it been?"

Winifred regretted the question as soon as it left her lips. They both knew how long it had been.

"Too long," Marie said.

Marie had been a firsthand witness to the worst moment of Winifred's life. She'd held Winifred's hand, rubbed her back, shared in her vulnerability and heartbreak. Nothing could connect two women quite like that. Except now, these facts embarrassed them. Winifred felt exposed, and Marie felt as though she'd somehow invaded Winifred's privacy with her mere presence, and Bruce lumbered in their minds as big as an elephant.

Winifred unclenched her molars, trying to regain some composure. "I'm throwing a party," she said. "I'd love for you to come."

The last thing Marie wanted to do was attend another party—especially in her state of dishevelment—but the promise of a free meal tempted her. "Oh? When is it?"

"Tomorrow," Winifred said. "Bring a friend, if you'd like. The more the merrier."

"All right, thank you."

Winifred smiled quick as a camera flash, and then she was strutting back to her convertible. Marie returned to the Plymouth, sank into the driver's seat, and let out a puff of breath. That wasn't so bad. Winifred probably had no clue about Marie's current living arrangements. Marie wasn't ashamed so much as she was afraid Winifred would try to intervene—and Marie wasn't looking for pity—or worse, a friend. Sleeping in her car was a means to an end that had nothing to do with Winifred Hurst.

Except Winifred—as she turned the key to her Pagoda—begged to differ.

9

By sunset, Winifred's kitchen was an absolute mess. Chocolate frosting and cherry juice had found their way onto the sink's hardware and hardened into sticky crusts. Glops of salmon mousse and raw egg daubed the countertop. Grated cheese littered the floor. There was flour everywhere, a fine dusting that dulled every surface; multiple white handprints decorated the oven handle.

Ever since Bruce died, Winifred had taken to watching Julia Child and cooking as often as she could. Focusing on a recipe was therapeutic; her mind could hardly wander when there were pots to stir, timers to silence, vegetables to carefully chop. Today had mercifully flown by. She'd hardly even noticed that she was alone. And now the kitchen needed cleaning—more distractions.

Winifred poured herself a gin and tonic and turned on the radio. She started with the dishes, then moved on to wiping down the counters, the sink fixtures, the oven handle. When finally she was finished mopping the floor, the sun was all the way down. Outside, the beach was a black expanse. Crashing waves ruffled the edge of the sand with frothy white flashes in the distant dark.

The first time Bruce had brought her here, they'd dropped their suitcases in the foyer and gone straight to the kitchen, parched after the long drive. Bruce had made her a gin and tonic, of which she had two sips before he was leading her out the back door. They walked past the pool, across the lawn, and—toeing off their shoes—over the gentle sand dune, past the rocks, and down the beach. The day was overcast, the sand powdery and cool underneath Winifred's bare soles. They stopped when they reached the sea, allowing the water to race along the hard pack and tickle their toes. Winifred had yelped at the sensation, and Bruce had swept her up into a tight embrace.

He had told her he loved her on that beach. Proposed to her on that beach. Held her hand, told her about his hopes and dreams, walking and talking and laughing for hours—all on that beach.

The beach called to her now, in spite of how fragile such memories made her. After pouring herself another drink, Winifred threw a shawl over her shoulders and walked out onto the patio. The air was balmy tonight, but the breeze had a chill to it. The ice in her glass clinked as she walked through the yard gate and onto the narrow path that led to the waves. Grit filled her sandals. Dune grass hissed all around her like snakes. At the waterline, she allowed the foam and froth to rush up and touch her feet. The wind lifted her hair all around her face.

Her eyes stung. Her lips pressed together, chin quavering. An ache settled in her throat, bringing with it the prick of tears. As of late, her grief was like a tide, rushing up unexpectedly to sweep her away. She almost missed the days when it had been more constant, less surprising.

In the early days, caught up in the swirl of lawyers and accountants and funeral organizers, Winifred had felt like she was floating on the surface of a whirlpool, the world spinning, but her body oddly weightless. Bruce's mother had been strangely calm, productive and focused in that way only someone truly hurting can achieve. His father had been as stoic as ever, though slightly less gruff when speaking to Winifred—a softness that revealed to her the true weight of his pain. Each night, Winifred had sobbed into her pillow until her chest wheezed, until she was well and truly empty and therefore able to make it through the next day without breaking down. She'd felt like a shaken-up Coke bottle, hard and shiny on the outside, but pressure building on the inside.

Staring out at the waves, Winifred wished she'd allowed herself some hysterics, because now she was beginning to acclimate to her life without Bruce. She no longer instinctually set out two coffee cups for the morning. She no longer reached for him in the middle of the night. She no longer smelled him on her pillow. These small things gave her grief a new shape: one of forgetting. It was worse, somehow. At least at the beginning, her grief had tethered her to him; now the grief was starting to fray, and Winifred felt her tether slipping.

She would not allow herself to get swept away into the vast emptiness of widowhood. Her parties would become her buoy. She couldn't possibly be lonely if she surrounded herself with people.

Winifred bent down, planting her bum in the damp sand. The waves crashed, slithering up her legs and wetting her dress. She set her glass beside her and buried her face in her hands, feeling so very sorry for the state of things.

Sorry for Bruce, who had died too young.

Sorry for his parents, who were so incapable of facing the loss of their child.

Sorry for Marie, who was clearly living in her car.

Sorry for Irene, who was too kind and sweet to be a widow.

And sorry for June, even, because she was nasty for a reason—perhaps because of her unsupportive husband, or the shame of the fertility struggles she tried so hard to hide, or simply because of the stress of trying to be everything society wanted her to be.

More than anyone, however, Winifred felt sorry for herself.

10

"So you want to have another baby."

June hated that her gynecologist, Dr. Applebaum, talked while examining her, rather than making eye contact. It gave her the sense that he was speaking directly to her cervix, rather than her brain.

"I'd like to give Bella a sibling," June explained, staring at the ceiling. "But with how . . . difficult the first time was, I wanted to make sure . . ." Harry had yet to agree to try for another baby, but June thought it was practical to be prepared—it's why she'd driven all the way into Providence on a Friday morning for this appointment.

"Ah, yes, I see."

Something pinched, and June gritted her teeth. Dr. Applebaum was not the gentlest with his hands, but he'd graduated from Yale and Harvard, and his wife had been on a few committees with June's mother. Having grown up in Rhode Island, she'd been going to Dr. Applebaum since young adulthood, and even though June was now a Duxbury—and therefore spent most of the year in either New York or Boston, as Harry bounced between the two Duxbury & Pierce offices—June still favored Dr. Applebaum over her doctor in Manhattan. At least he wasn't a stranger.

Still, it's not like either of her gynecologists listened to her concerns. In June's experience, that was just the way things were.

June glanced down at Dr. Applebaum's bald head between her knees. "So . . . should I be concerned?"

"A second child is usually easier than the first," he said without looking up.

June didn't know what to make of that statement—a nonanswer—but she couldn't bring herself to ask a third time as he prodded at her inner walls.

When Dr. Applebaum was done, he wheeled his stool away from June's pelvis and snapped off his gloves. He had an odd expression on his lined face, his lips sagging into a frown and his gray eyebrows rising high. Even the fold of skin that forever hooded his eyelids lifted slightly. With the elongation of his features, he looked like a thoughtful basset hound.

June lowered her legs and sat up.

"You're a bit . . . old to have another child," Dr Applebaum said slowly, as if he was trying for tact, "but there's little harm in trying." He swiveled on his stool and took up a clipboard.

June smoothed the hospital gown over her bare thighs and sat a little taller, mustering the courage to ask the question she always asked. "What about my pain, Dr. Applebaum?"

He was scribbling notes on her chart, not looking at her.

"My monthly pain."

"Every woman experiences monthly pain, June," Dr. Applebaum said—the same unhelpful phrase he'd been telling her for years and years.

"At times, I am . . . debilitated," June went on, the words as heavy as rocks in her mouth. "Unable to get out of bed."

Dr. Applebaum nodded but did not look up. "You've always been a sensitive girl, June."

June bit her lips together, mustering the courage to keep talking. Her desire and concern for a second child outweighed her embarrassment. "Sometimes I grow dizzy," she said, "and nauseous. Sometimes I . . . Do all women throw up from . . . ?"

Dr. Applebaum looked up then. "That *is* somewhat out of the ordinary."

After years of hand-patting and empty platitudes from every doctor she visited, his understatement felt like an absolute victory.

But then June's mind began to race. *Out of the ordinary* sounded a little bit like *problem*—and suddenly his acknowledgment made her fearful that something actually *was* wrong. Because if she wasn't just being sensitive, and the pain wasn't just in her head . . . what then? The question brought chills to her bare legs. If Harry didn't want her now, he certainly wouldn't want her once he found out the extent of her defects.

June clasped her hands in her lap, refusing to allow herself even a hint of tearfulness. She would not embarrass herself. "What could it mean, Dr. Applebaum?"

He was back to taking notes on her chart, his pen moving faster now. "It's probably nothing," he said, and June felt both relieved and dismissed.

"Nothing to worry about?"

"An anomaly." Dr. Applebaum stood up, causing the wheels of his stool to shriek. "That said, I'm going to prescribe a painkiller called Percodan to help you manage the pain; let's see if that doesn't make you feel better."

Make you feel better. As if it were her feelings that hurt, rather than every cell in her belly and hips.

Dr. Applebaum reached for the doorknob. "Send my best to your parents."

With that, he exited the exam room.

~

"May I help you find something?"

Spidery lace trim slipped through June's fingers. She looked up from the negligee and met the salesclerk's eyes. Was it obvious that she usually stuck with practical nightgowns?

"This one is very nice," the clerk said.

"It is," June said absently.

The clerk must've been barely twenty, with deep-plum eye shadow that made her eyes appear bruised. The look was distracting. "Are you looking for something in particular?" she asked, as if June hadn't heard her the first time. "An occasion in mind?"

June couldn't very well tell the girl that she wanted to seduce her own husband tonight. She couldn't think of an appropriate occasion to mention, anyhow—she was looking at lingerie, for heaven's sake. It's not like she was here to find a dress for a charity brunch, or a ball gown for an awards ceremony.

June touched the lace again. "I'm looking for something . . . nice."

The girl quirked a smile, as if she knew exactly what June meant. "I think I have something you might like."

It was still morning, and Maquette was practically empty. Without anyone around to witness her desperation, June followed the girl past various racks of silk and lace, ignoring the twinges of discomfort that lingered from Dr. Applebaum's earlier examination.

The salesclerk halted in front of a display of gauzy negligees. One had a puckering of polka dots across the diaphanous fabric. "What do you think of this?"

June pursed her lips. Did the girl think June was someone's mistress? June was a wife. A mother. And this was . . . What was the point of wearing something like this? She might as well be nude.

"Perhaps something simpler?" the girl asked, leading June to another rack.

This was more June's taste: a slender slip with a low enough neckline to tantalize but not embarrass herself. "I like this," June said, tracing a finger over the small rose bow affixed to the center of the bodice. The silk was a pale blush that would flatter her complexion.

"A mature choice," the girl said, supposedly meaning for her words to be a compliment, but they gave June pause.

She didn't want to appear *mature*, did she? She worried *mature* was only one step away from *boring*.

She glanced at the previous rack, the one with the see-through negligees. If June wanted to seduce her husband away from his actual mistress, perhaps the see-through option would get Harry's attention.

The girl clocked June's glance. "Why don't you take both?" she offered. "One safe, and one daring? That's what I would do."

June nodded. "Yes, all right."

The girl collected both negligees, and June followed her to the checkout counter, then watched her carefully nestle each piece in tissue paper. "He's going to love these," she said, handing June her shopping bag.

June was momentarily annoyed by her own transparency, but at least this was only a shopgirl. *Is there a money-back guarantee if he doesn't love them?* she wanted to ask, but she merely picked up her bag and walked out.

11

Irene was the first to arrive at the party, right at five o'clock on Friday evening, carrying some sort of Jell-O dessert covered in Handi-Wrap. When Winifred opened the door, Irene—standing there on the front stoop—had wide eyes and timid shoulders.

"I thought I must be in the wrong neighborhood."

Winifred raised her arms. "Welcome to the Seacastle!"

"Thank you for inviting me." Irene hadn't fully considered Winifred's address until she was driving down Ocean Avenue just now, past the shingle-style seaside mansions. She had known Winifred was well off, but she hadn't realized the extent.

"I'm delighted you could come." Winifred opened the door wider and stepped aside, beckoning. "Though you really didn't need to bring anything—you saw how much food I bought yesterday, didn't you?" She chuckled lightly—self-consciously, Irene observed.

"I never attend a party empty handed," Irene said, stepping past Winifred. Even the foyer was impressive, with its sparkling chandelier and expensive tile floor. "Besides, this was Wallace's favorite dessert: peaches-and-cream pretzel salad."

"Oh, *yum*. Not to be missed, then." Winifred took the dish from Irene's grasp. "Let's take this to the kitchen."

Irene tried not to gawk on the way, but that soon proved impossible. She'd never set foot in such an opulent home, with its excessive space and outlandish decor. As they passed open doorways, Irene spotted jungle-themed wallpaper, animal-print fabrics, gold-framed mirrors, and strange abstract artwork. On the walls of one room, bright birds of paradise stood out against a lush and leafy background; a massive magenta couch in the center of the room complemented their frilly feathers.

In any other arrangement, Irene would've deemed the house cluttered; but somehow, Winifred had managed to make the maximalist designs look . . . abundant. Joyful. Each room was a setting unto itself, a visceral experience, an escape.

In the kitchen—a breezy and utilitarian space—Winifred indeed had a massive spread of sweet and savory indulgences, including an oceanic pot of fondue and a Black Forest cake the height of a small child. It must've taken Winifred an entire day to prepare all this by herself (unless she'd hired help—but since she'd done her own shopping, Irene assumed she'd done her own cooking). There was barely room on the countertop for Irene's contribution, but Winifred wasn't shy about shoving plates out of the way to give the pretzel salad a prime location.

As she removed the plastic wrap, Winifred hummed indulgently. "Irene, this looks delicious," she said, drawing out the last word for emphasis. "This was so thoughtful."

Witness to Winifred's wealth, Irene appreciated her sincerity with new context. Winifred beamed down at Irene's modest salad as if it were the shiniest gem in the house, and Irene found her cheeks tightening with pride.

The doorbell chimed, a cascading song that echoed through the house. "Ah!" Winifred clapped her hands. "I'll be right back. Please, eat some food, make yourself at home," she said, disappearing through the double doors.

Irene found herself a plate, but the view outside caught her attention more than the food. There was a wide patio, a pool with twin lounge chairs, a lawn, and the sea far beyond. Even over the hum of a record singing in another room, Irene could hear the crashing waves and the gulls and distant children shrieking far down the beach.

She imagined Winifred fixing herself dinner for one in this kitchen; some nights, it must've felt as though the ocean might crawl all the way up the beach to swallow Winifred whole. That's how Irene's grief felt sometimes, even after so many years. At least her home was on a cozy suburban street where she was never truly alone, where a neighbor or friend was a mere shout away, and the walls pressed inward at night to make Irene feel melancholy but safe. Out here, she would feel as exposed as a crab on the open sand.

Suddenly, this party made even more sense.

At the front door, Winifred was delighted to find Fred—a bag boy from the Stop & Shop—standing ahead of two others. His cheeks were red. "I wasn't sure this was the right place," he said sheepishly.

"It is! It is," Winifred said, trying to sound welcoming to the shy boy. "And you brought friends!"

Fred visibly swallowed. "You said the more the merrier?"

"Yes, absolutely." Winifred stepped to the side, but Fred didn't budge.

"This is my older brother, Neil," he explained.

Neil waved. "How do you do?"

"And Neil's girlfriend, Mary."

Mary offered a small, unnecessary curtsy.

Winifred laughed. "No need for formalities. Come, Irene is here!"

At the mention of Irene, Fred's shoulders relaxed just a touch, and he followed Winifred into her house. They weren't halfway to the kitchen when the doorbell rang again.

The sound was like a gong sending her back in time. Suddenly Winifred was outside the parlor with Bruce, his lips lingering on her neck; their first guests had just rung the doorbell, but he'd held on to her hips. "You'll do great," he'd murmured into her hair.

She'd kissed his rough cheek, breathing his cologne. "Fingers crossed." Then she'd swiveled out of his grasp to greet their first guests, not knowing yet that this would be their last moment alone together.

Blinking rapidly, Winifred forced a smile on her face. "Hostess duty calls!" she said to Fred and the others, shaking off the lingering reverie. "The kitchen is through there." She pointed, and the little group disappeared through the parlor.

Opal had arrived, wearing a stylish miniskirt that was far more fun than her usual tailored-trouser uniform at Maquette; exquisite purple eye shadow brought out the green in her eyes. She introduced her friend Teresa, who appeared effortlessly cool with her round sunglasses and luscious leather jacket. Winifred was ecstatic.

"You live here?" Opal asked as Winifred led them to the kitchen, where the other guests were congregating.

Fred had already filled a plate with meatballs, and Irene was cutting into her pretzel salad. Fred's brother and his girlfriend had opened the back door and were lighting up on the patio; sea salt and sweet smoke wafted in. When Winifred appeared, Fred shot them a dark look, and they hunched a little but didn't extinguish their joints.

"You're fine," Winifred called out to them reassuringly. "Just fine."

"Look at that pool!" Teresa said.

"You're welcome to go for a dip," Winifred said, "but it's a bit chilly with the wind."

"Tempting," Teresa said, "but I think I'd rather try this fondue."

Winifred flashed them a toothy smile. Her chest already felt lighter from the hubbub that was gradually surrounding her. "Can I make anyone a piña colada?"

They all nodded, and the doorbell rang again.

Irene disappeared into the hall while Winifred worked on the drinks, filling a pitcher to the brim with the sweet liquid. The familiar chaos of hosting settled over Winifred like a silk robe. She loved this part of a party: guests arriving, introducing themselves, warming up to the space. Bashful but eager. The outgoing individuals paved a social path for the more timorous guests. She loved attempting to draw the nervous ones out—with friendly conversation, with alcohol, with introductions.

Irene returned with Lyle, the waiter from the Shore House. He'd brought four friends, two of whom Winifred recognized as his coworkers. Neil took the first two piña coladas from Winifred; his girlfriend asked Winifred if she could call a few friends to join them.

"Of course." Winifred turned. "Fred, have you met Opal and Teresa?"

The party went on like this—people arriving, Winifred and Irene managing the food and drinks, the youngest guests smoking on the patio and fiddling with Bruce's sound system until music blasted out of the parlor. The house filled with voices, laughter, and body heat. Conversation flowed like an Atlantic current, churned up by a storm of rum, vodka, and tequila.

The longer it went on, the less Winifred thought about Bruce, and it was a relief.

Pretty soon, some forty people were crammed into the kitchen. It was by no means the largest party Winifred had thrown, but with everyone congregated in one room, the crowdedness was distilled. Guests spilled into the yard. A game for which Winifred did not know the rules was played on the lawn with drunken exuberance. The gusting wind dispersed fragrant clouds of smoke.

Winifred recognized fewer than half her guests; friends of friends, siblings, and coworkers of her original invitees rounded out the attendees. When she *did* spot a familiar face, they were having fun. Teresa sat on the edge of the pool with one of Lyle's friends, her Levi's rolled up so she could kick the water. Fred's cheeks were bright red under Opal's attention as they sat in twin lounge chairs on the porch, but his gestures were loose and expressive. Neil's girlfriend had invited a whole gaggle of college girls, who were now sitting in the grass, passing a joint around the circle. Even Irene—the oldest of the bunch, aside from Winifred—was drinking a piña colada in between stirring the fondue and collecting dirty plates.

Winifred flitted from one group to the next, offering refills, cleaning up spills, giving directions to the nearest restroom. There was hardly a moment to think, but when there was, Winifred reveled in the fullness in her chest. One of her greatest joys was fostering other people's good times—even better if she could forget her own woes in the process. Wouldn't life be sweeter if it were forever one large party? If nights like these would never cease?

12

Not now, not now, not now.

June's core was on fire by the time she arrived home. Nausea had coiled around her esophagus and clouded her head. It was not uncommon for June to experience pain days before she bled, but this was still early. Had her examination triggered it? Of course it had to happen now. *Of course.* Harry was supposed to arrive at eight o'clock that evening. The one night she needed her body to comply, and it had decided to betray her.

Pain stormed in June's abdomen as she hurried through the front door. She dropped her shopping bags on the floor, blew past Peggy—Bella's nanny—and locked herself in the downstairs bathroom. She dug her new pill bottle out of her pocketbook, shook one into her hand, and swallowed it dry. Then she yanked her pantyhose down and checked herself for blood, glad to confirm that she had not started yet.

With her dress hiked up around her waist, June slumped on the toilet seat and cradled her head in her hands. Sweat pricked at the back of her neck. She breathed four short breaths, then one deep. She wasn't sure if breathing actually improved her pain or not, but her breath was the only thing that was within her control at that moment, and so she breathed as she'd been taught when she was pregnant with Bella. Lamaze breaths were, at the very least, something to focus on.

June waited like this—on the toilet, forcing her breaths into staccato patterns—while an electrical tempest raged through her. All the cramping gave her an upset stomach. Her thighs quivered.

None of this was new. Some months, a deep sorrow overtook her. It was a *why me?* sort of sorrow, pleading and desperate. Today, however, June was filled with anger. It wasn't fair. *It wasn't fair.* The defectiveness of her body brought on a primal fury. Were she alone in the house, she might've screamed—not in pain, but in rage.

Yet, as always, she did not scream. She didn't even moan. She choked it all back, swallowed it all down. Kept quiet, as she had been taught. *Society rewards mild women,* her mother and grandmother used to intone. An inner rebelliousness sometimes made her wonder if *mild* was just a nice word for *powerless*—but that voice was dangerous, and she'd gotten good at silencing it.

As she sat there not screaming, gradually, her shoulders released from her ears. The pill began to take effect, breaking the storm clouds apart like a miracle of God.

As if coming out of a daze, June reanimated. She tugged her pantyhose into place. Smoothed her skirt. Daubed her sweat with a tissue and emerged from the bathroom.

Peggy was tidying the living room—fixing the couch pillows, collecting Bella's toys. When June walked in, she looked up from her task, clutching Cotton, Bella's floppy stuffed bunny.

"Are you all right, Mrs. Duxbury?" Peggy asked.

"Where's Bella?"

"Upstairs, playing with her dollies." Peggy wanted to ask again if June was all right, but she didn't. June had arrived looking positively *yellow* and had spent the past half hour in the bathroom. Though her pains were a common occurrence, June rarely spoke of them, and Peggy knew better than to press.

"Has she eaten?"

"Yes," Peggy said. "I was just tidying up before I left—unless you'd like me to stay through the afternoon?"

"I'm fine, Peggy," June said tersely and retreated upstairs.

～

That afternoon, June decided to take advantage of the pill's effectiveness by taking Bella out for a Del's frozen lemonade by the beach. It was a tradition they'd started when Bella was first beginning to eat solid food. June and Harry had sat on a bench and given Bella a small bite of the cold lemony slush. The tart flavor made Bella screw her face up into the cutest pucker June had ever seen, lemonade oozing from pursed lips. When Bella reached out her tiny arms for another bite, June and Harry had laughed and cheered.

New motherhood had been so much harder than June expected—not just physically and emotionally, but socially too. There was pressure to lose the baby weight, pressure to maintain the house to the same standards as before, pressure for Bella to reach certain milestones at certain times. Before June had a baby, she'd imagined herself as the perfect mother—with a tiny waist, a spotless house, a thriving child—but after Bella was born, that ideal had felt completely out of reach. Once, on a particularly hard day, June had called her mother to ask *Why didn't you warn me?* over and over, her chest heaving with resentment while Bella screamed in the background. Of all the feelings she'd expected to experience as a new mother, failure had not been one of them.

But sitting there on that beachside bench, watching her husband and daughter giggle over the sweetness of lemonade, had been one of the first moments postpartum that June felt happy. Suddenly, her stretched and delicate body—with its soft belly, achy breasts, and dark circles under her eyes—didn't feel so embarrassing; the crumbs on her countertops were unimportant; her daughter was perfect. June had created a life, and she felt a flicker of the prenatal pride that had permeated her existence just seven months before.

Moments like that first lemonade had made all the hardship seem worthwhile—and worth doing again. Now that she truly knew what to expect, June felt ready for another baby—ready for a do-over. She imagined her family of four enjoying lemonade by the beach for many years to come, and it filled June with a sense of hope that was a little sour now, but she knew eventually would turn sweet.

If only she could convince Harry.

~

The pains returned in the early evening, just as Bella was finishing her bath. June had been crouched beside the tub for too long, and when she stood, a zap of discomfort had sprung up in her low back. It persisted as the evening trudged on, growing worse after an hour of playing with dollies on the floor.

By the time June could sneak away, her abdomen was twisted in a knot, and she hurried downstairs to take another pill. Now was the time June would start making dinner, but Harry was sure to have eaten by the time he arrived, and June wasn't hungry in the slightest. With Bella still preoccupied, June opted to stir herself a martini. Her skin was clammy, and it occurred to her that she should shower before Harry arrived—but it was only six o'clock in the evening; she had time for a drink first.

June wandered out onto the patio and sank into her favorite lounge chair by the pool. The warm breeze rippled over her legs and ruffled her hair. This time when she breathed, it was a deep and luxuriant sigh. The vodka made her limbs feel fuzzy, and the pill made her belly feel numb. Sitting by the pool all by herself, June was the most relaxed she'd felt in ages. The realization might have made her melancholy, if she weren't so peaceful.

13

By seven thirty on Friday night, June was fresh and showered. She tucked Bella into bed, bending to kiss her daughter's velvet-soft forehead. Bella had recently transitioned to a big-girl bed, and June still wasn't used to it. She had watched her friends' children transform into their own little people, but that wasn't the same as seeing her own child grow. It seemed like just yesterday Bella was wailing and helpless.

June missed feeling needed as only a mother was needed by a newborn. To have a tiny, sweet-smelling baby completely reliant upon her, giving June unconditional love and purpose.

June's recovery from Bella's birth had overshadowed those early motherhood pleasures she'd looked forward to for so long. At night, Harry had had to retrieve Bella from her crib to nurse, because June was still healing, unable to climb out of bed without fear of some fragile connection tearing open again. Those late nights put a strain on their marriage that hadn't lessened. June healed, and Bella phased out of nursing, but—aside from the occasional happy lemonade—Harry had only grown more distant.

What June wouldn't give for a chance to do it all over—do it right.

Moreover, she had felt so loved while she was pregnant. Cherished. June was certain that if she could seduce Harry this summer, she could recreate that early love feeling. She could prove to herself, her children, and her husband that she was capable of being a good mother. These modern feminists might've scoffed at her way of thinking, but this was all she'd ever wanted, and she was determined to succeed. She would do all she could to keep Harry home where he belonged, keep her family in one piece.

June crept out of Bella's room but not before taking one last lingering glance at her daughter's beautiful blonde hair and pursed pink lips. Bella needed her parents to stay together.

In the master bedroom, June carefully unwrapped the two negligees. She touched the sheer fabric of the more daring one. She wanted to be bold, and sexy, and free—but that just wasn't her. She liked the modest option—classy, sleek, and sophisticated—and she wanted Harry to fall in love with her the way she was. He'd done it before. He just had to remember.

June folded the see-through option in tissue and stuffed it into the back of her dresser drawer. Then she undressed and donned the safe negligee. The silk was cool against her lotion-soft skin.

It was exactly eight o'clock when June returned downstairs. She arranged herself on the couch—legs outstretched, a robe draped loosely over her shoulders—and sipped a fresh martini. She'd made a whole pitcher of martinis for them to enjoy. The windows were cracked, allowing the warm ocean breeze to slip through the curtains.

She waited.

Eight fifteen came along, and June plucked the olive from the bottom of her glass, sucking the brine from her fingers.

She waited another five minutes, then stood and refilled her glass.

At eight thirty, she ate the second olive.

At a quarter to nine, she felt the rumblings of pain deep in the recesses of her core. She waited a few minutes, paying acute attention to the sensation. It intensified.

"This can't happen now," she said to no one.

She stood and paced. Harry would be home any minute, she was sure, and she couldn't afford to take off her negligee and lie on a hot-water bottle all night. She hurried into the bathroom, placed the third pill of the day on her tongue, and swallowed it with a sip of her cocktail.

The living room was hot. Or maybe she was hot. The breeze coming in through the window wasn't strong enough. Maybe she should lie by the pool? Let Harry find her there, outside, looking beautiful. She stalked toward the door, wafting the fabric of her robe to fan herself—she didn't want to sweat in her brand-new silk. June looked down and was horrified to see that she already had. Dark mauve rings had formed under her armpits, in stark contrast to the delicate pink of the dry fabric.

"Damn it," she swore.

She rushed upstairs, untangling her arms from the thin silk straps. In the bedroom, she let the negligee fall down her body to the floor. Her skin was beginning to tingle. Dr. Applebaum had told her not to take the painkillers in quick succession. He'd warned that they were addictive. But what did that mean, exactly? And what choice did she have? Tonight had to be perfect. Besides, part of this floaty-fuzzy feeling was probably because of the martinis.

June dug the sheer negligee from the back of the drawer and shimmied it over her naked body. The floor-length mirror revealed everything. If she were sober, she would be embarrassed—all that smooth skin, veiled but not hidden—yet right now, well, she thought she looked rather appealing. Perhaps the mistress negligee had been a good choice after all. She couldn't save her marriage by doing the same old thing.

"Mommy?" Bella was in the doorway, rubbing her sleepy eyes.

June didn't think to cover herself up. She merely said, "Go back to bed, darling."

Bella wavered, clutching the wall.

"It's bedtime, sweetheart," June said.

Bella turned and toddled back down the hallway.

June waited ten seconds, twenty, and then she snatched the modest negligee from the floor, dropped it into her dirty-clothes basket, and returned downstairs. She poured herself a fresh martini and carried it outside, where the air was cool and she wouldn't sweat.

The fresh wind was a relief. She sank onto her patio chair and lay back. The sky was dark now. The stars shone like little diamonds on black velvet. They reminded her of going ring shopping when she and Harry were engaged.

June lifted her head and sipped her martini. The breeze cut through the sheer fabric on her body, caressing skin that never encountered the outside air: her inner thighs, her pubic mound, the undersides of her breasts. She adjusted her slip over her chest; her nipples were tight from the chill. Her body hummed with sensation. It felt good. She felt sensual. The pain was, miraculously, gone—and that only intensified her confidence. She delighted in the thought of Harry finding her out here. She closed her eyes and allowed the sea breeze to grope her skin.

Meanwhile, upstairs, Bella had had a nightmare.

She had gone back to bed as Mommy asked, but her chest was still clutched by worry. Every time she closed her eyes, she felt the dream catching up to her, and she'd open them again. After many minutes of this—to Bella, it felt like hours—she crawled out of bed in search of her mother again. She carried her stuffed bunny Cotton to the master bedroom first, expecting Mommy to be asleep, but she wasn't there. Bella called out in the hallway to no answer. She descended the stairs on her hands and knees, backward, dragging Cotton by the ear. Bella moved methodically until she reached the bottom.

She found Mommy outside on the patio, asleep in a chair. Bella liked the idea of a sleepover by the pool. The soft lapping of water against tile was lulling. Bella toddled close to the pool's edge, catching her own reflection in the ripples. She wanted to touch her reflection. Fixated on her own watery image, she dropped Cotton. The bunny plunked into the water.

A small noise emitted from Bella's throat. Panicked, Bella crouched to retrieve the bunny. She reached, and reached, and reached, teetering over the deep-blue pool water.

She did not think about how she wasn't wearing her water wings.

She did not think about how she couldn't swim without them.

She only wanted to save her bunny.

14

For a split second, Bella was weightless, nearing Cotton in a free fall toward the water. Then she was splashing, gasping.

"Bella!" Daddy was suddenly there, dragging her up.

Sopping wet, Bella wailed, extending her arms toward Cotton. With Bella clutched to his side, Daddy leaned down and seized the bunny from the pool, shoving it into Bella's arms. It made a squishing noise as she squeezed it tight, sniffling.

Daddy set Bella down on her own two feet, his body between her and the pool. His suit had a big dark wet patch where he'd held her close. "What have we told you about the pool?" he said firmly. "You always need Mommy or Daddy nearby."

Bella pointed to her mother lying on the lounge chair with an upturned glass resting on the tile beside her.

The next thing June knew, Harry was looming over her, a rough hand shaking her shoulder. "Jesus Christ, June."

She blinked. She must've fallen asleep. "Harry," she said, relieved he'd finally arrived. Then she noticed her daughter. "Bella, what are you doing out of bed?"

"She was about to drown, is what she was doing." Harry's cheeks were red with anger, his eyes wide with what June interpreted as a lingering scare.

"What are you talking about?" June sat up, and her chair swung underneath her like a swing. She touched a hand to her temple to steady herself.

"I can't believe you," Harry said. "I come home to find my wife passed out and my daughter in the pool."

June's stomach dropped. "She . . . *what?*"

Behind Harry, Bella stood with her toes pointed inward, her face blank with shock. She clutched her bunny close, shivering a little. They were both soaking wet, matted fleece and her little cotton nightgown dribbling pool water.

"She almost drowned," Harry enunciated, "reaching for a stuffed animal, while you lay drunk and oblivious mere feet away."

He spoke so matter-of-factly that despite the warm summer night, June could practically feel the ice radiating off him; her esophagus froze like a pipe in winter. In her daze, the shame hadn't yet caught up to her.

"Don't you have *anything* to say?" Harry shouted.

Bella squeaked in fright and surprise from the outburst. It was a sound June knew well, the same sound Bella made when she fell down and was yet to decide if she was perfectly all right or if she wanted to burst into meltdown tears.

"Harry, please." June didn't want Bella to cry. "Let's put Bella back to bed, and then we can discuss it."

"What's there to discuss?" he boomed.

"*Shhh,*" June hissed. "The *neighbors.*"

"You think I give a shit about waking the neighbors?"

"*Harry.*"

Bella began to wail, a soft moaning that made June's heart pop like a water balloon.

"She's scared," June said. "You're scaring her."

"She's scared because she fell in the pool," Harry said, scooping Bella into his arms. He kissed her head and turned his back on June, carrying their daughter into the house.

When she was alone, June wiped a hand over her face. She felt drunk and hungover at the same time—her mouth was dry, her head hurt, and yet she felt uncoordinated and a little dizzy. She clapped her hands on her cheeks, trying to wake herself up. The seriousness of what might have happened to Bella was yet unformed in June's addled head, her terror like a swelling wave offshore, yet to crash.

When June heard Harry's approaching footsteps, she smoothed her hair and sat a little straighter.

"What is this?" Harry asked, holding up June's pill bottle.

"Dr. Applebaum prescribed them."

He swiped a hand over his face, still raging. "How many did you take?"

June didn't want to say. Objectively, she knew her pain wasn't her fault, that her use of painkillers was justified, but the way Harry spoke to her . . . it made her feel like her *anomaly*, as Dr. Applebaum had called it, was a personal failing. If only she had better willpower.

"And drinks?" Harry gestured toward the martini glass by her foot.

"I don't know," she said, covering her mouth with her fingers.

The risk to Bella was beginning to wash over her. It could've been so much worse. So, so much worse. She could picture Bella flailing in the pool, and it made June sick to her stomach.

God, what had she done?

"I can't believe this," Harry said under his breath, reading the bottle.

"Harry, I—"

"Our daughter could have drowned," Harry said slowly, "and it would've been your fault. Think about that."

June began to cry, great ugly heaving sobs.

"I hardly recognize you anymore," Harry said, almost to himself, as if he was bewildered. "Who are you?"

June wanted to insist that she was still the same woman he'd fallen in love with, but perhaps the challenges of motherhood and the worsening of her pain *had* changed her. She did not feel as innocent or optimistic as she had when they were young; most days, she felt worn down. And she certainly didn't recognize herself tonight.

"I'm getting a lawyer," he said. "This divorce will happen. I've put it off long enough."

"*No*," June wailed, but he kept talking, going on about her actions, how she was an unfit mother, how he would vie for custody.

She wiped her face, the horror of Bella's scare clambering through June's chest like a sea monster. She couldn't keep up with this conversation, the lingering inebriation and the delayed but sickening realization that her daughter had almost just . . . she couldn't even bring herself to think the word. Her self-hatred was too great.

And now, Harry was leaving, and she couldn't do or say anything to stop him. In this moment, she didn't blame him for wanting to leave her, terrible mother that she was.

"I'm going to take Bella back to Boston with me in the morning"— June opened her mouth, and he held up a hand—"no arguments."

"Harry," June pleaded. "Please. Can't we work through this? Can't we stay together—for Bella's sake?"

"For Bella's sake?" His tone was mocking.

"I'm begging—"

"I can barely look at you," he said with a shake of his head. "You're not the same woman I married."

"I can be better, I can—"

"I'm going upstairs," he said. "I'm sleeping in the guest room, and I'm leaving with Bella in the morning. That's final."

A sob escaped June's lips, and she clapped a hand over her mouth. Her shoulders shuddered. If she could shrink into nothing, she would. If only.

"And for Christ's sake, cover yourself up," Harry bit off. "You look ridiculous."

15

Marie would never forget Winifred Hurst's house, but if there was any doubt that the hulking cottage was in fact hers, the noise of the party confirmed it. Marie heard the music and laughter before she even switched off her engine. Cars were crammed in the circular driveway, and to her surprise, they were not the usual swooping and jetlike convertibles that suited this elite neighborhood. No, the driveway was filled with rickety wagons and fifteen-year-old rust buckets like her own. Though it didn't appear as though the cars' owners were living in their rides, as Marie was.

Before her arrival, Marie had spent a half hour in a public restroom washing her face, wiping her underarms, changing into a clean shirt and trousers, and brushing her greasy hair. Marie had emerged with a newfound confidence and dignity, which were otherwise scarce these days. But she'd already managed to save a few extra hundred dollars, so the extreme measures were working. And they didn't have to work forever, just *for now*, until she reached her savings goal.

A big meal at the party would help too. It was her primary reason for following through on Winifred's invitation, although Marie wasn't so oblivious as to deny the fact that Winifred's company compelled her. Winifred was magnetic. And as long as nobody's husband died at this party, Marie would consider it a worthwhile way to spend an evening. Better than sitting alone in her Plymouth, at least.

On the front stoop, Marie raised her finger toward the doorbell and pressed. As soon as the chimes sounded, self-consciousness seized her. Clearly, this was not a high-society party, but Marie still felt like a vagabond. The thought of making polite conversation—answering small-talk questions about her profession as a failed artist—made her want to crumple down until she resembled a discarded piece of paper.

Marie cringed as the echo of the bells clanged and subsided. She glanced at her shoes. No one answered. Judging by the noise emanating from the back of the house, no one probably heard.

She could leave, and Winifred would assume she'd never shown, never gotten this far. Marie considered it, but then she reached for the doorknob, opened the door, and stepped through.

The last time she'd seen this house, it'd been filled with whispering partygoers dressed to the nines. Hurried, harried paramedics. Loud weeping. The clatter of shoes shifting on the hardwood. A drum kit accidentally bumped, the harsh sizzle of a cymbal taunting the silence. And Winifred, there in the middle of it all, shimmering in her shiny gown, tears and makeup running down her face. The hot skin of her shoulder under Marie's reluctant, comforting palm.

Now, the foyer and ballroom were empty, wide open and sad looking in their vacant ornateness. Marie didn't linger. She followed the voices and found everyone crowded in the kitchen and backyard. Loud laughter billowed, clouding her thoughts.

These partygoers were nothing like those at last summer's soiree. In fact, Marie thought she recognized a Stop & Shop employee—one of the sweet older clerks who rang up her cereal. These were working-class guests. College students with summer jobs. Regular people who wore regular-looking clothes and drove regular cars. No diamonds, designer dresses, or judgmental expressions to be found. Though the chaos overwhelmed Marie, the guests were far less intimidating than what she'd been expecting.

Marie pushed into the boisterous crowd toward the spread of food. Her arms brushed against cotton, denim, and bare skin that was a little sweaty. No one paid any attention to her. Everyone was drunk, or—judging by the smell drifting through the open patio doors—high. Everyone was flirting, cracking up, talking over each other.

Marie took up a plate and filled it: the last meatball, a glop of what looked like salmon dip, a piece of very cheesy-looking quiche, a big handful of mixed crackers. A giant cake had already been cut, and she flopped a slice on top of her savory selection. She dunked a piece of bread into a pot of fondue and stuffed it directly into her mouth. She was a vulture in bliss.

Shoving another cheese-covered hunk of bread into her mouth, Marie swiveled, considering her options for where to sit down and eat. Then she heard it: Winifred's unmistakable lilt of a laugh. Marie searched the crowd and finally spotted her, all elegance and charm, not fifteen feet away. Her back was to Marie. She was mixing refreshments, pouring juice and draining a bottle of tequila into a big pitcher.

Marie's sense of ease disintegrated. Aside from Winifred—a woman Marie had met in the upstairs bathroom on what was probably the worst night of Winifred's life—Marie didn't know any of these people. What if she hadn't read between the lines properly? What if Winifred had invited her just to be nice? Suddenly, Marie felt like an interloper. She didn't belong here. She didn't belong anywhere except in front of a canvas, but even that was futile. Creatively blocked and obsessed with a derelict racetrack—who would want to associate with *that*?

She shouldn't have come. She couldn't let Winifred see her.

Marie ducked her head and, ready to flee, turned hurriedly—only to run straight into someone. Her plate dumped down the front of his patterned shirt and clattered on the floor, drawing the attention of other people nearby. The man jerked backward, raising his palms.

"Sorry! Sorry. I am *so* sorry," Marie said.

"It's all right, no harm intended." He smiled an easy smile.

Marie pushed past him, abandoning her food and the mess. She hurried through the parlor, wiping her hands on her pants as she went. Her stomach pinched. A part of her wanted to run back in and grab another slice of quiche or cake to take with her, but she'd already created enough of a scene. Her only goal now was to abscond from the party before Winifred realized she'd come.

Of course, as soon as Winifred had heard the plate clatter somewhere behind her, she pivoted toward the sound. One of Lyle's friends—Lawrence, she thought she'd heard him say earlier—was covered in chocolate frosting, cheese, and barbecue sauce. His beautiful patterned shirt was probably ruined now, but he was still smiling. Winifred wet a dishrag, and when she spun back toward the scene, the woman who'd bumped into him was fleeing the kitchen and Lawrence was standing by the counter looking a bit bemused. A few people nearby had already crouched to pick up the mess at his feet.

Winifred raced over and pressed the rag into Lawrence's hands. "For your shirt," she said and was thankful to see Irene approaching with a bottle of soda, for the stain.

Meanwhile, the woman had disappeared into the parlor. Winifred ran after her, catching up just as she was entering the foyer.

"It's all right," Winifred said but stopped short when the woman looked over her shoulder, her face blotched with red.

16

"Rushing off to spend more time with the O'Keeffe?" Winifred asked Marie. It was obvious she was trying to leave, but Winifred wanted to ease Marie's embarrassment. "It's back that way." She pointed toward the stairs.

"I . . . ," Marie trailed off, looking as if she'd been caught stealing.

"You think that was the first spill of the night?"

Marie didn't speak, her wide eyes searching Winifred's face for . . . Winifred wasn't sure. Reassurance, maybe?

Winifred took a step closer. "I wasn't sure you'd show," she said. "I'm glad you did. Please stay. Let's fix you another plate, shall we?" Winifred extended her hand.

Instinct told Marie to sprint out the door. After all, most relationships seemed to be conditional, based on a set of rules Marie had never learned. When Marie was a child, life and friendship had come easily, but she'd quickly learned that true friendship was a rarity destined to be lost. It was foolish—painful, even—to expect anything different.

Yet Winifred's kindness compelled her to linger.

As Marie looked at Winifred, she could feel her heart screwing up, twisting tighter and tighter until she realized she was holding her breath. Marie wanted to leave; she really did. She did not want to return to the kitchen and have to apologize to the man whose shirt she ruined. But when her body finally unlocked, it did not shrink toward the door—she reached for Winifred's hand.

Upon contact, they were both briefly reminded of holding hands last summer, first as Winifred led Marie down the stairs, then as Marie led Winifred toward Bruce, and finally as Marie pulled Winifred away from her husband's body.

They were both also reminded of being young girls and holding hands with their friends—that feeling of power and solidarity in a world that felt big and unwieldy, yet full of promise.

The shock of contact faded, though. Marie went back to feeling nervous, dreading reentering the kitchen. A few people looked their way when they returned, but thankfully, the man she'd spilled her plate on was nowhere to be found. The mess had already been cleaned up, the party carrying on as if nothing had happened at all.

"Ah, Irene," Winifred said, approaching the familiar-looking older woman. "Do you have any pretzel salad left?"

Irene smiled, her eyes darting over to Marie before settling back on Winifred. "I saved you a piece."

"You're a peach," Winifred said. "My friend Marie, here, is absolutely *starving*. Mind if I relinquish my slice to her?"

"Of course not." Irene recognized Marie as the woman who slept in her car in the parking lot. "Would you like some quiche too? I just pulled the last one out of the fridge."

"She'd love a slice," Winifred answered for her.

Winifred and Irene led Marie around the food table, fixing her up with a hearty plate. When finally they seemed satisfied with Marie's bounty—a laughable amount of food, really—Winifred blazed a path through the patio door.

Outside, people were smoking and gabbing. Marie spotted the man from earlier and lowered her head, hoping he wouldn't see her. But out of the corner of her vision, he seemed perfectly happy. His shirt was a little damp, but the woman he was talking to didn't seem to mind.

Marie sighed as she shuffled behind Winifred through the fresh-cut grass. The cool beach breeze combed through Marie's hair, soothing her.

"There's a quiet place just this way." Winifred led her through a small wooden gate and along a narrow dune path surrounded by beach grass. The sounds of the party began to fade. "Here we are." Winifred gestured to a large flat-topped rock to the left of the path. "I like to sit here and watch the waves."

Marie took a seat with her plate, expecting Winifred to plop down beside her, but her host remained standing.

"It's perfectly secluded," Winifred went on, "yet you can still say you were at the party." She winked. "I'm going to head back and make more drinks. Just relax and eat. And if you want to leave, don't go without saying goodbye."

Marie nodded. "Thank you. I won't," she said, and she was telling the truth.

17

The party reached its crescendo when one of Neil's girlfriend's friends pushed one of Lyle's friends into the pool. Both the girl and the man in the pool were laughing, but Winifred heard whispers that a sexist comment had prompted the push. Of course, the splash encouraged others to make the plunge, and pretty soon there were more wet guests than dry, and Winifred was fishing musty towels out of upstairs closets.

In the midst of all this, her neighbor called to complain about the noise. For a brief moment, she shifted the stack of towels in her arms, feeling like a delinquent. Then a calm rebellion rose inside her, and she told her neighbor to quit being a bore—and hung up.

The last of the guests left around midnight, and then it was just Winifred, Marie, and Irene. The kitchen was littered with dirty plates, cups, and serving platters. The yard was strewn with wet towels and cigarette butts and beer bottles. Winifred hadn't had more than two piña coladas all night, but she felt giddy. The party had been a smash.

She'd never thrown a party with so much rowdiness. Before tonight, she would've said a successful party was one with a catering staff, expensive clothing, and minimal broken glasses. Bruce would've added that a successful party was one where he made a business deal. Now, however, Winifred thought differently. A successful party was one where people felt comfortable to be themselves, to let loose and make new friends and do something daring. A successful party now required at least one cannonball into the pool.

Winifred glanced around the kitchen. Now, the only proof of her success was the glorious mess that remained.

This was the part of the night when she and Bruce would turn on all the lights, put on a record, and clean together. They'd leave some things for the maid—the mopping, the linens, the sticky bannisters and invisible spills—but the rest was theirs. Winifred would pull on rubber gloves and wash dishes, Bruce would collect the trash, and they would dance and tidy up for hours.

After the first party they'd hosted together—a modest business dinner—Winifred had jumped right into cleaning. She wasn't yet accustomed to the luxuries of Bruce's world. He had told her to stop, said he hired people for that, but Winifred didn't like to go to bed in a messy house. Perhaps it was unconventional, she'd said, but he would feel accomplished when they were done. Sure enough, he did, and so it became their ritual.

Winifred's vision blurred with the thought of cleaning by herself tonight. But she couldn't ask anyone to stay. Irene was clearly exhausted; she stifled a yawn as she collected plates into a neat stack by the sink. Marie was hovering by the patio doorway with goose bumps on her arms, blinking sleepily, obviously waiting for an opportunity to escape. With the palms of her hands, Winifred rubbed the memory of Bruce from her eyes and then regarded the two women.

"It's time to go home," Winifred said. "Don't worry about cleanup, I'll handle it."

Irene appeared as if she might disagree but sighed. "I'll admit, I'm quite tired."

Winifred patted her arm. "You are an angel, Irene. Thank you so much for coming—and for all your help! I hope you had fun in between all that helping."

"I did," Irene said. More fun than she'd had in years. Though most of the partygoers had been younger than her children, she'd enjoyed their company. They hadn't treated her like an old woman, a mom, a widow, or a Stop & Shop checker—they'd treated her like just another party guest, like a friend.

Winifred handed Irene her pretzel-salad dish and escorted her to the door. "We'll do this again, and when we do, you'll have to make five times as much of this stuff."

Irene smiled. "I can do that."

When Irene was out the door, Winifred turned back to Marie, who was still hovering. "And what about you, Marie? Did you have fun?"

"Yes," Marie said. "Thank you for encouraging me to stay."

Tonight was the first time in a long time that Marie felt full and safe and relaxed. After her meal, Marie had actually joined the party. It reminded her of her gallery days, when she'd attended parties with other artists, freethinkers, and feminists wanting to make a statement. Marie didn't consider herself a political artist—even if that was the trend nowadays. She wasn't trying to *change* the world with her art—she was trying to understand it. And yet, those were the people she'd had the most in common with, because they knew what it was like to be consumed by their passion.

She'd found similarly minded people at the party tonight. Not artists, per se, but people who wanted to examine and question the world. Psychology majors, future defense attorneys, hippies, musicians. Marie had no idea where Winifred found these people—in fact, she got the sense that Winifred hadn't known most of them, either—but Marie was glad Winifred had invited her and convinced her to stay.

"Well, don't let me keep you," Winifred said now, reaching for the door.

Hesitation filled Marie's shoes with lead. She thought about the Plymouth parked out front, how uncomfortable it was. Given all the canvases crammed in the back, Marie slept crumpled behind the wheel. The night always compounded the kinks in her neck and the hardness of her seat and the cold air seeping through the windshield. The more tired she became, the more impossible it was to rest.

In the warmth of Winifred's home—the warmth of Winifred's *gaze*—Marie couldn't bear the thought of leaving. She would clean all night if it meant not having to go back to the Plymouth.

"I don't—" She coughed. The irony wasn't lost on her: only a few hours ago, she'd been reluctant to enter. Now she was reluctant to leave. She swallowed and tried again. "I don't have to go yet, if you . . . need a hand?"

Something shone in Winifred's eyes, a watery glimmer that Marie wouldn't dare identify. It could be nothing—sleepiness, perhaps—but it could also be something like hope, or gratitude, or endearment.

Whatever it was, Winifred was quick to answer. "I'd love some help, thank you."

Winifred latched the front door, and relief warmed her skin. On that terrible night last summer, Marie had saved her with her presence; now it seemed Marie would rescue her again.

Winifred led Marie back into the parlor, speaking over her shoulder as she went. "The way I normally clean is to put on some very good music, for motivation."

"Makes sense."

Winifred opened up a cabinet of records. "Why don't you choose?"

Marie crouched and carefully flipped through the covers. It was a great, eclectic collection, but Marie feared Winifred would judge her decision, whatever it was. She reached the end of the stack and began flipping back through all over again. She knew it shouldn't be so hard for her to select something, but little moments like this didn't come easy to her—it felt like a test, somehow. Winifred would think differently of her if she chose Sinatra versus the Rolling Stones versus the Temptations. What did Marie *want* Winifred to think of her?

"You don't have to take it too seriously," Winifred said. "You aren't choosing a husband."

Marie flushed and glanced up from her task. "Do you want to pick something?"

"No, no." Winifred waved her hand. "You're the guest."

Marie wanted to cry out from the pressure, but then she paused on *A Hard Day's Night*. She loved that album, and seeing the various expressions on the cover made her smile.

"That's a good one," Winifred commented.

"All right." Marie handed it to her. "Let's go with that." Marie liked the idea of Winifred thinking she was upbeat.

But Winifred frowned. "I didn't mean to rush you."

Marie shrugged. "If I had to choose a husband, I'd go with Paul McCartney."

Winifred snorted out a laugh. "Can't say I'd disagree, although I think he's a little young for me."

Marie laughed. "Me too."

Winifred slid the vinyl from its sheath and started the record. That single chord swelled through the speakers, and the Beatles launched into the title song. She set the album cover beside the player and adjusted the volume.

"Now what?" Marie asked.

"How about I start in on the dishes," Winifred said, "and you collect the trash?"

The Beatles proved to be a good choice. By the time "If I Fell" came into the speakers, they were both in the kitchen with all the lights on, singing along at the tops of their voices. Marie had a plastic bag and was combing the surfaces and floors for old food and paper napkins; Winifred wore rubber gloves and was bent over the steaming sink, rinsing plates for the dishwasher and hand-scrubbing the serving platters.

They worked like this for the whole album, feeling happy and sad and nostalgic. When they finished *A Hard Day's Night* for the second time, they put on *Rubber Soul* and continued cleaning. When they weren't singing along to the music, they were both lost in their own thoughts.

Marie hunched over her mop, swiping lopsided circles on the kitchen floor. She thought about painting. The mop could've been a big brush in her hand, the water like thin paint. She drew a curved cheek, plump lips. Then she dipped the mop in her bucket of gray water and slapped it onto the tile, erasing the imaginary figure. She started again, this time drawing the curved jowl of a Thoroughbred. Her high had faded hours ago—she hadn't taken more than a few drags—but she found herself transfixed by the wet splotches on the floor. Then she heard Winifred humming along with Paul's voice, and Marie blinked, breaking the spell to continue with her task.

Winifred was thinking about Bruce. The night before their wedding, she'd called him. They were staying in separate rooms at the resort, and she missed him. *Are you sure you want to go through with this?* she'd asked. His family didn't like her much. No one from his world did. *I am as certain about you as I am about the sun rising tomorrow,* he'd said. They ended up talking for hours—about their fears, their passions, their upcoming marriage. She told him she was glad it was the last night she'd have to sleep without him. Of course, she hadn't known that Bruce would leave her so soon.

But she wasn't alone now.

When Winifred or Marie paused in thought, each heard the other woman cleaning. The music, the clanking of dishes, the slap of the mop. Though neither of them spoke, the other's presence made internal musings less echoey. A thought or emotion couldn't swallow you up completely if you had company to pull you back into the moment. Winifred and Marie might've been barely a day beyond strangers, but neither of them wanted the companionship to end.

18

It was four o'clock in the morning when they both set down their cleaning tools. The whole downstairs and backyard were spotless; their skin was oily and gritty.

"I think that about does it," Winifred said, wiping damp hands on the front of her dress, which was already splattered with dishwater and cleaning solution.

"I don't think even a speck of dust remains in this house." Marie's sinuses stung with the scent of Pine-Sol. She was exhausted but also satisfied by this tangible sense of accomplishment, glad to have lingered here so long. But then it occurred to Marie that perhaps she had stayed too long. Had she been helping, or holding Winifred hostage?

"The sun should be up soon, I think," Winifred said, peering out the window at the star-flecked sky. "Gosh, when was the last time I pulled an all-nighter?"

Marie pulled all-nighters all the time—to paint, or because her car was so uncomfortable.

"You must be exhausted," Winifred prompted.

"I'm fine," Marie said, wondering if Winifred's comment was a hint that she should go. "Sorry if I overstayed my welcome."

"Are you kidding?" Winifred fixed Marie with a warm, crinkle-eyed expression. "I appreciate you staying so late. I hope I didn't make you feel obligated."

"Not at all." Marie glanced around the spotless kitchen. "In fact, this was a gas."

Neither of them was accustomed to asking for exactly what they wanted—that sort of brazenness had been trained out of them long ago, and they were both adept at skirting around a desire. Thankfully—standing in the spotless kitchen, surrounded by surfaces that were mirrorlike in their cleanliness—they both wanted the same thing: for Marie to stay.

"Care to stay up and watch the sunrise with me?" Winifred ventured. "I have the best view. And I think we have half a quiche left, if you're hungry."

Marie studied Winifred's face, searching for a falsehood, a hint of a counterpoint, a sign that she actually wanted Marie to leave and was only being polite. But Marie couldn't see it. All she saw were the wrinkled cheeks and pressed lips of optimism.

"That sounds like a fine way to start the day," Marie said.

Winifred brightened. "Wonderful. I'll grab the quiche from the refrigerator; you get a couple blankets from the closet there."

With their breakfast in hand, Winifred led the way out the patio doors and down the beach path until she reached the rock where she'd left Marie many hours before. This time, Winifred sat first, gesturing for Marie to sit down beside her. Marie handed Winifred one blanket and settled the second over her own lap. Winifred handed Marie a fork and held the quiche dish between them. Apparently, they were sharing. Marie stuck her fork into the edge of the quiche, breaking off a piece. When she lifted it to her mouth, Winifred went in for her own bite.

Winifred chewed, then sighed. "Bruce used to stay up and clean with me, after parties. We had a maid, but—I don't know, I can never sleep after a party. I'm always too energized, and I hated leaving such a mess for someone else, even if it *was* her job." Winifred looked at Marie for a moment, as if to see if she was listening. "A party isn't truly over until the house is clean, I suppose." She shook her head. "Maybe that sounds silly."

"That's not silly at all," Marie said. "Cleaning is like a conclusion."

Winifred broke another chunk off the quiche, her fork snapping against the dish as the crust gave way. "That's true," she mused. "There's satisfaction in doing a job and then seeing that it's done."

Marie thought about painting and how it was often impossible to tell when a piece was complete. One too many strokes, and it could appear overdone. She preferred to leave her paintings a little loose, a little unfinished. Better that than to push a piece past completion and ruin the whole thing.

Chores, on the other hand, were nothing like that. There was a mess, you cleaned it, and then there wasn't a mess anymore. Marie appreciated the simplicity of such tasks. They gave the illusion of order in an otherwise disorderly world. It seemed Winifred shared this sentiment.

"So many elements of life feel . . . endless," Winifred added.

Marie knew that feeling well. She recognized it as grief. "You miss Bruce."

"I do. Very much."

Close around them, crowding them, the beach grass rustled in the cool breeze. Without the sun, the sand and sea appeared indigo, nearly black. Waves burst with pops of frothy white, like ghosts tumbling onto the shore. Morning whispered pale across the horizon.

"I'm sorry," Marie said, "about what happened. The suddenness."

"Sometimes I wonder if that's better." Winifred smoothed the blanket on her lap. "Better sudden than to see it coming. A slow sickness would've been far worse, I think."

Her comment pierced Marie's heart with a familiar sharpness. Marie swallowed a bite of quiche, forcing the lump of emotion in her throat down, down, down. "I agree."

Watching a loved one die slowly, circling the drain for days on end, suffering, while you clung to a distant hope of improvement, the desperate chance at recovery . . . it was a torturous sort of heartbreak. One Marie knew intimately.

"It doesn't change the way I miss him, though," Winifred said with a sigh.

Marie disagreed with that. There was no *relief* in a sudden death, but there *was* relief in a slow one. Winifred's grief was pure, while Marie's . . . it was tinged with the understanding that *it's better this way*. Tinged with guilt too. And that changed the nature of the missing very much.

"It's the small things I miss most," Winifred went on. "I miss him pouring my orange juice. Resting his hand on my thigh while we read in the evenings. Hell, I even miss seeing his socks on the floor. In fact, I miss the small annoyances most. The stink of his cigars, and how he *insisted* on sleeping with the light on, and his perfect stoicism when we fought, which only made me angrier. And he always used the last of the milk and ate off my plate at restaurants." She blew out a long breath. "Those were the things that made him who he was, I think. More than the niceties. You know you truly love someone when you find even their worst quirks charming."

Marie's own grief was too old to remember any annoyances. All she could recall was the fierce love and awe she'd felt for the girl from her paintings. Then, that strange and horrible relief.

Marie stood abruptly, unable to bear the memory. Winifred's words had brought up a sudden surge of pain that Marie wasn't prepared to face. Like a spring flood, it knocked her down and sucked the solid ground from around her; sorrow rushed over her like white water. It got into her eyes.

"I just remembered I have somewhere to be," Marie said, which she knew made no sense, as it was not even five o'clock in the morning.

Winifred's brows pinched. "The sun isn't even up yet."

"I'm sorry, I—" Marie shook her head. "Thank you for having me." The blanket had fallen into a heap at her feet, and she stepped over it onto the beach path.

She wheezed with emotion all the way back to her car. It was only when she went to grip the steering wheel that she realized she was still holding her quiche fork. She dropped it on the floor. She shouldn't've left Winifred like that, but she'd panicked. The memory had overwhelmed her.

Back on the beach, Winifred was kicking herself. She'd made Marie uncomfortable with her grief. What was she thinking? Such topics were too vulnerable, uncomfortable, impolite. She should've kept the conversation light. She should've asked *Marie* questions, rather than babbling about her own problems. Winifred knew better than to talk about sadness with a stranger.

And that's what Marie was, wasn't she? A stranger? Their conversation in the bathroom, the tube of lipstick, the party, and their bout of cleaning—these moments hardly constituted a friendship. But Winifred had hoped, maybe, that they might lead in that direction. Because Winifred liked Marie. She wasn't judgmental like most other women here. Marie was kind, and accepting, and just shy enough to put Winifred at ease. And now Winifred doubted she'd ever see Marie again.

Winifred stayed on the beach and watched the sunrise, the sky paling into a delicate blue. Marie watched the sunrise, too, from her windshield as she drove back to the Stop & Shop parking lot. All day, each thought about the other.

19

June watched Mr. Duxbury drive away from their beach cottage with their daughter in the back seat. The last thing Harry said to her before he left was for June to hire a lawyer. She felt raw as she watched his car disappear. Her eyes were gritty with regret from the night before. She wasn't sure whether to feel heartbroken or afraid—or both.

In one day, all her plans had fallen apart.

She wouldn't have another baby.

She wouldn't save her marriage.

She had failed.

June turned away from the window, withdrawing into the dim house. The sky was gray, casting a pallor over the neighborhood. After a beautiful sunrise, clouds had rolled in; the air was heavy with heat and moisture.

June's body felt similar.

Her cramps had intensified overnight, and she'd started her period. June knew it before she rose from bed that morning—the bloating was obvious enough. Yet, later, in the bathroom, June had gazed into the toilet at the small red clots resting in the bottom of the bowl. The water had turned scarlet, the color dispersing like ink. The sense of failure had settled over her like a veil. She had witnessed the morning as if through black gauze, from her bloodstained underwear to the exhaust smoke billowing behind Harry's car.

June moved slowly after he left, making herself a cup of coffee that eventually went cold. She had no appetite. She prepared a hot-water bottle and collapsed on top of it on the sofa, clutching Bella's stuffed bunny close. It was still damp, but underneath the sharp scent of pool water, it smelled like her daughter.

June would not take any pills today. Not after Harry's rage and blame. She did not wish to dull the discomfort; she deserved every moment of self-hatred and pain.

Images from Bella's close call had haunted June all night. What kind of mother was she? June had been so fixated on facilitating an intimate evening with Harry that she'd put her daughter at risk. June felt a profound sense of horror, so deep that her bones ached. Thank God Bella was all right—but even June's relief was not enough to quell the sickening what-ifs that played in her mind's eye like a movie.

Lying supine, June rolled her head to the side, her ear meeting the rough fabric of an embroidered pillow. She stared past her mug on the coffee table and out the bay windows. A storm was riling. She had an unobstructed view of the ocean and sky, and both had deepened into a tumultuous indigo. While most of her friends found summer storms inconvenient, June had always loved the warm rain and rumble, ever since she was a girl. But now, as she carried a storm inside her, the threat of thunder made her uneasy. It felt personal, as if the heavens were growling directly at her.

June closed her eyes and tried to focus on the hot-water bottle under her back; the clammy heat numbed her skin even through her nightgown. Her belly pooched out, stretching with bloat. It made her look pregnant, an ironic taunt. She had the urge to move but knew that a change of position wouldn't help; it would only disturb things. She breathed and breathed and breathed.

Unlike the day before, when the pain had churned up an intense anger in June's heart, today, she was enveloped by powerlessness. For all her efforts, nothing ever seemed to change. Men—her father, her gynecologist, her husband—had all minimized June's pain. For twenty years, June had told them something wasn't right. And finally, *finally*, Dr. Applebaum had listened. For the first time in June's life as a menstruating woman, she had experienced relief.

But now her husband thought she was an addict.

Why was it so hard? June had done everything by the book. She fell in love, married a well-respected man, and made a place for herself in dignified society. She lived by the rule of her husband's needs, propping him up like the wire inside an umbrella, both supportive of his ambition and grateful for the shelter he provided. She mothered a beautiful child and gave her time and money to charity. She centered her decisions around elegance and grace—the prettiest dresses, the finest foods, the highest standards, the most respectable company. And yet, somehow, she had still failed.

A soft rain began to patter outside, and June shifted, ever so slightly, atop the hot-water bottle, so it would rest more squarely in the center of her lower back. Lightning flashed, not in a streak but a strobe; the world brightened for a mere moment; the clouds hung low and immensely textured. Over a minute later, the thunder growled. The distant sound was cut off by the ringing of the telephone.

She swung her legs off the couch one at a time, sitting up. Her head felt as cloudy as the scene outside. Still holding the bunny under one arm, she hobbled into the kitchen.

"Hello?"

"You'll never guess what Winifred did," Barbara said.

June smiled at her friend's lack of preamble. "What now?"

"She threw a party," Barbara said, as if she was shocked by the audacity.

"For what occasion?"

"Her *own*."

"Is that all?" June couldn't care less if Winifred threw a party for herself, but she welcomed the distraction. "Why do you sound so scandalized?"

"Well, apparently, it was a disturbance." Barbara was using her gossip voice: hushed, clipped, fast. "I called Bobbie this morning about a playdate, and she kept yawning, and finally I asked her why she was so tired, and she said that the noise from Winifred's party kept her up all night. So I asked Bobbie, 'What party?' And she said Winifred threw a raucous party that lasted well into the night. Apparently a few neighbors called to complain, to no effect. *Apparently* one call was answered by a guest who sounded . . . incapacitated."

"Drunk?"

"High."

The word pricked June's fragile emotions. She rubbed a gentle hand over her extended belly, as if she could smooth out the ripples of ache.

"It sounds just like Winifred to make a disturbance," June said, taking pleasure in the flicker of anger that roused inside her. Anger was more palatable than her sense of defeat.

"This is a new low," Barbara said. "Or maybe, without Bruce to hold her in check, she's finally showing her true colors."

"Maybe so."

"Grief has finally pushed her off the deep end."

The comment stirred the tiniest hint of pity in June—but grief didn't excuse being disruptive and disrespectful. If it did, the world would be chaos, because everyone had their grievances.

"That's not the worst of it, though," Barbara said, back to that gossipy tone.

"Oh?"

"After hours of noise, Bobbie convinced Mark to drive past the Hurst house—just to get a closer look—and her driveway was filled with junky cars. Apparently the guests were all . . . waiters. Service people."

June scoffed at that. It sounded like an invitation for crime. This was a nice neighborhood, after all.

"Drinking, drugs, riffraff . . . it's shameful," Barbara said earnestly.

"It is." June's dislike for Winifred brought her new energy, temporarily quelling the physical and emotional turmoil of her morning. Her spine straightened. "All the more reason to shun her from the committee. She's insulting the community that her husband brought her into."

"It's too bad. I always liked Bruce," Barbara mused.

"Me too," June agreed. "Until he married *her*, of course."

Mr. Hurst came from a good family, with powerful influence—a family that had known her own for generations. He was well mannered and charismatic but not boisterous, as many of the men in their circle were. Everyone had been shocked when he decided to marry Winifred; many claimed it wouldn't last. They'd told him she wouldn't belong, but he hadn't listened.

"I have a feeling it won't be her last party," Barbara said, growing serious again. "This is a problem that is only just beginning."

"There might be legal recourse—" June paused as a cramp swirled through her, then, through an exhale, added, "for her neighbors. If it escalates."

"Here's hoping there *is* recourse, and it doesn't escalate beyond repair. If I lived nearby, I'd lock my doors at night."

June was nodding. "Such a shame that—" A rumble of thunder overtook her voice, and they both paused, waiting for it to diminish. The storm was getting closer.

"Dreadful weather, isn't it?" Barbara asked.

June's eyes flicked up to the window. Rain was falling at a steady tempo on the patio. "The worst," June said. "I suppose I'll be staying in today."

"I forgot," Barbara exclaimed. "Did Harry arrive last night? You must be in bliss, having him to yourself for a few weeks."

For a moment, June considered confiding in Barbara about her marital struggles—it would feel good to get the truth off her chest. But before she embarrassed herself, June thought better of it. "Something came up," she said vaguely.

Barbara did not ask further. For how much of a gossip she was, she was fairly squeamish toward serious conversation; vulnerability was unbecoming.

The conversation devolved from there, the best gossip already out of the way. Victoria was having trouble with her in-laws, and Sandra was remodeling her master bedroom (much to the chagrin of her usually doting husband). June mostly listened, offering short remarks when Barbara paused for breath or laughter. June's life might've been falling apart, but it felt good to laugh at other people's problems.

But all the while, her cramps worsened. June knew because she was beginning to feel nauseated. She went cross eyed staring at the rain outside, the droplets appearing to move sideways. That was when she told Barbara—through a tight breath—that she had to go. They would talk again soon.

When they hung up, June slumped against the kitchen counter and released a low, guttural moan. To her own ears, she sounded primitive. And maybe she was—an animal baring her teeth to temporarily ease her own misery.

20

After two days of solid rain, Marie drove to the River Bend Cemetery to paint. Swans bobbed on the Pawcatuck River, their white bodies reflected in the dusty blue water; they sounded like a flock of trumpeting bike horns. Marie carted an easel, paints, and a four-by-four canvas across the lawn and set up by the shore. After four visits in the past week and a half, the cemetery had become her studio. The groundskeepers barely seemed to notice her presence anymore. She was quiet, at least; she blended in better than the birds.

People always seemed to think painters were peaceful. From the outside, Marie probably *did* appear contented: daubing paint, stepping back to observe her progress, daubing more paint, stepping back—as if she were waltzing with her work. On the inside, however, the process was more like boxing: two quick jabs of her brush, then bouncing back to reassess. Staying on her toes, trying not to get knocked out. Most often, Marie felt like the punching bag, raw as a slab of meat.

She was painting the girl again, of course. Dottie had been her name. After that conversation with Winifred on the beach, Marie had lost all ability to quell her memories of her childhood friend and Hurley Downs Racetrack. Painting the girl was the only way to ease her mind from the wakeful nightmares—except, well, they weren't really nightmares. Most of her memories were like a dream. The problem was that Marie knew how all those happy memories ended.

Marie had met Dottie outside their schoolhouse in 1943, when they were both five years old and new to school. They'd been paired up to clean the erasers and had gone out back, clap-clap-clapping the chalk dust. At first they were both shy and focused on their task, but then a gust of wind blew, and suddenly it became a game. Dottie would race upwind of Marie and smack the erasers together, causing a big cloud to engulf Marie; then Marie would do the same, switching her position so the wind would blow the dust onto Dottie. By the time the fifteen-minute chore was up, the erasers were clean, and the girls looked like pale ghosts, covered head to toe in a fine white powder.

Later that day, at lunch, a boy—Roger, Marie would never forget— snatched Dottie's sandwich from her hands and ran off toward the creek. As Dottie chased him, trying to retrieve her sandwich from his dirty fingers, Roger tripped and fell right on his lapels. The sandwich went flying, separating in the air. Bread and mustardy ham were strewn across the grass. Dottie looked like she might cry, but Marie got there before the tears did and tore her own PB&J in half.

They were inseparable from then on.

Roger sported a scuff on his chin for a week, but even after it faded, Marie and Dottie split their sandwiches and ate half of each kind, like they were performing a secret ritual. And in a way, they had been: a ritual of friendship.

When Marie was young, she needed merely to share a sandwich or a giggle and a connection formed as if out of thin air. But as an adult, Marie struggled with friendship. A laugh could be polite, or dismissive, or fake. And there were so many labels. Two people could be acquaintances or neighbors or even the same party guests but still not *friends*. Two people could share a traumatic experience and still not be friends. They could share lipstick and quiche and a conversation about grief and still not know where the other stood.

For the past two days, Marie hadn't been able to get Winifred out of her head. Not only had their chat on the beach reawakened Marie's grief with a vengeance, but it had also opened her up to a yearning that went much further back in time—that heady need for connection.

Marie ached to be Winifred's friend. She didn't know why. They weren't at all alike. They didn't come from the same backgrounds; they weren't in the same class; they didn't even seem to have much in common, besides sorrow and an appreciation for O'Keeffe. Marie only knew that she found herself drawn to Winifred like scrap metal to some sort of strong magnet. Winifred came into Marie's thoughts, and Marie smiled with admiration—it was the strangest thing.

If they were children, they would be friends already. Marie would've already shared her sandwich. Come to think of it, they'd already shared quiche. But Marie wasn't five years old anymore, and she didn't have any of the equalizers that children had, like school, or chores, or snacks. Winifred was a rich widow embedded in high society. Marie was a homeless artist who wished to purchase a racetrack. They couldn't be more different.

A nearby swan honked, and Marie startled. She'd been staring at her painting from five feet back but not really seeing it. She stepped forward again and pressed a splotch of burnt orange on the side of the girl's nose, deepening the dimension of harsh light and shadow. The whole painting was shades of cream and copper, like Winifred's skin and hair. A blend of Marie's thoughts, past and present.

Many of Marie's most acclaimed paintings from her *Girl* collection featured monochromatic palettes. One in particular, *Wildflower*, was nearly all shades of green-browns, from the faintest shade of sage to a dark, earthy moss. The painting was of a deep forest meadow, with splotchy trees around the edges. (One critic said the hazy framing *evoked a dreamscape.*) In the bright center, Dottie had her back to the viewer, her arms raised in a twirl. She wore an innocent yellow dress— the only color that wasn't green.

Wildflower had sold to a private collector, the sudden attention garnering enough buzz to launch her entire collection. It'd been left on the wall at the Iris Gallery for the duration of her showing, drawing critics and buyers from neighboring states, creating a surge of sales and prestige. Articles were written, museums were contacted, hands were shaken, parties attended. All because of *Wildflower*.

Sometimes she wondered if the painting had been so enamoring because it depicted a safe haven. There in that meadow, the girl was not only invulnerable; she was free. Marie didn't pretend to know much about people—in fact, most of the time, she thought she knew very little—but she knew this: everyone wanted security and freedom. The tragedy of humanity was that those two ideals were mutually exclusive.

But *Wildflower* put those ideals within reach; it harkened back to the days of childhood when naivete provided the illusion of their coexistence. Marie sometimes envied Dottie for dying before she grew up. Dottie never lived to an age when her confidence could be stolen. She never experienced a world where she couldn't scream at the top of her lungs anytime she felt like it. Dottie only ever knew her own power—that rural, wild childhood—and what a gift that was. Perhaps some of Marie's envy had dried in the paint of *Wildflower*.

After the collection's success, Marie had tried and tried to recall the unique ordering of thoughts and memories that brought her to that painting. Her obsession with Dottie had tapped into her creativity like tapping a maple; *Wildflower* had dribbled out of her, sweet as sap. If she could find that tree again, perhaps she could paint like that again—with love and yearning and envy and abandon. But that hadn't happened. Now, she was lost in a forest of grief, and she was beginning to wonder if she'd drained all her sap—if her source was dried up for good.

Marie stepped forward again, adding the same shadowy burnt orange to the girl's hair, down by her neck where the sun-kissed amber strands deepened to auburn at the root. All her early works were positioned far away, like *Wildflower*. As the years had gone by, Marie had gotten closer to the girl, going from full body to half to just her face, a cheek, an eyelash. Perhaps it was this zooming in that turned people off, but Marie couldn't help herself. She was convinced that if she studied the girl close enough, she might discover something new: a path out of the wilderness.

Marie moved her brush along the girl's neck, swiveled it in the giant nostril. On her palette, she mixed a burnt umber, stroking the brush through the pigment until the bristles formed a sharp edge. Then she reached up and tapped, arranging the hairs of the girl's dark eyebrow; vertical lines gradually tipped horizontally in a questioning arc. The girl had an open, quizzical expression that Marie thought she'd composed well—but, she realized, the color was too red. The shadows had become muddied, and she wasn't sure she could fix them.

Acid filled the top of Marie's chest, and she lowered her arm. This wasn't working. That's what the sickly feeling meant.

She stepped back, giving the painting some space. The new perspective and distance confirmed her fear: another failure.

Marie sighed. She needed to get on with her day, anyhow. The water glared, making Marie squint. The swans had gone, and someone had started a lawn mower. It sputtered and whined, the sound ping-ponging off the gravestones. Wind gusted a muddy scent off the river. Dried grass clippings from previous mows kicked up in the breeze and affixed themselves to the girl's wet, ruined temple.

Marie lifted the canvas from her easel, not caring that her palms smudged the paint along the edges. She rested it in the grass, where more clippings became stuck in the paint. She wiped her hands on a rag and collapsed the easel into a narrow bundle of wood and metal joints. She wrapped her wet palette in plastic so the unused paint wouldn't dry out; she preferred to waste paint on bad paintings, not dry palettes. It took two trips for her to cart everything back to her car. A hearse had parked next to her, and she admired all the space in the back; compared to her Plymouth, she could fit so many more lifeless canvases in there.

As much as she'd hated her old apartment, living in her car had proven to be more difficult than she'd anticipated—but her sense of choice in the matter made her less sympathetic to her own hardship.

It was her dream of buying Hurley Downs that had driven her to this existence; any discomfort she experienced was willfully self-inflicted.

Marie wiped the perspiration from her forehead. The day had grown hot. Marie needed to find a place to bathe. She needed to buy stamps. She'd drafted a letter to her old boss at the marketing firm, the one whom she'd drawn small advertisements for before the *Girl* collection got big. The chances of selling another fine art collection seemed slim at the moment, and steadier income would expedite this interlude of living in her car.

Marie climbed into her Plymouth and left the hearse in the dust. She drove with the windows down, airing out the scent of paint and her own body odor. The letter to the advertising firm rested on the passenger seat, already addressed:

Duxbury & Pierce
ATTN: Mr. Duxbury Jr.

21

On Monday morning, Winifred shuffled into Bruce's study to collect some paperwork from his filing cabinet. The Eckart Art Foundation had been operating on autopilot since Bruce's passing, and it was time she caught up. First, she needed to find all her files.

Though the Seacastle had been their summer cottage, Bruce often took his work home, and the study reflected his dedication. It was a serious space, filled with leather and oak. Floor-to-ceiling bookcases were cluttered with dusty tomes and personal memorabilia, including his high school wrestling trophy, a big jar of golf balls from his favorite foreign courses, and various plaques of education, achievement, and business recognition. There was a small dry bar that sported an etched crystal decanter and leather humidor.

The room's centerpiece, of course, was Bruce's behemoth desk: bare and orderly, adorned with an ornate stained glass lamp and a silly little snow globe that Winifred had gifted him. A pair of teak-and-tweed armchairs sat in front of the desk; when Winifred used to sashay into his office, she would always perch atop the chair on the left.

Winifred hated this room—not for its decor, but because it was so *Bruce*. The luxury, intelligence, and tidiness. The room represented a part of him she'd never truly reached: business professional, dealmaker, man's man. He had been an open book with Winifred, but she hadn't tried very hard to understand this side of him. Work-Bruce seemed abstract, unreachable, and perhaps a little confounding. Winifred was a sharp woman, but conversations about mergers and investments quickly became tedious, and he didn't like to bring business into their relationship. *I'd rather talk about you,* he'd say. *I'd rather talk about us. I'd rather talk about how ravishing you look in that new nightgown.* And Winifred had been fine with the separateness of their love and his work. Bruce was a kind, gentle soul, but something about his office made her suspect there was a hard, ruthless side of him, too, and she didn't care to see it.

Winifred riffled through the files, shimmied the large folder out of the cabinet, and balanced the papers in her arms. She turned to go, eager to seal this old tomb of her husband once again. But she paused. The only soft, welcoming part of Bruce's study was the painting on the wall across from the desk, a gift she'd given him for his birthday when they were newlyweds. It'd been Winifred's intention to display the painting in a more central location of their home, but Bruce wanted it in his study. *It reminds me of you,* he'd said. *Of joy and innocence, and God knows I need those reminders when I'm working.*

The landscape had been painted by the artist known simply as D, a mononym earned by the half-circle signature she used to sign all her paintings, like a filled-in D. Winifred had spotted it hanging in an obscure little gallery in Providence, a hazy field surrounded by dark trees. It was the perfect representation of how Bruce made Winifred feel: both sheltered and free, his love a secret clearing where she could throw her arms wide and twirl in the sunlight.

Bruce had had the painting assessed by his family's appraiser, who'd been impressed by the find. Winifred was sitting up in bed reading when Bruce came in to tell her that with her purchase, D was already receiving more attention for her work; she had the potential to become one of the most promising up-and-coming artists in New England.

Winifred had lowered her book to her lap, touched by an unexpected sense of pride in learning that her taste had swayed the opinions of others, had given another woman a leg up. If there was such a thing as anonymous kinship, Winifred felt it then—like an invisible cord connecting her to the greater world.

"You have a good eye," Bruce had said from the doorway to their bedroom. The light in the hallway was still on, causing his shadow to reach toward the bed.

Winifred made a show of appraising his imposing backlit form. "Do I?"

Bruce had stridden over to her, a wicked quirk to his lips as he yanked off his tie.

Later that evening, Winifred nestled against him, running her fingers through the hair that peppered the wide expanse of his chest.

"What if we set up an art foundation?"

She lifted her head. "What?"

He pressed a quick kiss into her hair. "You could run the whole thing. Attend gallery openings and auctions; invest in new artists. What do you say?"

The Eckart Art Foundation became her pride and joy, a magnifying glass that helped focus her passion for art. She'd helped launch a handful of talented female artists since then, visiting hole-in-the-wall showings in search of diamonds in the rough, then dusting off her treasures and watching them shine in deserved recognition. All because Bruce believed in Winifred enough to empower her to believe in others. Funny how he'd turned his own birthday gift into a cause for Winifred to cherish.

The stack of papers in Winifred's arms began to slip, and she readjusted them in her hands. She took one last look at the painting before turning off the light and closing the door. She settled on the magenta couch in her Bird of Paradise room, where she'd already placed a glass of lemonade on the side table. Compared to the coolness of the hall, this room always felt lush and humid. The weekend's rain had cleared, but moisture still hung heavy in the air, slipping through the open window. With a thunk, she dropped the papers on the cushion beside her.

Winifred supported a handful of small female-focused galleries in Rhode Island, Connecticut, and New York. After Bruce had died, she'd allowed herself to pull away from the joy of her foundation. She hadn't spoken with any curators in months, simply sent checks to the galleries to use and disperse to the select artists Winifred wished to support directly—including D. As she picked up the reins of her foundation once again, she planned to take it upon herself to be more engaged with her artists. She ought to commission a new piece, something just *hers*.

Her conversation with Marie on the beach—awkward as it had been—had made her realize how grim she'd become. On the heels of Bruce's death, Winifred's pleasures and interests had drained from her life like bathwater. Friday's party had reawakened her, and now, the idea of plunging back into the art world made her chest vibrate like a struck chord, ringing out with inspiration.

It was time she got back to living her life—and if art and parties distracted her from her sorrow, well, that was all right with her.

22

Late afternoon—after a productive day of sorting, organizing, and otherwise gathering the reins of her foundation once again—Winifred's phone rang. She picked up the line in the kitchen, tucking the phone between her ear and shoulder. The spiral cord stretched as she refilled her lemonade glass from a pitcher in the fridge.

"You don't have to keep calling," Winifred said, clunking ice into her glass.

"I can't call my own daughter?"

Her father still taught philosophy at NYU. He was a busy man—even in the summer—yet he'd been calling weekly since Bruce died. She didn't mind, but she didn't want him to feel obligated either. She was in her midthirties, after all. She didn't need her daddy to call and check up on her like a girl at a sleepover.

"You can call me anytime; you just don't *have* to," Winifred answered, closing the fridge. "I'm on to you."

He chuckled. "What scheme are you accusing me of? Loving my daughter?"

"It's been nine months," Winifred said, low. "Nearing ten."

"Ohhh," he drawled. "You think I'm checking up on you."

"Aren't you?"

"Oh, certainly," he said quickly. "In fact, I'm glad we're on the same page about it."

Winifred laughed. "Well, what do you want to check up on?"

"What's new?"

"Nothing's new. Everything is the same."

"Grief is never the same."

Though she didn't care to admit it aloud, her father was right. She missed the early days, when her sorrow was uncomplicated. The further she got from Bruce's death, the more complex the sadness became, morphing into listlessness, longing, anger—even resentment.

She didn't want to resent Bruce, but she couldn't help it. The more she thought about him, remembered him, *missed* him, the more her resentment demanded to be acknowledged. Because she had changed for him—changed in ways she hadn't fully realized, until he was gone, and she'd thrown a party for people she actually *liked*.

Bruce hadn't expected her to change—or perhaps he hadn't thought that her entering his life required any changes. But that was just it: *she* had entered *his* life. It wasn't a mutual merging. She'd had to morph herself into a new shape for him—and even so, she had never quite achieved a perfect fit. While she knew there wasn't any malice or expectation on his part, he also hadn't noticed. Hadn't realized that she had lost a part of herself on his behalf.

That part of herself had woken up on Friday night—and now it demanded to be heard.

Winifred didn't regret marrying him—she would give anything to have him back—but she did regret allowing Bruce's love to overshadow her sense of self so completely. She resented him for needing her to fit into his world—and then abandoning her in it.

She sank onto the barstool by the phone cradle. She really didn't want to talk about it; she felt better when she didn't think about it.

"Have you been keeping busy?" her father asked.

"You're particularly relentless today."

"You didn't answer my question."

"Whatever happened to small talk? Why do we always have to jump straight to—" She cut herself off before her voice broke.

"It isn't healthy to bottle it up."

Blinking rapidly, Winifred took a quick sip of lemonade.

"Have the ladies at the *spew* been playing nice?"

"S-P-W," Winifred corrected, spelling the abbreviation.

Pronouncing it as he did was his way of signaling to her that he didn't care for her involvement with them—but Winifred didn't like the joke. It reminded her that he didn't respect the organization that didn't even want her—a sort of double rejection, rather than the jab to June and the others he actually intended.

"They haven't been playing nice, actually," she admitted. While she didn't tell him *everything*, she was always honest with her father—even when it embarrassed her. It gave their relationship a rare sense of freedom. "They keep changing their meeting times and locations without telling me."

"On purpose?"

"On purpose."

"How do you know?"

"I overheard them talking about it." Shame heated her cheeks. She didn't like admitting to her father that she—a grown woman—still couldn't make friends.

"Please tell me you've decided to finally renounce your involvement."

"No, but perhaps I should," Winifred said, twirling the phone cord on her finger.

"Why don't you move back home? I could put a word in at the university, and—"

"Daddy," she said, "we've had this conversation a million times."

"Then what's a million and one?"

She sighed. She couldn't say she wasn't tempted, but somehow going home felt like a failure. She wasn't ready to turn her back on the last remnants of her life with Bruce. "I dusted off my foundation files today," she said. "I thought it would do me good to refocus on my own ventures."

"That's great to hear," he said. "Can I be of any help?"

"I don't think so," Winifred said. "I just have some catching up to do. Reaching out to the accountant and all that."

"All on your own?"

"Are you saying I can't run it on my own?"

"Oh, don't cast me off as a sexist. I'm asking if you'll get lonely."

"So what if I get lonely?" she asked, hopping off her stool. She wandered over to the window, her left arm folded across her body, fingers resting in the crook of her opposite elbow. Her right hand gripped the phone a little tighter.

"Loneliness," her father said at length, "is a rot."

He'd been saying that for as long as she could remember. Winifred stared at the distant ocean, flat and reflective as a sheet of metal. Everything outside the window appeared jagged and harsh in the summer sun: the sword stalks of beach grass, the hard-packed sand, even the twirling, sharp-winged shorebirds. She waited for her father to continue, because she knew he would.

"When your mother left us, the loneliness ate up everything. It infected my sleep, my work, my motivation. Even my resolve, which had once been strong as a crab apple, suddenly became mushy. Loneliness is worse than a hole that you might simply pack with something else—loneliness spreads. It eats away at the parts of you that used to be strong."

"You're still strong."

"Not like I once was." He paused, and she could picture him scratching his chin in thought. "Before she left, I fancied myself invincible."

"Well, what do you suggest, then?" Winifred asked, growing impatient. She spun away from the window, blinking the sunlight from her eyes. "I refuse to simply up and move home, just because I don't fit in with my snooty neighbors. I'm not a bullied girl about to change schools."

"Then find people with whom you fit."

Winifred shifted the phone to her other ear, just to buy herself a moment. If she fit in with any crowd, it was the one that had come over to her house on Friday night. Not elite, yacht-clubbing, tennis-playing ladies who lunched—but regular people with regular interests, desires, and problems. Winifred was, after all, a regular person. June and her fellow biddies had said as much about Winifred on numerous occasions, starting with the day Bruce had announced their engagement.

"Sometimes I wonder, had your mother not—"

"Dad—"

"—you would've had an easier time . . ."

He had the mercy to not finish his thought out loud, but Winifred finished it for him in her mind: *fitting in.*

"I get along fine," Winifred said, brushing off the comment.

But this was a soft spot of hers—a patch of rot. Though Winifred had been smart, and funny, and beautiful in school, she'd struggled to form a bond with other girls. She'd done all the things anyone would do to make friends: she'd joined clubs, attended dances, and thrown her own parties—popular, fun parties that everyone seemed to love—but she never grew *close* with anyone. No one ever stayed late.

Winifred often wondered if the absence of a mother was what tainted her. Mothers were meant to usher their daughters into womanhood, but hers had abandoned her right on the cusp of that transition. Winifred's father had done his best to fill the shoes of both parents—certainly more than the average father would have—but still. Winifred had spent her adolescence feeling like the women around her spoke a language she'd never learned, and the few connections she'd made in early adulthood had moved on as soon as they married.

Her father was still talking, suggesting a trip home sometime soon, a vow to tour galleries together and eat at her favorite restaurants. He knew she wasn't about to give up on her life in Rhode Island—and she knew that he still hoped to entice her. The familiar back-and-forth brought Winifred comfort—it was nice to know she had a place to go if life became too unbearable. But Winifred possessed too much pride to simply give up; she was determined not to run home to her father simply because the other man in her life had died. She was more independent than that.

Gradually, their conversation turned to more mundane topics—things they'd read, thoughts on politics, superficial reminiscing. She managed to hold her father on the phone for over an hour, and was relieved that when they hung up, it was time to make dinner and start her evening routine. Without committee meetings and errands, the afternoons were always the longest part of her day; she was grateful she'd managed to talk long enough to breeze through the time.

Winifred flexed her hand, which had cramped up from holding the phone so long. A gust of wind whipped up off the shore, and the house shuddered. The breezes and temperature fluctuations of the shore made the old wood settle and expand noisily. Sometimes she felt like she was dwelling inside a living being—the cottage expanded and contracted, creaking like an ancient rib cage. Most of the time, the sounds softened the silence; tonight, they punctuated it. Winifred put on a record to drown it all out.

After eating dinner with Diana Ross, Winifred drew herself a hot bath and settled into the suds. She closed her eyes, humming to herself as she languidly washed. Her mind wandered back to Friday's party and how happy she'd been. Twelve whole hours of laughter and merriment. The first she'd experienced since Bruce died.

Winifred didn't like to admit it to her father, but she *was* lonely. And it *did* eat away at her like rot. And *of course* she struggled socially. But somehow, the party on Friday had been different than all the parties before. More casual and relaxed. Less desperate on her part—with no one to impress, no impression to make, no expectation to reach. When she was a teenager, she was always trying to entice other girls into being her friend; when she married Bruce, she tried to entice the other women into accepting her. But on Friday, she'd merely put the word out. And people had come, and lingered, and had fun.

And—come to think of it—one person had even stayed late.

23

June was running late. It wasn't her fault—she'd been struggling with her pains all morning; sweat had created a necessity for her to reapply her makeup. As she breezed through the doors of the Shore House, heading toward the veranda, she opened her jaw until it popped. A headache was blooming behind her eyes and along the base of her neck, exasperated by her clenched teeth. Her mouth tasted like the vodka she'd sipped before leaving her cottage; the pill bottle rested at the bottom of her pocketbook, unused.

The other ladies had already been seated; she could see Barbara's favorite sun hat beyond the French doors to the patio, its brim quivering in the sea breeze. Rolling her shoulders back, June prepared to make her entrance—but stopped short when she heard them talking.

"—it's disgraceful, really," Bobbie scoffed.

"I don't know; I feel sorry for her," Rosie said. "I can't imagine what she's going through."

They must've been talking about Winifred. Ever since Barbara had called June three days ago, the party had been a central part of the neighborhood gossip, the ladies' words fanning the flames of their own hatred.

June found the topic a little tired. Her friends could pretend to be scandalized all they wanted, but was it any surprise Winifred was acting out, now that Bruce wasn't around to steer her straight? Sure, it was fun to see Winifred go down with her own ship, but June had a sneaking suspicion that Winifred gained some kind of satisfaction from being outrageous. June was beginning to wonder if it was better to ignore her; the less attention Winifred got, the sooner she'd quit haunting their summer colony and go back to wherever she'd come from.

Or maybe June was just in a sour mood. She couldn't stop thinking about Harry driving Bella away. The accident with the pool had been replaying over and over in her head; she didn't remember much from that night, but after days in the cottage all by herself, June's imagination had taken on a life of its own, taking turns that Alfred Hitchcock would've applauded. Paths that always ended with the same horrifying conclusion: that June was a bad mother.

"She should be embarrassed," Deanna said. "Ashamed."

June's lips curled upward. The topic of Winifred might've been tired, but there was nothing like someone else's shame to distract a person from their own. She started walking again, her heels clacking across the patio.

Barbara spoke up as June neared. "I'm surprised Harry didn't—"

The whole table looked up at her, and Barbara broke off.

June tipped her head, confused at first, and then—and then she realized who they'd all been talking about. Not Winifred, but *her*.

It's disgraceful.

I feel sorry for her.

She should be embarrassed.

Their words buzzed through June's head like a cloud of gnats, making her cringe and shiver. Thank goodness she wore her sunglasses, or her friends would've seen the hurt in her eyes. Thank goodness she wore a new dress, and stood tall, and was able to pretend she hadn't heard a thing.

"Sorry I'm late, ladies," she said, taking the empty seat between Rosie and Bobbie. She waved her hand dismissively, clinging desperately to her dignity even as she felt it slipping through her fingers. "The nanny was late returning from her errands." The lie rolled easily off her tongue. June knew that mentioning Peggy was the perfect hint that

Bella was still home, that whatever rumors they'd heard were, in fact, wrong.

"The . . . nanny?" Bobbie asked slowly, her thin lips pulling to one side, shrewd eyes narrowing in disbelief.

"Is your drink a little sour?" June asked. "You look as if you've swallowed a lime."

Barbara laughed.

June raised her arm, signaling for the waiter. Once she'd ordered her drink, she turned to the table. "So, updates on the fundraiser."

"Straight to business today, I see," Deanna said, watching June as if she were as fake and transparent as plastic.

But June was not unaccustomed to this game. "That's why we're here, aren't we? Unless you all would like to chitchat longer?"

A resounding chorus of *noes* lifted on the breeze, no one wanting to sound less serious about the SPW than June. She sat a little taller, knowing she'd successfully gained control of this runaway train—at least for the afternoon.

But as the meeting unfolded and they debated color schemes, centerpieces, and invitations, a seasick sensation spread through June's belly, as if the solid land upon which she'd once stood had dissolved into quicksand. The harder she fought against these rumors, the faster she'd sink. She'd have to stand still, stay calm. But that was easier said than done.

24

On Wednesday, Marie awoke to the low rumble of a delivery truck. She rolled her head off her shoulder, straightening against the driver's seat. Her spine popped and cracked as she twisted from side to side. The time couldn't be later than seven o'clock in the morning, condensation beading on the windshield.

She groaned. She hated early mornings—how they were filled with so much promise and expectation. If she were a busy, important person, she could imagine feeling motivated—ready to take on the day—but Marie was not a busy or important person, and therefore, the mornings were more like a taunt. A reminder that her days were aimless. The later she awoke, the less time she had to waste.

Silently cursing the delivery truck, Marie wiped the windshield with her sleeve, clearing away the fog. Fluffy clouds dotted the sky. A nearby crow was trying to open a bag of chips, and Marie reached for her drawing pad on the passenger seat. She sketched the shiny bag and black shape. No one saw her sketches; therefore, they were allowed to be smudgy and imprecise. Sketching was like stretching for an athlete, an essential but unmeasured part of her body's upkeep—successful simply by *doing*. The round pencil cradled in her fingers, the pulpy texture of the paper, the soft scraping of graphite—these things soothed Marie.

She drew the bird in various poses: hopping, pulling, bending, pecking. Crows were smart, and she tried to capture its use of problem-solving in its inquisitive positions. She was working on a fun pose—the crow's wings outstretched, guarding its bag from an intruder swooping overhead—when someone tapped on her window.

Marie startled, breaking her pencil tip against the pad. The sun had moved, glaring against the smudged glass; she blinked, unable to identify the backlit figure outside. Probably a Stop & Shop employee sent out to request she vacate her spot. She set down her notebook and turned the key in the ignition; the Plymouth sputtered.

"Wait," the person said. The voice was female, and Marie realized the woman was wearing a scarf on her head. Her eyes were obscured by large sunglasses.

Marie allowed the Plymouth to stall out, then reached for her door handle. The woman stepped back to make room for the door to swing open. Marie uncrumpled from the driver's seat, squinting in the sunlight.

"Winifred," Marie said, chest clenching around a sharp inhale.

Winifred's heart squeezed at the sight of Marie, with flushed cheeks and dark circles under her eyes. Marie didn't look good; she had a sleepless appearance, a pallid blush. Marie didn't appear happy to see her, either—she seemed caught off guard.

For a moment, Winifred felt like she was fifteen again, completely and utterly self-conscious. The last time she'd seen Marie, she'd made Marie uncomfortable. Marie had practically *fled* the beach—who was to say that Marie wanted to see her again? And now, Winifred had sneaked up on her.

"Hi, Marie." Winifred tried to sound friendly, but her tone came out as a nervous version of her party-host voice—high pitched and singsongy—and she consciously dialed it back to a calmer register. "Am I interrupting?"

Marie's eyebrows darted together, and she glanced back over her shoulder into the car. "Not really, no."

Winifred followed Marie's gaze, observing the clutter on the dashboard—candy wrappers, bits of charcoal, crumpled papers. It occurred to Winifred that perhaps Marie was not unhappy to see her but embarrassed to be *seen*.

After her conversation with her father, Winifred had come up with a brilliant idea, and she'd awoken this morning antsy to track Marie down. But Winifred hadn't paused to think about the intrusion from Marie's perspective. She hadn't thought about the time of day or the shame Marie must feel about her living situation. Their difference in economics couldn't be more vast, and judging by Marie's expression, she felt that disparity presently.

And here Winifred was, so wrapped up in her own desperation that she'd cornered Marie in the parking lot, wholly inconsiderate of the other woman's feelings.

"Oh my God," Winifred said, raising a hand to her mouth. "This is so rude of me, coming here like this." She backed up, giving Marie space. "Never mind, I—I should go."

"No, wait." Marie tipped her head, as if she was realizing something. "You came all this way to see . . . me? Why?"

"I came to . . . well, I came to apologize." It wasn't the exact reason Winifred had come, but it seemed like a good place to start, now that she was here. "I'm afraid I made you uncomfortable the other morning, on the beach." Marie's eyes widened—in surprise? horror?—and Winifred hastily continued. "All that talk of Bruce . . . I'm sorry if I made things awkward. I'm sorry if I'm making them awkward now too. I just . . . well, I don't like that the night ended the way that it did. And I wanted to thank you for—"

"You didn't make things awkward," Marie interrupted. Embarrassed as Marie was by the realization that Winifred knew where to track her down—confirming that Winifred *did*, in fact, already know about her living situation—Marie was touched that Winifred had cared enough to drive all the way here just to speak with her.

"I didn't?"

"No. You just . . . ," Marie trailed off, wondering how honest to be. Winifred had taken off her sunglasses during her rambling speech, and she appeared so earnest staring down at Marie from her elegant height. "Your talk about Bruce reminded me of my own loss."

Winifred's mouth parted into a little *oh*.

"It . . ." She swallowed. "Brought up a lot of memories."

This time, Winifred uttered the *oh* out loud.

"There's no need to apologize," Marie said. "I left because of me, not you."

Winifred smiled, mostly with her eyes. "We have something in common, then," she said. "Grief, I mean."

Marie chuckled. "Doesn't everyone have that in common?"

"No. No, I don't think so." Her words were gentle, thoughtful. "Unless you lose someone close to you, you don't really have a clue what it's like. The bottomless pit."

"I suppose that's true."

A crow swooped low, going for the one with the chip bag, each cawing loudly at the other. Marie and Winifred watched them squabble, both grateful for the sudden levity.

Winifred gestured at Marie's notebook, still splayed on the passenger seat. "Those sketches are really good. Are you an artist?"

What a loaded question, Marie thought.

"What am I saying? You must be." Winifred pointed to the back seat, where Marie had crammed all her canvases.

Marie wished her car didn't have windows. All her vulnerabilities— her finances, her failed artwork—were on display, right here in the parking lot. Shame crept up her neck again, flaming her cheeks.

But Marie didn't see an ounce of pity in Winifred's eyes. In fact, Marie saw inspiration . . . or excitement?

"I came here for another reason too," Winifred admitted. "I had an idea yesterday, and I haven't been able to get it out of my head. I think it's a brilliant idea, actually."

Now it was Marie's turn to say "Oh?"

"I have a proposition: I think you should move in with me."

25

"What?" Marie asked, certain she'd heard wrong.

"My house is far too big for just one person," Winifred went on. "I have all these spare rooms just going to waste, collecting dust. Beds that are far more comfortable than sleeping in a car."

"I'm not looking for a handout," Marie said, sounding more defensive than she intended. It's just that . . . well, she was perplexed. Utterly surprised. And she did not like how powerless to Winifred's allure she suddenly felt; Marie had a racetrack to focus on.

"Oh, it's not a handout. Not at all." Winifred pressed her lips together and glanced down at her painted toenails. Her voice became muffled. "Without Bruce, the house feels . . . empty." Winifred looked up again, her expression filled with light. "We had fun on Friday night, didn't we?"

"We did," Marie admitted.

"It's not a handout," Winifred repeated. "It's a plea. I could use the company."

Marie stared at Winifred's bright-blue eye shadow, her peach blush. Behind her pretty, done-up face, Marie recognized Winifred's genuineness. The absolute sincerity. Winifred didn't pity Marie—she needed her.

It was the strangest thing.

"I know you could use the space," Winifred went on, gesturing toward the paintings in the back seat of the Plymouth.

"I wouldn't want to impose . . ."

"That's my point, though," Winifred said quite forcefully. "You wouldn't be imposing. You would be welcome. I know we don't know each other that well, but it occurred to me that we both have a need, and this arrangement would answer both." She stepped forward and grasped Marie's forearm, just for a moment, for emphasis. "I wouldn't expect anything of you. No payment, no debt. And I promise I won't talk about Bruce."

Marie huffed a soft laugh. "You can talk about Bruce."

"Does that mean you agree?"

"I . . ." Marie almost agreed right there in the parking lot. Winifred was *that* eager. Yet something held Marie back. She didn't know what exactly, but she said, "I'd like to think about it."

Winifred straightened, her mouth pulling into a horizontal line. "Of course," she said, but Marie saw the disappointment in her eyes before Winifred covered it up with her sunglasses. "Take your time, and call me when you've decided." She dug into her purse and wrote her phone number on the back of a receipt, the pen shaking a little. Then she handed Marie the paper and took a step back. "I don't want to pressure you, but I think this arrangement could be the start of a beautiful thing."

Before Marie could respond, Winifred strode back toward her Pagoda, which was parked about ten spaces away. The convertible rumbled to life and, unceremoniously, sped away. Marie watched the tails of Winifred's headscarf fluttering at the base of her neck as she picked up speed down the street.

An odd sort of longing pulled at Marie's chest, squeezing her ribs like the tightening of shoelaces. She leaned against her car and closed her eyes. She saw Dottie on the pink backs of her eyelids, her childhood rope swing that swooped over the Susquehanna. If she listened closely to the breeze through the parking lot trees, she could almost hear Dottie laughing. The whinnying of horses. The ringing of the racing bell.

Up until she'd started school, Marie had never considered that growing up on a racetrack was abnormal. The track had been such a defining constant in her young life. Her father worked as a groundskeeper, the right hand and handyman to the barn manager. Because of his around-the-clock role, their family lived in a small home on-site. A compound had been built for the staff and track offices, located beyond the backstretch, behind the stables, and all the way north, by the river.

Marie overlooked the trainer track from her bedroom window. She used to rouse early to watch the exercise riders breezing horses in the predawn. White saddle pads flashed in the darkness; on dreamlike mornings, the full moon illuminated the animals to an almost supernatural glow. If she opened her window, Marie could hear the rhythmic snorting of their breath, the thump of their hooves, and the riders calling out to each other in the mist.

Marie's first memory was of horses. Her first smells, first sights, first fears and loves. The Thoroughbreds stabled at Hurley Downs were hot and high strung, with long faces and fragile-looking bones. Marie used to think the saddle cinches and dusty leg wraps were the only things keeping the horses' tendons together as they ran. Marie had not been allowed to touch or even approach the Thoroughbreds, but sometimes, her father would pick her up and allow her to pet the sturdy and stoic lead ponies that shepherded the skittish racers around the grounds.

Though the Thoroughbreds were off-limits to her, Marie loved to watch them breezing on the trainer track. They appeared almost peaceful when they were moving, floating along the rail before sunrise, as if it was their primal purpose. Marie respected that feeling—the inability to *not* do the thing you were meant to do. Her mother used to call painting Marie's *heart purpose*. The Thoroughbreds' heart purpose was to *turn loose*, as the jockeys called it. To run.

Marie hated the real races, which were loud and chaotic. Thousands of people crammed into the grandstands, all shouting and waving their hands as if they *meant* to spook the animals. Derbies turned the peaceful, primal beauties into prancing bundles of nerves. Marie had seen countless horses spooked and shy. Once, she even saw a horse go down, and she knew its leg wraps didn't contain the crack, and though her mother whisked James and Marie away from the scene and covered Marie's ears, she still heard the gunshot.

Even when Marie was young, she could see the cruelty of the operation. The ruthless inhumanity of gambling on a living thing. She felt like a Thoroughbred sometimes, her life as an artist a constant gamble. Meant to paint but not designed for the business of it. Her bones were delicate, and she shied easily, made frantic by onlookers. And yet she kept racing. Painting for her life, because she didn't have the luxury of standing still. She gambled on her own hide in hopes that it would all work out in the end, that her art would sustain those inescapable human needs: food, shelter, safety, and unconditional companionship. And all the while she'd dreamed of the day she could simply wake up and run with no bets and no stakes.

Hurley Downs—for better and worse—was a part of Marie, woven into the tapestry of her being. Sometimes, when she drove with the window down, she'd catch a familiar whiff of heady grains and hay, and it would take her right back to the barn—right back to that predawn magic—and her pulse would begin to pound like hooves.

It was pounding now. *Ba-dum, ba-dum, ba-dum, ba-dum.*

Maybe Winifred's house could be her trainer track. A place to paint freely and rediscover her purpose without so much pressure. She'd be able to explore new inspirations and make money off her advertising assignments (if Mr. Duxbury agreed, as she hoped he would), all the while continuing to save her patron funds to buy Hurley Downs.

It was a practical plan. For the both of them. Marie was not about to be flattered by the idea that Winifred wanted *her* company in particular; Marie's untethered situation made her a logical choice.

She glanced down at the paper still stretched between her pinched thumbs and forefingers. Winifred's phone number. She turned it over to read what was on the other side. It was a receipt for bed linens and new towels. Marie reread the itemized list, the numbers, the extravagant total.

Marie knew exactly what this meant: not only did Winifred hope Marie would say yes—she was betting on it.

26

A shiver cascaded down June's shoulders as she strode into Wave Watch's little general store and walked along a row of produce tables in search of fresh berries. In the city, she rarely shopped for her own groceries—the Duxburys had staff for that, people who cooked and cleaned and tended to all the errands that accompanied such tasks. But here in Wave Watch, June took pleasure in perusing. It gave her a sense of quaint simplicity that soothed her jittery, lonesome heart. And there was nothing so sweet as fresh berries on a summer morning. It was something she and Bella liked to enjoy together, and June was desperate for a sense of connection to her daughter.

The hole Harry had left in June's chest when he drove Bella away had only grown bigger as the days wore on, and no amount of brief and babbling phone calls with her daughter could ease the hot ache of such a wound. Try as she might to tap into her anger or pride—emotions that usually provided June with a bolstering sense of superiority—after overhearing her friends gossiping about her at lunch, June had felt only shame.

This was not an unfamiliar sensation to June; shame had peppered her entire upbringing, making her nose wrinkle and her eyes smart, a spice that seasoned everything she did. The first shame June felt was in relation to her appearance—little comments her mother made about her summer freckles, a scar she got on her knee from playing "like a boy," and when she gained ten pounds in tenth grade. She'd felt ashamed about her menstrual pain as a teenager, ashamed about a stain she got on her dress on graduation day, ashamed about her lack of experience on her wedding night, ashamed that her body fought so hard against her desire to get pregnant.

June had built her entire life upon the avoidance of humiliation, her worthiness predicated upon her role of behaving flawlessly at all times. Her father, grandfather, and the patriarchs before them had built the Clearmont family's prestige with rigorousness and pride, and they had all expected the same rigor in the wives who ran their homes, in the respectable daughters they sent out to marry into other prominent families. June had been acutely aware of such expectations from the first moment her mother chided her for not acting ladylike and onward evermore.

Once, while summering at the Clearmont house just down the road from here, June's cousin Doris—daughter of June's father's wayward sister, a wild child herself—had exclaimed, *There are so many* rules! *I just want to be free.* As if the propriety that upheld the Clearmont reputation—their money, their status, their way of life, the very slice of beach upon which Doris sat—was a burden and not a gift.

June still thought about Doris's comment. From time to time, she wondered where the girl was now; June had somewhat purposefully lost track of that particular branch of the family tree, as if their disease might spread to June if she so much as glanced in their direction. But sometimes, she wondered.

Times were changing. Traditions that had once meant everything to the wealthy families with whom the Clearmonts associated were fading like old photographs. The new generation of young Americans didn't appreciate what June and the generations behind her had built, the sacrifices made to rise to such heights. They lacked family values, patriotism, gratitude—the very tenets of virtue that gave June's life meaning. What would the world come to, without shame's governance? Without rules and decorum? June felt both fascinated and terrified by the idea.

June selected a carton of strawberries, worried about both the world and the threat of her own fall from grace. Her role as a wife and mother was all she knew, all she cared for; the fundraisers, garden parties, and trips to the Shore House were the only pleasures she cared to indulge in.

June concerned herself greatly with the boundaries imposed on her by her mother and society, but she found these guidelines comforting in a world that appeared to be quite frightening and lawless without them. The parameters within which she operated were what provided June with the comforts of this life, and she was determined to uphold them and fit herself within them the best she could. Because without them, she would have nothing.

June was leaving the store with her berries—still stewing on how to get her life back on track—when she ran into Deanna on the sidewalk. The other woman appeared immaculate as ever in a peony-pink sundress, her elbow hooked through the strap of a Chanel pocketbook. June had the overwhelming urge to ask Deanna how, exactly, she managed to be so perfect.

"Deanna, hello," June said.

But Deanna did not stop walking; Deanna did not even turn her head in June's direction.

June stood there on the sidewalk watching her idol, her mentor, walking away from her as if she didn't exist, the hole in her chest yawning wider.

27

As she sped away from the Stop & Shop parking lot, Winifred removed her sunglasses, allowing the wind to dry out her tears before they could fall. She didn't know why she was crying. Marie hadn't refused; she'd merely asked to think about the proposition.

A part of Winifred had wanted to shake Marie and ask, *What's there to think about? You're living in your car!* A part of Winifred felt insulted and hurt by the insinuation that Marie might find an old Plymouth preferable to her company—but she knew better. She knew it wasn't that simple, that Marie possessed pride, independence, shyness—just like Winifred did.

Maybe that's why Winifred was crying: not just the rush of adrenaline in admitting she needed someone but in placing her pride in someone else's hands.

She reminded herself that time was a reasonable request on Marie's part. Winifred had already had the chance to ponder the idea; Marie needed time to ponder too. It wasn't a conventional arrangement, after all. They were just shy of strangers.

Well, no, that wasn't true. Could Winifred truly call Marie a stranger anymore? She didn't think so. Not after Bruce, and the night of cleaning, and the depth of their conversations.

Marie had a quality Winifred hadn't encountered before: straightforwardness. Marie didn't operate in layers of judgment and expectation, as June and the others did. Marie was honest. Marie might've been the first honest woman Winifred had ever met. Perhaps that's why Winifred had hatched her brilliant idea—not just out of her own loneliness and Marie's convenience, but because Winifred wanted to keep Marie around. She wanted—oh, hell—she wanted to be Marie's friend.

Self-consciousness flared hot against Winifred's face. She was absolutely *desperate*.

She pulled into her driveway, parked the Pagoda, and hurried inside. She stopped short when she saw the shopping bags by the stairs, two huge bundles of bedsheets and quilts she'd bought for Marie's room. If Marie did decide to accept Winifred's offer, she vowed to never tell Marie just how desperate she had been.

She glanced at her watch—not even ten o'clock in the morning. Winifred would have to occupy herself. Stay busy. A few dishes had collected in the sink. She could skim the pool too. Wash the new sheets, make up the guest room. Perhaps even set up a makeshift studio—what did that entail? She might need to buy something to protect the floor from paint. Yes, she could do that. In the event that Marie agreed, Winifred wanted to be ready.

Energized by her newfound focus, she carried the shopping bags to the laundry room. She unbundled them carefully, read the instruction labels, and wadded the first load into the machine. She had just started the wash when she heard a faint knock—so faint that at first, she thought it was the machine. She checked the dials, then crouched down to listen to the water filling the drum. The knock occurred again—metallic and heavy—and this time, Winifred recognized the knocker on her front door.

She popped out of her crouch. No one ever came to her house. Had she forgotten about a committee meeting? It would be just like June to schedule a meeting at Winifred's house without telling her, so that when everyone arrived, she wouldn't be dressed or prepared.

Winifred wiped her hands on the front of her dress and hurried from the laundry room. Her makeup was probably smudged from earlier, but she didn't have time to clean herself up.

The knock occurred again, echoing through the foyer. "Coming!" Winifred called out. With a quick, steadying breath, she yanked the heavy wooden door open.

Marie stood on the landing, arms crossed over her chest in a self-embrace that made her appear utterly sheepish. "I couldn't find a pay phone."

A balloon of emotion swiftly expanded in Winifred's throat; she swallowed. "That's all right." Her inner fifteen-year-old was bouncing with glee. Marie had come! She'd agreed! "I'm glad you're here, actually," Winifred continued. "I was wondering what supplies you might need for a studio—if you need anything at all, that is. Perhaps something to protect the floor?"

"I have a drop cloth," Marie said, perplexed by Winifred's sudden practicality. "I could use a stool, though. Or a small table."

"I have those." The corners of Winifred's mouth quivered ever so slightly. Excitement, Marie realized. Winifred was *excited*. Joy spread through Marie's chest like warm honey, golden and sweet.

Winifred clapped her hands together. "Well, gosh, come in! Come in. Let's get you settled."

"Thank you." Marie's heart was still pounding—*ba-dum, ba-dum, ba-dum*—but the clip was different. She felt freer already.

Winifred stepped back, ushering Marie inside. Marie had forgotten just how cavernous the foyer was, how magnificent.

Winifred opened her arm to the space, as if in presentation. "Welcome home, Marie."

28

Winifred hurried up the stairs, gesturing exuberantly. "I'm delighted, Marie. I think this'll be the start of a wonderful arrangement."

Marie trotted behind her, carrying a small duffel of clothing.

What was she doing? One minute, Marie had been standing in the parking lot thinking about Thoroughbreds, and the next, she was on Winifred's doorstep. The only explanation she could come up with was that she was compelled, and it went deeper than Winifred's candy-coated exterior. Winifred had magnetism. From their first meeting in front of the O'Keeffe to eating quiche on the beach, Marie had been drawn to Winifred's warm and welcoming nature.

More importantly: the arrangement was practical. One might say that Marie hardly had a choice in the matter. Winifred's offer was an open door in an otherwise long, dark hallway; Marie didn't know what lay beyond the threshold, but anything seemed preferable to sleeping in her Plymouth and painting in a cemetery.

"Here we are," Winifred said, opening a door to their right.

Marie slipped past Winifred's outstretched hand and into the spacious upstairs bedroom, which possessed more square footage than her previous apartment in its entirety. A queen-size bed stood across from her, stripped of its sheets. There was a writing desk in one corner, a green velvet reading chair in the other. A black dresser with a lemon-colored vase of fresh-cut hydrangeas atop it. The walls were a buttery yellow, adorned with artwork in gold frames—originals, no doubt, which Marie promised herself she'd investigate later.

"The sheets are in the wash," Winifred said.

Marie allowed her duffel to slide off her shoulder onto the floor. Then she turned back to Winifred. "Thank you."

Winifred blinked rapidly for a moment—then she led Marie back into the hall, opening the door directly across the way. "I thought this might make a good studio space."

This bedroom had slanted ceilings and a huge window that overlooked the beach.

"There's so much natural light in here," Winifred went on as she tied the floor-length curtains all the way back, revealing the full width of the view. "You're welcome to sleep in here, of course, but I figured: Why limit you to just one room? I'm certainly not using them."

Marie walked farther into the space. Winifred was right: this would make an excellent studio. Unlike the rest of the house—which was heavily, spectacularly decorated—this room was sparse. Unfinished. The walls were a creamy, neutral white; the only hint of Winifred's maximalist taste was the ceiling, which had been painted a deep azure and dotted with fluffy clouds. Soft, indirect sunlight filtered in; on hot days, Marie could open the windows to air out the scent of paint, replacing turpentine with the sea breeze.

Marie approached the window; her easel could go here, just to the left of the pane, where the light was bright, and Marie's shadow wouldn't block the canvas. She turned, observing. In-progress paintings could line the wall by the bed, out of any direct sun but still well lit, so Marie could stand at the opposite end of the room to consider them from a distance. The writing desk in the corner would make a great worktable for her illustrations; the low top of the dresser could house sketches if the desk became cluttered, and the drawers could hold tubes of paint, extra brushes, all the supplies she needed.

Marie pressed her lips together in an attempt to quell the moisture that blurred her vision. This room would be the best studio she'd ever had—by a long shot.

"This is . . ." Marie turned back to Winifred. "This is too much."

"It really isn't, though," Winifred said, placing her hands on her hips. "It's too much for *me*. The least I can do is share it with someone else."

"But why?" Marie shook her head, dumbfounded by her luck—or whatever had brought her here to Winifred's house. "Why me?"

Winifred seemed to consider that for a moment, her lips pursed in thought. Finally, she asked, "Why not you?"

The question stumped Marie, and Winifred used Marie's pause as an opportunity to continue the tour. She led Marie out into the hallway, pointing as she went. "My bedroom is that door there, next to yours, and you remember the bathroom with the O'Keeffe. I figured we could share it—it's the best room in the house, really—but if you want your own bathroom, there's one through here."

"Thank you," Marie repeated, because what else could she say?

Winifred, who seemed to be on task now, walked Marie back downstairs. Marie had the sharp memory of walking these stairs last summer, and the terror that followed, but when they reached the landing, the morning remained peaceful.

"Can I help you unload your things?"

"Oh, I . . . ," Marie trailed off. She really didn't want the help—didn't want Winifred to see the shame of her possessions, all crammed into the back seat—but she couldn't think of a worthy excuse to refuse her offer. Except: "I'm sure you have a busy day; I can—"

"Busy?" Winifred was already bustling through her front door toward Marie's car. "I have nothing happening today—not one thing. I'd love to help. It'll go faster with two people, anyway."

Marie followed her outside. The morning had become muggy but not uncomfortably hot. Marie could feel herself perspiring nonetheless, a clammy dampness developing under her arms and along the back of her neck. It was nerves. The car was a mess, and Winifred was about to see it all. Marie didn't have much, but it was the state of things—the chipped kitchenware she'd dumped into a shoebox, the tattered and stained art books, the framed pictures wrapped in old T-shirts—that made Marie self-conscious.

But none of it could be helped, so she opened the back passenger door. "Perhaps you can move the canvases?"

29

The driver's-side back seat was crammed with upright canvases, mostly two by twos and three by threes. Larger rectangular canvases rested horizontally on top, spanning from the front headrest to the rear window. Most had paint on them, but none were what Marie would consider "paintings." They were failures—underpaintings at best. But they weren't heavy or hard to maneuver, nor were they as embarrassing as Marie's other items, so they made a good task for Winifred.

At the Stop & Shop, Winifred had tried not to look too closely into the back seat, to respect Marie's privacy—but now, well, it couldn't be avoided. Winifred opened the car door and was astounded by what she saw. Marie had clearly taken more care with the canvases than her clothes or trinkets. A few boxes and bags of personal items were piled on the floor, while tens of canvases had been stacked neatly on the seat, frame by frame, organized by size. All the canvases had paint—some appeared unfinished, others had bits of grass from (Winifred presumed) painting outdoors, and a few made Winifred's heart flutter.

First, she grabbed a pair of large canvases resting atop the stack and eased them out. "May I rest them against the car?"

"Of course," Marie said, hastily gathering clothing and loose toiletries into an existing box of what Winifred could only refer to as a bathroom drawer dumped into cardboard.

Winifred pretended not to see the disarray. She didn't want Marie to feel embarrassed or exposed, though clearly that was *exactly* how

Marie felt. So Winifred made a point of not looking in Marie's direction at all.

Instead, she kept her eyes on the canvases, on her task. It wasn't hard. The paintings—even the obviously unfinished ones—were exceptional. At least, some of them were. Some were clumsy or unemotive, but others stunned her. Winifred could see herself spending hundreds of dollars on some of these, and yet here they were, crammed into the back of Marie's car. How had Marie become such a talented painter? Why wasn't she in local galleries? And why hadn't Winifred heard of her? If anyone deserved Winifred's patronage, it was Marie.

Upon seeing the canvases up close, Winifred was certain that this arrangement was kismet. The familiar thrill of discovering a new artist echoed through Winifred's chest like a gleeful shout. Winifred had always wondered if the privacy of her anonymous foundation was worth the trade-off of working with artists more directly. But now, with an artist under her roof, what if Winifred could learn to help Marie develop her talents further? Winifred certainly had the connections to give Marie a leg up.

Winifred lifted more paintings out of the car, observing them as she went. None of them were signed, which Winifred took to mean that none of them were considered done. But the style was oddly nostalgic, wistful. Loose and sweeping brushstrokes, primarily monochromatic palettes, with odd angles and harsh shadows. A bit derivative of other styles Winifred had seen, but that was common among budding artists who were still finding their creative edge.

Winifred lifted another painting out, a peach-and-copper portrait. The girl's features were young, but the colors almost matched Winifred's hair. Bits of grass had dried in the paint, and finger smudges had muddied the edges. Winifred's stomach wobbled with a strange form of excitement, as if she'd just uncovered something important.

"Marie," Winifred said slowly, "these are . . . these are lovely." Not all of them were, but clearly Marie had skill. "Have you sold to galleries?"

Marie stopped, straightened. She couldn't stand Winifred's inspection, even if her comments were favorable. The paintings weren't finished, and they weren't any good. Either Winifred was lying about liking them, or she had terrible taste—and if Winifred's home and outfits were any indication of her tastes, Winifred was definitely lying.

"They're works in progress," Marie said, evading her question. "Just doodles, really. They aren't any good."

Winifred met her eyes from across the back seat. "I beg to differ."

"Yeah, well . . ." Marie hefted a box. "The canvases are easiest to carry by their frames," she added. "Don't worry about touching the paint; they're all dry. Just don't stack smaller ones on top of larger ones—the weight will stretch the fabric, and the bottom canvases will end up needing to be restretched."

Winifred appeared mildly perplexed, as if she were trying to remember a word in a different language. But all she said was "All right."

With that, Marie headed up the porch steps and into the cool dimness of the house, relieved to be out of the sun and out of Winifred's scrutiny. She set the box just inside the guest room door, still a bit disbelieving that she was here, that this was her new temporary home.

She shouldn't have been so curt with Winifred about the paintings. Whether Winifred actually liked them or not, she had extended a kindness, and Marie should show some gratitude. On her return trip, Winifred passed her on the stairs and smiled brightly; Marie smiled back.

They carried on like this for a while, unloading boxes and canvases. Up and down the stairs, up and down. Marie placed her personal items in her bedroom while Winifred deposited the canvases in the studio.

As Winifred unpacked the paintings from Marie's Plymouth, she felt like an art historian discovering a secret stash in a forgotten attic. She couldn't wrap her mind around what she was seeing, how familiar the paintings seemed. Marie hadn't answered her question about galleries. Was it possible that Marie had had showings before? If so, her finances suggested that she hadn't in a long time. She seemed self-conscious, embarrassed. Winifred was saddened to think that the world had stolen the joy from Marie's artistic practice. She clearly had a lot of promise, but it was obvious that Marie didn't want to discuss the matter.

And Winifred wouldn't ask. She *couldn't*. If she did, she would risk putting Marie on the spot—or, worse, make her feel *watched*. Winifred had the sense that it wouldn't take much to scare Marie away.

Meanwhile, Marie felt as though Winifred was picking through her dirty laundry. She tried not to look at Winifred's face or wonder what she was thinking as she observed each failed painting. When she'd done gallery openings, Marie had hated seeing the creased foreheads, half frowns, and quizzically tipped heads of observers. Even when someone liked a painting, their expressions made Marie squirm.

She had been thrilled to show her work, to have it become so explosively coveted, to make a few hundred dollars in a night. But the money and the praise didn't ease the knots in her stomach. This was the cruel paradox of Marie's existence: she wanted both all and none of the attention. She wanted her paintings to excel so she could justify painting more of them. The more acclaim she received, the easier it was to shrink back into her studio and focus on the heart of her passion. The discomfort of success guaranteed the comfort of her life as an artist.

But the attention had dried up, moving on to abstracts and pop art, and she'd gradually become frustrated and dissatisfied with her work, and now she was here, watching Winifred's face as she studied an unfinished canvas. Marie wanted to reach out and snatch it from Winifred's fingers. At the same time, she wanted to ask Winifred if she thought it was any good.

When the back seat was unloaded, Marie opened the hatchback, where more canvases were neatly stacked, along with two easels, a box of paints and brushes, and her drawing materials. Most of these canvases were blank, save for a few works in progress she had not yet given up on. Winifred exited the house from her recent trip and floated over to Marie with that graceful gait of hers.

"Is this really all you have?" Winifred asked.

"This is it."

Winifred chuckled—an odd reaction, Marie thought. "Ninety percent of your things are related to painting."

To her surprise, the comment made Marie chuckle too. It was kind of ridiculous, when she thought about it. "I suppose you're right."

"You must really love it."

Marie looked into her eyes; even with smudged makeup, Winifred was still flawless. "I really do."

"How lucky you are," Winifred said, wrapping her arms around the box of paints, "to have something you love so much." She lifted the box and carried it inside, leaving Marie behind.

Marie just stood there, immobilized by the comment. Lucky? Most days, it felt like a curse. But on occasion, well, perhaps Marie *did* feel lucky. Some people went their whole lives without a passion. Marie had folded her life into such an odd shape, all for the sake of her art. Why else would she do that, if not for love?

The slam of a car door jolted Marie out of her thoughts. A hundred yards to the left, Winifred's neighbor had arrived home and was standing in his driveway staring at her. Marie bent her elbow, raising her hand in a modest wave. He visibly huffed and stormed into his house. It occurred to her that though she might be welcome in Winifred's cottage, she might not be welcome in this neighborhood.

"Don't mind him; he's a stodgy prick," Winifred said, somehow at Marie's side again.

Marie tried to suppress the smile that came to her lips. "You aren't worried that your neighbors will take offense at my . . ." She spread her hands.

"Existence?" Winifred supplied.

"Our arrangement might stir up talk."

Winifred patted her arm. "Oh, it certainly will. But the thing about this neighborhood is that they'll talk whether you're here or not." She surveyed the car, resting her fists on her hips. "Looks like one more trip, don't you think? I've become a canvas-moving expert, so why don't you grab the easels?"

When Marie had disappeared into the house, Winifred pivoted back toward her neighbor's driveway, staring at their impossibly green front lawn as if she could scorch the grass with her gaze. For some unexplained reason, she felt protective of Marie. Vicious.

Winifred gathered the last of the canvases and hurried inside. Marie was upstairs in her studio, already setting up an easel by the window. It warmed Winifred's heart to see.

"Why don't I let you settle in?" Winifred said, leaning the last canvases against the wall. "I need to tend to the laundry, anyhow."

"Thank you," Marie said, and Winifred knew instantly she was thanking her for a lot more than the moving help.

"Thank *you*," Winifred returned and closed the studio door behind her.

30

It was the way the sunlight slanted through Rosie Kirkland's sunroom that made June think of it: the day she'd met Harry.

They were both attending a birthday party on a mutual friend's yacht. She was eighteen, and he was twenty, and he'd offered to refill her punch. Backlit by the sun, his blond hair had looked like 24-karat gold, and his white polo had made his tan skin appear warm and inviting. He'd been horsing around with the other young men all afternoon, and the earnest manner with which he'd given June his sudden, full attention had been so disarming that she'd fallen for him right then and there.

Throughout their courtship, June had often scoffed at Harry's boisterousness; she'd been careful not to appear too naive or swept up in his charm. But secretly, June found it thrilling. He drove a little too fast, stayed out a little too late, kissed her a little too deeply. She'd imagined herself as the calm to his storm—wasn't that the role of a wife?—and had assumed that one day he'd mellow out. In the meantime, there was nothing so enthralling as being the focal point of his wildness.

He'd given her the same intoxicating smile on their wedding day when he lifted her veil, and on their wedding night when he removed her dress, and while sitting across from her at numerous café tables on their honeymoon in Paris. But none of those crooked, boyish smiles compared to the one he'd given her when she announced to him that she was *finally* pregnant. The victoriousness and excitement with which he'd swept her up into his arms had filled her with a giddy elation that at the time, had felt like it might last forever. He'd kissed her lips, her cheeks, her hair, before kneeling on the floor to kiss her belly too. She'd never felt so cherished, so loved, so filled with purpose.

From the time she'd received her very first baby doll, June had known that she was meant to be a mother, and she had never been so happy as when she was pregnant. She had waited so long, tried so hard, and the news had been a relief, a confirmation of who she was meant to be. For nine beautiful months, the anticipation of the love to come had eclipsed all the discomforts of expecting. It was the one and only time in her life that her future seemed clear, bright, and certain.

Today, as June waited for Rosie to prepare a pitcher of iced tea, she both envied and pitied her former self. Had the loss of her rose-colored glasses driven Harry away? There was a certain femininity in innocence, in the naivete she no longer possessed.

"I'm glad you could visit today," Rosie said, bustling into the room with a serving tray.

She wore a pretty floral housedress that picked up the blush on her cheeks. Rosie wasn't particularly fashion forward, but June thought the traditional style flattered her. Generally speaking, June liked Rosie—she was five years June's junior, and she could be a little tiresome at times, but she had a wide-eyed enthusiasm that June found charming in a nonthreatening sort of way.

"I'm afraid I can't make heads or tails of the list Deanna gave me," Rosie went on, "and I don't want to make any mistakes. Sugar?"

"Please." Trying to ignore the twinge she felt at the mention of Deanna's name, June watched patiently as Rosie poured tea into two ice-filled highballs and dropped a sugar cube into each.

June had entrusted Rosie with the invitations this year; the young woman was so keen to please that June knew she'd take the task seriously. Last year, Deanna had asked Bobbie to do it, and the invitations had gone out late. Due to the kerfuffle of Deanna's impending retirement, everyone had excused the snafu—but June hadn't forgotten. As the new head of the committee, she couldn't afford to forget.

"Is it the names that are tripping you up?" June asked. "Deanna cataloged both married names and maiden names to cover all her bases—but her system created a lot of repetition."

Rosie lifted her hands. "That must be it," she said, sinking deeper into the wicker love seat across from June. "I might need your help in clarifying a few, if you don't mind."

"Of course not."

"I can't thank you enough for trusting me with such an important task," Rosie said. "Sometimes I fear the other ladies think I'm dim."

"Not at all," June said, though she *did* think that, just a little. "You're . . . green."

"I'm hoping I can prove myself this year," Rosie said. "Don't tell Deanna I said so, but last year seemed a little . . . chaotic? Maybe it was just because it was my first year on the committee."

"Running a large event is not for the faint of heart," June said.

"Yes, well"—Rosie ran her hands over her skirt, smoothing it out—"now that you have things fully in hand, I'm sure it'll go smoother."

In spite of Deanna's snub earlier this morning, June had the instinct to defend her—after all, Deanna was the yardstick by which June measured herself—but she was flattered to think that Rosie saw *June* as the example. June recognized Rosie's eagerness as something she could cultivate.

"Would you like to go over the list now?" June asked.

"Oh, no need to rush; let's finish our tea first." Rosie's eyes widened. "Unless I'm keeping you?"

"Not at all," June said.

"Besides, the SPW isn't the only reason I invited you here."

"Oh?"

Rosie glanced down at her hands in her lap, curling and uncurling her fingers. "I wanted to apologize for what you overheard at the Shore House yesterday." She met June's eyes, her brows creased with concern.

June did not like feeling pitied—especially by Rosie. "And what did I hear?"

Rosie's gaze darted back down to her hands, to the pitcher of tea, to this month's issue of *McCall's* and a book called *The Feminine Mystique* resting on the glass-topped table between them. "I'm not sure, exactly," she said slowly, "but they mentioned Harry, and—"

"I don't concern myself with silly rumors, and neither should you," June said tightly. "It's childish."

"I agree," Rosie said emphatically. "I guess I was just concerned that your feelings had been hurt?"

June stiffened. "You know, you *are* keeping me," she said. "I have many tasks to accomplish today."

"Of course. I'm so sorry."

"Stop groveling, Rosie. It's unbecoming."

Rosie rolled her shoulders. "I'll go get the list."

When Rosie had disappeared into the other room, June lifted her iced tea to her lips, angry to find that her wrist was a little unsteady. First the gossip, then Deanna, now this. Even if Rosie was genuine in her concern, June did not like the implications of it: the newest member of the SPW already doubting her.

She would have to nip this in the bud.

31

When Marie emerged from her new studio a few hours later, the sun was slanting through the kitchen windows above the sink, causing the silver tap to glint and shine. The patio door was open, and Winifred was sitting by the pool, sipping what appeared to be iced tea. Sheets were clipped up on a clothesline, fluttering gently in the breeze. Marie walked over and sank into the empty lounge chair beside Winifred.

"Unpacked?" Winifred asked without turning her head. Her eyes were shielded by those big Jackie Kennedy sunglasses of hers.

"Mostly," Marie said. "I organized my canvases and paints."

Winifred rolled her head against the back of the lounge chair until her glasses were pointed at Marie. "Did you even go into your bedroom?"

"No."

Winifred's lips split open, teeth flashing. "Of course you didn't."

Marie laughed and kicked her feet up. Her skin was grimy. She hadn't bathed in days, and all that moving in the midday sun had made her sweat. But it was late afternoon now, and the sun was on its descent. The ocean breeze was fresh and cool. For the moment, Marie was content.

Content.

When was the last time she'd felt like this? Relaxed and unworried? Dottie and Hurley Downs were hundreds of miles away. For the first time in months—maybe even years—Marie was excited to paint. Her new studio beckoned.

Winifred tipped her glasses down, glancing toward the clothesline, then replaced them on her nose and took a sip of her tea. "Your sheets are probably dry by now," she observed. "Though, perhaps I should leave them up awhile longer. Our neighbors get irritated when I hang laundry within their view."

"Why do y—" Marie cut herself off. It wasn't her place to ask.

"Why what?"

"You don't seem to like your neighbors," Marie ventured.

Winifred stared up at the sky. "Whatever gave you that idea?"

Marie didn't dare speak further.

"You're wondering why I stay, if I'm not liked here." Winifred still wasn't looking at Marie, instead favoring the wispy clouds above. She sighed. "It's okay; I think everyone is wondering the same thing."

Marie watched Winifred's profile, the freckles dusted across her pixie nose.

"This is all I have left of him," she said simply. "All my happiest memories of Bruce are here." She glanced at Marie. "But I recall promising that I wouldn't talk about him, so that's all I'll say."

"I never wanted you to stop talking about him," Marie said.

Winifred smiled against the rim of her highball glass, then sipped her tea.

"When did he first take you here?" Marie prompted.

"Our second date, if you believe it. Our first date had been interrupted by a rather rude coworker of his, and he thought taking me here would be a nice escape. It was still the offseason, and the town was empty. Peaceful." She set her glass beside the leg of her lounge chair. "He'd been coming here since he was a boy. This cottage was a family home, a summer escape. Part of three generations' worth of tradition, just like the rest of this neighborhood."

"But now it's yours?"

"Now it's mine," Winifred said, sounding almost regretful to have broken the chain. "My consolation prize."

"Is that why the neighbors . . . ?"

She giggled. "Oh, the rich folks here hated me long before Bruce put my name in his will." She waved her hand in a dismissive manner. "You wouldn't believe how uptight his parents are. Their whole social circle, really. Bruce grew up in an elite ecosystem, cut off from the rest of the world. I was his act of rebellion. A normal girl. A smart and independent girl."

"Why does that matter?"

"Beats me," she said. "But if I had to pose a guess, I think his circle saw me as a harbinger of change."

"And that's so bad?"

"The *worst*," she said ominously. A few fine smile lines, barely visible, feathered out from under the sides of her sunglasses. "There is nothing so threatening as an independent woman."

Marie didn't understand the world of wealth, summer colonies, inheritances, and traditions. Her life had never been conventional. But she saw society reflected in Winifred's experience. The hatred for independent women, child-free women, women's lib on the whole. It made no sense to her, but then again, there was little about the human experience that *did* make sense to Marie.

"Bruce used to refer to this place as our safe haven," Winifred said. "I heard him call it quaint once. Thirteen thousand square feet, *quaint*."

"But it's not a safe haven, is it?" Marie asked softly.

"When he was alive, it was. Or maybe *he* was my safe haven."

"And now?"

"And now . . . well, now nobody is forced to play nice anymore." Winifred removed her shades and turned to Marie, the brown in her irises standing out in dark contrast against her skin. "You know, I tried so hard to fit in. For Bruce, I mean. I tried to wear the right outfits and say the right things and joined all the committees, and June and her posse—the housewives here, Bruce's peers' wives—never welcomed me.

They treated me like a stain. I could've poured bleach on myself, and they still would've called me dirty."

Marie didn't recognize the Winifred she was describing. As far as Marie was concerned, Winifred was the most stylish, charming woman she knew. Who were these women who deemed Winifred not good enough? "They sound like witches."

"They're brainwashed," Winifred said. "They've been told since childhood that they're to be good little housewives and broodmares, and I don't fit that mold. Never have." The wind ruffled Winifred's hair, and she tucked a red strand behind her ear. "On good days, I like to think they're all a little jealous that Bruce never held me under his thumb like their husbands do to them."

"And on bad days?"

Winifred stared at the ocean for a few beats. "On bad days, I *do* feel like a freak. I'm all alone." She turned to Marie and grinned. "Well, I *was* alone."

"Now I'm here."

Winifred's eyes lit up, brows rising. "You don't exist inside their box either, Marie. You're a freer spirit than I am, living life for your art. It's admirable."

"It's exhausting," Marie said before she could even think.

"At least you're not trying to be someone you'll never be."

"Are you?"

"You know what?" Winifred sat up. "*No*, I'm not. Not anymore." She grinned again, all teeth. "See? You being here is good for me already."

Marie could hardly wrap her head around Winifred's story. Her self-image was so different than how Marie saw her.

Marie wanted to ask Winifred why, why, why. Why did she linger here when Bruce was no longer around? Why did she think these women were worth her time, anyhow? Why was she so self-conscious, when everything about her—from her silky copper hair to her neatly painted toenails and all the warmth, friendliness, and charisma in between—proved that she was magnetic?

"There I go again, blabbing on about myself," Winifred said. "Tell me about you, Marie. What brought you here?"

Marie froze like a frightened rabbit, wondering where to run. But Winifred had opened up to her, and maybe she ought to do the same. "I—" Her stomach growled, interrupting her.

Winifred straightened, eyes going wide. "I forgot to plan dinner."

So? Marie wanted to ask, but instead she waited for Winifred to clarify.

"You're starving," she said emphatically. "When was the last time you ate?"

Marie thought back to the cereal she'd bought earlier. "This morning?"

"A *real* meal."

"Your party?"

Winifred rocketed to her feet. "I'll start dinner," she said. "It's early, but hell, we both skipped lunch. I'll make a casserole; it won't take long."

Marie stood, too, and followed Winifred back into the house, leaving the lounge chairs and the empty tea glass behind.

"I can help," Marie said.

Winifred pulled a Pyrex dish from a cabinet. "No, no, it's easy enough. Just relax."

"Relax?"

"Yeah, Marie, *relax*," Winifred said, gathering things out of the cupboard. "Sit by the pool, take a warm shower, whatever you want. This is your house now too."

Marie thought about it a moment, then said, "I could use a shower."

"I already left clean towels on your bed. There's soap in all the upstairs bathrooms."

"You sure you don't want help?"

Winifred waved her away. "Get fresh. When you're done, we'll eat."

32

Winifred put the casserole in the oven and then sank into the chair at the head of the dining room table. All day, Winifred's blood had been racing. First, with nervousness over whether Marie would agree to her idea. Next, with excitement when Marie arrived on her doorstep. Then, with curiosity toward Marie's paintings, the mystery of who she was as an artist. Some of the canvases Winifred had seen revealed true potential; at the risk of scaring Marie away, Winifred was tempted to try to help. Marie was exactly the type of artist that Winifred aimed to support with her fund. And if not in an official capacity, perhaps Winifred could support Marie in other ways: encouragement, suggestions, and the obvious one, a home.

Winifred's blood was also racing because she couldn't believe what she was doing. When she'd had her brilliant idea yesterday, she didn't see the fault in it. She still couldn't, really. But it was unconventional. Her neighbors would call her a hippie. And maybe she was. All she wanted in life was peace, love, and freedom. She'd spent so long trying to fit herself into the box Bruce lived in, but enough was enough. It was time Winifred expressed her *true* self—June Duxbury and the rest be damned.

She hadn't lied to Marie when she said she needed company in this lonesome existence of hers, but it was more than that: Winifred admired Marie. Marie was calm, and mysterious, and so . . . *brave*. Winifred had no idea why Marie had been living in her car, but clearly it had something to do with her dedication to her art. Had Winifred *ever* gone to such lengths for something she was passionate about?

She had criticized the neighborhood women earlier, but in many ways, Winifred was just like them. She'd never imagined herself a proper housewife, but she'd always wanted to find true love. Winifred had adored her husband. She had adored making his dinners and sharing his bed—not because she saw herself as his subordinate, but because she enjoyed doting on him. It felt like throwing a party for two. Like playing house.

But that was it, wasn't it? She'd been playing. June Duxbury wasn't playing—if anything, she was being played. Everyone knew her husband was cheating on her. Even Winifred, isolated as she was, knew that Harry wanted a divorce. She'd felt sorry for June when she'd overheard the gossip. Because unlike Winifred, June believed wholeheartedly in the system. Become a wife, have children, live happily ever after. Nobody warned June that a lack of purpose could dull a woman into melancholy. June was unkind, but she'd also been fed a lie, and no woman deserved that. No woman deserved to be as helpless and miserable as June Duxbury.

Sometimes Winifred wondered if being a woman was defined by sacrifice. Women sacrificed their autonomy for their husbands. Their bodies for their babies. Their dreams of *more* for domesticity. They sacrificed their individuality for status. They sacrificed each other to get ahead in a world designed by men.

This was the part of Winifred's grief she couldn't stand: missing Bruce but also feeling like Bruce had contributed to this stalemate she'd found herself in. Either try to fit in with the only other women around or run home to her father in defeat.

And then there was Marie.

She was outside the box that walled Winifred's life. She didn't do things as she was supposed to. She didn't even do things for her own vanity. She lived life by the beat of her own drum. Marie didn't claim to be a hippie, but Marie was the most far-out person Winifred had ever met.

And Winifred wanted to know everything about her.

33

Upstairs, in the shower—enveloped in steam and suds and gratitude—Marie started having doubts.

Was this situation too good to be true? Marie had only ever had one true friend in her entire life, and the world had taken her from Marie. Winifred seemed so *keen* on connecting with Marie, but Marie wasn't sure if she could do it all again. She had kept herself locked away for too long.

People had wondered, over the brief months of Marie's skyrocketing fame, why she fixated on the age of ten. The leading theory among male critics was that it had something to do with wanting to capture youth—a sentiment that made Marie's eyes roll every time someone brought it up (this sexist take at odds with the common secondary assessment that Marie's *Girl* paintings were part of a feminist agenda). Others thought Marie was focused on the past, which was closer to the mark, except she wasn't painting herself. *Innocence* was a word art professionals used a lot—it was a word that made Marie cringe a little, because it made her sound somehow predatory.

The truth was, Marie was mostly just grasping.

Grasping for a memory. For that brave time in a young girl's life before she learns the full, devastating capability of the world. Not as a means of examining *innocence*, but the opposite. Marie had never felt so powerful as she did at ten years old, running through the Pennsylvania fields. Not knowing her limitations had given Marie a fearless sense of freedom she would never get back.

The fact that nobody who viewed her paintings understood what she was *trying* to capture proved that not only did Marie's inner sentiments make her an outcast, but that she also wasn't a good painter. Maybe her work was pleasant and evocative enough to warrant high price tags (for a while), but no one *got it*, got *her*. No one ever did.

Winifred had *wanted* to, though. Just this morning. Marie had seen the way Winifred studied the canvases as she moved them; her curious gaze had made Marie wince. Paintings were meant to be seen, but Marie didn't want to witness the scrutiny. She had no idea whether Winifred truly *got* her paintings—her recent works were failures, anyhow—but Marie couldn't overlook the way Winifred's face lit up upon seeing them. As if she had discovered something special.

Dottie had looked at Marie that way, on occasion—an expression of gladness and wonder. Something she could never paint, not if she tried forever, because it was more than muscles and shapes—it was a thought passing across a face. Only a living person could express that sort of energy.

Dottie had been such an expressive child. At turns bold, funny, timid. She was like a bird tracing the path of wind. Her lips might as well have been the flicker of wings: turning up, frowning down, angling. Taking something invisible—a breeze, a thought—and moving over it with speed and grace. (*You have opinions,* Marie used to tell her, making the word sound like a sack of onions, heavy and smelly. *So do you,* Dottie would taunt, but then she'd give Marie that look—that look that said *I like your opinions. I want to hear them.*)

Dottie had opened Marie's world. Things that had once concerned Marie became small and inconsequential. Every day felt like an opportunity. The fields were greener, more golden. The night sky grew more vast and prismatic. Even the Thoroughbreds were no longer so untouchable.

By the time school ended for the summer, Marie and Dottie spent every day together. Dottie lived a mile from Hurley Downs, in a small home on the outskirts of Nisbet. The track property stretched three hundred acres widthwise and was shrugged right up under the west branch of the Susquehanna River. They would meet in the fields on the edge of the Downs, where an old barbed wire fence with a yellow No Trespassing sign marked the end of the property. To the north, a small forest obscured the river; to the south and east, cattle fields.

The girls were often accompanied by their older brothers. Marie had only James, but Dottie had three older brothers and one younger. The boys would romp in the fields and dare each other to run up behind cows. On the track side of the fence, the girls would crouch in the tall grass to catch crickets or run off into the woods and look for frogs in the creek, a small offshoot of the Susquehanna. They spent the whole summer this way. Chores in the morning, play all afternoon, dinner bell at six o'clock, and then sometimes they would meet again to catch fireflies in the twilight.

Marie only saw Dottie's house one time. Early in the summer, Dottie invited her over for dinner, and the next evening, Marie's father drove both James and Marie to Nisbet. Marie had expected a rowdy affair—all those brothers—but when Dottie's mother opened the door, the house was quiet.

"Good evening, Mrs. Evers," James said politely. "Our mother made cake." He handed the worn, heavy cake pan to Dottie's mother.

"Well, wasn't that thoughtful?" Mrs. Evers said.

"It's vanilla," Marie added.

"My favorite." Mrs. Evers lifted onto her tiptoes and waved at their father idling in the driveway; he waved back and then drove off. "How nice of your father to drive you."

"Ma worried we'd drop the cake if we walked," James said.

Marie had never met Dottie's parents before, but her own mother had spoken to Mrs. Evers on the phone and afterward commented on how nice she seemed. Mrs. Evers wore a white ruffled apron with little blue flowers on it. The apron appeared well used and well loved.

Already, Marie had an eye for color—an appreciation for that specific shade of azure. She'd gone on to paint many iterations of those flowers.

"I like your apron," Marie had said.

"Why, thank you."

Marie wondered if Mrs. Evers's hazel eyes were always so red-rimmed, but instead, she asked, "Where's Dottie?"

James elbowed her, probably to signal that she was being rude, but Marie just elbowed him back.

"Outside, with the boys," Mrs. Evers answered, smiling, but her voice sounded strangled. "Run along. Dinner will be ready in a half hour."

"May I ask what we are having?" James asked.

"Meat loaf. My specialty." She pointed toward the kitchen. "The back door is that way."

James grasped Marie's hand and led her through the kitchen and out the screen door.

Dottie and her brothers were all in the backyard, except the middle-oldest, Henry. They were standing around as if the fun had been interrupted. A shiny red Radio Flyer wagon was turned on its side in the dead lawn grass, its front wheels crooked due to the handle being wrenched against the undercarriage. Croquet mallets and balls were strewn everywhere, along with a few baseballs and a stray mitt with loose stitching. No one spoke as James and Marie stepped off the back porch.

"Where's Henry?" James asked.

Dottie let out an odd squeak. Her eyes shot to Marie's, and they were red like her mother's.

Dottie's oldest brother, Adam, clenched his jaw. "He's with Pa."

Marie waited. When he didn't say more, she approached Dottie. "My mom made vanilla sheet cake."

Dottie smiled, a bird turning in the wind. "I *love* vanilla."

James picked up the baseball at his feet and tossed it to Kenny, Dottie's youngest brother. Kenny caught it with his bare hands. At only five, Kenny was really good at baseball. His older brothers were always saying he had a *good arm* and that someday soon Kenny would play for a Williamsport Little League team.

Kenny tossed the ball to Finn, the third brother, who dropped his palm to absorb the slap of leather on skin. All the older boys did that. Finn tossed it to Adam, Adam tossed it to James, James tossed it to Marie, Marie tossed it to Dottie, and Dottie returned it to Kenny. They went on like this—throwing the ball randomly across their six-point circle—until Henry sulked into the yard.

His eyes were red, too, and his pants were scuffed.

"He stole a hot dog from the fridge," Dottie explained.

Marie didn't understand how a child could steal food from their own family's fridge, but she didn't say anything.

Adam tossed Henry the ball. When he caught it, he examined the faded red threads and sniffled. When he looked up again, his lip quavered, and he caught it between his teeth. Then he dropped the ball in the brown grass and walked inside.

"He'll be all right," Adam said.

By the time dinner was ready and they'd all piled around the table, Henry was still quiet. Marie tried not to look directly at Mr. Evers. He had a stern face and didn't speak—he just ate his huge piece of meat loaf and sucked at his beer bottle. Henry didn't seem to look at his father, either, but when Mrs. Evers brought out the cake, Henry brightened. Once the tin was empty and they were all outside again, Henry was back to his normal self. They spent the evening in the empty lot across the street, catching fireflies and taking turns in the wagon.

"What happened to Henry?" Marie whispered to Dottie while they sat on a rock in the twinkly dusk, watching the boys shouting and jumping on each other's backs.

Dottie was usually so sunny and frank, but she frowned then. "He was punished." Marie expected her to elaborate, but she didn't.

An hour after dark, Mrs. Evers rang a bell, and the kids all ran back to the house, except Kenny, who'd fallen asleep in the wagon and had to be dragged back by the girls. Marie and Dottie walked side by side, each with a grip on the handle. When they arrived a few minutes after the boys, Marie's father's car was in the driveway. Marie and Dottie hugged fiercely, their twiggy arms twining.

"Thank you for dinner, Mrs. Evers," James said.

She handed him the clean cake tin. "Please thank your mother for the cake. What a treat that was!"

James nodded and climbed into the back seat of the car. Marie scooted in after him and closed the door.

On the road, their father's headlights carved yellow cones out of the dark.

"Did you have fun?" he asked.

"So much fun," Marie said.

"We had meat loaf," James added.

That night, after her mother had tucked them in, Marie crept out of her bed and into James's. He scooted over to make room.

"What did Mr. Evers do to Henry?" she asked.

"He beat him," James said flatly.

"Beat him how?"

"With his fist, I reckon."

Marie had been spanked before, but only once, with an open hand on her bum. She winced. "Dottie said he stole a hot dog from their fridge."

"Their dad's a drunk," James said.

Marie didn't understand what being a drunk had to do with it.

"He gets angry," James explained. "Drinking makes him angry."

Worry pushed on her chest, and she rolled from her back to her side so she could stare at James's profile, outlined by the dim moonlight streaming through the window. "I don't know if I want to go to their house again."

"He'd never hit *you*." James said it as if she were being silly, but then he whispered, "We don't have to go back there if you don't want to."

"Can they come here sometime?"

"We'll have to ask Ma," James said, "but I'm sure she'll say yes."

34

Marie toweled off, allowing the memory to evaporate. She'd spent years trying to bury her memories in the dirt, shoveling on more resolve when they tried to poke through. But now they were sprouting up everywhere. The closer Marie got to buying Hurley Downs, the harder they were to hack away. It didn't help that Winifred reminded her so much of Dottie. She hadn't seen it before, but the more she thought about it, the more similarities became apparent.

Her amiability.

Her humor.

Her charm.

And more than anything else, it was the way Winifred made Marie *feel*: seen, heard, welcomed. Dottie had done all those things, too; she'd made Marie invincible with her friendship.

And then Marie lost her.

Marie wasn't sure she was ready for another love like that—the kind that had the power to split her open like a seed. But maybe she was getting ahead of herself. Maybe Winifred wasn't trying to be her friend at all. Maybe Winifred was just *nice*. Somehow, that thought made Marie sad. She wanted Winifred's care, but she also wanted Winifred's indifference.

Marie audibly growled at herself. She was thinking in circles.

She wrapped the towel around her body, and with the self-consciousness that comes only upon being naked in someone else's house for the first time, she quickly tiptoed across the hall into her new bedroom. Past the threshold, the carpet was plush under her bare feet. The line-dried sheets were on the bed, and the room smelled like beach brine and fresh-cut lawn. Winifred must've made the bed while Marie was in the shower, going in and out of the room like a ghost.

Marie found a semiclean T-shirt and a pair of jeans from her duffel. Both were covered in paint, but they didn't smell too bad. Her skin was soap-smooth as she slid them on, and despite her jumbled thoughts and once-forgotten memories, she felt refreshed.

When Marie emerged downstairs, Winifred stood from the dinner table. A casserole was steaming on a trivet. Two place settings had been prepared, one at the head of the table and one to the left, facing the ocean. Winifred gestured to the ocean-view seat.

"Can I get you some water, Coke, lemonade?"

"Lemonade, thanks," Marie said, sinking into the chair.

Silence leaked into the moment like water into a boat. Marie stared out the window at the pool, listening to Winifred clinking and breathing in the kitchen. She delivered a pitcher of lemonade and filled the glass in front of Marie. Then she sat beside Marie and slid a cloth napkin into her lap.

"Please," Winifred said, gesturing to the casserole.

Marie grasped the serving spoon that had been stuck into the noodles. She scooped two helpings onto her plate.

Winifred did the same.

They ate.

"Did you have a nice shower?"

"I did, thank you."

"Did you have everything you needed?"

"Yes, everything."

More chewing, more silence. Their social boat was sinking fast.

"You'll feel more settled in a few days," Winifred said.

"Thanks again."

Winifred gestured at the food. "Do you like it?" She was still wearing her apron. The perfect picture of domesticity.

"I feel like a husband home from work," Marie quipped.

Winifred's brow creased.

"I just mean, I walked in, and dinner was already waiting. I might as well have had a briefcase in hand. And your apron—it's so frilly." Marie frowned, afraid she'd insulted her host.

But after a long pause, Winifred laughed. It started out as a low chuckle and grew into a full-on gasping cackle. "You're right," Winifred croaked, wiping her eyes. "I'm sorry, this must be so . . . *uncomfortable* for you. I promise I'm not using you to replace Bruce." Her breath hitched, and they both chose to ignore the awkward comment. "I guess it's just an old habit—being a wife, that is. I'm fine in a crowd, but one on one . . . ," she trailed off and shook her head. "I'm not used to it."

"I'm not used to *having* a wife."

They smiled at each other.

"It's horribly quiet in here, isn't it?" Winifred stood abruptly and flipped on the radio. A staticky rendition of "Satisfaction" gave the room some oxygen again.

"So tell me about you," Winifred said, resettling her napkin over her lap. At Marie's brief pause in chewing, Winifred added, "What, you thought I didn't notice you evading the question earlier?"

Marie poked at her noodles with her fork. "I'm not very interesting, is all," she mumbled.

"*Pah.*" Winifred waved her hand as if swatting at a bug. "I don't believe that for a second."

"It's true."

"You know," Winifred said, leaning forward dramatically, her thin wrist bending gracefully backward as she settled her chin in her palm, "if you keep evading my question, I'll start to think you might be hiding something."

Marie's eyes reflexively widened, and Winifred leaned back, giggling.

"I'm kidding," she said. "But I do deserve to know *something* about the stranger I've invited into my house, don't I?"

Marie frowned at her nearly empty plate. She owed it to Winifred to open up a bit—she just didn't like talking about herself. What was there to say? "I don't know where to start."

"Why don't you tell me about your paintings?"

Her cheeks flamed. The last thing she wanted to talk about was her artwork.

"Or . . . your childhood?"

Her whole past was a minefield. So much destruction that even the happy memories carried an edge of foreboding.

"Where'd you grow up?" Winifred asked gently.

Marie felt as if she was being interrogated, but Winifred—she was just trying to connect. Was that so awful?

"I grew up on a Thoroughbred racetrack," Marie answered. "In Pennsylvania."

Winifred's strawberry blonde eyebrows rose. "Really?"

"Yes." Just to occupy her hands, Marie grasped the serving spoon and heaped another pile of noodles on her plate. Etiquette be damned. Even with second helpings, the casserole would last them days. She shoved a big bite into her mouth, and it went down like a sticky brick.

"Did your family own horses?"

"No," Marie said. "Too rich for our blood. My father worked as a groundskeeper, and we lived in a staff compound behind the stables."

"Oh, wow."

"What?"

"I'm just thinking that you are very interesting, indeed."

Marie smothered a smile. While she didn't like the spotlight, *Winifred's* spotlight wasn't so bad.

"Was it just you and your parents?"

"I have an older brother, James."

"Where is he?"

"Philly."

"And your parents? Are they still at the track?"

Marie didn't know how to sweeten her phrasing, so she just said the facts. "My parents are dead."

"I'm sorry to hear that," Winifred said, and she really looked sorry. Her eyelashes swooped in slow, compassionate blinks. "Were you close with them?"

"Yes."

"Me too," Winifred said. "I mean, I'm close with my father. My mother left when I was a girl."

"Died?"

"No, left."

Marie didn't know what to say.

"It's all right, there's nothing you can say," Winifred said, reading her thoughts. "It's just a fact by now, you know? It happened so long ago."

"Time doesn't always heal," Marie said.

Winifred smiled sadly, as if she agreed but didn't want to affirm. Instead, she asked, "What was it like growing up on a racetrack? I imagine it was exciting."

"We weren't allowed around the horses." Marie felt like a barn swallow swooping over a pond, dangerously close to a crash landing. "They were hot, as the breeders say. Lots of nervous energy. Not safe for kids."

"Did you watch the races?"

"Some," Marie said. "I didn't care for them."

"I used to think races were thrilling," Winifred said. "But then you watch the horses on the sidelines, all frothy and wired, and it seems . . ."

"Cruel."

"Exactly." Winifred chewed a dainty bite. "So, what did you and your brother get up to?"

"It was a rural childhood," Marie said, surprised when her voice came out a little wistful. "Running through the fields, exploring the woods, catching frogs and fireflies."

"That sounds like a dream," Winifred said.

"It was," Marie admitted. "While it lasted."

Neither of them spoke for a moment, but this time when the silence crept in, it was amiable. The radio hummed in the background.

"Why didn't I see any paintings of fields, woods, and fireflies?"

Marie looked up from her plate.

"What you describe of your childhood," Winifred went on, "it all sounds so picturesque. And yet I didn't see any Pennsylvania paintings. Just portraits. Why?"

Marie laid her fork down, realizing she was overfull. "I don't know," she answered honestly. "I never considered it. I usually just paint what's on my mind."

Dottie. Always Dottie. Marie had done her best *not* to think about her childhood, but when the fields and the fences and the forest fell away, Dottie was still there.

"Did you always love art?"

"All children love art," Marie said. "Creativity is natural—built right into our DNA. Artists are always waxing poetic about '*Oh, I always loved to paint.*' Of course they did. We all did." Marie's words came of their own volition. "It's the world that kills a child's creativity, I think. Life and expectations dim the wonder. Or maybe it's just our faith in the wonder that dims."

"But *you* kept going."

Marie knew what Winifred was implying: that Marie's sense of wonder hadn't dimmed. Except . . . that wasn't it. Marie painted because she was trying to make sense of the senselessness of life. To find that last remaining glimmer of light, like the sun after it sets, but before the night falls fully. She wanted to explain her feelings to Winifred, but they were as indefinable as twilight.

When Marie failed to reply, Winifred asked, "Were your parents encouraging?"

A tide of nostalgia rose in Marie's heart. "My parents were the epitome of encouragement. I know the career choice worried them—put some strain on my brother to look out for me—but they were nothing but supportive."

After Dottie died, Marie had spent hours in her bedroom drawing her friend's face. At first, she'd been trying to remember how it looked, the fleeting expressions it made. Trying to capture her forever. But then the portraits grew compulsive—a means of quieting her creeping sense of culpability, a way to reconnect with a more innocent feeling. Her mother found a drawing one day and bought her a proper pencil set. When Marie's skill improved, her parents bought her watercolors, then children's acrylics, then professional oils and real canvases.

Marie had often wondered if her parents had encouraged her because she was talented, or simply because they knew she was trying to paint away her grief. Either way, she was grateful. To deny Marie would have meant denying her a piece of herself. Most parents of their time would've told her to lay down her brush—chiding her for its impracticality—but they had handed her one instead. Pushed it into her fingers. Bought her the paint.

Marie lifted her head; Winifred was watching her openly, about to ask something else.

Before she could, Marie gestured toward her empty lemonade glass. "If you're going to ask more questions, I might need something stronger."

35

In the kitchen, Winifred retrieved a liquor bottle from a high shelf. "Grasshopper?"

After all the lemonade she'd just drunk, Marie thought the cream might curdle in her stomach, but she nodded. The conversation had gotten away from her, answers to Winifred's questions flowing freely. Marie had never spoken about her childhood so openly. Winifred had a disarming quality that Marie was powerless to, a curiosity so genuine that Marie felt . . . safe.

"So, your brother." Winifred obtained a pair of etched glasses, which caught the evening sunlight and sent it skittering across the countertop. "If he's still in Pennsylvania, why did you move to Rhode Island?"

"I didn't, really. I moved to New York City to illustrate for an advertising firm. Then a gallery in Providence wanted to show my paintings, and—"

"A gallery?" Winifred stopped midpour, the cocktail dribbling on the counter. Her pause only lasted a moment before she was wiping up the spill with a rag. "Did much come of it?"

Her voice was tight, restrained, and the sharpening of Winifred's interest caused Marie to retreat into herself once again. "No," she lied.

"But you're here."

"Last year, an associate suggested I attend a few shindigs out here. Rub shoulders." *Seek patronage,* she didn't add. "I liked it better than the city, so I . . . came back."

Winifred bobbed her head, knowing better than to show too much interest. Who had sent Marie to last year's party? Which gallery in Providence had shown her work? Why hadn't Winifred *heard* of Marie Clarke before? She had the faintest inkling of familiarity, like the whiff of a scent she couldn't place, but then again, maybe she was imagining it.

"Here." She handed over the finished cocktail. "Care to sit outside?"

Winifred led Marie onto the patio, her thoughts whispering like the wind through the beach grass. Winifred found Marie endlessly fascinating—not just the mystery of her artwork but her childhood on the racetrack, her philosophies on art in general. Marie was like an agate, beautiful and rare. Winifred wanted to pluck her out of the sand, turn her over in her hands, hold her up to the light. Study every striation and weathered chip. Winifred liked people, but she rarely met people who captured her interest to this degree. She could tell that Marie was special.

"Do you care where we sit?" Winifred asked.

"Anywhere is great."

"How about right here, in the grass?"

Marie seemed surprised by the suggestion.

"Oh, come on, I'm not so uppity that I won't sit on the ground."

Marie's mouth quirked. "It's just . . . not what I expected."

Winifred slipped her sandals off her feet and plopped down. "I like the feeling of the grass on my toes."

"Me too."

Marie was already barefoot; Winifred had spotted her ratty shoes in her bedroom, when she went in to replace the sheets. Maybe she should take Marie shopping. When was the last time Marie had felt the joy of a new pair of shoes?

Winifred was careful not to look directly at Marie when she said, "I don't mean to pry, but how long had you been living in your car?"

Marie lifted her cocktail to her lips and sipped quickly. "Not long."

"Did something happen?"

"Not one particular thing . . ." She drank again, as if deciding whether to say more. "I chose to."

"You *chose* to?" That's not what Winifred had expected. Was it some sort of Eastern spiritual belief that had made Marie live so simply? Was she more of a hippie than Winifred thought? No—had it been on principle, Marie would've refused Winifred's offer. *"Why?"*

"I'm broke," Marie said simply. "And I'm trying to save up for something big. Paying rent on an apartment with the same square footage as my car didn't make sense anymore." She met Winifred's eyes, searching for something—maybe empathy, or understanding?

Winifred digested that information. "You must want that 'something big' quite a lot," she remarked.

Marie stared off toward the ocean. From their spot on the lawn, all they could see was the gull-speckled sky and the swell of the sand dune that led down to the beach. "I do." She looked at Winifred again with that same searching expression, as if she wanted so badly for Winifred to hold her secrets, to be humane.

No one had ever looked at Winifred like that—as if she had power. As if she could somehow be destructive or reckless with Marie's admissions. She realized, perhaps belatedly, that these personal details were not things Marie commonly shared. Winifred was determined to be delicate with such gifts.

"What is it?"

"The racetrack."

"You want to buy . . . the racetrack?"

Marie took another long sip of her grasshopper.

"What would you do with it?"

165

Marie's eyes glittered as she stared far off, no doubt seeing her childhood home instead of the sand. Her tone was unexpectedly hard when she turned back to Winifred. "I would bulldoze it."

"Bulldoze it?" Winifred repeated, certain she'd heard wrong.

"That's right."

"I don't understand."

Marie finished her drink and set the empty glass down between them. "I don't expect you to."

Winifred heard the locked door in Marie's voice, then, and did not ask anything more.

Nestling her feet in the grass, Winifred wondered how much Marie had already saved for this outlandish venture; even a run-down racetrack would be expensive. But however much she had—and by whatever means she'd earned it—she wasn't going to tell Winifred. Not yet, at least.

"When do you think you'll have enough?"

Marie shrugged—her movements were a little looser from the alcohol. "I don't know. Soon, I hope."

Winifred's whispering thoughts picked up, a sudden gust of questions hissing over the dune grass. She'd mentioned galleries before, *shindigs*. Had Marie sold much of her work? Did she have any patrons? Winifred couldn't see another reason why Marie would've come all the way out to Rhode Island.

"Can I get you another drink?" Winifred asked.

Marie met her eyes, squinted, then shook her head. "No, thank you. In fact, I think this one nearly put me to sleep."

The summer sun was only just now setting, the sky a pastel blue fading to peach near the horizon.

"Go to bed early," Winifred offered, sensing that Marie might feel the need for permission. Her shyness was endearing, but Winifred didn't want her to feel that way forever. "I'm going to sit out here awhile longer. We'll catch up in the morning."

Marie stood. "Thank you, Winifred."

Winifred smiled and watched her disappear inside the house again. When Marie was gone, Winifred finished her own drink and lay back in the grass. She watched the stars gradually reveal themselves as the sky faded from blue to black.

Fields, forests, fireflies—that's how Marie had described her childhood. With her supportive parents, Marie's home in Pennsylvania sounded idyllic. Why would she want to buy the track only to destroy it?

A realization made Winifred press her fingers to her mouth: something bad must've happened. Something bad enough to make Marie desperate with anger, or sadness, or rage. Marie was carrying a weight Winifred couldn't see. Winifred wondered how big it truly was.

36

A week had passed since Harry took Bella away. June missed her daughter with an ache that radiated all day long, pulsing at the sight of a stray toy, Bella's closed bedroom door, her tiny spoons in the silverware drawer. But it was her smell that June missed most: that fresh, powdery, almost floral scent. June had smelled plenty of babies over the years—one by one, each of her friends had given birth before her, while June struggled hopelessly to conceive—but when Bella was finally born, she smelled the sweetest. When June tucked Bella in at night, she always pressed her face into her daughter's soft neck and inhaled that scent because she knew that it wouldn't last forever.

June had always thought time would slowly take away that delicate aroma; she never would've guessed that her own recklessness would snatch it away. But now Bella was gone, back with Harry at their home in Boston. Their absences had disgraced June, and after Deanna's snub outside the grocery and Rosie's pity, June was beginning to panic.

What if she deserved the ruin about to befall her?

The question had badgered her day and night until June's defiant *I won't let this happen* attitude toward Harry's divorce madness had been replaced by a clutching fear that maybe it really *would* happen. Just yesterday, he'd called to ask who June had chosen as a lawyer. (She hadn't chosen anyone yet, and he knew it—how was she even supposed to begin such a process?) The sound of a woman's voice in the background had made June's agony flare like a flame, bright and quick. She'd told herself that the voice had belonged to the nanny, or a maid, but she didn't know for certain.

People were already talking. Harry hadn't been discreet about his affair, and he wouldn't be discreet about a divorce. June felt like a particle of dust floating in a sunbeam: suspended, helpless, and on display. Never had she imagined her life would turn out like this.

But she couldn't avoid the facts of her body. June's struggles with fertility had cost Bella a community of children her own age, delayed as she was compared to June's friends' children; they had cost Bella a sibling too. And June's pain had driven Harry away. She hated her body for everything it couldn't do, for the love and normalcy it had stolen from her.

But June wouldn't let her life fall apart that easily. She was finished bleeding, the sun was shining, and she was determined to clean up her social messes before they made a permanent stain.

June arrived at the Shore House early. She'd put on her favorite cherry red gingham dress, the one with a smart collar and a cinched waist that accentuated her figure. The feminists who wore miniskirts and T-shirts with no bras would call June's style dated, but she preferred the words *elegant* and *timeless*. And it made sense to dress her best on this day in particular, the day she would get ahead of the rumors by telling her story.

Barbara arrived at ten past the hour. "Sorry I'm late." She plopped beside June and flopped her pocketbook into the remaining empty chair at their table.

Her lipstick was a little smudged, and June said as much.

"I've been racing around all day," Barbara said, flicking open a small mirror. The waiter came by, and without looking at him, Barbara ordered "whatever she's drinking."

"Wet martini," the waiter confirmed and swiveled away.

Barbara glanced at June's half-empty martini glass, then met June's eyes. "A martini? This must be serious."

"It's about Harry."

Barbara frowned and put her mirror away. "Is it the . . ." *other woman*, she mouthed.

"More than that," June said, taking a deep breath in preparation for the free fall. "We're getting a divorce."

Barbara's face quaked—but not in pity, so much as . . . disgust. The worst part was that June couldn't blame Barbara for it—had June been in Barbara's shoes, she would've been disgusted too.

But June sat tall and did her best to lie to herself and to Barbara. "It's for the best." Her voice wavered, but she kept on. "He's been unfaithful, and it's only gotten worse. I won't stand for it any longer." June wanted Barbara to think that she was in the driver's seat; that way, the words of gossip would be that June was not pitiful, but brave and in control.

"All husbands have blips," Barbara said, "but that doesn't mean a marriage is doomed."

"Well, mine is doomed. In fact, it was doomed years ago."

To her credit, Barbara's tone was compassionate when she said, "Can't you look the other way?"

June thought of Harry's recent declaration: that Evelyn wanted to get married. "Not anymore."

"What about Bella? You can't possibly think a broken home is better than—*what?*—telling her that her father is working late again?"

June had known her friend wouldn't respond well, but she'd still hoped for a little more solidarity. "That might work while she's little," June said, "but eventually Bella will discover the truth, and I don't want my daughter to learn that adultery is acceptable. It's a bad example."

"Breaking your vows, turning your back on commitment, giving up when the going gets tough—aren't those bad examples too?" Barbara looked around the deck, her eyes flitting to all the other tables. *What will people think?* That's what she was wondering. When Barbara's gaze returned, her eyes pierced June like sewing pins. "What will this do to our summers? Our charities? The SPW? June, this will upset the entire . . ." Barbara's voice dropped to nothing as the waiter delivered her martini.

Both women watched the olive bob along the bottom of the glass until the waiter was out of earshot.

Then Barbara leaned in. "You've always been such an example to us, June. I don't recognize the woman sitting here today. The old June would've fought for her marriage."

I've been fighting, June thought. "He's in love with her." The words were poison on her tongue: tingly, sharp, bitter.

Barbara sat back, shaking her head dismissively. "It's puppy love; it'll blow over."

"It's been *years*," June said. "He's not even trying to hide it anymore. He invited her to Winifred's party last year—she was *there.*"

After Harry's declaration at the party, June had done her best to delay him, to make him reconsider. Bruce's death had also shaken him. One night shortly after the funeral, Harry had told June that his friend's sudden absence had given him a new perspective on what was important in life. June had thought Harry meant her and Bella, but now she wondered if he'd meant Evelyn instead.

June had managed to keep him home for nearly a year, but now it all felt futile. She could slow him down, but she would never change his mind. It was time to concern herself with the proceedings. How far would he go to prove she was unfit? To prove his grounds for divorce? Better that June rise above his claims, get out ahead of his efforts, maintain control.

Barbara frowned, and for a moment June thought Barbara was softening, but then she said, "Are you giving him what he needs?"

June had tried and tried. She'd showered him with love, affection, attention. Then, in her desperation, the negligee—which had almost ended in disaster. The familiar agony of her failure to reseduce her own husband threatened to swallow her heart whole—only this time, the agony was tinged by something new: rage. Not horror or even humiliation—June was filled with rage over Harry's actions, for doing this to their family. For abandoning the mother of his child and scarring their daughter in the process.

It made her want to rip him to pieces.

But the rage was short lived, like a flame crumpling through a single strip of newspaper, with nothing left to catch. The ash fell away, and June felt alone. She had known Barbara would bristle at the word *divorce*, but she hadn't anticipated needing to convince her friend to feel for her. She'd hoped her friend would be understanding, or at least console her. June and Barbara had been close since senior year of high school—over fifteen years—but all she saw on Barbara's face now was blame.

"It's better this way," June said, her voice coarse. She finished her martini and stared straight into Barbara's vacant, judgmental eyes. "I've done everything I can to make my marriage work, made every effort and sacrifice. The truth is that Harry doesn't care about us. He'll never step up."

For the first time since they sat down, Barbara's expression softened, opening like a plum blossom: the tautness of her forehead released, and her frown morphed into an empathetic pout. "What are you saying?"

Harry's cruelty was his absence. June didn't know how to explain the feeling to Barbara. Barbara preferred it when her husband wasn't home. But June—June had loved Harry. She still did. The ultimate betrayal wasn't sleeping with the other woman—it was falling for her.

"I'm saying Bella and I are better off on our own."

If Harry wanted a divorce, he'd get a divorce. June was determined to protect Bella from his inevitable disappointments. It was important that people understood that he was at fault for everything. That June and Bella were the victims.

Barbara touched her arm, but June wasn't comforted. "Albert will know a lawyer."

"I would appreciate his recommendation," June said, sincere.

Barbara often said Albert was a bore, but June had always liked him.

"And that reminds me," June added, "please keep this between us? Albert can know, but no one else."

Barbara nodded emphatically, her diamond earrings flashing through her wispy hair.

Everyone knew Barbara couldn't keep a secret. The more serious it was, the faster she'd tell it. It's why June had called Barbara in the first place. She wanted the whole beachside village talking about how Harry was a villain, how he'd chosen a mistress over his own family. How the grounds for divorce were June's and not Harry's.

June raised a hand at a passing waiter and said to Barbara, "How about some lunch?"

Barbara sighed audibly, thankful for the end of that subject. She couldn't stand to see June ruined like this—not to mention the blow to her own reputation by association. Barbara was of a mind that marriage vows were for life; otherwise, the sanctity of tradition was meaningless.

Barbara made a silent note to talk to Albert—not just about a lawyer but to see if he could speak with Harry about the whole ordeal. This couldn't've been June's idea. Harry had always been an impulsive man, but maybe Albert could talk him down from this particular ledge. God knew Albert had talked Harry out of plenty of other stupid things, from boyish impulses to bad investments.

Both ladies scanned the menu, though they already knew it by heart. In the end, Barbara went with a warm salad, and June ordered the scallops. They both sat there as the waiter collected their menus, feeling the sun on their heads and the breeze on their faces, letting the mild ambiance of white tablecloths and beach views distract from the tension between them.

"Have you heard the latest on Winifred?" Barbara finally asked.

37

June was relieved by the change in subject; her problems would always pale in comparison to Winifred's.

"She's living with a *woman*," Barbara said, sounding both scandalized and elated by the quality of her gossip.

June choked on a sip of her new martini. "You're kidding."

"I'm not." Barbara grew expressive, enlivened. "Mark and Bobbie saw them unloading a junker of a car and carrying boxes into Winnifred's cottage."

"Who is she?"

"A bohemian." Barbara's voice grew breathy and quiet. "Mark said he could practically *smell* the woman from their driveway."

June rolled her eyes, but inside, her mind was churning like saltwater taffy. Ribbons of disdain and curiosity melded together. Winifred had never fit June's mold for what a woman should be—in fact, most of the time, she was the opposite. Too loud, too tacky, too brazen. Still, June never would've expected *this*.

June wanted to scoff and rant about how Winifred was ruining the neighborhood—because she *would*, if she kept inviting riffraff into her home—but another, more surprising part of June wondered what was behind Winifred's decision. There was a possibility that the question came from a place of empathy, though June never would've admitted that to Barbara. June knew what it was like to live alone; she'd done so for the past week, trapped in a cage with the hungry lion of her own thoughts, afraid it would consume her. Winifred had been living in her big, empty cottage for nearly a year—including the blustery, lonesome offseason. June could hardly imagine.

She wondered if Winifred's post-Bruce existence was a glimpse into her own future. The idea horrified her, but she also couldn't stop thinking about it, like candy stuck in her molars.

"And that's not all," Barbara was saying. "They were unloading paintings."

"Paintings?"

"The woman is an *artist*." Barbara hissed the word as if it were a slur—which was a little much, if June was being honest. There were plenty of respectable artists.

"What kind of art?" June asked.

"Does it matter? Bobbie said it looked as if the woman had been living in her car!" Barbara took a bite of her recently delivered salad, speaking after she'd finished chewing. "First the parties, now the artist. Deanna's worried that Winifred is going to start a commune."

June frowned. "I almost feel sorry for her."

"*Why?*"

"Clearly, she's lost her sense," June said, and she regretted her words immediately.

She felt as if she was in a similar state of uncertainty. Her world was splitting apart, like a tree root was boring through the smooth sidewalk that had once been June's life. Now everything felt uneven, unstable. She wanted to reach out and grasp Barbara's arm for support, but June knew that Barbara wasn't that kind of friend.

June took a bite of her lunch, trying to think of who in her social circle *was* that kind of friend. Victoria, probably. Rosie, though June hated to admit it. Either one of them would sit with anyone in a rainstorm—but neither was the sort to think ahead and carry an umbrella.

Barbara continued to spout her venomous rumors while June ate, nodding and replying on occasion but not really listening. June had been floating through her empty vacation house all week, but at this moment, she couldn't imagine feeling any lonelier.

38

Over the course of their first weeks together, Marie and Winifred fell
into a rhythm. They met in the kitchen in the morning to retrieve coffee, then retreated into their own spaces: Marie to her studio; Winifred
to the room with the magenta couch. They ate lunch and dinner on
the patio together: crackers and cheese and salmon dip, or simple sandwiches, or elaborate casseroles, or leftovers. They spoke of nothing in
particular. Often, it seemed, they allowed the awkwardness to swallow
up their words completely, and they ended up listening to the ocean,
the birds, and each other chewing.

Winifred didn't know what she was doing wrong, why Marie had
become so closed off.

Marie had the vague sense that she was disappointing Winifred.

Their first night together, Marie had said too much. The words
had tumbled out of her like river stones, sediment clouding the water.
Marie had escaped upstairs, feeling gritty with the mud of her past.
She dreaded the day the particles would settle, and Winifred would
see through her, straight to the bottom. Marie wasn't ready to reveal
herself like that, but she had been spellbound. Winifred's compassion
and curiosity, paired with the rawness of the day, had opened Marie up
in a way she normally resisted.

So she overcompensated by holing herself up in her new studio.

She didn't make any progress on paintings. She spent two days
daubing halfhearted strokes on one; another day, she stared at a portrait

for two hours before crossing it out with a thin white layer so she could start over. But she *did* make progress practicing illustrating. Her hand wasn't as sure as it had once been, and she figured she ought to resharpen her skills if Mr. Duxbury responded to her request.

In that time, Marie had also called her brother to let him know about her new lodging. He didn't understand. He might've scolded Marie for the suddenness of the decision, but one of his children had the chicken pox, and James had been overtired from two consecutive sleepless nights. *Who is she?* he'd kept asking. A crying child had cut the call short—but not before Marie got the latest update on Hurley Downs. It still wasn't officially up for sale, but the rumblings of such a move were growing louder. *Don't worry,* James had said. *No one would buy a money pit like that except you.* Marie was comforted. Soon enough, she would bury her grief and guilt and put the past to rest—for good.

One day in early July, Marie awoke later than usual. Ever since her first night at Winifred's, she'd been dreaming about horses, and last night, the threat of dreams had made her afraid to succumb to rest. Judging by the brightness of the sky outside her window, it was already midmorning. Marie rolled out of bed and yanked on a pair of dirty jeans. Winifred would've already retired to some other part of the house with her coffee, and therefore Marie didn't bother to smooth her hair or put on a bra.

She shuffled down the stairs, stretching and yawning. When she rounded the corner into the kitchen, the sun was streaming through the windows, and she squinted against the onslaught of light. Ducking her head, she blinked away the purple spots that filled her vision. She went straight for the coffeepot and poured herself a mug of tepid left-over coffee.

"Late night?" Winifred asked.

Marie touched her chest, startled.

Winifred was perched on a stool at the kitchen island, backlit by the brightness.

Marie swore under her breath. "How did I not see you?"

Winifred shrugged. She was fresh-faced and cheerful, her hair loose and flowing. "I thought we might do something together today."

"Oh?" Marie sucked down a big gulp of coffee, a little desperate for the caffeine. Her head still felt cloudy from her restless night.

"You need clothes," Winifred said. "And I'm a great shopper. I thought we could go out and buy you some new pieces."

The word *pieces* sounded ridiculously fancy to Marie. "I can't afford new clothes," Marie said, "and besides, they'll just get paint on them."

"My treat," Winifred said.

Marie was shaking her head, protesting, but she already knew Winifred wouldn't budge.

"Come on, it'll be fun," she said. "We've hardly spent any time together. Let's get to know each other."

Marie stared into her mug, searching for an excuse, but her mind was as black as her coffee. "I'll need to shower first," she said finally.

Winifred clapped her hands, grinning, and Marie couldn't help but feel a little lift from the other woman's excitement. Winifred was so genuine it hurt. Marie downed her coffee and hurried upstairs.

39

A half hour later, Marie and Winifred were on their way in the Pagoda. The sun was fierce, beating down on them as they drove along with the top down.

"I'm thinking a few outfits, a bathing suit for the pool, shoes"—Winifred regarded Marie, one too-long glance from the road—"and sunglasses. Anything else?"

"I can't imagine I need—"

"Yes, you do," Winifred insisted, but her words were kind. "How many times have you worn those jeans since you moved in?"

Marie pressed her legs together, running her hands over the tops of her thighs. "I get paint on everything," she said, "so why bother getting anything new?" But she had to admit—even just to herself—that the promise of a new wardrobe excited her. It was an unexpectedly feminine excitement, and it made her feel silly. Uplifted.

Her reluctance had waned in the shower, and when she climbed into Winifred's convertible, she'd been eager. Happy, even, that Winifred had asked her to come along. Two women shopping together was incredibly pedestrian, yet Marie was delighted. In all her adult life, Marie had never gone shopping with another woman. She'd never really had a *girlfriend*, not after—

The air whooshed out of Marie's lungs like a collapsing balloon.

Befriending Winifred felt dangerous in a way only grief could distort, as if just by being Marie's friend, Winifred would suffer. There was no logic to it, only instinct: that quaking urge to cower when thunderclouds appeared on the horizon.

But the summer sky was clear. The air whizzed warm across Marie's cheeks. A sweet song Marie didn't recognize sprang out of the convertible's radio. When Winifred caught Marie looking at her, she smiled so big her sunglasses shifted on her nose.

Marie's shoulders relaxed from her ears; Winifred's attention returned to her hands at ten and two on the steering wheel and the pale ribbons of the road lines.

Winifred was thinking about high school again: all those shopping sprees she'd never gone on with the girls in her grade. That morning, she'd wanted to finally realize that teenage dream—and while she knew Marie was shy, she also knew the look of someone who was quietly excited, and she'd seen that look on Marie's face as soon as she'd returned from the shower, bright eyes and a coy smile. It was then that Winifred knew for certain that Marie was glad to have been asked.

Their first night, Winifred had pushed Marie too hard. The next morning, after Marie had retreated into her studio, it had been obvious Marie regretted telling Winifred so much about her family. Winifred had done her best to let Marie recuperate; she told herself she'd wait until *Marie* suggested some bonding time. Winifred had spent time on her art foundation, calling around to her favorite galleries to inquire about new talent. Time passed, but Marie still hadn't opened up. Winifred didn't know if Marie's introversion was a part of her creative process or what, but this morning, she'd grown too impatient to wait any longer.

Winifred could've taken Marie to one of the small boutiques closer to home, but instead, she opted to drive all the way to Shepard's in Providence. It was a long drive, but she loved to speed in the Pagoda, and she wanted to give Marie a department store experience, the unique rush of endless rows of trendy styles.

By the time they arrived and Winifred spotted the clock out front, she was downright giddy. She led Marie through the arched entrance.

The place was abustle with young women, voices echoing off the shiny floors. Winifred walked past the makeup counters, aiming Marie for the women's clothing department. She loved the smell of department stores, the mix of perfumes and fibers and floor wax.

When they arrived at the racks and tables, Winifred said, "First thing's first: What's your style?"

Marie's eyes were wide as a rabbit's.

"Marie?"

She blinked. "Sorry, what?"

"You all right?"

"I'm . . . not a fan of crowds."

Winifred made a show of looking around the room. Women clustered around various displays. "They're just friends we haven't made yet," Winifred said.

Marie regarded her for a moment, eyebrows pinched, head tilted— then her face opened, brows softening, neck straightening. "That's a nice thought."

"It's the truth." Winifred put her hands on Marie's shoulders and pointed her toward the clothes. "Now: What's your style?"

"I'm not sure."

"Well, what do you feel most confident in?" Winifred gestured to herself. "For example, I love dresses. They make me feel feminine and confident—and I hate those pink marks that the waistbands of pants leave on my stomach."

"I don't mind the pink marks." Marie paused to think. "I like feeling covered but not encumbered. And I don't want to feel bad about getting paint on things."

"Great. That's a start."

For the next hour, Winifred loaded her arms with clothing for Marie: patterned pants made of soft denim, simple T-shirts, and two blouses that Winifred pushed Marie to try "for special occasions" when she wasn't painting. Winifred made the horrifying discovery that Marie only had one bra, so she took Marie to get fitted and ended up buying a new one for herself too. Underwear was discreetly added to the list, and to Winifred's surprise, Marie selected an elegant maillot bathing suit in a stunning shade of blue. They found slingback sandals to replace Marie's tattered shoes, and Winifred bought a matching pair. Marie found a pair of round yellow-tinted sunglasses, and Winifred replaced her oversize pair with wire-framed aviators.

Winifred had never had so much fun shopping. As a girl, she'd always gone with her father, who was helpful and engaged but also clueless. Before she married, she'd mostly gone alone, with no one to ask *What do you think of this? Do you find this flattering? Does this color work for my skin tone?* When she met Bruce, shopping became an anxious affair, as she tried to find pieces that might impress his parents or his wealthy friends. His mother always criticized the quality of her fabrics; his friends' wives dressed with a modest elegance that Winifred could never quite match. She was always too colorful, or cheap, or revealing.

Marie was encouraging and—unsurprisingly—had an excellent eye for color.

They were all done and walking toward the exit when a mannequin caught Winifred's attention. The thin, stiff body sported the most beautiful flowing dress Winifred had ever seen.

"Wow, look at *this*." Winifred reached out to touch the deep-blush fabric, tracing its geometric pattern, which had been painted in shimmering reds and golds.

Marie came up beside her. "That color would look great on you."

"You don't think it's too . . ." But Winifred couldn't find the word. This was the sort of dress that June Duxbury would despise: casually shapeless but, with the thin texture, sensuously flattering. Winifred instantly loved it. "Sometimes I wonder if reds make me look pale."

Marie seemed to consider this seriously, her eyes darting from Winifred's face to the dress and back. Then she shook her head. "No, the mauve compliments your tan. And the reds are deep enough that they won't wash out the color of your hair—in fact, I think the gold accents would make it look brighter."

Winifred studied her.

"Painter's eye," Marie said with a shrug. She walked over to the rack where a whole row of the dresses hung. She found Winifred's size and handed her the hanger. "You should get it."

"In my neighborhood, I'll stand out like a sore thumb."

"But it clearly makes you happy."

Winifred held the hanger up to her collarbone, smoothing the fabric across the front of her body. The fabric was soft as a petal. She felt her cheeks tighten. "That's true."

"I think you should get it," Marie said. "You aren't trying to fit in with them anymore, anyway."

Winifred lowered the hanger. "You're right; I'm not. In fact, I think I've been holding back in here."

"Oh?"

"Yes. I saw some cropped tops over that way that looked fun. Mind if I shop a little longer?"

"Not at all."

By the late afternoon, their arms were tired from carrying it all. Winifred had found a whole new wardrobe—clothing that was youthful and trendy and all *her*. Bright colors, loud fabrics that neither her father nor Bruce's associates would approve of. Cuts that bared her childless stomach; textures that were ruffled and pleated and flowing.

All the while, Marie offered her tips on colors and shapes, and Winifred delighted in how seriously Marie took the task. Clearly, she had a talent for art that transcended paint. Winifred wondered if Marie might help with the foundation—her eye would be useful—but Winifred didn't want to push.

In the makeup department, Winifred's gaze was fish-hooked by a palette of pretty eye shadow. She doubled back for a closer look. The counter girl was assisting another customer, so Winifred turned to Marie.

"In your professional artist's opinion, do you like this blue?"

"Definitely."

"What would you call it? If this shade were a paint?"

Marie leaned closer. "Topaz."

"I just love bold eye shadows, don't you?"

"You know I don't wear makeup."

The casualness of the statement—*you know*—made Winifred smile. Because she *did* know. "Let's get you some!"

"Oh, no thank you," Marie said. "I don't need it."

"I'm not saying you *need* it. You already have such pretty features," Winifred said, knowing that Marie's comment was not made in self-confidence but practicality—and hoping her subtle compliment might give Marie a boost. "All I'm saying is that it's fun. We could do makeovers when we get home."

Marie dubiously eyed the makeup display. "I don't like the gucky feeling on my skin."

"You can wipe it off as soon as we're done."

Marie scrunched her nose.

"Well, at least let me buy you some brushes. You can use them for painting."

Marie laughed, plucked a tester brush from the counter, and waved it in the air. "This is *not* a paintbrush."

"What's the difference?"

A counter girl called out, "Please don't take that!"

Marie set the brush back down, flushing a shade of pink that Winifred couldn't name, but Marie would know if she could see it.

Winifred waved at the girl and headed for the door. "Let me buy you some real brushes, then. There has to be an artist-supply store nearby, don't you think?"

"You'd do that?"

"I had my fun," Winifred said, looping her arm through Marie's. "Now it's time for you to have yours."

40

Back at Winifred's house, in the O'Keeffe bathroom, Marie was seated on the edge of the tub, and Winifred was bent over her, tickling her eyelids with eye shadow.

"You'll have to hold still for this next part," Winifred said, coming at Marie with a sharp brush tipped in inky black eyeliner.

Marie closed one eye, lifted her brow, and tried her best to hold still.

"You're shaking," Winifred said.

"No, I'm not."

"Yes, you are. You'll ruin the cat-eye if you move."

Marie's eye twitched, and Winifred jerked back.

"It's involuntary," Marie whined, thinking of her new brushes waiting for her in the next room.

Winifred tried again, and Marie twitched again.

Winifred let out a low, frustrated growl. "I feel like I'm putting makeup on a child."

Marie frowned.

"Not really," Winifred said softly. "But you know what, it always tickles more when someone else does it. Why don't you try?" She held out the brush.

Marie took it and stood.

"Just stretch your lid like this and do one smooth sweep." Winifred mimed the movement, holding her linerless eyelid taut.

Marie leaned toward the mirror, close enough for her breath to fog the glass. Her eyelids shimmered in an alien way—with all this makeup, her face didn't look like her own. It felt worse than she remembered, oil slick and caked on. But Winifred was watching her with a girlish glee, and Marie had to admit, the process was . . . fun. Almost like painting.

She used her left hand to pull the skin at her right temple outward, stretching her eyelid until the faint wrinkles were gone. She used her right hand to paint a thin line of black from the inner corner to the outer edge, flicking the brush at the end in one fluid swipe. Just as Winifred said, she wasn't so twitchy under her own touch. She repeated the process on the other eye, which was a little more awkward with her hand across her vision, but the final result was relatively symmetrical.

When she set down the brush, Winifred was staring at her.

Maybe Marie had messed it up. "Did I do it right?"

"Perfectly," Winifred said. "I mean, wow, Marie. Can you do mine?"

"You can't be serious."

"You have the steadiest hand I've seen," Winifred said. "Must be all the painting."

"Or illustrating," Marie offered.

Winifred sat on the edge of the tub where Marie had been seated. "My turn."

"Are you sure?"

Winifred nodded, her hoop earrings swinging.

Marie picked up the brush again and dipped it in the pot of eyeliner, smoothing the tip into a point. Her heart pattered as she approached Winifred's face with the brush, but her hand was steady from all those days she'd learned to paint through her nerves and emotions. Winifred closed her eyes.

This close, Marie felt the other woman's breath on her face. She could see each individual eyelash, a graceful fan of copper-blonde hairs that were slightly darker at the roots and—as they were not yet coated with mascara—dusted with errant eye shadow shimmer. She could see the deep pores and ocher freckles around Winifred's nose, a single blackhead on the bridge. This was the detail her close-up portraits had been missing: the flaws that conspired into beauty. The realness.

She wondered what Winifred had seen on her own grimy face. The intimacy scared her, like that feeling of almost rear-ending someone in traffic but braking at the last possible moment: the aortic jump start of seeing for a split second what could have been disaster.

Marie couldn't bring herself to touch Winifred's face.

"Want me to hold the lid?" Winifred asked, sensing her hesitation.

"Yeah," Marie breathed.

Winifred reached up and pulled the skin outward, unfurling Marie's canvas.

Marie placed her pinky on Winifred's cheekbone as an anchor and swiped the brush across the left lid. It skittered too far at the end, and Marie pulled back sharply.

"Did you mess up?" Winifred asked. "We can fix it with remover if we have to." She stood and studied the line in the mirror. "Oh. Oh, Marie, *look at it*. So dramatic. I feel like Cleopatra." She plunked herself back down. "Do the other side."

This time, Marie's hand was more sure; she tried not to look too closely at Winifred's skin. "Done," she said and set down the brush.

Winifred studied herself in the mirror, turning this way and that. "From now on, you're in charge of the liner."

Marie laughed.

"Come on, let's put on new outfits and get dinner at the Shore House. This liner deserves to be seen."

41

At the Shore House, Winifred floated in on a cloud—or maybe *she* was the cloud—shimmering sunset pink in her new dress. Marie wore a pair of cherry red trousers and one of the peasant blouses Winifred had talked her into. It always amazed Winifred how a new outfit could change her confidence for the better, and tonight, she felt like a piece of fine art. She hoped Marie felt the same.

Out on the deck, Winifred and Marie sat such that they shared a corner of the square table and could both look out at the view. They wore their new sunglasses, but even the tinted lenses weren't enough to keep the sun's glare out of their eyes. It sat low in the sky, big and orange and dancing in its own heat.

Lyle came by with a pitcher of water. "Well, aren't I lucky?"

Winifred tilted her head up to meet his velvety brown eyes. "Why's that, Lyle?"

"Isn't it obvious?" Lyle asked, gesturing around the deck. "The foxiest ladies here were seated at my table."

"Oh, stop." Winifred had always had a rapport with Lyle. When she used to come here with Bruce, Lyle warned him that he'd steal his wife away someday, and the three of them would laugh and laugh. She was probably ten years Lyle's senior, at least.

He flashed a grin. "Your husband always said I had impeccable taste—and not just on the wine list."

Without Bruce, the flattery felt a little . . . sad. Winifred's composure wobbled briefly, like a bike tire hitting a rock. With the distraction of Marie, she had temporarily forgotten her sorrow.

Lyle noticed her change in demeanor. He sobered, straightening his spine and tie. His brown eyes were genuine when he said, "Anyway, it's nice to see you again—truly. Both of you."

Marie's face creased. "Do I know you?"

Lyle smiled a lazy smile, heavy-lidded and languid. "From the party. You hit it off with my friend Lawrence?"

Marie visibly flushed under her makeup. "You mean I hit him with my dinner?"

Lyle shrugged. "It made an impression." He looked at Winifred. "You sure know how to throw a party, Mrs. Hurst. Planning another soon?"

"Winifred, please." She knew he meant to be polite, but she wasn't Mrs. Hurst anymore, was she? "And maybe I *will* plan another party."

His smile spread like honey on toast. "Care for a drink, *Winifred?*" Every syllable snapped.

Always the flirt. "Tom Collins."

He looked at Marie.

"Water for me."

"Oh, c'mon now," Winifred said. "It's my treat. Have whatever you want."

"It's been your treat all day."

"So?"

"So . . ." Marie couldn't seem to come up with an excuse. "Fine. I'll have a Tom Collins too."

"You don't have to get what I get."

"They're my favorite, actually."

"Oh, yeah?"

"I like the cherries."

Lyle was still smiling. "Extra cherries. Anything else?"

"That's all for now, Lyle." When he was gone, Winifred said to Marie, "It sounds like you have an admirer."

"Lyle was flirting with *you*, not me."

"I mean Lawrence."

"What? No."

"You're blushing."

"*You* put the blush on me."

"I don't mean the *makeup*; I mean underneath."

Marie rolled her eyes.

Winifred nudged Marie with her arm.

For a split second, they both felt like quibbling sisters—and they relished the moment.

Marie looked around before whispering, "I think *you* have an admirer."

"Lyle admires everyone."

"Especially you."

Winifred didn't want to think about anyone other than Bruce admiring her. "Today was fun," she said. "Wasn't it?"

"More than I thought," Marie admitted. "Thank you for the supplies."

In addition to the brushes—which were, admittedly, much different than makeup brushes—Winifred had bought Marie an armful of paints, big fat metal tubes of ivory and cobalt and moss green. She'd had no idea that paint was so expensive, but the look on Marie's face—Winifred had never seen someone glow like that before. "Paint something amazing with them, all right?"

Marie stared at the napkin in her lap. "I'll try."

A small vase of daisies rested on their table, and the white petals and yellow heads bobbed in the breeze. Winifred watched them with casual fascination.

She decided to open up a little. "You know," she said, "I'm a bit of an art buff. I don't flaunt it, and I'm in no way an expert, but if you ever want a second set of eyes on—"

"That's kind of you. Maybe."

Clearly, Marie didn't like the idea, but the topic was dispelled as Lyle arrived with their drinks. Marie laughed when she saw five cherries bobbing among the ice in her glass. Lyle took their appetizer and dinner orders and left—but not without a cheeky wink.

The conversation meandered after that. Winifred spent a lot of their dinner telling Marie about her father: what it was like to grow up with a single dad after her mother left, how she missed having a woman in her life but was also grateful to her father for teaching her how to be independent. He was the reason Winifred had pursued a college degree; he had also introduced her to Bruce.

In turn, Marie spoke a bit more about her art. Winifred learned that Marie had a letter out to her old boss at the advertising firm, in hopes of getting back into illustrating. Marie talked about the painting process, how images were built in layers: first she prepped the canvas, then she worked on an underpainting of shapes and shadows, then she gradually defined the image from there. Marie told her that sometimes the best underpaintings were really just failed first attempts. Winifred liked the idea of painting over the things that didn't work. Marie didn't divulge to Winifred whether or not she'd found any success at the endeavor over the years.

After sharing a complimentary slice of red velvet cake from Lyle, Winifred paid the bill, and the two women exited the restaurant. Winifred was buzzing from multiple drinks but something else, too: the breathlessness of time passing. It seemed that one moment, she'd been drinking coffee in her robe this morning, and the next, she was here wearing this stunning outfit, getting to know her new friend. Winifred hadn't forgotten time in so long; she'd counted every hour since Bruce died. How strange it was that time moved so slowly when she was alone and so quickly when she was in the company of someone who made her smile.

Outside the restaurant, Marie and Winifred were walking down the steps when none other than June Duxbury, Barbara Aldridge, and

Bobbie Coldwell came into view by the valet station. They were deep in a giggling, chattering conversation—but when they spotted Winifred and Marie, they halted in speech and step.

"Hi, ladies," Winifred said, looping her arm through Marie's as if that might protect her from their ugly opinions.

"Winifred," June said stiffly.

"You missed the meeting," Bobbie said, and Barbara actually sniggered.

"What meeting?"

"Today's committee meeting?" June enunciated.

"I wasn't informed of a meeting," Winifred said, knowing full well that they had willfully excluded her again. "In fact, I wasn't informed of the last meeting either. Are you sure you have my phone number correct? Which one of you tried to notify me?"

None of them answered.

"That's what I thought," Winifred said.

"Who's your friend?" Barbara asked.

"Her name's Marie," Winifred said, tightening her arm on Marie's.

"Does she not speak for herself?"

"Not unless prompted," Marie said.

"You're the artist, aren't you?" Bobbie asked. "Welcome to the neighborhood." Her tone was anything but welcoming.

"What do you paint?" Barbara asked. "Anything we'd recognize?"

"Nudes, mostly," Marie said without missing a beat. "Say, any of you want to model?"

June scoffed; the other two frowned. Winifred glanced down at Marie in pride, trying to mask her surprise and delight. For how shy she was, Marie had a quick wit. She must've sensed that these were the women Winifred had tried so hard to please.

"If you'll excuse us," Winifred said, stepping sideways to walk around them.

But June blocked her path. "Make your choices carefully, Winifred, or there will be consequences."

"Such is life," Winifred said, pushing past her. Over her shoulder, she added, "Oh, and I forgot to mention: from now on, consider me resigned from the SPW."

To Barbara's credit, she actually gasped. But June didn't put on airs. She swiveled around and said, "Isn't that outfit a little *young* for you? The hippie look is unbecoming on women our age."

Winifred's face blazed hot, but she didn't turn around. She hated, hated, *hated* how June could so easily make her feel flimsy and cheap. She refused to give June the satisfaction of a retort—because that would only demonstrate that June's words had gotten under her skin. Winifred marched toward the street, Marie trotting behind her.

"We always knew you were low class," June called. "We always knew Bruce only married you because you were easy, and he was desperate."

Winifred halted, a tide rising in her chest, ready to flow through her and knock June down—but Marie was at her side, then, tugging her arm, urging her to ignore the words.

"Be careful with those loud parties," June continued, "or you and your little lesbian friend will face consequences."

Marie continued to hold Winifred's arm, and finally, the valet delivered Winifred's Pagoda, and the other women disappeared into the Shore House.

Wordlessly, Winifred tipped the valet, dropped into the driver's seat, and slammed her door.

"Wow," Marie said. "They were nasty."

Winifred gripped the steering wheel and forced a deep breath. She itched with heat. "Usually they're more . . . subtle in their vitriol."

Gently, Marie said, "It was wrong of her to bring up Bruce like that. I'm sure he—"

"Bruce couldn't have children," Winifred said. "It's an old refrain: they think I was a gold digger and that he settled for me because I was the only woman who'd knowingly marry a man who . . ." She sniffled and wiped furiously at her face.

"Shit."

Winifred's eyeliner—the wings Marie had drawn on—was smudged and ruined. "I'm sorry they were cruel to you," Winifred said.

Marie watched as Winifred ran her fingers under her eyelashes and smoothed her hair. Marie didn't like to see her like this; Winifred didn't like to be seen like this.

"You don't look cheap, and you don't look old," Marie said. "You look like a goddess."

"You think so?"

"Of course," Marie said. "You always do."

Winifred met Marie's eyes. "Nudes, huh? Where are you hiding those?"

Marie laughed.

"You really held your own with them," Winifred said. "How did you do that?"

Marie shrugged. "I don't care about them."

"You're saying I do?"

"Of course you do. I'm sure it mattered back when—"

"You're right," Winifred said curtly. "I cared about them because of Bruce. But you know what? I don't have to." She adjusted the gear shift, and the Pagoda purred like a leopard. "From now on, I don't care about them anymore. If they think I look like a hippie, well, maybe they'll be right."

"If that's what you want."

"I don't know what I want," Winifred said. "Except that I want to be free and have fun. And I'm going to start by throwing another party. A moving-in party." Winifred pulled onto the main road. "A giant party to celebrate you, Marie. We'll even invite Lawrence."

"Oh, I don't need . . ."

"You definitely *need*. You need to be celebrated. You've freed me."

"Won't another party anger them?"

"That's the cherry on top." Winifred peered at her from over the rims of her sunglasses. "After all, you like cherries."

42

"You eviscerated her, June," Bobbie said, tossing back the martini that had just been delivered. "What got into you?"

"I don't know," June said. "I suppose I'm simply tired of hiding my frustration at her blatant disregard for the well-being of this community."

It wasn't a lie, but it wasn't the complete truth. June had spoken with a lawyer today. She hadn't said anything to her committee friends, but the call had ignited a flame in her. Her anger—at herself, at Harry, at the world—was a brush fire, catching on any stray piece of kindling: the maid who broke a dish, the secretary at the law office for incorrectly saying June's maiden name, and then Winifred. June would've burned Winifred down, had it meant one moment of relief from the scorch of her own bitterness.

The only good that had come out of the day was Bella. June's new lawyer had insisted that Harry could not keep Bella from her as he had; a call was placed with Harry's lawyer, and in turn, it was arranged that Harry bring Bella back to Wave Watch. If Harry wanted to continue living in Boston, then he'd have to travel back and forth. Until the divorce was settled, June and Harry would share Bella's time. When it was all over, June would have Bella full time; custody always went to the mother. Always.

In the meantime, June could look forward to seeing her daughter the week after next. The day might as well have been a million years from now, but still, a tangible date was a balm to the stinging burn of Bella's absence. A mother wasn't meant to be without her child for so long.

"It's a midlife crisis," Barbara was saying.

Bobbie scoffed. "Women can't have midlife crises."

June blinked, watching the conversation bounce between the two women like a tennis ball.

"Yes, they can."

"And what, pray tell, would that look like?"

"Same as a man: unnecessary purchases, erratic behavior—"

"*Barbara!*"

"I said *erratic*, not *erotic*. Although I'm sure that's part of it too."

Bobbie laughed. "June, talk some sense into Barbara."

"I'm afraid that ship has sailed," June said congenially, but Barbara shot her a warning look that Bobbie didn't clock.

Ever since their conversation about June's divorce, Barbara had been more brusque. June had hoped a dinner out with Bobbie would assuage Barbara's tension, but clearly, June would have to tread carefully tonight. Play her cards right. The social game was never over.

"Winifred is not *middle aged*," Bobbie argued. "She's younger than we are."

"*My point*," Barbara enunciated impatiently, "is that her behavior resembles a midlife crisis."

"A midlife crisis is just an excuse to act impulsively," June said.

"Amen," Bobbie agreed.

Barbara's mouth was screwed up into a little pucker. "It's a crisis of *identity*."

"So, what, you want to excuse Winifred's behavior because she's going through a not-so-midlife crisis?" Bobbie asked.

"*No*," Barbara said. "I'm just saying . . . I'm saying . . . you know, I forgot my point."

All three women laughed, leaning back as a waiter came by to refill their water glasses.

"Oh!" Barbara exclaimed. "I remember my—*AAH*!" Barbara jumped up as ice water spilled across the table and directly into her lap. Ice cubes clattered on the deck.

"My apologies," the waiter said, using a napkin to daub at the tablecloth.

"What is *wrong* with you?" Barbara said, wringing water out of her skirt.

"An accident," the waiter said, but he didn't seem remorseful. In fact, his lips were tightened into the tiniest smile.

"What is your name?" Barbara demanded.

"Lyle, ma'am."

"I'd like you to apologize, Lyle."

"I did, ma'am."

Barbara's cheeks nearly matched the color of her crimson lipstick. "I think you owe us a round of drinks, *on your dime*, for your clumsiness. Otherwise I'll have a word with your manager."

"Oh, calm down, Barbara. Clearly, it was an accident," Bobbie said, using her napkin to dab the remaining liquid from the table. "But a free dessert wouldn't hurt."

When the water was mopped up, and he was gone, Barbara settled into her seat again. "I can't believe you took his side."

Bobbie waved a delicate hand. "Accidents happen."

"Waiters are *not* supposed to be clumsy."

They went back and forth like this for a few minutes, then finally changed the subject to their children and husbands. June remained quiet; she didn't have much to say on either topic. But eventually, as always, the conversation swiveled back to Winifred.

"I can't believe she quit," Bobbie said as their dinners were delivered.

"I can," Barbara said. "She never cared about the SPW. Deanna once overheard her call it *pointless*. Pointless! Can you believe that?"

"I wish she'd quit sooner," June said.

The other two nodded.

"Except now she has more time for disruption," Barbara said.

"We should've seen it coming," Bobbie said. "Bruce always encouraged her weird tastes. Mark said Bruce married her to spite his parents."

"Bruce told Mark that?" Barbara asked.

"Oh, who knows." Bobbie shrugged. "But Bruce seemed to revel in her . . . quirks . . . didn't he?"

"Quirks." Barbara scoffed at the understatement.

June shook her head. "You really think Bruce is to blame?" June's and Bruce's families had known each other for generations—she didn't like the thought of Bruce knowingly sabotaging the community by marrying someone that no one had approved of. Despite what she'd suggested to Winifred about Bruce's rumored infertility, June preferred to think that Winifred had tempted him, and he'd been blinded by love.

"I feel sorry for him, mostly," Bobbie said. "Who else could he attract? She married him knowing full well she'd never have a child. What kind of woman would do that? Women are meant to have children—and not just one."

June cringed. All her friends had given birth to multiple beautiful children—all in their twenties. At nearly thirty-five, June had barely survived Bella.

Bobbie's eyes widened, seeming to realize her slight. "Oh, except you, June. We know you've tried and tried—that's different."

Is it? June wanted to ask. Suddenly, her earlier slight seemed cruel. It was neither Bruce's nor Winifred's fault that they hadn't had children. In fact, rumors told that Bruce's impediment was a war injury—which, by all standards, made him a hero.

"Kids aside," Bobbie continued, "I've always suspected Winifred was a hippie. Her embarrassing sense of style, her grimy parties, her peace-love attitude. I always thought she'd divorce Bruce—she seems like the kind of woman who'd get a divorce, right?"

June met Barbara's eyes. Did Bobbie not know June was getting divorced? The comment seemed too on the nose for Bobbie to have intended it. As Bobbie blathered on, Barbara held June's stare, her eyebrows tipped upward in an expression that might've been sympathetic if June looked hard enough. Or maybe pitying.

Had Barbara kept her secret? June had expected—*planned*—for Barbara to tell the whole committee behind her back; she'd spent today's meeting in an edgy state, hoping that her calculated move had worked. Hoping that sympathy was in their hearts, rather than disdain.

But June had encountered little evidence that Barbara had told them. Could it be that June's situation was so embarrassing that even the biggest gossip of them all wouldn't dare spread the word? Judging by Bobbie's monologue about only children and divorce, June ought to be ashamed of herself. What if they never came to understand or sympathize with her situation?

She looked away from Barbara's face and stared at the beach. A family was walking in the surf, a husband, wife, and two girls. The smaller of the two was perched on the father's shoulders. The elder girl bent down to pluck something from the sand, then presented the small treasure to her mother. June wondered if her heart would ever stop breaking.

She also couldn't help but contemplate what Winifred would think. She'd probably congratulate June on exiting an unhappy marriage. She'd probably commend the failure.

As she considered Winifred's perspective, June experienced an odd expansion in her chest. It resembled relief—and that scared her. The thought of Winifred approving of June made her want to shrink into the surf, bury herself in the wet-cement sand. June both hated and was fascinated by Winifred's ability to slip outside the norm, to live beyond the expectations of the world. How freeing it must be; how lonely; how embarrassing.

June finished her drink. If she felt any envy or sympathy for Winifred Hurst—even the slightest bit—she was clearly in a bad way.

43

Bruce had told Winifred about his infertility quite early in their courtship.

They'd gone for a walk in Central Park, taking in the fall colors and crisp breeze of a sunny October afternoon. They'd sat on a bench, and he'd explained his injury—a silly accident during basic training that resulted in what the doctors had referred to as *probable infertility*. When the war ended, he'd come home to women desperate for children; the last woman he'd gone steady with had left him when she found out, and he didn't want to put Winifred in the same position.

"It's not impossible, just unlikely," he'd said, adding that he had long since come to peace with his reality. "But I don't want to dash your dreams or waste your time."

Unlike most women, Winifred hadn't spent her adolescence dreaming of babies—she'd spent it wondering why her mom left—so this news was inconsequential to her. Besides, she was already far too smitten with Bruce to turn back.

After a moment of consideration, a mischievous smile had tugged at her red-hued lips. "Does . . . *it* still work?" she enunciated.

Bruce's eyes widened a little—in surprise, in amusement—and he grasped her hand in his. "Yes," he'd said slowly, grinning. "Yes, it works."

His previous girlfriend had been the one to tell the others, the gossip spreading quickly. Bruce knew people felt sorry for him; he also knew that a "war injury" made him sound noble—heroic, even—and while it hurt his pride to think that anyone might pity him, he was not so insecure as to let it occupy his thoughts.

His stoicism and quiet confidence had only made Winifred love him more.

Just the thought of Bruce now made her eyes hot, her throat tight. Winifred scrubbed a hand over her face and sank a little deeper into the bath, covering her mouth to keep the high notes of her sobs from permeating beyond the bathroom door.

But it wasn't the memory itself that made her upset, nor was it June's cruel words from earlier. It was the realization that Winifred had been *happy* today. The distraction of Marie's presence had worked: Winifred had briefly forgotten her grief—but somehow it now felt like a betrayal of Bruce. She had been so desperate for relief from her loneliness that she'd lost sight of the fact that her sadness was her last true connection to him. Strange as it was, she feared the day she forgot to think of him at all—because that would be the day he was well and truly gone.

~

The following morning, Winifred's sadness still lingered, complicated and heavy in her sternum.

Marie had heard her weeping last night, soft little sounds that echoed faintly off the tile; when Winifred shuffled into the kitchen for breakfast, the shadows under her eyes confirmed for Marie that Winifred had not yet shaken off the sting of June's words.

A day ago, Marie would've left it alone—allowed Winifred space. But after seeing firsthand how nasty those women could be to her, Marie thought that maybe space was the opposite of what Winifred needed.

Without giving herself a chance to talk herself out of it, Marie announced to Winifred, "I'd like an ice cream."

Winifred swiveled away from the coffeepot, her dressing gown billowing as she squared her shoulders at Marie. Her red hair was a nest of frizz. "Right now?"

"Yes, now."

Winifred tipped her head, and Marie could see the hopeful reluctance in her squinting eyes and rippled forehead. "It's ten in the morning."

"We'll put on fresh outfits." Marie hoped she sounded convincing when she added, "It'll be fun."

"Do you feel sorry for me, Marie?"

Marie balled her fists at her sides. "What if I do?"

Winifred seemed vaguely entertained by that answer. "Is that a yes?"

"June and her set were horrible to you," Marie said. "You deserve an ice cream."

Winifred's eyes crinkled with a smile, and to Marie, it felt like a win. "Well, I'm not sure I can argue with that," Winifred said. "I'll get dressed and be back down in twenty minutes. Why don't we invite Irene along too?"

"The more the merrier."

When Winifred had disappeared back through the doorway, Marie took a quick sip of her coffee. A mix of regret and joy buzzed behind her ribs. When had her determination to remain unattached deteriorated? Doing something nice for Winifred would only further entrench Marie in this arrangement, but after witnessing the extent of Winifred's isolation—not to mention the lengths Winifred had already gone to to welcome Marie—ice cream seemed like the least she could do to cheer the other woman up.

~

Irene was surprised to receive Winifred's call—but also grateful. She had been about to head off on a series of errands, and driving down to the harbor sounded far preferable. She arrived early and lowered herself onto a bench; her joints had started to ache in the mornings, but the sunshine softened them like cold butter left on the counter to thaw.

She spotted them before they spotted her. Winifred, with her long bronzed legs on display, and Marie wearing a plain T-shirt. They couldn't appear more different, and yet the amiability between them was apparent in Winifred's exuberant gestures and Marie's coy little chuckles. Their companionship reminded Irene of her own friend, Kat, who was her polar opposite and yet had been her dearest confidant for going on forty years.

Irene stood, her right knee groaning, and waved at the other women.

"Irene!" Winifred exclaimed, giving her an airy embrace. "So glad you could come."

"Ice cream for breakfast? How could I not?" Irene said, adding, "Marie, nice to see you again."

"Likewise."

Marie didn't know Irene that well, but she remembered the older woman as kind, calm, and self-assured—qualities that made Marie feel safe. It was becoming clear that, in her own way, Irene had been looking after Winifred, and Marie found the responsibility endearing. Not to mention that she was also an amazing cook.

Marie allowed Winifred to lead the way, her arm looping through Irene's as they walked across the street to the ice cream shop. Winifred insisted on paying, which seemed counter to the spirit of the whole trip—but in fairness, she did possess the most money by far, and it seemed to make her happy to treat them.

Once they had their ice creams in hand, they arranged themselves back on Irene's bench with Winifred in the middle.

"Dare I ask what prompted this outing?" Irene asked.

Winifred licked a spot of strawberry cream off her bottom lip. "Marie felt sorry for me."

Marie straightened. "That's not the whole . . ."

Winifred was giggling. She quickly explained to Irene the ugliness of last night's interaction. "The good news is that I quit the SPW," she ended victoriously.

"So this isn't pity ice cream; it's celebratory ice cream," Irene said, offering Marie a subtle wink.

"I like the way you think, Irene," Winifred said.

"Well, I'm glad you thought to invite me," Irene said.

It struck Marie how automatically inclusive Winifred was, an instinct that stood out starkly against the other women in her neighborhood—or, really, most people in general.

"And, oh! I've decided to throw Marie a welcome home party." Winifred went on, launching into a long list of considerations and menu ideas. Irene seemed eager to help, interjecting with possible dishes she could make and offering to lend a hand with the setup.

"We'll have to invite that young man that Marie . . . ran into," Irene said.

Marie winced at the literality of her words.

"What was his name?"

"Lawrence," Winifred said, drawing out the syllables. "He seemed to like you, Marie."

Marie's cheeks flared at the memory of ruining his shirt. "Doubtful."

"Why do you think I mentioned him?" Irene said, raising an eyebrow. "He was charmed."

"He was just being polite."

Winifred nudged her with her elbow. "He was *staring* at you."

Marie lapped at her scoop of chocolate, willing her heart not to beat so fast.

Thankfully, Winifred dropped the topic. While she and Irene continued with their party-planning conversation, Marie passively listened, her tongue numbing from the cold, rich sweetness of her ice cream. How quickly living in her car had morphed into shopping and ice cream and talk of men. How strange it was for these two kind women whom Marie barely knew to be discussing a party for *her*.

It was worrying. It was surreal.

Worst of all, it was also heartening.

Try as she might not to enjoy the company too much, to remain focused on her goal, Marie was acutely aware of how rapidly her resolve was melting, like the scoop in her cone.

44

The day of Marie's party, Irene came to the house to help Winifred cook and set up. Marie had tried to help, but they banished her from the kitchen, because "the guest of honor doesn't help set up." Apparently it was a party rule.

So Marie hid away in her studio, working on the painting she'd started last week. It was a close-up like the others, but this time she was painting Winifred. Heavy blue eyelids and thickly mascaraed lashes looked off toward her left; her pupils shone with a bold, free expression, serious but at ease. When Marie painted the giant flick of Cleopatra liner, the memory was a thread tied to her heart; it ran from her chest down her arm to her brush's tip, tugging as it met canvas.

It had been a long time since Marie had painted a memory that wasn't painful. She stood back to study the painting's full effect and was pleased—*pleased*—with what she saw. The painting had a looseness to it, the brushstrokes varied and imprecise, giving it a dreamy appearance. The colors were as bright and strong as the subject.

"Is that me?"

Marie jumped toward her easel, throwing her arms up to block Winifred's sight line. "It's not finished," she mumbled over her shoulder.

Winifred was standing in the doorway, all done up in a puffy-sleeved top that bared her midriff and a pair of high-waisted lime-green trousers. She'd parted her hair down the middle, and it hung glossy and straight just past her collarbone. It was like she'd walked off the page of a catalog.

She crept a little closer. "I came to ask if you'd do my liner again."

Marie had been doing Winifred's eyeliner since their shopping spree, yet the request still made the breath leap out of her throat. "Sure."

Marie hoped Winifred would turn around, leave the studio, and lead the way to the bathroom—but she didn't.

"Is that me?" she asked again.

As Winifred inched nearer, Marie shifted, ensuring that she still obscured the painting with her body. "I—"

"It is, isn't it?"

The canvas was a five by five. Try as she might, Marie couldn't realistically block it with her small frame. "I lost track of time. I should get dressed for the party. What time is it?"

"*Marie*," Winifred said, enunciating both syllables equally.

Marie dropped her arms. "It's not finished," she repeated, "and it's not *you* per se, just a woman who—"

"—looks a lot like me?"

Marie hung her head.

Winifred touched her shoulder, moved her aside, and stood back to look at it. She might as well have been reading Marie's deepest thoughts as she studied the painting. Marie stared at the floor, afraid to see the look of horror on Winifred's face. The utter discomfort.

But then Winifred whispered, "I love it," and when Marie looked up, she saw that yes, indeed, Winifred loved it. Her words were confirmed by the shimmer of her pupils.

"Really?"

"Marie, it's lovely. Can we hang it in the house? There's a bare wall in the kitchen where this would go perfectly."

Marie's mind felt like a record that needed to be flipped; her thoughts crackled like a needle on a silent edge of vinyl. "Of course," she managed. "You really want—"

"You'll have to sign it, though." Winifred gestured at the canvas. She meant for Marie to sign it *now*. "And then we'll get you ready. Guests should be arriving any minute."

Marie repeated, "It's not finished."

"I beg to differ." From the nearby stool with Marie's palette, Winifred retrieved the water cup and rattled the protruding brush handles. "I like that it's a little undone. Seems more true."

Marie couldn't argue with that. The painting toed the line between freedom and obscurity, and that's what made it compelling—it just took Winifred's reassurance for Marie to see that.

Marie selected a line brush from the cup, scraping the excess water off the bristles with the edge of the cup. She dipped the brush in a smudge of orange paint, something to stand out against the blues in the bottom right corner of the canvas. She couldn't remember the last time she'd signed a painting; to mark her signature was to declare a painting finished, and it was too proud an act for how she'd felt about her art lately. But now, as she filled in her mononym with Winifred watching, Marie *did* feel proud; the feeling was a tiny rosebud, full of promise.

Winifred saw Marie's pride blaze across her face in a flush of bright pink. Her brows were drawn in focus. Winifred wondered what had made Marie so insecure about her art. Sure, many of the ones Winifred had seen on moving day were flawed, but there was potential, an undercurrent of skill and beauty. But this—Marie had unlocked something with this painting. This painting was a river of white water, fast flowing and breathtaking. Winifred didn't love it because it was a painting of *her*; she loved it because the painting was *free*. It had energy and power.

Marie set down her brush and faced Winifred. "I should get changed."

Together, they turned away from the painting. "I picked out a dress for you—from my closet."

"A *dress?*"

"Just try it," Winifred said, holding the door. "It's in my bedroom. You can do my liner in there too."

"All right."

As Marie slinked down the hall, Winifred paused in the doorway to take one last look at the painting. Her gaze found the signature and snagged, the shape like a thorn catching the fabric of her mind.

Because she recognized it.

Marie was disappearing down the hall, but Winifred stalked closer to the easel and peered at the shape: the simple filled-in *D*.

It couldn't be. Was Marie the mysterious artist D? The one Winifred still sponsored through the Iris Gallery to this day? The semifamous artist she'd practically *discovered*? Winifred thought of the painting that hung in Bruce's office: *Wildflower*. Had Marie really painted *that*?

Marie could've faked the signature, of course. It was a simple half circle, after all.

Winifred knelt down in front of Marie's easel and stared at the orange dot, the pattern of brushstrokes that had filled in the shape: first the outline, then concentric circles moving inward, before a scribble and daub in the middle. How many times had Winifred studied *Wildflower* and that exact systematic pattern of lines? So simple, yet also consistent across all the works she'd viewed.

D was not quite famous enough to have imposters, Winifred reasoned, and it seemed unlikely that Marie would fake her artistic identity in a moment like the one that just transpired. Winifred might not know much about her house guest's past, but she knew Marie was more honest than to pretend to be another artist, and hiding behind a mononym did seem like something Marie might do.

Winifred was certain now that Marie and D were one and the same.

Winifred hurried out of the studio and closed the door, trying to school her face into a sunny mood. Through the doorway of her bedroom, Winifred spotted Marie, and her stomach dropped. Marie was running her fingers over the outfit Winifred had left out for her, a polyester minidress.

When Winifred came closer, Marie looked up at her and said, "I don't know about this. It's not really my style."

Winifred couldn't believe it. She'd been living with an incredibly accomplished artist—an artist she *sponsored*. How had Winifred not known as soon as she unloaded that first painting from Marie's Plymouth?

Sure, some of the paintings she'd glimpsed had seemed a little familiar, but something had happened to Marie's work. It'd become stagnant since that debut collection. Too precise, too self-conscious. Nothing compared to the looseness of her earlier works. What had happened to Marie, to ruin her confidence like that? What had caused Marie to lose her magic touch?

Marie seemed to take Winifred's silence as insistence. "Fine, I'll try it." She lifted the hanger from the bed and disappeared behind a folding screen in the corner.

Winifred puffed out the breath she'd been holding. The painting she'd just seen had the magic touch, that was for sure. Winifred wasn't so self-absorbed to assume it was her charity or company that had awakened Marie's talent again, but she wondered. What made some paintings different than the others? Why did the one of her *work*?

Another thought launched in Winifred's mind, fast as a rocket: *her foundation*. There were no terms to the artistic agreement, beyond the idea that the artist use the funds for living expenses so they could focus on their art. Marie hadn't done that, though. She'd been living in her car and *sacrificing* her art for the discomfort, despite large payments being issued every month. Winifred pondered the facts . . . but there was no need. Marie had already told her what she was doing with the income: she was saving it for a racetrack.

A fucking racetrack.

Winifred was probably single-handedly buying Marie that track, and it had nothing to do with art, nothing to do with *anything*. In truth, she couldn't care less about the money—what she couldn't stand was the idea that Marie would waste such profound talent for the sake of an irrational pipe dream.

Winifred's brow tickled, and she wiped a hand across it to find that she was sweating. She wiggled her elbows; her underarms were damp too. This was too much. This was too strange.

Did Marie *know* that Winifred ran the Eckart Art Foundation? No. Not possible. Winifred had barely mentioned her interest in art to Marie, and even so, the foundation's name had no clear connection to Winifred Hurst. She'd used her maiden name on purpose, opting to lie low and—unlike the rest of the folks in Bruce's world, who preferred to flaunt their do-gooding—allow the philanthropy to speak for itself.

Which meant that Winifred knew her connection to Marie, but Marie didn't know her connection to Winifred. That fact made the whole situation more innocent but didn't absolve Marie of Winifred's frustration.

But then Marie reappeared from behind the screen wearing the dress, and the sight of her disarmed Winifred's frantic thoughts. Marie was still Marie. Shy and kind and genuine.

She looked lovely. Her hair was loose and flowing. The dress formed perfectly to her slight figure. And—"Your *legs*," Winifred said aloud, despite herself.

Marie looked down, pointed a toe, and twisted it this way and that to inspect her skin. "What about them? Do I have paint . . . ?"

"You have great legs, Marie," Winifred said, coming closer, trying not to think about art or money or racetracks. Trying to think only about her friend. Her *friend*. "That dress is stunning on you."

"I feel ridiculous."

"Lawrence will love it."

Marie glanced away. "I'm not trying to impress Lawrence. Or anyone."

What was it like to not want to impress anyone? To Winifred, the concept seemed as far away as the moon.

"You'll impress him anyway, though," Winifred insisted.

Marie smiled. "It *is* comfortable." She swung her arms back and forth like a child, clearly convincing herself of the outfit. "You were right about pants. This is freeing."

"See?" Winifred said. "You just needed my guidance."

Winifred decided she wouldn't tell Marie about her revelation. Certainly, this track obsession had derailed Marie's art, but now that she was living here, perhaps it wouldn't occupy her thoughts so much. And with Winifred around to encourage her, *guide* her, Marie was certain to put out another collection. That was the point of Winifred's charity, anyway. For Marie to keep painting. For Marie to find success again.

"We should get downstairs," Winifred said. "I can hear people arriving."

"I still need to do your liner," Marie said.

"Right." Winifred sat on the edge of her bed. "Of course."

Marie took up the liner brush and rested her palm gently on Winifred's cheek. Her warm breath floated over Winifred's skin, tickling the wispy hairs at Winifred's temple and drying the remaining beads of panic sweat.

Winifred closed her eyes, allowing Marie to pull one lid tight. Another realization passed across the horizon of Winifred's mind, one that sent her spiraling once more: *if Marie finds success again, then there's an expiration date on her being here, with me.*

45

Over the next four hours, Marie was stunned by the influx of people. Winifred had asked Lyle to spread the word, and he'd done just that. Irene couldn't refill food platters fast enough, and Winifred's phone was ringing with constant complaints from the neighbors. Marie recognized a few familiar faces from the last party: Fred from the Stop & Shop. Fred's brother, Neil, and his girlfriend, Mary, and Mary's girlfriends. Lyle and his coworkers. Then there were the college students, who were working nearby for the summer, and the hippies who were friends of friends of friends.

Someone knew a band and had invited them to play. It was a sticky-sweet summer evening, and they set up their amps on the patio, running long extension cords into the kitchen. The drum kit rattled on the stone pavers, and the cymbals echoed across the surface of the pool. The beach grass vibrated with the chords of the bass guitar, and though the music was mostly mellow, it was loud. There were people in every corner, it seemed: lounging in the yard, laughing in the parlor, packed into the kitchen.

And Lawrence.

He arrived late, his lean shoulders filling the open doorway that led to the patio. When he spotted Marie, he descended the shallow patio stairs, heading right for her. Fred, who she'd been chatting with, noticed Lawrence's approach and wandered off in search of another drink.

"Did you come to collect a reimbursement for the shirt I stained?" Marie asked.

Lawrence laughed. "Not sure it would be polite for me to shake down the guest of honor. Marie, right?"

"Yes. Yeah. Marie," she said, not entirely sure why she was so flustered.

The band had reached a crescendoing bridge, blasting the yard with sound. Lawrence leaned in close enough for her to smell his cologne, which was deliciously floral. "I should confess: I already knew your name. I was just trying to seem less eager."

"Eager for me to ruin another shirt?"

His mouth pulled to the side in an amused, if slightly suppressed, smile. "Do you want to sit by the pool, Marie?"

They spent a good hour sitting on the edge of the pool. He wanted to hear about how she ended up in Wave Watch and told her about how he was getting a degree in economics. They talked about the band, and Irene's cooking, and how nice the weather was this evening.

Every time he looked at her legs swinging through the crystalline pool water, Marie thought of Winifred's exclamation: *Your legs!* Marie felt pretty in the dress, and prettier when Lawrence complimented the way it flattered her shape. The crowd was overwhelming, overtaking the yard with shouting, dancing, and raucous laughter—but sitting beside Lawrence with her toes in the water, Marie was temporarily content.

The vodka didn't hurt either.

After dark, Marie pretended not to notice a few smokers using their lighters to ignite candles on a big cake in the kitchen. Irene and Winifred carried the cake out to a table on the lawn, their arms straining under its immense weight. It was red velvet with creamy white frosting, and it said *Welcome Home, Marie!* in big chocolate-piped letters. Birthday candles flickered and dribbled wax.

"It's not my birthday!" Marie shouted into Winifred's ear over the din of so many party guests, but her sternum was filled with happy air.

"Tonight it is!"

The crowd cheered when Marie leaned over and blew out the candles. Never in Marie's wildest dreams did she think she could feel so celebrated—not even at the stiff parties put on by the gallery when the *Girl* collection was taking off.

Of course, most of the guests weren't here for her, but the way Winifred looked at her from across the blaze of candles—with giddiness and appreciation—made Marie feel like maybe they were becoming best friends. Had Marie been sober, thoughts of Dottie would've crept into her joy, but she was too buzzed tonight to pay them mind.

Irene quickly cut Marie a giant piece of cake, then asked a few people nearby to carry the rest back into the kitchen for butchering.

Marie turned to Winifred and Lawrence, the heavy dessert plate already straining her fingers. "I can't possibly eat all this on my own."

"Beach?" Winifred asked.

Marie nodded.

Lawrence ran inside for forks and then followed them down the dune path.

Marie found Winifred's usual spot, the wide boulder overlooking the breakers. Winifred and Lawrence sat on either side of her. Together, the three of them wielded their forks and ate. The red velvet was moist and sweet. It was a corner piece with gobs of extra frosting, which Winifred hogged, but Marie didn't comment on.

She was trying not to measure the tiny sliver of air between Lawrence's leg and her bare one. She couldn't tell if the goose bumps on her thighs were from the ocean breeze or his nearness. A low part of her belly squeezed in a way she hadn't allowed in a long, long time. Soon, the cake was gone, and Winifred's warmth on Marie's left disappeared. A small panic rose in Marie. She wanted to call Winifred back to them. She hadn't realized that the safety of her friend had been buffering Marie against a quake of nervy attraction.

But then Lawrence turned to Marie, and his warm hand found her chilled thigh, and his nose found her nose. He tasted like sweat and cake. Her nerves disintegrated like frosting on his tongue, and her panic morphed into ecstasy.

"You taste like red velvet," Lawrence murmured.

"So do you," Marie whispered back.

He squeezed her thigh sensuously, and after more kissing, he procured a joint from his patterned shirt pocket and passed it to Marie. He held out his lighter and shielded the flame, so all Marie had to do was breathe. She inhaled and held, then exhaled. She did this three times, until the edges of her vision became soft brushstrokes. Lawrence's hand returned to her thigh. Absently, she considered what paints she'd mix for him. His skin was an exquisite raw umber, with perhaps a touch of purply Mars violet. All richness and warmth.

"If you could do anything right now, what would you do?" Lawrence asked.

"Paint." His eyes widened just a little, and it satisfied her in a curious way. "Paint you."

"Me?"

The colors of his shirt were pure: cerulean, lime green, tangerine. "Yeah."

He seemed to consider this, his lips wrapping around the joint again. Then he said, "Okay."

She led him upstairs, fully intending to turn left into her studio. But when they crested the stairs, his hand met the small of her back, and Marie turned into her bedroom instead.

46

Winifred tucked Irene into a spare bedroom around midnight and helped the band pack up their amps sometime after two o'clock. The cottage grew quiet at three o'clock, and around four o'clock, Winifred gave up trying to work through the dirty dishes, afraid she'd wake the guests sleeping on the couches in the nearest rooms and those dozing in the grass outside the kitchen window. She spent a little time quietly tidying, until she found a pack of cigarettes, at which point she lit one on a stove burner and sauntered outside into the night.

She sat on the pool tiles for a good long while. Winifred had known when to leave Marie and Lawrence alone. Their shyness and attraction had reminded Winifred of her own with Bruce. The thrill of light contact. The pounding need in her abdomen. The intoxicating tastes and smells when learning a new body. Falling in love with every breath and hitch of breath and sigh. If Winifred's heart were a scale, her present happiness for Marie and Lawrence would weigh the same as her sorriness for her own broken heart. Winifred loved love. Romantic, platonic, in friendship or family. Love made heartbreak as sweet as cake.

Winifred finished her cigarette, stubbing it out in a little puddle on the tile. She extended her legs into the pool, a chill spider-climbing up her calves until her skin pulled tight. She shivered and kicked a little, her feet *ka-thunking* on the silver surface. Whispers mumbled across the yard, and Winifred stopped splashing, letting her legs simply dangle. The water tickled her ankles.

She lay back, resting her head in the basket of her interlocked hands. The sky was a deep black dome. Light softened the stars toward the east, but daybreak was still a ways off. A forceful sigh rushed past her lips.

"You all right?" Marie asked, lowering herself beside Winifred on the other side of the stubbed cigarette.

Winifred sat up. "Did he leave?"

Marie was wearing a pair of shorts and a baggy, paint-spattered T-shirt. "He has work later."

"Did you have a good time?"

Marie glanced away, gently slapping her feet on the water.

"I'll take that as a yes." Even in the predawn darkness, Winifred saw Marie's cheeks darken.

"I forgot to tell you: I heard back from my old contact at the advertising firm. I received the letter yesterday."

Winifred was aware of Marie's interest in making a little extra money this way; she thought it was a waste of Marie's time and talent, but she appreciated that Marie would share such a development with Winifred. It was a sign of closeness, of trust, that Marie would think to tell Winifred at all.

"And?" Winifred asked.

"He sent a brief for a small assignment. A logo for a toy company."

"You don't look glad."

"I should be glad."

"But?"

Marie lay back as Winifred had. "I forgot how boring it is," she said. "I need the extra money, but the assignments . . . they don't make my heart sing."

"But painting does."

Marie stared up at the sky, the skin around her eyes tightening as if she was straining to see something that wasn't there. "Sometimes."

Winifred wanted to ask why Marie did anything other than paint, especially when the foundation paid her so handsomely—but she couldn't. Marie didn't know Winifred knew about that hefty source of income. And if she admitted to Marie that she was writing the checks, the balance of their friendship would be ruined. Winifred didn't want to lose Marie—not now, not yet, and (if she was being honest with herself) not ever.

"Why seek the work, then?" Winifred asked.

"The track," Marie said simply.

Winifred didn't understand why the great D needed to reduce herself to a regular job. Her first collection had been a showstopper, a rocket launch. Why couldn't she do that again? Why was she allowing herself to plummet into a free fall back toward Earth?

"Could you try to sell your paintings?" Winifred asked.

"None of them are good enough."

Winifred looked down at Marie, her heart wobbling on its axis like a spinning top about to tip over. "Which paintings make your heart sing?"

Marie propped herself up on her elbows, her gaze still trained on the stars. "There's this feeling I get sometimes, of losing myself in the art. Time fades away, and I forget about the world. It's just me and the brush and the canvas and the paint. When I can get to that place, the paintings just . . . *work*."

"Did you feel that way about the one of me?"

Marie picked at a thread on the hem of her shirt. "Yeah."

"How do you replicate that feeling?"

"I wish I knew," Marie said. "I wish I could stay in that feeling forever, of time being lost."

Winifred understood, then. She knew that feeling. Not from any sort of art but from other things, like dancing to a great song, or hosting a party, or making love with Bruce. It was the feeling of time racing and slowing simultaneously.

"I wish for a lot of things, I guess," Marie added with a self-conscious chuckle. "I should seek out more birthday candles to blow out, or shooting stars to wish on, or a fountain to fill up with coins."

Winifred sprang to her feet. "Wait right here."

Marie sat up and watched as Winifred hurried toward the house, her dress fluttering behind her as she ran through the grass and up the patio steps and through the door. The wind gusted, sending ripples across the surface of the pool. The lapping water was almost musical, like a liquid chime. Winifred returned in a flurry of perfume-scented wind as she carried a jar full of nickels and pennies.

"What's this?" Marie asked.

"You said candles, stars, coins." She paused, and when Marie didn't reply, Winifred elaborated. "You had candles earlier. And"—she pointed up—"we can watch for shooting stars. The only thing missing was a fountain and coins."

"I didn't wish on those candles."

"Why not?"

"It's not my birthday."

Winifred waved her hand. "A technicality."

"We don't have a fountain."

"You're such a wet blanket."

Marie scrunched her nose at Winifred, not bothering to deny it.

Winifred gestured at the crashing waves beyond her yard. "We have something better than a fountain."

"What's that?"

"The *ocean*."

"You want to throw pocket change into the ocean?"

"I want to make *wishes*."

Marie laughed. It was a silly idea, but she was charmed. "Isn't that littering?"

"Is that a *no*?" Winifred's eyes were wide and warm and a little wild as she offered her hand.

Marie considered it for a moment, then took her hand, allowing Winifred to haul her up. With gasping, cackling laughter, they ran—hand in hand—for the beach.

The wind had picked up, and the ocean was a surge of sound and energy. Winifred's dress whipped around her legs, and Marie's hair floated all around her head as if she were weightless. When the tide rushed up to meet their toes, they jumped back, squealing. Meanwhile, the vast expanse of space glimmered above their heads.

Winifred hefted the jar of coins, holding it out to Marie. "Ready?"

Marie reached into the jar and raised up a quarter. "I will if you will."

Winifred beamed, white teeth flashing in the dark. She retrieved a dime and held it up. "On the count of three."

They counted together—"One, two, three!"—and the coins soared, disappearing into the froth.

"What did you wish for?" Winifred asked.

"I can't say it out loud. It won't come true."

"That's stupid."

"You've never heard that before?"

Winifred planted the jar in the wet sand and retrieved two nickels, handing one to Marie. "If people were more willing to share their wishes with the world, we'd realize that we're all the same, and *pow*"—she clapped her hands once—"we would achieve world peace."

Marie's lips quirked. "That simple, huh?"

"What does *anyone* wish for, Marie? Love, security, freedom. We all want the same things."

"Fine, then tell me *your* wish," Marie said.

Winifred squinted at her, like the glare of an older sister. "I wished for love."

"Love?"

"Love."

"I thought Bruce—"

"*Not* romance," Winifred clarified. "Platonic love."

Marie wasn't sure how to read into Winifred's words.

Thankfully, Winifred didn't give her time to ruminate. "Your turn."

"I didn't agree to share my wish."

"It was implied."

Marie rolled her eyes. "I wished for security, I guess." Marie had wished for her art to work out.

"See? Universal things." Winifred held up her nickel. "Another? This time out loud."

"No way."

"Come on." Winifred nudged Marie's hand.

Once they were both holding their nickels to the sky, they counted again: "One, two, three!"

They called out their wishes over the rush and hiss of wind and waves:

"Love!" Marie shouted, as she boldly wished for this friendship with Winifred to be a long one—to not be stolen from her as Dottie had.

"Security!" Winifred shouted, as she wished to find a place where she belonged.

They met each other's eyes and giggled at their inverse wishes, then reached inside the jar for more coins.

"One, two, three!"

"Freedom!" Marie said, and she wished to escape her grief.

"Cheese!" Winifred said.

"Cheese?" Marie asked, practically shrill.

Winifred offered a cheeky grin. "Don't we all want more fondue in our lives?"

They burst into howling laughter.

"Again?" Marie asked.

This time it was cake and weed.

Then it was clothes and paint.

Then it was belonging and friendship.

Then it was friendship and belonging.

They went on and on like this, until sleepy partygoers shouted from the lawn for them to stop. Until all the coins disappeared into the sand and saltwater. Until they felt like they understood each other, after all.

47

The next day, after the guests were gone and Marie and Winifred had cleaned the whole house to the Temptations, Marie decided that she would accept the logo job. The opportunity wasn't exciting, but the extra money would get her one step closer to buying Hurley Downs. Living with Winifred was a surprisingly joyful whirlwind, and Marie was beginning to dread the inevitable day she'd have to leave—but it would come eventually. She couldn't mooch off Winifred forever.

Besides, Marie had been working toward buying the track for the better part of seven years—longer, if she included all the time before Hurley Downs fell into disrepair, when destroying it was more a fantasy than a tangible possibility. The track had taken so much from Marie, and for so long, she had been powerless to its destruction; to own it would be to reclaim her power. Living with Winifred had perhaps softened her fixation a little, but the parties and good-natured company were distractions. Leveling Hurley Downs was the true answer to Marie's strife. It was the only way she could take control of her past once and for all. Of this, she was wholeheartedly convinced.

So Marie would work for Mr. Duxbury again—just for the extra buck. And perhaps his assignments would be good for her painting somehow. Perhaps having deadlines on mundane pieces would make her true creativity itch.

In the late afternoon, after a shower and a nap, Marie came downstairs to find Winifred sitting in the dining room, sipping coffee. Her cheeks were puffy, and a faint bluish hue shaded under her eyes.

"How are you feeling?" Marie asked from the doorway.

"Hungover?" The word lilted into a question.

Marie sank into the chair kitty-corner to Winifred's. "You sound surprised."

Winifred gave her a flat, humorless glance.

"Any more calls from the neighbors?"

"I'm sure they're drafting a formal letter as we speak." Winifred's eyes sank to the folded paper Marie was absently clutching. "Speaking of letters, what's that?"

"It's the logo-job contract."

"They already sent a contract?"

Marie shrugged. "They included it with the brief, just in case."

"You're going to take it?"

"I have to."

Winifred opened her mouth as if she might argue, but then lifted her mug to her parted lips instead.

"It won't be much," Marie said, wondering why she felt the need to explain but doing it anyway. "Just the occasional illustration. I need the income."

Winifred sipped her coffee again, clearly not interested in voicing her opinion.

"It's on a project-by-project basis, so I'm not locked into anything." Marie waited a moment for Winifred to reply.

"You don't need my permission, Marie."

"You seem disappointed."

"So?"

"So . . . why?"

"Because you should be painting."

"Yeah, well . . ." Marie tore her gaze from Winifred's, redirecting it outside, to the black-capped terns swooping toward the ocean. "Painting isn't easy right now."

"What about the painting upstairs?"

Marie scrubbed a hand over her face. "A fluke."

Marie could feel Winifred studying her, but she didn't turn. Didn't look.

After a long moment, Winifred asked, "Do you really believe that?"

Marie met her eyes. "Yes."

"So you need to get unstuck."

Easy for Winifred to say, when she wasn't the one caught in a creative sinkhole. "And how do you suggest I do that?" Marie asked, her voice all doubt and sarcasm.

Winifred regarded Marie, trying to think around her pounding headache. The mission of her foundation was to make artists' lives easier. To support them so they had the time to create. But of course life expenses weren't the only things that could stand in the way of creation. It was clear that Marie's creative stalemate had something to do with her childhood scars and that godforsaken track she was so obsessed with acquiring.

Winifred straightened in her seat. "Why don't you paint something new?"

If money hadn't helped Marie break out of her blockage, there were other ways Winifred could help: encouragement, ideas, emotional support.

"Judging by the paintings I saw when you moved in, you're stuck on those close-ups, and it sounds like they aren't working for you. Why don't you paint something else?"

Marie's brow crumpled in confusion, or maybe uncertainty.

"You want to buy the racetrack," Winifred reasoned. "Why don't you paint horses? They're so elegant, and I bet they'd be fun to paint." Winifred wasn't sure that a new motif would satiate Marie's obsession with the track, but it couldn't hurt, right?

"Horses." Marie didn't sound convinced.

"It's just an idea," Winifred said casually, but she could see that Marie's interest was piqued, that she was turning the idea over in her mind. Winifred changed the subject before Marie had a chance to dismiss the suggestion. She gestured to Marie's contract. "Did you need an envelope for that?"

"And a stamp."

Winifred made a face and stood. "Mooch."

"Ha ha," Marie enunciated, following her into the kitchen.

Winifred kept a stack of envelopes and stamps on a shelf above the telephone. But she stopped short of retrieving them when she spotted a scribbled note on the notepad by the receiver: a phone number, a peace sign, and the letter *L*.

"Well, look here," Winifred said, showing Marie.

Her face instantly flushed. Winifred giggled and reached for the envelope and stamps.

Marie was still blushing as she copied the address on the firm's letterhead to the face of the envelope. Winifred watched her write, about to ask if she would call Lawrence back, but the words died in her throat. She recognized that address. Or, rather, she recognized the name.

"Duxbury & Pierce?"

Marie nodded as she stuffed the contract into the envelope and sealed it. "You know them?"

"That's June's husband's firm."

"The June who made those comments about Bruce outside the Shore House?"

Winifred met Marie's eyes.

"I didn't know he was married."

Winifred quirked a worried brow. "Were you hoping he wasn't?"

Marie scoffed. "God, no. It's just—I worked for Mr. Duxbury for years when I was younger. All the times we met, he . . ."

Winifred felt her chest grow hot. "He *what*?"

"He didn't *act* married," Marie said.

Winifred waited for her to go on.

"He made a pass at me. More than once."

In spite of everything June had said and done, Winifred's stomach dipped. Everyone said Harry had dalliances—hell, look what he'd done at Winifred's wedding—but Harry's conduct had taken on a mythic quality among his elite community, the stuff of disbelieving whispers, more entertainment than fact. But now: further confirmation. June was a sour woman, but no woman deserved an unfaithful man. Especially if she loved him, as June seemed to love her husband.

Winifred sighed. "You see? This is exactly why you shouldn't—"

"What does my boss being a misogynist have anything to do with it? As I said, I've worked for him before. He's harmless"—she waved the envelope—"especially by mail."

"But Marie—"

"Why are you so against me taking this illustration job?" There was an edge in Marie's voice.

"I didn't mean—"

"You've been discouraging all morning."

The comment smarted; Winifred was only trying to help. "You said yourself last night that you didn't want to—"

"I need the money."

"*No*, you don't," Winifred said.

They stared at each other.

"You live here," Winifred said gently. "What money could you possibly need?"

"I can't live here forever." Marie's brow was creased; she shook her head as if to dislodge a thought. "Besides, I have a goal, a life plan."

You can't hold me captive. That's what it sounded like Marie was saying. And she was right. Winifred had been so absorbed in enjoying this arrangement that she hadn't fully considered the fact that it was impermanent. Marie didn't *want* to live here forever. And the thought made Winifred's heart tremor.

"I'm not trying to trap you here," Winifred said, low.

"I didn't mean it like that. It's just . . . a job will be good for me."

"Fine, all right. But be careful."

"It's just a job." Marie turned away.

"Did you have a fun party?"

Marie stopped and faced her again, leaning against the doorjamb. "Yeah, I did. Thank you."

"For what it's worth, I'm glad you're here." She lifted the notepad. "And it sounds like I'm not the only one."

48

Another weekend, another party.

This time, Winifred decided to make it a theme party—but instead of the elegant masquerade balls of the elite, this theme had been cheese. She'd wished for it on a coin, after all, and Winifred had told Marie that some dreams were well within their control of realizing. Irene had brought no fewer than five different kinds of cheese; Lyle and a score of other restaurant workers had smuggled wheels of expensive brie and parmesan from their workplaces. Winifred had taken Marie to Stop & Shop to scour the shelves for anything and everything they could dip in cheese: bread, meat, vegetables, fruit.

Winifred's neighbors on both sides had conspired to call the police, complaining of the noise—some college students had invited another band to play—but by the time the police arrived, most of the guests were comatose. It seemed the cheese and bread had put them all to sleep. Irene had sent the police away with morsels of brie, bacon, and apples for the road.

Perhaps it hadn't been the rowdiest party, but word had gotten out about the widow on the coast, and buses of hippies had driven in for the occasion. Lawrence said he'd counted approximately three hundred people between the lawn, the ballroom, and the many open doorways on his journey to Marie's bedroom. Half asleep in his arms by then, she wasn't surprised by the number.

Two days later, Marie's stomach was still not quite right from all the cheese and alcohol—but, then again, it might've been nerves over the tight deadline Mr. Duxbury had given her.

If I recall correctly, you work fast, he'd said on the phone, when she'd called to accept the job. *If you nail this timeline, Marie, I might have a bigger project for you next.*

No flirting, no innuendo. After the call, Marie had the vague urge to tell Winifred *I told you so,* but she knew it wouldn't change Winifred's opinion. Besides, she was more worried about the deadline. She ended up working all week long, sunup to sundown, much to Winifred's silent but obvious chagrin. It'd been a while since Marie had illustrated professionally, and she wasn't as fast as she'd once been, but by the end of the week, she felt she'd done her best.

On the last Monday in July, Marie was packaging a whole folder of mock-ups to mail when Winifred knocked outside Marie's open studio door.

"You need a break," she said, carrying a tray of breakfast into Marie's space.

"I need to focus," Marie said, but she'd already set down her pen and pushed back from the desk.

"I've barely seen you since the cheese party. Have you even called Lawrence?"

Marie rolled her eyes and leaned back in her chair. "Did you come up here to nag me?"

Winifred smiled. They hadn't spoken about Mr. Duxbury since Marie had mailed the contract, and for the most part, the warmth between them had returned—along with some added banter. Marie was glad. She didn't want any tension with Winifred. The growing ease she felt around Winifred was like a hot bath to Marie's sore heart.

Winifred set the tray on a side table and plucked a strip of bacon off the plate. "Have you thought more about painting horses?"

Marie stood and eyed the spread of food Winifred had prepared. "You're really hell bent on the idea, aren't you?"

Winifred had mentioned it another two times, always with an air of casualness that Marie saw right through. But to Marie's dismay, the reminders wouldn't have mattered; she hadn't *stopped* thinking about the idea. That was the problem.

"I'm going out this afternoon." Winifred wiggled her fingers. "For a manicure. Since you decided manicures are *pointless*—"

Marie held up her own ink-stained fingers in proof.

"—I'm assuming you won't come." Winifred smiled a smug, saccharine smile. "So you'll have the house to yourself. You can paint horses, or call Lawrence, or do whatever else you might want."

Marie wiped her dirty fingers on a wet rag by her easel, then dried her hands on her pants as she approached the breakfast tray. "Can you mail my mock-ups while you're out?"

"Of course," Winifred said.

Marie selected a strip of bacon and ate it in one rather unladylike bite. "These are good."

Winifred smiled. She appeared as if she might say something but didn't.

"I think I'll do some painting this afternoon—while you're gone, I mean," Marie said, plucking a strawberry from the tray. She said it to make Winifred happy, and she wasn't exactly sure why that suddenly mattered to her so much.

When Marie looked up from the food, Winifred was watching her. They held eye contact for a moment, Winifred's gladness apparent in the creases beside her eyes.

But then she scoffed and turned away, throwing a cheeky "You're so predictable" over her shoulder as she left.

～

Once Winifred was gone, Marie poured herself an iced tea and returned to her illustration desk. She retrieved her notebook from the drawer, and past the sketches of the cemetery and parking lot crows, she landed on her latest drawings. They were quick-sketch portraits, mostly: a chin lifted in pride, eyebrows pointed with worry, curiosity portrayed in an arched neck. In all of them, the horses were without bridles or halters or blinders. Just their expressive faces: soft eyes, telling noses, warning ears.

The images had come easily to Marie. Too easily.

She carried her sketchbook and a stubby pencil over to her painting easel, where a primed three-by-three canvas waited. With her sketchbook tucked into her left arm like a baby, she wielded the pencil in her right hand. The lines were faint and loose as she roughly translated one of the sketches into a bigger version on the blank canvas. Her heart pounded in her tongue, and she swallowed.

The horse's face was all angles and cheekbones. An ancient, skeletal face, with eyes that were both innocent and wise. Framing his close-up were the jail bars of his stall. Marie could feel his breath on her cheeks as he stood in his open doorway, reaching out toward the two girls who'd sneaked into the stable. Marie had been petrified staring up at him—his long face was the size of her torso; his shoulder a distant mountain peak. A single rope had been strung across the gap—the only thing keeping him in. It seemed illogical—futile, even—to expect a thousand-pound-plus racing giant to be held back by a single clip and twine.

Panic clutched her. Marie dropped her pencil with a clatter and placed a hand at the base of her throat. She could feel her pulse in the hollow, fluttering like a frantic moth. She forced a breath, then another, reminding herself where she actually was. Not there, not at Hurley Downs, but here in Wave Watch, in the Seacastle. Her vision darted around the room, finding her palette on a stool, the white window frame. A desk, a carpet, clouds painted on the ceiling.

Somewhere downstairs, the phone rang. She jumped.

"Get it together, Marie," she demanded out loud, making her voice firm. "It's just the phone."

Relief spread through her numb limbs as she hurried out of her studio. Her panic eased with each step; by the time she reached the landing, she'd removed her hand from her neck and was breathing normally again.

In the kitchen, she lifted the receiver. "Hello?"

"Hi, is Marie there? This is her brother, James."

Despite herself, Marie huffed a single ironic laugh. She might not have wanted to think about Pennsylvania, but here it was, calling.

"Hi, James," she said.

"Oh, hi, Marie. I didn't recognize your voice."

"Well, it's me," she said, fists clenched. She both knew and did not know that he was calling about the track. She felt suspended in water, waiting to see if she rose to the surface or sank. "How are you?"

"I'm fine," he said. "Listen, I'm just going to cut to the chase. I heard from Eddie. The track's going up for sale this week."

Marie slumped against the wall. "It's . . . what?"

"I'm sorry."

"But you said six months. It hasn't been six months."

"That was a guess, not a guarantee."

The handset slipped from Marie's grasp, clattering on the side table. She pressed her fingers into her eye sockets until she saw purple spots.

"Marie? Marie?" James sounded small and far away, his voice floating up from where the receiver now rested. "Are you still there?"

Marie pinched the bridge of her nose between her steepled fingers. "I don't have enough money yet, James."

He kept talking, but without the phone to her ear, she couldn't make sense of his tiny words. Marie pushed a breath out through parted lips. Dottie's voice filled her head. *He's beautiful,* she'd said of the Thoroughbred in the doorway. Dottie had loved Hurley Downs, right up until it killed her.

Marie snatched the phone. "I get paid by my patron in a few days, and that'll bring me up to nine thousand dollars. Could you . . ."

"I see where you're going with that thought, but I don't have anything to spare."

"Nothing?"

"Look, you might still have a shot, Marie. I doubt anyone is going to want to snatch up a run-down racetrack immediately—maybe, after a while, they'll be willing to settle for less."

"So that's it? I just . . . wait and see?"

"Well, I'm no expert, but . . . yeah, Marie. Keep saving and wait and see. Eddie said he'd keep his ear to the ground."

Marie nodded, heart galloping.

"But, Marie, that's a lot of money to just—hell, I'll just say it—that's a lot of money to waste on a bad investment."

"James—"

"No, listen. I'm your big brother, and I'm supposed to look out for you, and I wouldn't be doing my job if I didn't tell you what a bad idea this is. I've been patient up until now—"

"Hah."

"—but you're being foolish. No, not foolish, downright *stupid*. Buying Hurley Downs won't make you feel better. You know that, right? I mean, logically, you must know."

Marie shook her head as if she could shake herself free from the agony of reality. "What else am I supposed to do with my life, James? Seriously. I'm washed up. I'm a failure."

"You're not a failure, Marie. You're a wonder. Don't waste that on a grudge with the past. Use that money you've so diligently saved and buy yourself a nice house somewhere, paint more paintings."

"It's not that simple," Marie said.

"Why not?"

She wiped the tears from her face. "It doesn't matter where I go, James," she said. "I can't shake her. I can't . . . *forget*. She's a ghost. This is the only way I can lay her to rest."

Marie heard the creaking of floorboards under James's feet. She could picture him standing there, in his modest little house, looking out at the backyard, where his children were no doubt playing in the summer morning sun. Somehow, he'd found his way out of the grief and wreckage of their past; but somewhere along the way, he'd left Marie behind.

When he spoke again, his voice was so delicate—so filled with pause and pity—it made Marie want to weep. "Why do you *want* to forget, Marie?"

"Because it's all my fault."

49

"He's beautiful," Dottie had said, stepping toward the Thoroughbred with an outstretched hand. How she'd managed to convince Marie to sneak into the stables, Marie wasn't sure. Dottie was like that, sometimes—too convincing for her own good.

"Be careful," Marie hissed from three feet back, her knees and ankles locked in place. Terror shook Marie, but it was a reverent terror. An awestruck terror.

Dottie only crept closer. The Thoroughbred lowered his nose to her face and blew puffs of curious breath. He nudged her ear, wiping a wet smear of nostril grime on her temple. Dottie giggled, petting his cheek. A huge pink tongue lapped over her chin and mouth. "His whiskers tickle."

Marie approached her friend, her joints stiff and mechanical. When she reached Dottie's side, she stroked a reluctant hand down the horse's nose. It was soft as velvet—and warm. He breathed his heady oat breath across their faces, and the girls continued petting him, giggling when he nudged and nosed their necks.

Voices far down at the opposite end of the stable interrupted the fun. The horse looked up, ears perked, his neck extending so high that Marie was reminded of her terror. He stomped a deadly hoof and tossed his head, impatient.

"We're not supposed to be in here," Marie whispered to Dottie, her eyes trained down the long hallway of horse stalls. "If we get caught—"

A pair of men—one tall and broad, the other small and birdlike—entered the stable. They were caught up in a conversation, grunting and gesturing, voices competing.

"In here," Dottie whispered and darted under the rope into the horse's stall.

"Dottie!" Marie squeaked, trying to be quiet despite her horror.

"Quick! Hide!" Dottie said, now out of sight inside the Thoroughbred's shadowy stall.

Marie glanced from the men approaching to the long pillars of the Thoroughbred's legs, her heart throbbing inside her throat. She let out a little choked sound and ducked inside, dodging as the metal shoe of the Thoroughbred's hoof flashed in the low light, pawing at the ground. Panting, Marie scampered over manure and dusty straw, her shoulder brushing against the wood wall as she gave the horse a wide berth.

Dottie was crouched in the back corner, her small body enveloped in darkness. Marie sank down next to her, breath ragged. The burning-sweet scent of horse piss hit the back of her throat. They weren't *allowed* in the barn. Seeing the horses might've been Dottie's idea, but Marie knew better.

"We shouldn't be in here," Marie whispered.

Dottie raised a finger to her mouth, her eyes wide.

The men were walking past now, still arguing. The horse stomped and tossed his head, tail swishing; Marie felt the air whistle and scatter as the strands swiped close to her face. From their place behind him, Marie saw the power of his haunches, a ripple of shadow accentuating muscle. His long legs couldn't seem to stand still, bones and tendons straining with energy.

"I think they're gone," Dottie said quietly, creeping forward on her knees.

"Careful, careful, careful," Marie pleaded.

Dottie continued, her eyes trained on the bright square of sunlight that was the horse's open door. He was in their way, blocking their exit.

Dottie moved with her back against the wall, inching closer to the door and the Thoroughbred's sinuous front legs.

From down the way, a metal clang and rattle tore through the quiet stable. The Thoroughbred, with Dottie now practically underfoot, whinnied and stomped and—

"Marie, are you crying?"

Marie blinked, her canvas materializing before her. Red browns and shadow blues came into focus, and there he was, the kind, inquisitive face of the Thoroughbred staring back at her. Marie turned, paintbrush still in hand. Wetness tickled her face.

"I came to pick up my platter," Irene explained from the threshold of the studio, "but I don't know where Winifred put it."

Marie started breathing again, settling her fear one ragged gasp at a time. She set down her brush and lifted her elbow to dry her damp face on the shoulder of her T-shirt. "I'll help you look."

"I'm sorry to interrupt." Irene wavered, her eyes fixed behind Marie.

Marie didn't look back, afraid of what she'd see, afraid it would start a flood behind her eyes again. After her call with James, she'd returned to her easel practically in a trance, the memory bubbling up inside her and spilling out through her brush-wielding hand.

"That painting . . . ," Irene began, sounding awestruck.

"It's nothing," Marie said, ushering Irene out of the studio.

In the kitchen, Marie found Irene's dish in the cabinet, mixed in with Winifred's other serveware.

"Ah! Perfect," Irene said, taking the dish from Marie's paint-smudged fingers. Irene's gaze seemed to linger on the rich ocher and midnight blue that filled the indents of Marie's knuckles. "I had no idea you were such a talent, Marie."

Marie lifted her hand toward the door. "After you."

Irene hesitated, then led the way to the foyer. Out on the porch, she said, "I'm sorry I interrupted."

"No, it's fine," Marie replied. "Painting can get emotional for me, is all."

"I didn't mean to pry."

"Don't sweat it, Irene. Really." Marie touched her shoulder reassuringly and then thought of the paint on her hands and pulled back.

Irene pressed her lips into a fond, creased smile. She took the porch steps one at a time. At the bottom, she glanced back at Marie. "You know, you're just like Winifred."

Marie frowned. "How so?"

"You both sell yourselves short," Irene said.

Wordlessly, Marie watched Irene climb into her car, wave, and drive away.

Irene's words clanged in her head like a racing bell.

Marie retreated into the kitchen, poured herself a lemonade, and stood by the window. Heat emanated from the glass windowpanes, and sweat beaded along her hairline. Beyond the crisp lawn, the dune grass swayed in magnificent, shifting shades of sage and tawny brown. And past the shaggy dunes, the flat sand and sea glimmered the palest yellow in the sunshine.

Marie closed her eyes, listening to the distant hiss of the tide. She pretended the sound belonged to the Susquehanna River instead of the Atlantic, and when she breathed in, she didn't smell salt—she smelled orchard grass and manure and the earthy wet muck of the riverbed.

Marie's throat squeezed, and she blinked her eyes open, breaking the spell before it could break her first.

50

On the last Monday of July, June crept into Bella's room and kissed her daughter's head. Harry had dropped her off three days ago, and tears had sprung to June's eyes upon the sight of her husband and daughter, equal parts sorrow and joy. Breathing in the sweet, powdery scent of Bella's hair, June felt the prick of tears once again, a sharp stinging in her nostrils.

The pain had returned to June last night, the warning bells of a new cycle. Racked with a deep, radiating ache in her hips this morning—the strength of which made it hard for her to stand—she'd finally given in and had taken just one pill to remove the sharpest edge of her discomfort. She was determined to be careful, to not lose control of her senses as she had before. In order to be present for her daughter, June knew that she couldn't allow pain *or* painkillers to fog her mind. This week would be a tightrope, but June would walk it perfectly. There was no room for error. Bella was home again, finally, and June wasn't going to let her body ruin it.

June kissed Bella's head again, her daughter's soft hair tickling her cheeks. "Bella," she sang sweetly. "Bella, Bella."

Her daughter stirred, stretched, yawned. "Mama," she squeaked.

Bella's voice was enough to make June's heart melt. "Are you ready for the best day ever?"

Bella nodded sleepily, sighing.

According to June, each of the past three days had been the best day ever, because Bella was home. They'd already taken three trips to Del's Lemonade, visited the lighthouse, and tossed bread to the shorebirds. June was eager to give her daughter another fun-filled day, and this was going to be the best yet.

"How about we start with some pancakes?" June half sang.

Bella lifted her head, a squinty smile transforming her features from sleepy to gleeful. "Pamcakes?"

June scooped her daughter into her arms, wincing as the strain sparked through her abdomen. "They're in the kitchen! Let's go!"

Bella shrieked with joy as June carried her downstairs to start their perfect day.

~

For a while, June's pain remained mostly under control.

After pancakes, they made sandcastles on the beach. The warm summer wind gusted against June's back, and she managed not to feel queasy.

After rinsing off the sand and restyling her hair, June painted Bella's toenails a delicate shade of baby pink. With her daughter seated on the bathroom counter, June remained upright, her vision clear and her hand steady.

June was beginning to feel hopeful about the rest of her day, but then they reached the carousel. There, her discomfort bloomed, and the spinning platform and bobbing horses made her pain feel like it was elevatoring up and down her legs and torso. It stuck with her as they disembarked from the ride and ventured to the toy store.

As Bella deliberated over which toys to select, June rested her hand against a display stand, fighting the lingering floaty sensation of the carousel. In the end, Bella picked out a new Barbie doll and a stuffed horse, clutching them both in her tiny arms on the way out; June was glad for the opportunity not to carry anything more than her pocketbook.

At the playground, June's pain flared hotter. While Bella played on a slide with another little girl, June sank onto a bench, fanning herself. Children shrieked, exhaust fumes drifted through the trees from the parking lot, and the intense sun beat down on June's forehead. Her back had grown damp with sweat, and she wished she'd brought a sun hat.

"Good job!" June called as Bella braved the slide—then winced. Even her own voice seemed to rattle her insides. A head-spinning nausea rose, and she hunched forward, panting through her mouth, gripping the edge of the bench to ride out the worst of the fire in her stomach.

"Hi, June!"

She blinked, realizing she'd had her eyes squeezed shut. Rosie Kirkland was standing before her in a flawless fuchsia shift dress.

"Hi, Rosie." Ever since the tense moment in Rosie's sunroom, they had been cordial bordering on friendly; June had to admire Rosie's ability to move past it.

"Mind if I sit?" Rosie sat, ankles crossed, and adjusted the white-and-mauve scarf tied around her neck. She smelled like Shalimar. "Enjoying the sunshine?" she asked, not bothering to pause long enough for June to actually answer as she continued, "Our nanny had a family emergency, so I'm on my own today."

As Rosie continued talking, June forced a smile, clenching her fists through another tremor in her lower back.

"I heard Winifred resigned from the committee," Rosie said. "I know everyone considers her an odd duck, but I have to admit, I quite liked her creative ideas."

June was in too much pain to counter Rosie's appalling assessment.

"Do you have any idea why she—*Robert*, be nice to your brother!"— Rosie pointed a finger toward a boy throwing clumps of grass at another boy, her diamond watch glittering on her tiny wrist—"why she resigned? Barbara said that Winifred threw a fit outside the Shore House and then stormed off."

June watched as Rosie's oldest son dropped a wad of dirt from his filthy hands and darted off toward the slide. Like most other women in their circle, Rosie already had three children older than Bella. Rumor had it that she and her husband were hoping for a fourth.

"Winifred was a poor fit for the committee," June said, the last word slightly guttural.

"Are you all right?" Rosie asked, fixing her ice-blue eyes on June. Her long lashes fluttered. "I hope it's not rude of me to say, but you look . . . uncomfortable."

"I'm fine," June said through her clenched jaw.

"You're in pain," Rosie insisted.

If June hadn't been doubled over with her elbows on her knees—and wasn't so ashamed of her own lack of decorum—she would've laughed at the utter obviousness of Rosie's statement.

"June, I've never seen you like this." Rosie placed her hand on her own chest, the perfect picture of concern. "You're positively *pale*. What's wrong? How can I help you?"

It was humiliating, having Rosie want to help her. June twisted away from Rosie to dig through her pocketbook. Finding the bottle, she tried to open it without lifting it high enough for anyone to see, but the cap wouldn't budge. With her head bowed, the world seemed to tip sideways, and June had to rest a hand on the bench to steady herself.

Witness to all of it, Rosie sprang into action, circling to June's other side so she could help with the bottle. June wanted to shove Rosie away, to get up and leave, but her hands had become feeble and shaky; all she could do was let them fall into her lap as Rosie opened her prescription bottle for her.

"One pill, or two?" Rosie asked.

June blew out another breath. *All of them,* she wanted to say, but then she heard Harry's words in her head: *Our daughter could have drowned, and it would've been your fault.* "One," June answered.

Rosie read the bottle. "It says you can take up to two at a time."

June was too strangled by pain to snap at Rosie for questioning her judgment on her own prescription, so she merely took the two pills Rosie offered and swallowed them dry. It would be fine—the night of Bella's almost-accident, June had mixed the pills with alcohol. She hadn't had a drink today and didn't plan to. June was a responsible woman. She certainly couldn't care for Bella in her *current* state, and beyond that, it was embarrassing to be panting like this in public. This was merely a wobble on the tightrope; the two pills would set her right.

Beside her, Rosie was still chattering. "What else can I do for you, June? What's going on? You're scaring me."

June surveyed the areas surrounding the playground; other nannies and mothers were watching them with curiosity and perhaps even a little disgust. It was unseemly for June to be doubled over like this, with Rosie's high-pitched worry carrying through the air like a chime.

"Calm down, Rosie," June ground out, forcing herself to sit upright. She crossed her legs and clasped her hands in her lap and squeezed her knees and fingers until the joints ached. "Just a little monthly discomfort, is all."

Rosie flushed, but there was only kindness in her voice when she said, "I understand completely. Before I had Robert, my pains were excruciating."

June balked at Rosie's frankness, but strangely, the comment soothed June's shame a little. She was unaccustomed to receiving any sympathy when it came to her pain—then again, maybe it was pity.

"It must be really bad, to need a prescription."

No matter how understanding Rosie tried to be, June didn't want to keep talking about it. This visit had been embarrassing enough. June glanced around, trying to spot Bella in the crowd of children swarming the play structure.

When she didn't immediately see her daughter, a small panic twanged in her chest. "Have you seen Bella?" June asked Rosie.

Rosie craned her neck. "Ah, there." She pointed. "Do you want me to get her for you?"

June didn't know which was worse: accepting Rosie's help or the certain nausea she'd experience having to walk across the playground in the afternoon heat and carry her daughter back to the bench. Ultimately, she decided that Rosie's help would be less humiliating.

June drew a long breath into her lungs as Rosie navigated the uneven grass in crisp white shoes. She heaved another as Rosie stooped in front of Bella. When Rosie scooped Bella into her thin arms, rising up on slender legs, June's heart cracked. Rosie might've been naive, but she was a natural mother: sweet, dainty, but charmingly outgoing. It stung to see Bella cradled against another woman's chest, while June waited, incapacitated, on a bench.

When Rosie returned with Bella, she offered June a small, private smile. While June understood the smile as condescending, Rosie was nothing but sincere, uncertain of exactly how to express her solidarity to someone as proud as June.

June stood and accepted Bella into her arms, straining under her daughter's weight on her hip. "We better go," she said, unable to spend one more moment with Rosie. This encounter had been shameful enough.

Rosie leaned in close enough for June to smell her Shalimar perfume again. "Do you need help getting home?"

"Of course not," June snapped, insulted. Did she really appear so incapacitated that Rosie didn't think June could drive herself home? June's abdomen was raging against the pressure of Bella's weight on her hip, but she schooled her face into an expression of haughty boredom. "And it's really none of your business."

June strode off before Rosie could reply, hurrying toward the parking lot. Bella pointed back toward the playground, whimpering. "We're going to get ice cream," June sang into her daughter's ear.

"No," Bella said, wiggling in June's arms.

The shifting weight sent a cascade of tremors through June's left side, crackling like a bonfire. She prayed the pills would kick in soon.

"Ice cream," June repeated. *"Yummm."*

Bella squealed, throwing her arms over June's shoulder and reaching for the playground behind them. June's sandals reached asphalt, and the heat emanating off the blacktop made her seasick. They were almost to the DeVille. Almost, almost, almost.

Bella began to cry, thrashing in June's arms. Excruciating pain blazed through her. She bent forward, setting Bella on the hot pavement. Bella threw herself onto her stomach and wailed.

"Bella, stop that," June said. "Please stop." She crouched—only to clutch her back in agony. Her vision swam, the sun beat down, and she would've cried if it weren't for her perfect mortification over the ordeal. She should've taken the pills earlier; she should've insisted Bella nap before the playground; she—

"Bella, dear," Rosie cooed, now at June's side.

Bella, noticing the three older boys in tow with Rosie, paused in her wailing. June glanced around; a pair of mothers were watching, whispering. It was bad enough that Bella was in the midst of a tantrum; now that Rosie was here, it would be obvious to any spectators that June was a terrible mother with no control over her daughter. To accept Rosie's help would confirm that fact.

But this time, Rosie didn't wait for June's acceptance. Unceremoniously and without asking, Rosie scooped Bella into her arms. "Where's your car?" she asked June.

June pressed her lips together in a mix of disgrace and relief. Wordlessly, she waved toward her convertible.

Rosie started off toward it, Bella's suspended feet bobbing with Rosie's bouncy gait. "Come, boys," Rosie called, and all three of her children stalked after her, poking and prodding each other even as they obeyed their mother.

June simply stood for a few moments, waiting for the bonfire in her stomach to diminish. When it did, she strode after Rosie, trying to hold her head high as she swallowed the tears collecting in her throat.

51

At her car, June watched as Rosie eased Bella into the back seat, bending in a way that made June's stomach wrench just watching. Rosie handed Bella a candy from her pocketbook, then closed the door.

"I hope you feel better," Rosie said, then turned away, sons in tow.

June didn't watch Rosie walk away. She stalked around her car and collapsed into the driver's seat. The pills were finally softening the edges of her pain, making room for anger to flare up in its place.

That was humiliating, and Rosie had only made it worse. Was Rosie really so naive as to think that no one at the playground would notice what just happened? Or had her help been a strategic move against June, a show of superiority over the new committee head?

June wouldn't allow it. June would keep her head held high and—if need be—remind Rosie who was the superior woman.

June started her car and pulled out onto the street. Bella was already fighting sleep in the back seat, so June decided to drive straight home. The pills were watering the fire inside her, abdominals finally uncoiling and cooling as June drove. The road became a soft haze. Even her anger dissipated, the pills sweeping away all her heat until only a calm and hazy steam remained.

June turned on the radio, humming along. Here and there, tall cedars and oaks shaded the pavement, and neatly trimmed privacy hedges were broken up by little ponds, driveways, and manicured lawns.

Where was June going again? Home. She was going home. Had she taken a wrong turn?

"Mama," Bella cooed, seemingly calmed by the candy and the smooth, slow car ride.

June glanced back; her daughter was smiling at her, pointing.

"Mama," she said again.

June pointed right back. "Bella."

Bella's smile morphed into a gaping frown. "MAMA," Bella screamed, right as their car slammed into something with a nasty metallic crunch.

~

On the day of Winifred's wedding to Bruce Hurst, June and Harry had had a row. Their arguments had become more common since Bella had been born, the sleepless nights piling on their nerves until even minor inconveniences became mountainous. *Isn't she supposed to be sleeping through the night by now?* was a common refrain of Harry's, as if Bella's tantrums were June's failing.

And maybe they were, but not for the life of her could June figure out why. June, herself, had been a restrained child, mild and well behaved. Harry had been the little terror, according to his mother. So maybe it was his genetics—an idea she'd muttered to him over coffee that morning, setting off an argument that morphed from topic to topic, always somehow coming back to June's inadequacies: her failure to pack the right snacks for Bella for the trip here, her inability to quiet their screaming daughter, and so on.

All June's friends assured her that Bella would grow out of it, but the Duxburys had gone through three nannies in two years, each one more useless than the last—also, somehow, June's fault. Their newest nanny, Peggy, had done her best last night, but Bella's voice carried through their beach cottage either way.

All this—the cumulation of two years' worth of arguments and exhaustion—rested on the shoulders of the Duxburys when they arrived at the wedding. June had never actually met Winifred, but she already didn't like the other woman. The rumors had been enough to sour June's opinion.

Bruce Hurst had been a pillar of June's and Harry's families' particular corner of East Coast elite. June first learned his name when she was a girl; he was heir to his family's wealth. While she played with her dollies on the lawn, Bruce was already wearing suits and learning his father's business. Once, at a family cookout, when June was fifteen and Bruce was twenty-five, June's mother had pulled her aside and murmured, *Someday, we'll find you a husband like that.*

No one understood why it took Bruce so long to marry. June's older sisters and friends' older sisters pined after him; he could've had anyone he wanted. Some accused him of sowing his wild oats, an insistence that carried a flavor of humor and pride, rather than disdain. Then Patricia Hainsworth spread those rumors about his inability to have children, and—well—perhaps that perpetuated his solitude.

Then Winifred came along, with her college education, her independence, her *commonness*. His infatuation with her sent shock waves through their social circle. It didn't take long for people to start whispering that Winifred had seduced and snared Bruce solely for his money.

Between the collective unease and June's tiredness, June was particularly irritable and critical at the wedding. The valet station was disorganized, causing a pileup that forced them to wait nearly fifteen minutes just to hand over their keys. The flower arrangements were huge and gaudy. The seating made no sense. The menu was atrocious. And Winifred's dress was cut inappropriately low.

But the most insulting incident came after the toasts, when June spotted Harry speaking with Winifred and Bruce on the edge of the dance floor. A woman stood with them, her dark hair pinned up in an elegant French twist. She wore a scarlet dress that accented the sharp slant of her tiny waist.

June was just returning from the powder room, her bladder control irreversibly weakened since Bella. When she arrived beside her husband, Winifred turned toward June and introduced herself.

"I don't think we've met," Winifred said, holding out her hand as if she expected June to shake it.

June simply stared at it, then blinked back up to Winifred. "June Duxbury," she said tightly. "Congratulations on your nuptials."

"*You're* June Duxbury?" Winifred said, glancing at Harry, then the woman in the red dress. "I thought—"

Bruce squeezed her arm, knuckles whitening, and Winifred looked to him, confusion racking her forehead. June glanced around, too, spotting Barbara not far off, openly staring at the scene unfolding.

"My apologies," Winifred said, but there was an obvious bite to her tone. She narrowed her eyes at Harry. "What I saw just now, in the courtyard, wasn't—"

"Winifred, dear," Bruce said, effectively cutting her off. "Why don't we get you another champagne?"

Expertly, Bruce whisked her away—but the damage had been done.

"What did she see?" June asked Harry, already primed for more arguing.

"What do you mean?" Harry asked sharply.

The brunette in the red dress hurried away, her cheeks flushed.

"What happened in the courtyard?" June hissed.

"Nothing. She didn't see a thing."

Even back then, June was privy to Harry's wandering eye. She opened her mouth to argue, but Harry kept talking.

"You're really going to believe *her* over your own husband?"

Someone touched June's back: Victoria. "June, dear, people are staring."

June glanced around, horrified to see that Victoria was correct. Other couples were eyeing them, whispering.

Winifred had baited June into making a scene.

"Of course not," June said, answering Harry's question. "Of course not," she repeated, looping her arm through Harry's, making a show of leaning her head lovingly against his shoulder.

The onlookers went back to their respective conversations.

"That's a handsome tie, Harry," Victoria observed.

"Thank you, Victoria," Harry said.

"Benjamin has been talking about having you two out on the boat," Victoria said.

"Has he, now?" Harry asked, cinching June close as Victoria led them to their table.

June assumed a countenance of pleasant amiability, a familiar mask.

But on the inside, she was seething, stewing, plotting retaliation against Winifred Hurst. Because how dare she attempt to embarrass June Duxbury.

52

June's head snapped forward with such force she thought the world would spin forever, but then everything steadied and came into soft focus again. June had rear-ended a cream-colored convertible. Bella was crying in the back seat, shrieking with fear.

"It's all right," June said to her daughter. "We're not even moving anymore, dear. You're safe, you're safe." But Bella continued to wail, a bruise blooming on her forehead.

June gripped the steering wheel tighter. The world was liquid, rippling like pool water as she surveyed the scene through the windshield. The convertible sat in front of a stop sign. She couldn't see any visible damage. She'd been driving so slowly, after all. Probably too slowly for this road.

"What the hell?" a voice said from beyond June's open window.

June squinted, finally recognizing the street. She'd overshot her own home, driving farther down the beachfront into . . . into Winifred Hurst's neighborhood.

"What the *hell* is wrong with—" The words died on Winifred's tongue when she reached the Cadillac that'd just rear-ended her beloved Pagoda. June—*June Duxbury*—was behind the wheel. Winifred had half a thought to wonder if she'd rammed into the Pagoda on purpose, except for the fact that June's upper lip was sweating and her knuckles were pale. She looked downright ghastly—far from the prim, perfect housewife she usually portrayed—but rage still simmered under Winifred's skin.

"Didn't you see me at the stop sign?"

Still staring straight ahead—presumably at the damage she'd just done—June simply shook her head. Winifred's fury threatened to boil over, but then she studied June and her pinched but vacant expression. It was one of someone in . . . pain. Winifred couldn't see any injuries from the accident—although Bella was whimpering in the back seat, she merely had a goose egg on her forehead—and yet the strain on June's face and slight glassiness of her eyes made her look like a woman in labor.

"Are you all right?"

June blinked up to Winifred's face, recognition finally spreading across her features. Her apparent confusion transformed into hostility in an instant, like the flick of a light switch. She yanked her door open, flung it wide, and stepped out, wobbling slightly, but indignant, with hands on hips. "You were just sitting there!"

Winifred prickled. "And that gives you the right to rear-end me?"

June pushed past her to study the damage. "That's barely a dent," June said, waving her hand. "I can give you the name of Harry's mechanic, if you—" She turned as if to return to her car, but lost her balance, catching herself on the side of the Pagoda.

"Are you drunk?" Winifred asked.

"Of course not," June snapped, but she remained half bent. She silently begged the world to firm up. Winifred—wearing another one of her *horrendous* dresses—couldn't know about the pills or June's fuzzy-headed state.

"If you're not drunk, then—"

"I'm *fine*." But even as the words escaped her, June winced at the dulled edge of pain in her belly. *Home*—she just wanted to get *home*, so she could curl up in bed with Bella and let sleep steal away this awful, watery discomfort. June breathed through her teeth. She knew Winifred was watching her, measuring her, but June refused to be pitied.

Winifred sighed. "Look, you're right, the damage isn't too bad." Her voice was considerate. "Let's pretend it never happened."

The pity stained June's relief, but it was better than Winifred reporting the incident.

"Good," June said primly, though she still sagged over the side of Winifred's convertible. She needed to get a hold of herself. June heaved a breath, girding herself to stand fully upright again, but something on Winifred's passenger seat snagged June's interest: a large envelope.

With her husband's name on the front.

Pushing off the car, June pointed. "What the hell is that?"

Winifred's awful dress fluttered in the breeze as she tracked June's finger. "Oh, the envelope?"

"My husband's name is on it."

"That's none of your business, is it?"

"What's *that* supposed to mean?"

"It means what it means."

"You—"

"If you're curious," Winifred said, speaking over her, "why don't you ask *your husband* about it?"

June pinched her lips, her spine going ramrod straight. "How did you find out?"

"Find out what?" Winifred sounded exasperated.

"About our . . ." June couldn't even say the word out loud, not on the side of the road, not to Winifred.

But Winifred's glance slanted toward June's ringless hand—she'd removed the diamond before Harry had dropped off Bella, in the hopes of appearing strong—and understanding smoothed Winifred's features. June felt as if she'd just handed her enemy a weapon of truth: the knife that would inevitably become lodged in her back.

But Winifred didn't wield it now. She simply said, "Go home, June."

"Fine," June said. "At least my home isn't empty, like yours."

"Excuse me?"

"Oh, wait," June said, pretending to have just stumbled upon the thought. "You have that bohemian mooching off you. I forgot."

"She's not—" Winifred's face flushed, and she cut herself off.

"She *is* mooching off you!" June resisted the urge to cackle. "Who would've thought that killing Bruce with your reckless behavior would result in *you* becoming a pushover?"

"How dare you."

"Oh, I'll *dare* all I like. Everyone's thinking it—I'm just brave enough to say it."

"You're a coward," Winifred said.

"Am I?" June said sweetly, mockingly.

"You know why I have that envelope in my car?" Winifred smirked. "Because your lying, cheating, pig of a husband is *working* with that so-called bohemian. He hired her to illustrate an ad campaign."

June opened her mouth, but nothing came out.

"*And*," Winifred continued, sounding so pleased with herself, "he tried to sleep with her. Multiple times. But unlike you, that bohemian had the sense to stay far away from him."

June got into her DeVille and turned the ignition.

"But wait," Winifred continued, hovering over June's car. "That was years ago, when he *first* hired her! In fact, that might've been around the time that your dear Bella was born." Winifred leaned over June's car door. "Tell me, June, at my wedding. Were you simply blind to Harry's blatant disregard for you? Or were you in denial?"

June saw red. She *burned*, a wildfire catching on dry grass. She shoved her foot on the gas, hot fury raging in her bones, and tires squealed as her bumper crunched into Winifred's.

Winifred leaped backward, a shriek erupting from her chest, shock showing in the whites of her eyes as June put her car in reverse, backed up, then shifted into drive and stomped on the gas pedal again, slamming so hard into Winifred's Pagoda that it lurched beyond the stop sign and into the intersection. Winifred was screaming, her face as red as her atrocious outfit. June backed up again, but Winifred leaped between the two cars, holding up her hands, and for a flash of terrifying desire, June imagined slamming her car into Winifred instead.

But then Bella's terrified mewling permeated June's rage.

At the sound, June forgot all about Harry and Winifred and the cars, her vision tunneling on Bella. Beautiful, perfect Bella, who appeared physically all right but was shaking in her seat.

"What have I done?" June whispered, so softly that only she heard it, her voice reedy with shock and regret.

Sirens swelled in the distance; someone in the neighborhood must've heard the commotion. Winifred stormed up to her window, her hair tousled and voice hoarse as she growled, "You'll pay for this."

But June was ash by then, burned out by her own fury, so frail she might blow away in the breeze.

53

Winifred was still seething when she pulled into her driveway an hour later. She couldn't believe it—that someone like *June Duxbury* would just . . . ram her car. On purpose. With her own child in the back seat.

In her statement to the police, Winifred had explained their argument and how June hit the Pagoda again—but she'd left out June's apparent inebriation. She didn't know why. Something about June's mussed hair and vacant eyes had drawn out Winifred's compassion, she supposed. Such dishevelment was not something June would willingly allow others to witness. June had been in severe pain—Winifred was sure of it.

Considering all the snide remarks and undermining behavior that June had aimed at Winifred over the years, Winifred should've been ruthless as a viper in her charges. But sympathy had softened her strike. June was going through a divorce, after all. Winifred didn't know that particular heartache firsthand, but she knew what it was like to feel alone, and she could practically see the loneliness wrapped around June like a coat. Those fake friends of hers were probably ostracizing her, making her jump through hoops similar to those they'd held up for Winifred. She was intimately familiar with their particular brand of disdain, one that made you feel like you had a chance of doing better next time. One that kept you on the hook.

Probably the only true support June had in her life was her own shame, pride, and force of will; for her to use substances for pain relief wasn't entirely surprising—or damning, in Winifred's opinion. Besides, after easily baiting June into a frenzy, hitting June where Winifred knew it would hurt, a sourness had spread into Winifred's stomach, and she'd realized: she pitied June. Maybe Winifred was foolish, but she just couldn't bring herself to be cruel to someone she pitied. Even her own bully.

But now, as she stood in her driveway staring at the damage to her beloved Pagoda, Winifred overflowed with pity and rage in equal measure, volcanic. A growl rumbled from deep inside her belly, rattling her teeth as it escaped and echoing through the quiet neighborhood.

"Winifred?"

Marie had opened the front door, wearing jeans that were more paint than denim. Her plain white tee was speckled with watery blue splatters and dark-green smudges. "Is something wrong?"

Marie's creased face made the temper inside Winifred hiss and cool. Her heart sputtered. "I'm okay," Winifred said, but her voice sounded hoarse, all steam.

As Marie approached, she spotted the crumpled bumper of the Pagoda and swore. "Oh my—what happened?"

"I'm not sure you'll believe it."

Marie stared up into Winifred's eyes, dipping her head as if to study her more closely. "Are you sure you're okay? You look . . . shaken."

"I suppose I am shaken." Winifred rubbed her face, only to stop abruptly when she realized she was smudging her makeup. "But I'm fine, I—*shit*."

"What?"

"I'm so sorry, Marie. I forgot to mail your illustrations." Winifred buried her face in her hands, this time not caring about her makeup. "After the police left, I just . . . came home." She looked at her watch. "And, *shit*, now it's too late."

Marie's lips thinned. She studied Winifred for a beat too long, but then her brow furrowed. "Police?"

Winifred sighed a shaky breath. "Let's go inside, and I'll explain."

Marie couldn't help but wonder if Winifred had forgotten the errand on purpose—after all, she didn't approve of Marie working with Mr. Duxbury. But as she followed Winifred through the front door, stealing one last glance at the damage to the Pagoda, relief cut through her suspicion.

She didn't like how her pulse thrummed just a little too fast as she wondered what had happened. It was easier to be angry over her missed illustration deadline. She preferred anger over the raw, vulnerable concern of caring about a person and knowing they'd been in danger.

This arrangement between them was supposed to have been transactional. When had Marie lost her emotional distance? She had tried, that first week, to avoid Winifred—but who was she kidding? Marie had been drawn to Winifred since their first encounter. And now . . . well, now she truly cared.

In the kitchen, Winifred poured them each a glass of lemonade and told Marie about the accident, argument, and how June had gone haywire. Gradually, Marie's anger about the illustrations and worry for Winifred dissipated as she wrapped her mind around the complete and utter strangeness of the ordeal. She hardly knew June, but intoxication? Rage? If it weren't for Winifred's sincere—and slightly frazzled—demeanor, plus the proof parked outside, Marie wouldn't have believed any of it.

"Do you think she's hiding a more serious addiction?" Marie asked. Dottie's father had been prone to rage in his drunkenness—but never sweaty and pale, as Winifred had described of June.

"Like what?"

Marie shrugged and finished her lemonade. "I don't know. I suppose it's none of our business, anyhow."

Winifred carried both their empty glasses to the sink. "No, it's not," she agreed.

Marie absentmindedly rubbed at a speckle of paint on her arm.

"You've been painting," Winifred observed.

Marie glanced up. "It's nothing." As soon as the words left her mouth, she realized they were the same ones she'd uttered to Irene.

You're just like Winifred, Irene had said. *You both sell yourselves short.*

"Nothing, huh?" Winifred leaned a hip against the counter, her arms crossed. "Must've been a productive afternoon, for you to undersell yourself like that."

Marie should've been irritated by how easily Winifred saw through her lie, but instead, the familiarity warmed her chest. Just a little. Just enough.

"Can I see?" Winifred asked.

"I—" Marie thought of a million ways to say no, but none of them escaped her lips.

Against her better judgment—in defiance of her shyness and grief and fear—Marie *wanted* to show Winifred. She valued Winifred's opinion, but more importantly, she valued the encouragement. If it weren't for Winifred, Marie wouldn't have dared to paint the Thoroughbred. And she had a startling hunch that the painting was good.

"Sure," Marie said. "Yes, you can see."

Winifred tried not to express her excitement as she followed Marie upstairs. She could tell by Marie's slow, heavy steps that whatever currently resided on her easel, it mattered a great deal.

Outside the door, Marie paused and faced Winifred, her arms lifting defensively, as if guarding the entrance. "The painting isn't done," she said. "It's rough."

"All right," Winifred said.

"I'm trying something new, and I'm not sure it works."

"That's great; new is great."

Marie shifted nervously on her feet. "Just—"

"Marie, do you want me to wait to see it?" Winifred asked.

Marie lowered her arms. "Well—no, it's fine. I—I'd like your opinion."

"Well, all right," Winifred said, charmed by Marie's admission. She reached for the door handle.

Marie wavered, then stepped aside, allowing Winifred to walk through ahead of her. Winifred's eyes immediately found the painting—and how could they not? It stood in the middle of the room on the lone easel. Afternoon light zinged through the windows like a natural spotlight.

Winifred approached slowly, astonished by the textures and details. How Marie had managed to capture the curious innocence and dangerous wild of the Thoroughbred, Winifred had no idea. The dichotomy was unexpected, and yet more honest than anything she'd seen before. Art these days might have been leaning toward abstracts, but this—this transcended trends. Marie had done it. This was the breakthrough Winifred had been certain Marie could achieve.

It was a masterpiece. A marvel.

Whatever Marie had been missing amid her creative funk, she'd found it. Winifred had no idea what Marie had done differently, but—

"You hate it," Marie said, coming up beside her. "I knew it."

Winifred blinked, tearing her gaze away from the painting to meet Marie's pinched, pained expression. "I—what?"

"You look horrified."

Winifred laughed, which only made Marie frown harder. "I'm sorry, I shouldn't laugh, I just—"

"It's okay, you can tell me the truth."

Winifred placed a hand on Marie's upper arm. "Marie, I'm in awe," Winifred said. "I'm, well, I'm speechless."

Marie pivoted her shoulders so that they were no longer square with Winifred's, as if to study Winifred at a different angle. "What are you saying?"

"I'm saying it's a masterpiece."

They both faced the painting again, standing side by side as they'd done so many months before with the O'Keeffe.

"You really think so?"

"Yes," Winifred said. "I think it's the start of a new collection."

Marie stiffened in Winifred's periphery. "I don't know if this is something I can . . . recreate."

"Of course it is," Winifred said. "If you did it once, you can do it again."

Of course, Winifred didn't know the emotional torment Marie had undergone to tap into the energy now captured in this painting.

"You just want to get rid of me," Marie joked.

On the surface, the sentence was innocent enough. But like all self-deprecating humor, there was a kernel of fear behind it, a serious question, a testing of the water. Marie's words were like stones tossed in a lake, sending ripples. And somewhere in the weeds of Winifred's mind, those ripples were a disturbance.

Winifred turned away from the painting to look at Marie, using the action as a chance to settle her emotions. "How do you mean?" she asked, working to keep her tone light.

"A successful collection would be enough for me to . . . ," Marie trailed off, her words dying on the vine.

Enough for Marie to buy the track.

Enough for Marie to *leave*.

Winifred had thought that a taste of success would compel Marie to abandon the idea of the track—but she had been wrong. Winifred's encouragement had only empowered Marie toward her outlandish goal—and *away* from Winifred. That was clear now.

After all the time they'd spent together, Marie still wanted to leave. And by supporting Marie, Winifred had orchestrated that loss.

An odd, covetous sort of panic gripped Winifred's throat. She was not ready for Marie to leave; she was not ready for Marie to throw her life away on some senseless pipe dream. She was not ready to be alone all over again, a widow in double. First by the death of her husband; second by the death of this friendship.

She wouldn't let that happen. She *couldn't*.

But what *could* she do? Winifred wasn't sure. She needed time to think. And in the meantime, she needed *people*. Lots of them. Noise was the perfect solution to her impending solitude.

Winifred clapped her hands together. "We should celebrate your breakthrough," she said to Marie. "We'll throw another party. Invite all the usual suspects."

Marie's lips twisted. "You just want to throw another party."

"Perhaps. But your success is the perfect excuse."

54

Winifred stared at the ceiling, the night's shadows catching in the creases of the molding that lined the upper walls of the bedroom.

In her mind's eye, Marie's future played out like a movie. More paintings would turn into a full collection. The collection would make it into a prominent gallery. On opening night, critics would come and offer their acclaim. Headlines would state that the great, mysterious D was back. And private collectors from all corners of New England would flock to Marie and fund her silly dream.

The worst of it was that Winifred wanted all the creative success in the world for Marie. With a passion and talent like hers, she deserved creative success. Who was Winifred to wish ill on that? It was in her very nature to want to support artists like Marie—Winifred found joy and fulfillment in the act. The charity of her wealth and encouragement.

But, she realized now, there would be no convincing Marie out of purchasing Hurley Downs. It had been naive of Winifred to think otherwise. Marie already knew how impractical it was, how *pointless*. Winifred had once thought that such pointlessness would eventually sway Marie into a different decision, but no—the impracticality wasn't a crack in Marie's foundation; it was a sign of the strength of her resolve. Reason was no argument for emotion.

Winifred had overheard multiple phone calls between Marie and her brother, the arguments. Marie had spent years and years working toward her goal. And Winifred—with her parties and dinners and shopping sprees—couldn't compete with that.

It was stupid of Winifred to have ever harbored such hope. She didn't want to end up like June Duxbury, near-manic from exile. She didn't want to return to her father's home, defeated. She didn't want to let go of this house, this last relic of her love for Bruce. She didn't want to be abandoned. She didn't want to be alone.

Winifred retraced familiar shadows along the seams of the ceiling. As she did so, it occurred to Winifred that Marie's down payment probably hinged not only on the sales from a new fine art collection but also on her patron income. Income that *Winifred* supplied.

Income that Winifred had the power to take away.

At first, the thought scared Winifred, like finding a gun in an old desk drawer.

Winifred knew she had no right to control Marie's life. She couldn't make that decision for Marie, couldn't steal the opportunity.

But it was *her* foundation. Her donations were meant to support artists in their artistic pursuits, not to help them make bad investments that had nothing to do with their careers. If anything, cutting Marie off could *help* her—force her to refocus on what mattered: not a pipe dream but her art. Her talent. Her potential.

Winifred told herself she'd sleep on it and make the decision in the morning, when she was fresh. She told herself she'd take time to reflect.

But the truth was that Winifred had already picked up the gun. Hesitating on the trigger would only soothe her conscience, not change her mind.

55

June nudged the hot-water tap with her foot, moving only the bare minimum in order to reheat her bathwater. The tub steamed, warmth permeating her aching muscles. She lowered her leg and sank down until the waterline slid along her lower lip.

Her special week with Bella had been a disaster. Her daughter had spent more time with the nanny than with June. When she wasn't half-bedridden with pain, June had taken her car to the mechanic and paid a visit to the police station. Chief McCurdy knew June's father and had immediately dismissed her incident with Winifred as a fluke, but since Winifred had pressed charges, June had needed to write a check for the fine. As McCurdy munched on one of June's homemade cookies and guided her out of his office, she'd smiled up at him and thanked him for his discretion.

After her errands, June tried to push through her head-spinning discomfort to play with her daughter, but at best, she was only half-there, caught up weathering the tempest in her belly. When, yesterday afternoon, Bella had begun to emulate June's deep, rhythmic breathing, June's sense of failure had been a high whistle announcing the runaway train of her life.

What did it mean to be a good mother? What did a clean kitchen matter if she was in too much pain to play with her daughter? If her husband didn't love her anymore? June used to have a clear sense of it, like a page in an old magazine, but now the gloss had worn off.

A crusade against traditional families was sweeping the nation, and June was determined to uphold the foundation upon which her own sunny childhood had been built—but even when she was a girl, she could see the cracks in that foundation. The arguments her parents had when they thought she was asleep. The outbursts of frustration. The stained dresses. How much of it was real? How many women—her grandmothers, her mother, her peers—were merely pretending for the sake of propriety? For the sake of men?

Such thoughts scared her.

June straightened her legs, sliding her shoulders out of the water, steam rising all around. She had cookies in the oven; Bella would wake from her afternoon nap soon; Harry was due to pick her up in an hour. June had eschewed her painkillers again—nothing good happened when she took them—so she'd done her best to uncoil her muscles with the hottest bath she could stand. The radiating pain in her hips and low back had dissipated, but it always diminished by the end of her cycle. Of course her relief would coincide with the day Bella went back to her father.

June sighed, her chest deflating. She wasn't sure exactly what'd gotten into her that day with Winifred; after the pain, disappointment, and humiliation, she'd felt more animal than person. All week, she'd been reliving the incident, the memory at turns frightening and confusing. Her anger had been primal, as if she'd been backed into a corner and had no choice but to snap her teeth.

That rage, that anger, that uncontrollable emotion—was that the real June? How much of who she was came down to training? Was it possible that the June who'd rammed Winifred's car was her true self?

June sat forward and unplugged the tub drain, then stood up before her thoughts could spiral with the bathwater.

It was a pain-induced outburst, nothing more. June was under a lot of pressure. The SPW fundraiser was next month, and as the new head of the organization, it was up to June to ensure the event was a success. It was a lot to manage. Harry's behavior had added an undercurrent of distress and frustration to her already hectic responsibilities. That was all.

After toweling off, June removed her shower cap and restyled her hair. She was fully dressed and applying makeup when she heard a shriek downstairs. June dropped the tube of lipstick without finishing her bottom lip and raced into the kitchen.

Bella stood in the doorway and was bouncing on her feet, pointing. June pushed past her daughter and saw that the oven was smoking, gray plumes escaping from the seams in the door.

The cookies.

"*Shit*," June said, rushing forward. "Stay back, Bella."

June opened the oven, and a huge burst of burnt-cookie smoke wafted out, making her cough.

"No, no, no," she whispered and yanked the kitchen window open. She snatched a dish towel off the counter and waved it, trying to disperse the smoke. When she could see inside the oven, she used the dish towel to grab the smoldering cookie sheet and dropped it into the sink. She turned on the tap, and the hot metal hissed.

"June?" Harry's voice carried from the foyer, echoing off the high ceilings.

Bella ran toward her father's voice, and June slammed the oven shut, racing toward the back door to allow more fresh air into the kitchen. She swung the door open and shut, fanning the smoke outside.

Harry strode into the room, Bella on his hip. "What the hell is going on?"

June let go of the doorknob with the door still agape. "I was baking cookies, and they caught fire," she said.

Harry's lips pinched. "Are you kidding?"

"It happens," June said, smoothing her dress. "No harm done."

"Did you forget I was coming?"

"Of course not," June said, taking one step toward him. "Bella's bag is packed. It's upstairs."

Harry bounced Bella in his arms, shifting her weight. With his free hand, he wiped his face. June tracked the movement, his ringless finger, and regretted putting her own wedding ring back on.

"How was your week?" Harry asked tightly, not moving.

"We had a wonderful time," June replied.

"Chief McCurdy called me," Harry said, and June's stomach shriveled. "He said you got into an accident."

"We did, but we're both fine, thank goodness."

"Yes, thank goodness," Harry said, setting Bella down. Once her little white shoes were firmly planted on the kitchen tile, Harry strode forward, stopping a foot away from June. She backed up slightly, her rear bumping into the still-open door.

"Thank goodness you were there to put our daughter in danger," Harry growled. "Thank goodness you *rammed Winifred Hurst's car.* Thank goodness you baked cookies to smooth over your *mess.* I hope the chief's weren't as burnt as those," Harry added, gesturing at the still-smoking pan in the sink.

Harry peered into June's eyes, as if trying to spot something that wasn't there. "What's happening to you?"

"Nothing's *happening*," June said, pushing past him so he wouldn't see the sudden sheen in her eyes. She bent down in front of Bella and tucked a strand of hair behind her daughter's ear. "Why don't you get your things, dear?"

When Bella had run along, June straightened and faced her husband again. "It was a minor accident. Winifred blew it out of proportion. You know how she is."

Harry laughed a single disbelieving huff. "This string of odd behavior is only making me more certain about a divorce. You're unfit." He turned, tracing Bella's path toward the front hall.

June glanced toward the window, catching a glimpse of herself in the reflective glass. Her hair was frizzy; in the chaos, she'd only applied lipstick to her top lip. She looked like a clown, a caricature. Her cheeks heated into a rosy red that only worsened her appearance.

Wiping her lips on the dish towel, June stormed after Harry. He was in the foyer again, affixing a sun hat over Bella's curls while she sat on her tiny suitcase.

Whatever June had been about to say to Harry died under the crushing weight inside her chest. Her daughter would grow up in a broken home—it had already begun—and there was nothing June could do to fix it. The family she'd longed for was over. She could only watch as the world around her crumpled like paper.

Harry pinched Bella's cheek, eliciting a giggle. Then he stood, hefting her luggage in one hand and grasping Bella's tiny palm in the other.

"Every day, it's something new with you," Harry said to June. "I fear for Bella's safety—"

"Harry," June went to protest, but he spoke over her.

"I've decided I want custody. It's clear that Evelyn and I can provide a far more stable environment than you can on your own."

His words hit with a locomotive force. She blinked, breathless, seeing stars. "Harry. You can't . . . *replace* me. I'm her *mother.*"

"Bella needs stability." Harry led Bella out into the sunshine and toward his car.

June followed, hovering over him as he loaded Bella's things into the trunk and settled Bella in the back seat. When he was out of the way, she bent, kissing her daughter's cheeks, her hair. "I love you, Bella-Boo," she whispered.

Harry sank into the driver's seat and slammed the door.

"I won't let you take everything from me," she said to her husband.

He dangled his hand out the open window, his gold watch glinting in the sun. A new watch. "I have a strong case against you, June. Stronger now, after your car *accident*. Don't fight it. Just take the deal my lawyers draw up and be grateful that our daughter will grow up in a safe home." He started the car. "Take the deal, June," he repeated over the rumble of the engine, and then he was driving down the quiet road, taking June's baby away from her.

June hung her head and noticed that she was still wearing her house slippers. She rested her hand over her mouth, refusing to break down. This was just a hiccup, a misunderstanding, a mistake. Harry was wrong. He was the one at fault.

Blinking rapidly, June scurried back up her porch steps and inside. She needed to call her lawyer.

56

Winifred's self-reproach was akin to walking on shattered glass. Every step emitted a crack, a crunch, a new cut.

The day after the accident with June, Winifred had called her father. "What is one's moral obligation to a friend," she'd asked, "if that friend is doing something that is clearly to their disadvantage? Is it right to intervene?"

"I'd think not," her father had said carefully.

"Never?"

"Consider Aristotle's *Ethics*: friendship is a state of character."

She could always count on him to quote men who'd been dead for centuries.

"Friendship requires respect," he went on. "A friend might disagree, or offer an opinion, but in the end, you have to let the other person make their own decisions."

"But isn't life more complicated than that?"

He'd chuckled softly.

Winifred was not convinced. Not by her father, not by Aristotle. What did these men know about fine art, racetracks, or—hell—friendships between women?

And so she'd done it: she'd called the Iris Gallery and informed the curator, Petra, that she was pulling her funding from D. *I'm surprised you held out as long as you did,* Petra had commented. *As much as I hate to say it, I fear that she's officially old news.* After the call, as Winifred slipped out of Bruce's office, she'd run into Marie in the hall. Profound pity and guilt had coursed through Winifred like a geyser; she'd had to bury her face in her hands and scurry off to a bathroom to pull herself together.

Now, four days later, Winifred wondered if losing Marie to Pennsylvania would've been less painful than hurting her friend on purpose. But Winifred knew, deep down, that beyond the pain of losing the track, Marie would eventually thrive. If it kept Marie living here longer, working in her studio and filling Winifred's upstairs hallway with the smell of paint, building a catalog of more horse paintings, well, clearly it was for the best. Winifred only hoped that when Marie received the call from the gallery, she'd be able to spot the silver lining.

Winifred busied herself with the early stages of another just-because party, trying to tune out her own loud guilt. While some might say that the first hour of a shindig is dull compared to hours in, Winifred begged to differ. There was an unspoken energy among the first guests, a reluctant hopefulness. As sobriety dwindled, people would become more bold—but early on, timidness ruled. People made awkward introductions and fixed each other drinks and broke the ice with menial setup tasks, and the rooms of Winifred's house hummed with possibility. It reminded her of her wedding day, right before walking down the aisle: that peak of excitement, of stopped time, the moment just before losing yourself in an experience. It was the stuff memories were made of: anticipation.

"Hey, Winifred, where should we put this?"

She pivoted to see Lawrence and another man wrestling with a keg. "Outside, please. Last time we set it up in the kitchen, my floor was sticky for days afterward."

Lawrence flashed a smile before the two of them grunted their way out onto the porch.

Winifred lazily followed, squinting when the sun hit her face. She lifted a hand to shadow her eyes and surveyed the yard. Two separate rock bands were setting up their instruments beside the pool, running extension cords through a nearby window.

A girl in cutoff shorts halted by the pair of drummers and gestured at the pool. "Hey, what gives? Why is the pool empty?"

Their shrugs turned to winces as one of the amps came to life with a shriek.

"I finally remember to wear my bathing suit, and the damn pool's drained."

Winifred was about to walk over and explain that the pool had been drained because some broken glass from a previous party had caused a problem with the mechanism—but then Opal approached the girl and handed her a cup. "You'll have to drown in booze instead."

Winifred lowered her hand from her face and retreated inside.

She was mixing a third pitcher of spiked lemonade when Irene came into the kitchen, her arms stacked with casserole plates. Glad for a new distraction, Winifred sprang to her aid, taking half the load and setting the dishes on the counter.

"Wow. What would I do without you, Irene?" Winifred asked.

"Starve," Irene said with a grin, but as she removed the Handi-Wrap from the first dish, her brows pinched. "I saw Marie in the hall. Is she all right?"

"What do you mean?" Winifred asked.

"She was crying. Ran upstairs."

"Did she say why?"

"No, but I think she'd been on the phone."

Winifred pressed her lips together. Of all the days for Petra to call. "I'll go check on her."

Winifred wiped her hands on her apron as she wove through the thickening crowd of partygoers. Every movement felt like another slice against her skin. By the time she made it to Marie's studio door, she felt shredded. She could hear Marie's soft whimpers coming from inside, and it was all Winifred's fault. She'd done this. How could she comfort Marie knowing she had caused her pain?

Winifred rolled her shoulders back, forcing the doubt from her thoughts. The trigger had been pulled. Now, she needed to make Marie see how this could be a good thing.

Winifred opened the door and stepped inside, momentarily overwhelmed by the scent of paint thinner that assaulted the backs of her nostrils. Marie was slumped in the lone armchair in the corner, her face buried in her hands, shoulders shuddering. When Winifred closed the door with a click, Marie looked up, her cheeks splotched with red. Her eyes shimmered.

Winifred winced. What if Aristotle had been right? After all, there was a reason people still remembered his name.

"Irene said . . . ," Winifred trailed off. Her guilt was a chant inside her skull. *You did this. You did this.*

Marie's face crumpled, lips pursing into a pitiful frown. Devastated.

Winifred forced herself to take a step forward, then another. She deserved to walk on glass. She deserved all the guilt in the world for doing this to Marie. But wallowing wouldn't help either of them; they both needed to focus on what was ahead.

Winifred crouched in front of Marie's chair and grasped her hand. It was cool and damp from wiping at her tears. "Tell me what happened."

Marie sniffled. "My brother, James, called."

Winifred hadn't expected that.

"The other day, when you got in the accident. He called and said the track is officially on the market." A shudder. "And then, just now"—her voice went high—"my last remaining patron dropped me. Three payments before I could . . ."

"Oh." It was all Winifred could force out of her constricting lungs.

"I was so close, Winifred," she said, meeting Winifred's eyes.

The tears made the amber in Marie's brown irises glitter like gold. Winifred couldn't stand it. She looked down at their tangled hands.

"What am I going to do now? I'm at least a thousand dollars short of the bare minimum."

This is your chance, Winifred told herself. It was time to remind Marie of who she was destined to be.

"Marie, dear, all is not lost," Winifred said, catching those red-rimmed eyes and holding them.

"All *is* lost, though. I've been working toward this for *years*, Winifred. Practically my whole life, it seems"—a hiccup—"all those sacrifices—only to come up short."

Winifred bit her lip. "But try to see the silver lining," she said. "You just made a major breakthrough. You're right on the precipice of a grand collection. You have a roof over your head, a studio, a—a friend who will let you stay as long as you like." Winifred smiled. "It'll be okay."

Marie stared at her, lip trembling. Then she exploded out of her chair. "You don't get it," she said, pacing back and forth in big clomping strides. "You don't get it, Winifred. You never have. You've been against me buying the track this whole time, so of course you don't think anything of this setback." Marie spun to face her, pounding her chest. "But I've just lost my dream, and—and you want me to see the silver lining?"

Winifred rose to her feet. "That's not what I'm—"

"*Why* does no one respect my decision?" Marie ran her hands along her scalp and tugged at her already-tangled hair. "Not you, not James, nobody . . . ," she trailed off, dropping her hands.

Winifred approached, daring to place her palms on Marie's upper arms. "I can't speak for your brother, but Marie, I respect you."

"No, you don't." Marie yanked herself out of Winifred's hold. She spun, pointing at a half-finished painting on the easel: a horse with a curved neck, tucked chin, and one foreleg striking out. "You respect *this*," she said. "My talent. Not *me*. If you respected me, you'd respect my decision to buy the track."

"That's not true," Winifred said, and suddenly she felt as if she was arguing with her father as much as she was arguing with Marie. "I can respect you as a person without condoning a stupid decision. And, yes"—she held up a hand, stopping Marie from interrupting—"I think it's stupid."

"How dare you pass judgment on me," Marie said, seething. "You hardly know anything about me."

"It's a waste of money, Marie. A pipe dream. *Pointless.* Don't you see? Your patron did you a kindness." Guilty as she felt, Winifred believed that wholeheartedly.

Marie shook her head, her brow and lips scrunching closer together as she seemed to will herself not to cry.

"Listen." Winifred approached again, but this time didn't reach out to touch her. "I know it hurts. I know you're upset. I'm just saying . . . try to see the upside. You're free of the track. You don't need to concern yourself with it anymore."

Marie opened her eyes and fixed Winifred with a surprisingly level stare. "But I'm not free of it," she said. "I'll never be free of it." She crumpled forward, then, right into Winifred's arms.

Winifred caught Marie, practically holding her up as the dam broke, as she sobbed and sobbed.

One thousand dollars. Winifred could fix this for Marie, and the bottomless well that was Bruce's fortune, her inheritance, would be unaffected. But as she ran a hand along Marie's shuddering back, she knew she wouldn't do it. She *couldn't.* It wasn't fair of Winifred to make this decision for Marie, but she was the only person who could. The track wasn't a dream for Marie—it was a nightmare she wanted to destroy. But Winifred knew, deep in her bones, that if Marie got what she wanted, she wouldn't feel any better. *That* was the true tragedy.

Either Marie would be disappointed now, or she would be haunted later. Ultimately, that's how Winifred justified her actions. Maybe this made her a terrible person, but if it meant saving Marie from herself, then so be it. Winifred was cutting Marie loose. With time, Marie would look around and realize what a gift that was.

57

Hours later, after Winifred had gone downstairs and the sun had set and the party had grown incredibly loud, Marie still lingered in her studio. From the window, she could see the yard filled with people and hear the electric guitars wailing, the empty pool catching the sound and scattering it up into the boughs of the trees and the eaves of the house. The drums pounded through Marie's skull like a headache, rattling her fragile, tear-swollen sinuses.

She closed her eyes, tears seeping out to wet her lashes. On the backs of her eyelids, she saw the crowds at Hurley Downs, the line of cars clogging the driveway on racing day. She heard the cheers, the announcer on the loudspeaker, and the earth rumbling under the Thoroughbreds' hooves. When she breathed in, she didn't smell paint—instead, she caught the familiar whiff of her father and the workday he brought home on his skin every night: sweat salt and tangy engine grease and the earthy sweetness of manure. She could feel the squish of Susquehanna sediment between her bare toes and the clammy leather of a toad's skin cupped inside her palms. She could hear Dottie's lilting laugh, a high melody over the rhythmic chortles of their brothers.

Sometimes Marie wondered if she'd imagined the worst parts, like how shadows in the twilight woods could take the shape of monsters but only out of the corner of an eye. Back then, when she faced what haunted her periphery, it was always nothing: a funny-shaped log, or James hiding behind a rock.

But the bad memories—those only grew more grotesque with observation: the black eye that Dottie's dad gave her eldest brother, Adam, the collective gasp of the racing day crowd when a horse inexplicably went down, or the painting kit Marie's mother placed in front of her after she went six weeks without speaking.

And that day in the Thoroughbred's stall: the way Marie's heart became lodged in her throat when the horse struck out with his powerful front leg, and the acidic taste of bile in Marie's mouth as she watched Dottie dodge the blow. Even at ten, the horror of what could have been had rattled Marie's bones.

She and Dottie darted out of the stables and around the back of the building. Out in the harsh daylight, Marie's heart still strangled her airway. She saw a smudge on Dottie's cheek from where the Thoroughbred had licked her face. A strand of straw was tangled up in Dottie's hair, but Marie was panting too hard—hands on knees, heaving with the horror of what could have been—to reach over and pluck it from her friend's curls.

"That was close," Dottie said, but she was grinning, as if her own mortality wasn't a nightmare but a thrill. "Are you all right, Marie?"

Marie nodded, still gasping. "You could've died, Dot."

She only stuck her tongue out. "Last one back to your house is a rotten egg!"

Dottie took off running, but Marie didn't move. Her hands were still shaking, so persistently that she wondered if they would ever stop.

It's not like she hadn't been afraid before. She remembered the tingly rush she'd felt the first time she dropped off the rope swing into the river. Or the time James had hidden under her bed and grabbed her ankle, and she'd involuntarily shrieked so loud her mother had burst into their room, bleary eyed, to make sure both kids still had all their fingers and toes. Or when she'd been playing in the hay barn and had fallen into the crack between bales; she'd had to wait in the cramped, scratchy darkness for her father to move half the stack just to reach her hand to lift her out.

Marie had been scared many times but never like when she saw Dottie almost get trampled to death by a giant. Marie hadn't known it was possible to be so frightened—the tingling numbness, the lack of muscle control—but of course, it wasn't long after that day that Marie experienced an all-new sort of terror, the worst terror of her life: watching her friend waste away while Marie remained trapped between hindsight and the inevitable.

She'd wanted to bury that terror, just as that terror had buried her heart. Bury it all.

But now, in her studio, Marie felt herself giving in and giving up on ever defeating the legacy of Hurley Downs.

She reached out and touched the semidry canvas propped on her easel. She still needed to finish shading the sinuous tendons of the horse's outstretched leg, but what was the point? Without the track's promise of closure, she could paint thousands of horses and never find relief.

Marie glanced out the window again. Down below, dark shapes danced in the yard. The moon glinted off the liquid in their cups, little round glimmers like mirrors in the night.

Marie could use a drink.

She peeled herself away from the window and out of her studio, locking the door behind her as if that would keep the memories contained. She rushed through the house, downing a finger of whiskey from the decanter in the parlor, then pushing through the crowd in the kitchen to refill her cup with vodka from the cupboard, and finally tumbling out onto the porch to breathe in the smoke that wafted from the yard.

She spotted Lawrence standing by the empty pool, chatting with another man that Marie didn't look at long enough to know whether she recognized or not. She stormed up to Lawrence with the confidence of someone with nothing left to hope for, no dreams left to dream beyond her most basic wants and needs. Without so much as a pause, Marie reached out and grasped Lawrence's pink silk shirt and pulled him into a kiss. The man he'd been talking to stopped midsentence and let out a low whistle. Marie barely gave Lawrence a chance to breathe before she was yanking him along, back upstairs.

58

Winifred and Marie threw seven parties over the next four weeks, with every party more outrageous than the last.

One party ended early after a man broke his clavicle jumping from the roof into the (freshly filled) pool; another was busted up when Winifred's neighbors looked out their bedroom window to see a trio having sex on the lawn, and promptly called the police. Someone brought a pony to one party; a llama to another. At the mid-August two-day party, a group of theater actors painted their bodies in glittery gold paint and put on absurd improvisational skits. The following week, one of the actors invited a French circus performer, who hung from aerial silks out an upstairs window and contorted herself into impossible shapes for two hours straight.

They received so many complaints from neighbors that they unplugged the phone. Angry notes were left on windshields, letters from lawyers delivered; someone tacked the ephemera up on the wall in the foyer like a bulletin board of debauchery. Police were called, and sometimes they were sweet-talked, but other times the party broke up.

None of it mattered. Winifred and Marie drifted through the crowds in a half daze, consumed by their woes.

Winifred—racked with regret over Marie's unhappiness—tried to numb her guilt by losing herself in her role as host. If someone's cup waned, Winifred was there with a pitcher or bottle. If they ran out of quiches, Winifred ordered takeout. If a French circus artist needed a better anchor for her aerial silks, Winifred hung out an upstairs window to drape the fabric around the chimney.

Without Marie as a cleaning partner, Winifred was unable to keep up with the mess; she hired house cleaners to erase the damage and slept all day to the sound of their scrubbing. The less she could think about how she'd ruined her friend's dreams, the better. It didn't matter if she thought she'd done the right thing—she'd hurt Marie, and now Marie wasn't even painting. The only way for Winifred to escape the blame that consumed her thoughts was to immerse herself in the chaos.

While Winifred darted from room to room, Marie distracted herself from her disappointment by drinking and smoking out on the lawn. The other party guests were a spectacle, like a strange play; Marie was just a part of the audience, sequestered in the shadows, participating only when someone spoke to her directly. When she grew bored of the absurdity, she sought out Lawrence, and they ducked into an empty room to be alone—her bedroom, a bathroom, and once, a closet.

Whether a party or hangover was raging, her studio was one room Marie did not enter. She hadn't responded to any more illustration assignments, nor had she picked up a brush. What was the point of working when the track was out of reach? It hadn't sold yet, but she knew it was only a matter of time. It might've been derelict, but land like that was valuable in and of itself.

But after the party guests went home, and the blood and vomit were hosed off the pool tiles, and it was just Winifred and Marie in that big lonesome house, and all Marie wanted to do was sleep it off—she couldn't. Without a creative outlet to dispel her grief, true rest was impossible.

On the second day of September, Marie was hovering on the edge of sleep in a sweat-drenched tangle of sheets, fighting a nightmare. She tasted sickness on her tongue, sour as death. Memories flashed like lightning.

Dottie in a horse stall.

Dottie in a hospital gown.

Dottie in a black box in a hole in the ground.

Marie's eyes flew open. She wrenched her clammy limbs free of the blankets, practically stumbling out of bed. She blinked, getting her bearings. The taste in her mouth wasn't death—just a hangover.

Marie clutched the front of her head and stumbled over to the window. She wrenched it open, and the fresh air that swept inside her bedroom cleared away the fog of her fitful sleep.

Every night for the past month had been like this. Sometimes the dreams were so realistic it was like living it all over again. When she awoke—every time—she had the urge to paint.

This very moment, she could feel the temptation tingling in her fingers, hear the squirt of paint out of a tube, feel the texture of the canvas through the handle of her brush. Ever since her mother had bought Marie that first set of painting supplies, the act had been an outlet, a mode through which Marie could take her sorrow and put it to use.

Marie hadn't picked up a brush in weeks. She knew that painting could often ease the intensity of her nightmares but only because painting was a waking dream, a lucid nightmare, more vivid than her subconscious could ever produce in sleep. Painting the *Girl* collection had been a tour through her memories of Dot, a therapeutic reminder of all Marie had loved. Yet after the collection dropped, her artwork had slowly begun to feel . . . false. Built on memory, yes, but a rose-colored, watered-down, cloying version of reality that wasn't actually *real*.

And now, the Thoroughbreds . . . well, so far, all she thought of when she painted them were the things she didn't want to think about.

Marie placed her hands on the windowsill and hung her head. Without the track, Marie's future was a wide-open field, stretching into a distant horizon. The thought was not a comfort. She was an aimless field mouse, vulnerable to hawks and ermines and plowing tractors. She was no longer heading somewhere, and that made her feel all the more exposed in the endless swaying grasses of existence. Without something to run toward, the grief would eventually snatch her up. Then what?

Marie released her grip on the windowsill and raked her fingers through her tangled hair. She glanced down, realizing she'd fallen asleep in her clothes again; she still wore corduroy trousers and an old T-shirt.

Without bothering to change, she stumbled downstairs and into the dining room.

Winifred was seated in her usual spot, wiggling a pen between her fingers. A pad of paper rested beside her coffee, which emanated a steady tendril of steam. Her hair was a red halo of chaos around her crown, but her eyes were bright.

Marie retrieved her own mug of coffee. "Morning," she croaked, surprised by how hoarse her voice was. She sank into the chair beside Winifred's—but not before removing a used napkin and a single shoe from the seat. "Whose shoe is this?"

Winifred shrugged. "Pool cleaners come at ten o'clock today."

Marie slurped her coffee.

"Last night was fun," Winifred said.

"Was it?" Marie asked. "I feel like I got pushed out of a moving train."

Winifred chuckled.

As host, Winifred never partied as hard as Marie did. Some nights, Marie didn't even see Winifred with a drink. This morning, her eyes were a little bloodshot, but otherwise, her sunny demeanor was fully intact.

"I've decided to throw an end-of-summer bash," Winifred said, gesturing at her pad of paper. "Just shy of three weeks from today, the last official day of summer."

"Isn't that the same night as June's fundraising thing?"

Winifred lifted a shoulder. "So what if it is?"

Winifred had gotten the invitation a few days ago—a taunt, if she ever saw one. She hadn't heard from the SPW since that night she quit the committee. They'd excluded her from everything, and *now* she was invited? No, Winifred refused to give them the satisfaction of crawling back to them. It was insulting that they even thought she would. She'd already decided to donate to the silent auction—an excellent contribution, just to spite June—but there was no way she'd attend.

"I want this party to be our best yet," Winifred added, drawing a little star next to the header at the top of her lined page, *End-of-Summer Bash*.

Last year, she and Bruce had thrown their summer party with the hope that it would become a new tradition—now it would.

"I'm thinking of hiring some performers this time," Winifred continued, tapping her pen on the pad of paper. "What did you think of the performers at last week's party?"

"They were great," Marie said absently, still staring into her coffee.

"What about Giselle, with the silks?"

"Also great."

"And maybe one of Irene's quiches could play the guitar."

"Sure."

"Marie," Winifred said.

She lifted her head. "What?"

"You're not listening, are you?"

Marie blinked. "I'm sorry. I didn't sleep well."

"Again?"

Marie nodded at her mug.

Winifred frowned and glanced down at her bulleted list of party ideas. She'd expected Marie to be upset for a while, but it'd been a full month now, and still Marie hadn't shaken off her funk. Winifred hadn't scented paint thinner, or seen any new splotches of color on Marie's clothes, since Petra had called.

"Marie," Winifred said, "why haven't you been painting?"

A flash of shock widened her eyes. "How do you know I haven't?"

"Come on," Winifred said. "We've been living together all summer; you don't think I know when you're not painting?" When Marie didn't respond, Winifred enunciated, "Why haven't you picked up a brush?"

"What's the point?"

"You seem pretty miserable. I think that's the point."

"I'm not miserable." But even she didn't appear convinced. She sipped her coffee, avoiding Winifred's gaze.

"Look, I know you're disappointed about the track—"

"*Disappointed?* I'm . . ." She shook her head, not finishing her thought.

"Devastated? Heartbroken? Sad?" Winifred pressed.

"Congratulations on noticing."

"I'm *worried*, Marie," Winifred said, feeling that cut-glass guilt slicing at her heart again. "You've been in a funk all month, getting high out of your mind and sleeping all day long."

"Oh, you're one to talk," Marie shot back. "Some days you sleep even later than I do."

"I'm *tired*. From hosting."

"And why *have* you been hosting so many parties, Winifred?"

"To try and cheer *you* up," Winifred said, even as her face heated. Guilt parties, that's what they were. But she couldn't admit to that.

It's for the best, she told herself for the millionth time. Winifred's job, now, was to help Marie see that. "Obviously, partying isn't helping you face your disappointment," she added. "In fact, I think you're avoiding it—and that's why you've avoided painting too."

"So what?"

"You're wasting your potential."

Marie pulled a face. "Why do you *care* about my potential?"

Winifred flinched, then felt her shoulders soften and drop. "Because I care about you," she said gently. "And I believe in you. You're clearly happier when you're working on something."

Marie met Winifred's eyes with a sideways glance, reluctant as a stray cat. "Why do you think that?"

"Because it's true."

59

June crossed another item off her list—*Call florist*—and set her pad of paper down on her mess of a kitchen table. All around, SPW committee members were carrying boxes of decorations, organizing silent-auction sheets, and triple-checking the place cards against the confirmed RSVPs. Her house was fundraising central, and they were just one day away from the big event.

For the past few weeks, the chaos of her role as head organizer had been a welcome distraction from Harry's custody threat. She'd enjoyed two more visits with Bella, and June cherished them, doing everything she could to spoil her daughter and imprint the happy memories on both their hearts. The thought of Harry taking Bella away from June was a horror she could not face.

Especially not now, in the midst of the SPW's event frenzy.

A few other ladies were already packing up their cars with decorations and supplies for the morning, to haul over to the Shore House, where every year, they rented the same airy and elegant space for the fundraiser.

June consulted her list, reading the next item: *Confirm linen delivery.*

She set her pen and pad beside the kitchen phone. She was dialing the number for the linen company when Rosie walked by, carrying a box full of newspaper-wrapped vases. "What an operation," she commented, her gaze sweeping over the commotion throughout June's house. "I can't *wait* to see how this all comes together tomorrow."

A platitude? Or a barb? June smiled tightly and turned away from Rosie, hunching over the phone receiver.

She'd seen Rosie numerous times since that humiliating day at the park, and Rosie had said nothing of the matter; she'd been overly polite and sunny, but that was par for the course with Rosie. Still, June had been waiting for the other shoe to drop—surely Rosie had told *some-one* about June's embarrassing display. Anyone else on the committee would've spread that gossip like wildfire.

And yet: *nothing*. June wondered if Rosie was waiting for a better opportunity. She was new to the committee, after all. Perhaps Rosie intended to burn June at a more opportune time. Deanna had warned June that the lead role would come with at least some level of covetous-ness from the other members.

June pushed the concern from her mind; now was not the time to be paranoid. Tomorrow was a big day, and it was important to take each challenge one step at a time, lest she become overwhelmed.

After June confirmed the linen delivery, the phone had barely rested in its base for ten seconds before it rang. "Duxbury residence," June answered.

"Mrs. Duxbury, it's Mr. Carlisle." Her lawyer.

June's stomach swooped. "Oh, hello." She glanced over her shoul-der, where people were packing boxes in her kitchen and sorting papers in the conjoined dining room.

"Let me take this into the other room," June said softly and set the phone face down on top of her to-do list. "I need to take a call," she intoned a bit louder, to no one in particular, and hurried toward Harry's study.

Her heels clip-clopped on the hardwood floor, strides quick and purposeful. She closed herself inside the study, not bothering to turn on the light. Leaning against Harry's bare desk, she picked up the phone.

"Mr. Carlisle?" she said.

"I'm here," he replied, and though she did not know him well, she could tell by the delicacy of his tone that he bore bad news.

"I'm guessing it's not good news," she said, just to preempt her own discomfort, and her voice—it sounded distant to her own ears, high and wispy and filled with more air than sound.

"Afraid not," Mr. Carlisle said. "I've heard from Mr. Duxbury's lawyer. Your husband has a strong case. He's going to use everything he can against you: the medication, the accident with Mrs. Hurst, everything."

The phone quivered against her ear; her wrist felt too weak to hold it up. "But I'm her mother," she said thickly. "I'm her *mother*."

"I know you are, dear," Mr. Carlisle said, and that *dear*—June hated it. Men loved to wield *sweethearts* and *dears* to patronize and pity women. June could usually let those pet names roll off her back, but this time—this time that *dear* sank into her skin like a bullet, cutting through clothing and flesh. It angered her.

"I'm sorry," he added.

She balled the fist that wasn't holding the phone. "I'm not paying you to be sorry," she said, her tone as flat and sharp as a knife. "I am not prepared to give up my daughter. I *will not*."

"Of course," Mr. Carlisle said. "I'll do everything in my power. But June, I'm not going to lie to you." A weighted pause. "Your husband has a strong case."

A few months ago, June might've balked at those repeated words but not today. June had not struggled to conceive Bella for years upon years, and labored until her body tore and bled, only to lose Bella to the woman Harry had betrayed June to be with. She would not. It was not acceptable. June was a force of nature, a volcano of lava and ash. She would bury the world with her rage if she had to.

"I will not lose my daughter," June repeated, her whisper muted by the four crowding walls of Harry's study.

But outside the door, back down the hall, seated at the dining room table, Barbara had just finished her task of sorting the guest list and organizing the corresponding placards into alphabetical order. She paper-clipped the whole bundle together, along with the master seating chart. June had trusted Barbara with the guest list task as her right-hand woman, but it was tedious, and Barbara had been working on it for the past two hours. She wandered into the kitchen to seek out June and perhaps pour herself a drink from the bottle her friend hid in the cabinet above the fridge.

But June wasn't in the kitchen.

Oh, well. Barbara looked around for a stool so she could reach the vodka. The small nook that housed the phone had a stool tucked under the lip of the built-in counter. Barbara reached for the stool, ready to carry it away, but paused.

She saw June's pen and pad resting there, with the phone face down. That was odd.

Barbara picked up the phone, about to set it back on its base, when she heard voices coming from the speaker.

She held it to her ear and heard everything.

60

At daybreak the next day, June blinked at the ceiling. The clock on her nightstand ticked steadily; she'd been counting those clicks for the better part of an hour, watching the white ceiling of her bedroom transition from cobalt black to the pink-tinged gray of morning. Her alarm—already set for an ambitiously early time of morning—wouldn't go off for another thirty minutes, but she knew by now that sleep was a hopeless cause.

There was so much to do. Her mind had been mapping her day step by step, from her first sip of coffee to event setup to her gracious acceptance of *congratulations on a successful fundraiser* from various attendees at the end of the night. Everything was planned, stacked as neatly as bricks; June was the connective cement, holding everything together and yet crushed under the immense weight.

Her first time running the annual SPW summer fundraiser on her own, as the new head of the organization, was pressure enough—but now the last shred of her social standing seemed to rest upon tonight's event. If it went well, everyone would be reminded of June's virtue; if it went poorly, everyone would point to her divorce and say *no wonder she failed—she's a failure.*

June heaved a sigh and swung her legs out of bed; her feet tingled as she stood, the tired muscles in her heels tender as she padded across the carpet.

What joy was there to find in the start of her day, without spending it making breakfast for her daughter? In the absence of Bella's mewling morning voice and Harry's snores, the house was eerily quiet. Before Harry left, June would've been grateful for the silence, but now it felt all wrong. The silence wasn't fleeting—it was indefinite. If Harry won . . .

No. June wouldn't let him win. June had a lawyer—a good one. Mothers always won. Her house wouldn't be silent forever, just this morning. Just until she turned on the radio.

Downstairs, June acted out the tasks that she'd been thinking about in bed, from coffee and fruit to packing up her car and driving to the Shore House to start setting up. She arrived first, of course, and was shown to the ballroom. The chairs and tables were already set up just as she'd planned months ago, when she surveyed the space. The room was long and wide, with a set of double doors at one end and a stage at the other. All along the side were huge windows framed by velvet drapery and glass panels that opened onto a ground-level patio and manicured lawn.

All of it—from the tassels holding the curtains open to the ornate chandeliers above—filled June with a sense of reverence and familiar awe. June's first glimpse of this room had been when she was a child, perhaps nine or ten. The nanny had been late—a family emergency, though June's mother had scoffed when she got off the phone—and her mother had taken her along to help set up the space. Her mother had thrown many events here, paving the way for her daughters to do the same. Since her sisters had moved away to other states with their own families and husbands, the family legacy of the Clearmonts at the Shore House had fallen to June.

Countless esteemed women had walked across this old emerald carpet, made speeches on that stage, hired singers and caterers. Now June was here, following in their high-heeled footsteps; it was her turn to prove her legacy.

After requesting a bellboy help with her boxes, June hurried toward the parking lot. She probably ought to have been thinking about her to-do list, but her mind remained in the ballroom. That first time she'd seen it, her mother had been frantic, scurrying around in a frenzy to get everything ready in time, but June—June had just stared up at those chandeliers, imagining all the ladies in gowns she wouldn't see later that night, because by then she'd be home with the nanny again, getting tucked into bed.

She could still smell her mother's perfume, hear her parents' new-shoe footsteps in the foyer back at home, voices echoing their goodbyes. Her mother had worn a long black dress with pearl earrings that June had thought about all night long—the elegance, the beauty. All the stress of earlier had been combed smooth, painted over with makeup. Her mother's shoulders held a rigid line, but her eyes sparkled as she and June's father exited the house, leaving June behind.

June had eventually grown up to take her mother's place, leaving Bella behind to sleep and dream of the sophistication she, too, would one day help organize. Except tonight, Bella would not only be with her nanny but Harry—and, possibly, his mistress too. The thought of Bella with some other woman—a woman poised to *replace* June—made June's assured strides falter. What legacy *would* Bella live, if June lost custody to Harry? Would the Clearmonts' long-standing family tradition of hosting respected events end with her?

"Today's the big day!" someone called out, and June pivoted.

Bobbie was exiting her car, all fresh-faced and bubbly. "You walked right past me."

June doubled back, plastering a smile on her face; she felt like a puppet, the muscles going tight as if pulled by strings, with no feeling behind the expression. "I'm in my own world this morning," she said breezily. "Lots to do."

Barbara pulled into the parking lot, then, flapping her wrist in a little wave as she sped by and whipped into a parking space a few empty spots away from Bobbie's Mercedes. When Barbara got out, she lifted her sunglasses onto her head, appraising June with a faint little frown.

"You look tired," Barbara said.

Bobbie giggled. "Always so direct."

"Oh, stop. I'm fine," June said, but Barbara's manner didn't break or soften like it usually did after a harsh, jesting comment like that—and June suddenly wondered if Barbara had been kidding at all. "You two ready to get started?"

"Yes, ma'am," Bobbie said, standing at attention.

Barbara's expression remained exacting. It was the same icy, disapproving face she donned with inept waiters and—June's chest clenched—with Winifred.

"What's gotten into you?" June asked Barbara, opening the back seat door of her car. She bent forward to grab a box and then straightened, balancing it on her hip.

In a flash, Barbara's tense demeanor vanished. "Nothing at all," she answered, turning toward Bobbie. "Let's track down a bellboy to help us with these boxes, shall we?"

Without waiting for Bobbie's response, Barbara walked toward the Shore House, her long strides barred only by the narrow width of her dress. Bobbie sprang after her, leaving June behind with her box of decorations.

Not for the life of her could June guess why Barbara was in such a tiff this morning—but it unsettled her. Barbara was the most in touch, gossipy person June knew, and a change in demeanor that sharp must've meant Barbara knew something about June—knew more than what June had allowed her to know.

And she didn't approve.

61

The upper field glittered with frost. Delicate white stalks of grass remained eerily still in the chill breeze. Fog obscured the lowland, a bright smudge beyond the barbed wire fence, practically glowing in the faint morning sunlight. Beyond the fog, cows bellowed, their solemn voices echoing through the mist.

Marie looked left, over her shoulder, back toward the woods. The trees had blanketed the field's edge in leaves of honey yellow, pumpkin orange, brick red. The scent of the Susquehanna—all loam and rot and decay—soothed Marie's nostrils as she breathed in; she filled her chest until it stretched and burned with the cold, cold air of autumn.

She hugged herself, the soft fabric of her nightdress bunching under her fingers. The hem was dirtied from her trek. She wore her brother's boots, which were sturdier than her own, a better match against the frostbitten ground. It was early. Earlier than even her father got up, and Marie had come out here to . . . what *had* she come here to do? Stand, freeze, grow numb? Perhaps cry and wonder at the world (she'd done a lot of that lately). Or perhaps sink to her knees in the hard mud, stain her nightdress beyond her mother's repair. Wait for a coyote to find her curled up in the grass.

"Marie."

She turned. James stood behind her, already shrugging out of his heavy winter coat. He draped it over her shoulders.

"You can't keep doing this," he said, breath clouding around his face.

Her mouth quaked, pulling into a grimace that threatened to split her cheeks apart. She pinched her eyes closed before tears could escape.

"Marie," James repeated, pityingly, and pulled her into a tight hug. His body was bed-warm.

Marie gripped his shirt; she gripped her duvet.

She opened her eyes and saw her bedroom in Winifred's house, the spread of mattress under her cheek. Beyond that: rumpled blankets, her nightstand, and the window. Outside, the sky was still inky black, the darkest part of morning.

Her heart raced so fast it felt as if it could stumble at any moment. In her half-sleep state, Marie heard the hooves of Thoroughbreds running that same risk, the possibility of falling, breaking, gunfire and a gasp.

She rose, startled by the repetitiveness of her recent dreams. They'd grown more vivid over the past few weeks, pushing at her consciousness as only real memories could.

Wiping her face, yawning, Marie wandered toward the window and stared up at the star-flecked sky. Nights like these, she felt as if time was both long and short, a thread spooled over and over itself. Unspool her life, and that morning with James in the field would seem far away. But with her life rolled up in a memory, her childhood was a mere coil from where she was now. Practically parallel.

The only thing that unwound Marie was painting. It drew her out of her tangled thoughts. Helped her weave a new self.

This morning, the last morning of summer, Marie couldn't remember why she'd been avoiding painting. If the memories came anyway, she might as well capture them on canvas. It was the only thing that ever made her feel better.

Marie wandered toward her bedroom door, careful not to make a sound as she unlatched the knob. She kept the frosted field in her mind's eye, cradling the details as carefully as she could, so she wouldn't forget. By the time her brush met a fresh canvas, Marie was nearly dreaming again.

She felt the wet hem of her nightdress fluttering against her bare legs and the weight of James's jacket across her shoulders.

62

The morning of Winifred's end-of-summer bash, she crept out of her room just before dawn, as the stars were starting to fade into the paling horizon. She slipped on a dressing gown and mentally ran through the things she needed to accomplish before her guests arrived: dishes and caterers, amps and musicians, a staging room for the performers she'd hired, a first aid kit. She scratched the back of her head, her hair tangled from sleep, and yawned as she made her way out into the hallway.

Halfway down its length, she stopped dead in her tracks.

She smelled . . . paint.

Fresh paint.

Winifred tiptoed nearer to Marie's closed studio door, breathing in the scent until her nose burned. Then, she smiled to herself.

After cutting off Marie's funds, Winifred had worried that she'd broken the other woman's spirit for good—but now, she sighed, relieved and hopeful that this marked a new and brighter chapter for Marie's artistic career. A venture that Winifred would support not by funding a pointless diversion but by housing Marie and giving her all the encouragement and support Winifred could muster. She might've done a bad thing on the surface, but Winifred wholeheartedly believed that now, the both of them could thrive.

Yes, Winifred told herself, *it's better this way.*

A shiver washed over Winifred's shoulders and arms as she hurried downstairs. She'd never been so happy to smell paint in her life.

63

"What is she *doing*?" Bobbie asked as she drove herself, June, and Rosie past Winifred's house. They were heading back to June's for one last load of decorations—something June could've done on her own, but Bobbie insisted on making it a social trip. Now, Bobbie slowed slightly, allowing the three of them to stare at the yard they passed.

Out the window, June spotted a cluster of cars in Winifred's driveway. Streamers had been hung out of the home's top windows. A pair of men in white shirts—*caterers?*—were carrying an unwieldy-looking tray in through Winifred's front door. Around the side of the house, a woman clutched a guitar case to her chest while a grungy-looking man hefted a large black box.

"It looks like she's throwing a party," Rosie said as they drove past, sounding genuinely confused.

June scoffed. Of course Winifred would throw a party today, of all days.

"The audacity." Bobbie picked up speed again.

"Do you think she knows tonight is the SPW fundraiser?" Rosie asked.

June briefly wondered if Rosie's ignorance was willful.

"Of course she knows," Bobbie answered.

"It's despicable," June bit out.

"So she's not coming tonight?" Rosie asked.

"Clearly not," Bobbie said.

"I don't understand. Didn't she donate to the auction?" Rosie asked.

"She's doing this to spite us," June said. "But it only makes her look uncharitable and sour."

"She did this last year too," Bobbie pointed out. "You'd think she would've learned her lesson."

"Bobbie, her husband *died*," Rosie whispered. "Besides, last year's party wasn't on the same day as—"

"Stop defending her," June snapped.

Rosie startled, flushed.

June adjusted her sunglasses, staring straight ahead as Bobbie turned down her street. "She's never respected how anything is done in this neighborhood, so now she's throwing a tantrum. That's all this is."

"But we all know how *disruptive* tantrums can be," Bobbie said, pulling into June's driveway. "Do we need to worry about tonight?"

"You think she'll come and make a scene?" Rosie asked.

June waved her hand dismissively, even as her friends' words permeated her calm. "She won't leave her own party," June said, exiting the car.

"She might not have to," Bobbie said, hurrying after June up the porch steps. "Did you see those huge speakers they were carrying? It's not like she lives far from the Shore House."

"So we'll call the police if we have to," June said, waving her off—but her assured footsteps wavered. The police had been called numerous times, formal letters written and sent, yet still Winifred had succeeded with her disruptions. What if Winifred *did* intend to ruin everything? What if she got away with it?

June didn't say more as they loaded Bobbie's car with the last of the papers and leftover decorations. It was a silly task for three of them to do, but ever since June had become head of the committee, she'd noticed a shift in behavior from the other women, some chummier, some colder and more calculating.

With a twinge, she tried not to let Bobbie's overt helpfulness, Barbara's judgments, nor Deanna's snub cloud her focus today. The looming threat of Winifred's party was enough of a concern.

Grinding her teeth, she sifted through a stack of left-behind place cards on the dining room table. It was a small mercy that June's parents had stopped attending the SPW events when her mother retired—*that* pressure would've been one too many.

She barely heard the phone ringing until Bobbie called from the kitchen, "June, should I pick it up?"

It was probably someone from the Shore House. "Sure," June replied.

A niggling frustration twisted her lips as she wondered how these place cards could've been separated from the others. Who had been in charge of them? Barbara? June would have to check her master list.

"June?" Rosie said, entering the dining room. She held a box of fabric: the runners for the silent-auction tables. She opened her mouth to say more, but Bobbie's call from the other room interrupted her thought.

"June, it's a man named Mr. Carlisle. He's a . . . lawyer?"

June froze, her heart clanging in her chest.

Rosie's brows lifted, and with her mouth still open from her interrupted question, she appeared overly surprised.

June turned, leaving Rosie behind in the dining room as she made quick strides around the corner and into the kitchen. Bobbie had the phone pressed to her chest, her face screwed up in an equally quizzical expression as Rosie's, brows high and mouth open like a fish.

June took the phone from Bobbie's fingers and answered, "Hello?"

Rosie had followed June into the kitchen; she and Bobbie stood side by side, watching her. June assumed Barbara would've told the whole neighborhood about her divorce by now, but Rosie's and Bobbie's expressions had a flavor of worry that suggested otherwise. Could it be that June's divorce was so shameful that even Barbara couldn't bear to share it?

"Mrs. Duxbury? It's Mr. Carlisle." The abruptness of his voice startled her.

June wanted to scream, but she forced a deep breath instead. She was accustomed to folding herself up into the smallest shape imaginable, never showing her true feelings. Doing it now was the most natural thing in the world for June—but for some reason, in this moment, it felt all wrong. The worry and shame and fury inside her were becoming more unwieldy by the day; she couldn't bottle them up the way she used to, and in spite of her effort, she felt her forehead quake.

June placed a hand over the phone. "It's nothing," she told Bobbie and Rosie. "Just give me a minute, all right?"

"Are you there, Mrs. Duxbury?"

She hunched over the phone. "Yes, I'm here."

"I'm calling with an update," he said. "I'm sorry to say, it's not good."

~

On the way back to the Shore House with Bobbie and Rosie, June assumed a placid, indifferent expression—at least, she hoped that's how she appeared. On the inside, June was falling apart. Mr. Carlisle had spoken with Harry's lawyer. Apparently, Harry's case was ruthless. They intended to paint a picture of June so horrible that her chances of winning full custody were almost nonexistent. Mr. Carlisle had used words like *drugs, negligence, neglect.* Words that could easily be explained with compassion, context, truth, and yet they were words that stained June's heart and pride like wine spilled on a white dress. They soaked into her, tainting her, ruining her.

Mr. Carlisle insisted that June's best option was to settle and give Harry whatever he wanted. Harry was—to use her lawyer's term—*kindly* willing to share custody, with he and Evelyn assuming the majority of Bella's time. But that didn't seem kind at all. That sounded like June's baby girl being stolen from her and given to a home-wrecker. June was being unfairly depicted as the villain.

The worst part was that Harry's lawyers weren't lying about any of it—June had done all those things and more, not in malice but in desperation. She was being punished for having pain, emotions, opinions—for *struggling*. How had trying her best and keeping it together morphed into such an upsetting outcome?

Perhaps June didn't deserve her daughter, after all—only, no. She couldn't think like that. If she indulged those thoughts, June would lose all reason to live.

June came from a long line of respected women. Her mother had taught her how to be polite, productive, and measured. The model housewife. And she *had* been. She couldn't lose sight of Harry's role in all this—his unfaithfulness. She might've made mistakes, but *he* was ultimately in the wrong. His lawyers could try to convince everyone otherwise, but she was determined not to lose sight of the true telling of this story: Harry was the villain.

So why did it feel as though June was the one who'd failed her family? Her body, her painkillers, her shortcomings—all *hers*.

June gritted her teeth again, her molars aching. Her thoughts were circling the drain; she needed to get a grip.

Behind her sunglasses, June's eyes watered, but she refused to show emotion. She balled her shaking fists, pressing them hard into her lap to keep them still. Rosie and Bobbie were back to chattering about Winifred's goings-on, and June was glad for the distraction. They hadn't asked what June's call had been about, but she knew there would be talk behind her back. Her only hope was that Barbara—in spite of what she might now know—would set the record straight and tell them what June had told her: that June was the victim.

As they drove, June held on to that precarious glimmer of hope. But something deep down in the pit of her belly told her that hope meant nothing when it came to best-laid plans. And she feared that all her plans—from her happy life to the SPW to getting to keep her daughter—were about to go very sideways.

64

People were already parking down the block, and the party wasn't supposed to start for another hour. The actors were painting each other's bodies with metallic paints—gold, silver, bronze—in one of the guest bedrooms. Irene was instructing the caterers in the kitchen; she'd brought her own pretzel salad at Winifred's request, six whole casserole-size Pyrex dishes sure to disappear within the first hour. Winifred had already asked the three bands to arrange themselves in the yard in the usual location by the pool but with more speakers set up along the patio. Giselle, the aerial-silk artist, had enlisted the help of an electric guitar player to string up her silks out an upstairs window again, but this time with sturdier knotting. Chairs and picnic blankets had also been set out. Along the path to the beach, a girlfriend of one of the actors—an installation artist— was setting up little paper lanterns in the sand.

Upstairs, Winifred had donned a gold sequin minidress and was sitting on the edge of the bathtub. Marie was only inches away, her lips pressed together, eyes focused on her task. Her hand rested against Winifred's cheek as she dragged the eyeliner brush across Winifred's lower lash line. Winifred had told her to go for a chic, double-winged mod look; Marie's level of stillness and care promised a stunning result.

"You painted this morning," Winifred said, her words slightly mumbled in order to keep her face as motionless as possible.

Marie's brush paused ever so slightly before landing at Winifred's outer corner and flicking out toward her hairline. Marie had done her best to wash her hands and change into paint-free clothes before she arrived downstairs for breakfast this morning.

"I smelled the paint," Winifred explained.

"Ah." Marie dipped the brush into the little pot of black liner. She smoothed the bristles against the lip of the pot, rolling the brush in quarter turns to form a sharp point. She did this for two rounds, three. Stalling.

"I'm happy for you."

Marie did not meet Winifred's half-made-up eyes; even as she leaned forward with the brush, she focused on the near-translucent skin of Winifred's undone eyelid, the way it rested closed, fluttering slightly. Marie was close enough to count each one of Winifred's lashes, hyperaware of her breath on Winifred's face. How many times had she done it now? Drawing Winifred's eyeliner was a pre-party ritual, and yet Marie still squirmed with the intimacy of it—the trust of proximity.

Winifred, even with one eye closed, seemed to scrutinize Marie at this distance, seeing through her evasiveness. *I'm happy for you.* Her words weren't a compliment but a challenge. Marie had no idea why Winifred wanted so badly for her to paint, but admitting her recent progress made Marie feel like a child again, the same embarrassed sort of pride as when her mother praised her first drawings.

"It's no big deal," Marie finally said, only—*damn*—it sort of was. She'd painted the field as she remembered it: the gentle slope into thick fog, the dark shapes of cattle in the mist, and the foundation for delicately textured grass. The underpainting was all dark hues and shadows, but next she would add glittery pops of white, cream, fawn, and sage green to highlight the frosted stalks and half-bare trees.

The only differentiation from the memory was that she'd painted three figures staring out at the field instead of two. Her lanky brother wearing only an undershirt, the planes of his back and shoulder blades cutting through the thin fabric. Her own shorter figure, bulky in James's too-big coat, with a frilly nightgown peeking out from under its hem. And the third figure, ghostlike: the same height and build as Marie but dressed in the white gossamer she'd been buried in, the ivory paint translucent over the green-black background of saplings and slumped autumn grass.

The memory had clung to her all morning, but rather than feeling as dense as the fog in the valley, Marie was clearheaded. Fresh. As if this painting had been weighing her down like a rock in a lake and even getting the underpainting out had somehow helped her get her head above water again.

"I beg to differ," Winifred said, countering Marie's disparaging comment. "I'm glad you're painting again."

Me too, Marie wanted to say, but it was still so easy to fall back into the self-pitying state. So what if she was painting again? Without the end goal of Hurley Downs, her artistic practice had no tangible purpose.

Marie flicked the liner brush in a final flourish, then leaned back, assessing her line work. "All done."

65

Soft jazz wafted through the event hall as two hundred of the area's wealthiest sipped champagne, socialized, and meandered past the silent-auction tables. June, dressed in a boat-necked evening gown, greeted and exchanged pleasantries with all the biggest donors and cherished guests. She demurely accepted compliments—on the scrumptious appetizers, the excellent but subtle four-piece band, the quality of the auction prizes—while secretly beaming on the inside. Family friends were in attendance, all of whom seemed pleased. Even Deanna had offered a respectable nod, noting how smoothly things seemed to be running.

From the outside, the night—though it was early—thus far was a success.

But in between the cracks of laughter and chatter, when the band faded out of one song and had not yet started another, June heard a distant rumble to the west. It sounded like a rock and roll concert, peppered with car horns and shouts. Fundraiser guests whispered about the noise, speculating on its origin. But June knew the source, and it made her cheeks grow flame-hot under the bright chandelier lights.

June had had enough of Winifred's disturbances. Terrorizing the neighborhood with her disruptions was one thing, but tonight—of all nights—was too far. June would not allow Winifred to ruin this fundraiser, June's chance at redemption.

With her skin ablaze, June politely excused herself from the conversation she'd been having with two of the SPW's longtime donors. She tried to hide her anger underneath a mask of amiable calm as she made a beeline for the double doors that led into the hall. She practically itched with rage, her placid smile fracturing at the corners of her mouth the closer she got to privacy.

When she finally burst out of the ballroom and into the carpeted silence of the wide hallway, June felt her smile crack into a wicked, vengeful frown. She stormed toward the Shore House lobby. She would call the police, file a complaint. Certainly, this noise warranted a visit from the law. She'd call again and again until the racket from down the street ceased.

When she was almost to the end of the hall, a man appeared in the doorway, wearing a fine suit . . . and a tie June recognized. A tie *she* had picked out. June came to a halt, immobilized by the sight.

Harry wasn't supposed to be here. She'd asked him not to come, to pardon himself so he wouldn't spoil this night for her. For some odd reason, Barbara hadn't blabbed their divorce to every housewife in a ten-mile radius—but June and Harry's separation was still *known*. Harry's absence from the event would've been noted but forgotten; his presence would enliven the gossip, divert focus from the event itself.

Harry, here, now, would undermine the success of her event and undercut her chance to change the neighborhood's perception, to get herself back in everyone's good graces.

She glanced around, a hare surveying the best means of escape. But it was too late. Harry was walking straight toward her, and under his steady gaze, June had nothing to do but stand there like a stunned animal as he approached.

"June." His voice was gravelly; it pierced her belly in a way she hadn't felt in ages, a way that didn't make sense.

She was struck, then, by the horrible realization that she still loved him. It made her feel stupid, and weak, and she hated herself for it.

She glanced around, worried that someone had already seen him. "What are you doing here, Harry?"

"My mother insisted."

"She's here?" June had invited Claudia, but her mother-in-law had RSVP'd *no*. The senior Duxburys were attending a wedding in Italy—a friend's niece, June recalled. Claudia had pressured June to change the day of the fundraiser, which had fallen later than usual—*the Duxburys have proudly attended every SPW fundraiser since the organization's founding*—but Deanna had been the one to reserve the date. No matter the Duxburys' status, it couldn't be changed.

Harry folded his arms. "Shouldn't you know whether or not she's here?"

June gritted her teeth. "I—"

"My mother asked that I be here in her stead—it's not like I could say no."

"I don't have a place card for you." It was the only excuse she could think of as she tried not to stare too long at his handsome face, to not think about how soft his hair was and how she used to love running her fingers through it.

"Then *find* a place card for me. You must have extras."

His patronizing tone dried up her longing. "Do you need one? Or two?" June bit out. "Did you not bring your mistress?"

"She's home. Looking after Bella." He stepped a little closer, speaking low. "You can pretend that I'm the villain, June, but we both know the role you've played in this."

"My only *role*," June snarled, "was of a perfect wife and mother."

Harry huffed a laugh, but when he saw the unmovable seriousness of June's face, his eyes narrowed. "I didn't need you to be perfect, June," he said. "I needed you to love me."

What was he talking about? "I *did* love you," she protested. "I did everything I could to . . . ," she trailed off, bemused.

"You expected me to become a different man, entirely."

"Do you mean a father?" June shot back. "A serious—"

"—wet blanket," he interrupted. "Your ridiculous expectations were stifling."

"Stifling," June exclaimed, anger rising. What did Harry know about stifling expectations? He wasn't the one expected to manage the household, to cook *his* dinners, to never voice his true feelings because they were too inconvenient or ugly or *unfeminine*. If anything, the expectations that Harry resented were his own. Expectations that *he* benefited from.

He ran a hand over his face. "You're the one who changed, June. You became relentless, obsessive, completely fixated on Bella."

Fury rose up in her body like a geyser. "You have no idea the physical and emotional toll that—"

"You left our marriage by the wayside," Harry interrupted. "You lost all spontaneity, all *fun*."

"Is this about my pains?" June whispered. The question humiliated her, but she had to know.

"Your pains?" He shook his head, as if she was delusional. "Are you not hearing me? You cared more about appearing perfect than being present. And then you started drinking."

She opened her mouth to protest, but he continued.

"You think I didn't know about your hidden bottles? You always chided me for being irresponsible, but while I was out providing for my family, you were at home getting drunk."

June pressed her fingers into her temples. Suddenly the hallway felt unbearably hot. "That's not fair," she said. "That's not *true*. You were the one who started working late. You're the one who ruined it."

"So you agree with me, then," Harry said. "That it's ruined."

"Don't—" June balled her fists, trying to keep her voice from betraying her emotion. "Don't twist my words, Harry. We took vows. Bella deserves to grow up in a happy home. She deserves an intact family. A sibling."

"You're right, she does. And she can have all those things," Harry said, "with me and Evelyn."

He brushed past her, pushing through the double doors into the ballroom.

The doors swung, releasing the sounds from within: jazz brushes on a snare drum, glasses clinking, and many, many competing voices. The din muted as the doors closed behind him, leaving June in the solitude of her own shock.

He really meant to marry her. His mistress. No matter what people said or thought, it was clear that Harry would find a way. June felt as if she were caving in on herself, crumpling like a parachute with no air. June had done everything she could to love him, support him, and care for their daughter—even through immeasurable challenges. If she had changed, it was only in her effort to cope with the demands of her life.

And she still hadn't done enough.

Meanwhile, his mistress was home with Bella. It was a slap in the face, a punch in the gut, a stab in the back. June's daughter, spending time with the enemy—the woman who broke their family apart. If June were a different woman, a less controlled woman, she would've cried out. She would've slapped Harry across his handsome face, pounded her fists on his solid chest, wailed at the top of her lungs until the whole event crowd poured into the hall to see the spectacle of June Duxbury falling apart. They would've covered their ears to bar against her screams.

But June was not that woman.

June was the woman who remained immobile, willing herself not to cry. Too concerned with the threat of public embarrassment to run after Harry and cause more of a scene.

June was the woman who forced a deep breath—shaky as it was—and told herself to focus on the fundraiser.

June was the woman who called upon years of childhood scoldings and etiquette classes to rein in her emotions. Her heart was a rearing, stomping, aggravated beast, chomping at the bit, striking out; as she stood there not moving in the middle of the empty room, she yanked her own spirit into submission.

The only outward sign of her struggle was the set of her jaw and the rigidness of her shoulders, which no one—not even Harry—would know to recognize as any sort of inner torment or distress. June's jaw was always clenched. Her shoulders were always rigid. Whether she displayed a smile or carefully controlled upset, the creases beside her eyes were a constant. She was well versed in the art of silencing her fury.

But as she worked to control herself, a small voice inside her wondered if that fury was worth listening to—if that fury was trying to tell her something important.

66

"June, there you are," a woman exclaimed, her mature voice echoing off the walls.

June turned away from the empty space Harry had left in front of her to see Yvette Kent, one of the SPW's most fervent supporters.

"Yvette," June breathed. "What a delight to see you."

"I hear you're responsible for tonight's success," Yvette said.

June feigned bashfulness even as her heart ached. "I owe it all to my committee."

Yvette patted June's arm. "Always so humble."

June offered a meek little smile.

"It's a shame there's so much noise coming from down the road," Yvette said. She leaned in, lips quirking mischievously. "Is there any way you can send someone to investigate the disturbance?"

June dipped her chin. "I—"

"I'm kidding, dear, of *course*," Yvette said. "Pay it no mind."

Yvette was one of the few women who seemed to actually mean what she said—at least, most of the time—but June wondered now how much truth was contained within the jest. If June's anger toward Winifred was on a dial, Yvette's comment turned it up another notch.

June's fingernails bit into her palm, bringing her back into the present. Better to move on from the topic of the noise and pretend it truly was no matter; to apologize would be to show undue responsibility and, therefore, ineptitude.

"Tell me, Yvette, I'm just dying to know: Do you have a favorite auction item this year?" June asked.

The committee women often liked to wage guesses about what might catch Yvette's eye. She always chose one of the grandest prizes and bid an inordinate amount of money—not out of ignorance but in the name of charity. Last year, she'd bid double the value of a yacht and then—having won the boat, no contest—donated it to the local yacht club to use for their youth programs.

"You haven't made my decision easy," Yvette said. "I was torn between the Parisian vacation and the Jaguar, but then the most exquisite painting caught my eye." She paused with a small, private smile. "Ultimately, I decided to be a little selfish this year and put a generous bid on the painting. I couldn't resist."

June's brow creased; many paintings had been donated, but she didn't recall any of measurable significance. "Oh? To which painting are you referring?"

"Why, the original D, dear! It's quite the popular bid too. I had to request a second bidding page from one of your dear committee girls—and you know, I might go back to ensure I'm still in the lead. The competition has been hot."

Not for the life of her could June picture which painting Yvette was talking about—how had June missed such a gem when she was compiling the final donation list?

"Will you show me?" June asked.

"Of course."

June followed Yvette back through the double doors. The temperature in the event room was many degrees hotter than the hallway; it made her feel clammy. All around, husbands in black ties and wives wearing glittering diamond necklaces sipped sparkling champagne from the delicate flutes June had picked out. Beyond the expensive drapery and gold-splashed windowpanes of the patio doors, the sand dunes and sunset reflecting on the ocean appeared similarly lavish, shimmery, and warm.

See? June told herself firmly. *A success.*

Yvette looped her arm through June's. Her hand was wrinkled and velvety, holding tight as they navigated the crowd. June had always admired Yvette's kind, charitable nature. She had two grown daughters who were around June's age, each with their own families. Yvette's husband had passed away, and now she lived alone. This past summer, June had come to learn just how lonely life could be without a husband or children around. She wondered if Yvette enjoyed the solitude, if she was able to fill it with friendships and causes or if the emptiness of her life echoed as cavernously through her rib cage as June's currently did.

June had focused all her energy on growing a family and community of her own. But now, walking beside Yvette, she wondered what life might look like with so many of the *shoulds* of womanhood behind her. June had never thought that far ahead, past Bella's adolescence and fledging, and into her own twilight years. Sure, she'd thought about the idea of growing old with Harry—the wrinkles that would form, the happy memories they'd look back on—but now she looked upon that future and saw herself alone.

The idea was disturbing.

Fascinating.

Maybe even liberating.

"Here we are," Yvette announced.

A cluster of socializers stepped aside to make room for Yvette and June by the auction table.

The painting rested on the satin tablecloth, propped up against the wall. It depicted a girl lying on her back in a field of wildflowers. She wore a gingham blue dress with a white ruffle around the collar; bright-white socks contrasted with black Mary Janes. Her legs were straight, and her arms were bent up to clutch a single purple coneflower to her chest. She appeared as one might in a casket, and indeed the grass and earth beneath her were dark and cradling—but the wildflowers were vibrant, and the girl's eyes were open.

June wasn't much of an art collector—she preferred arts that took place on a stage, like ballet and opera. In fact, normally, she felt rather dense when it came to paintings. She wasn't sure what people saw in them—beyond the picture itself—and always felt as if she was missing something. Of course, she knew the necessary facts about fine art— enough to make polite conversation and appreciate the pieces that had been passed down within her family—but beyond that, she had no instinctual sense of what made a painting great and what made it worthless.

But there was something haunting about this girl, and it touched June. The symbolism of death was not overt but clear. The girl herself, however—and the flowers surrounding her—were full of life. Her face was pink, not pallid; her freckles were a lively smattering across the bridge of her nose, which was slightly crinkled with her peaceful smile. The girl's gaze was bright and somehow a little wondrous. Even her fingers grasping the coneflower stalk appeared relaxed.

"Isn't it magnificent?" Yvette asked.

The painting made June feel something and feel it deeply. A squeeze in her lungs, a twinge in her heart. It reminded her of fragility, innocence, girlhood—qualities that, for some reason, also came with feelings of sorrow and grief. The painting both soothed and roused June. It made her wistful.

She couldn't tell Yvette all that, so June nodded, leaving her sentiments unspoken. "Are you still in the lead?" June asked, directing her attention to the auction sheets.

She had single-handedly reviewed all donations—why didn't she recognize this one? How had it slipped past June's discerning eyes, and who was the donor? June bent, reading the donation details.

Type: Painting, Oil on Canvas
Artist: D, 1960
Title: Coneflower Cradle, *from the* Girl *Collection*
Estimated Value: $600
Donor: Winifred Hurst

67

June peered at the name, disbelieving. Her lingering wistfulness melted into magma.

First, Winifred had joined the SPW and sullied it with her obvious disregard for the institution.

Then, Winifred had quit—insulting the opportunity she was granted by being approved for the committee in the first place.

Now, Winifred had sunk to pettiness by donating a valuable piece just for the attention.

It was insulting—that Winifred would shirk her invitation to tonight's event, disturb the affair with her raucous party, and yet still insert herself into the whole thing by donating what appeared to be a showstopper.

June didn't get Winifred's logic, but it made her muscles bunch. Lava radiated in her sternum. She stifled a growl, feeling as if she might combust. She couldn't show her displeasure on the outside—especially not in front of Yvette, who was clearly excited about the piece.

June flipped to the second page of bids. The amounts had surpassed a thousand dollars. She ran a manicured finger down the list of names until she found Yvette's, which was second to last.

"Someone outbid you," June informed Yvette. With her finger still marking the spot on the page, she leaned back so Yvette could see.

The older woman studied the list. "Damn," she swore, and it sur-prised June to hear Yvette's intensity. The older woman snatched the pen up off the tablecloth and scribbled her name under the competing bid.

"There we are," Yvette said, straightening once more. She had a lively expression pulling at the corners of her wrinkled eyes and cheeks. "I see this is Winifred Hurst's donation. Do you know how it came into her possession? It's quite impressive."

"I . . . I'm not sure."

"Do you know where she might be hiding? I'd love to chat with her about it."

"She's not in attendance," June bit out, unable to strip all the bit-terness from her voice.

"Oh?"

"She quit the SPW," June added.

"You're kidding," Yvette said, laying a hand on her chest. "Did she give a reason?"

June recalled their barbed exchange outside the Shore House. The memory reminded June of the car accident, when Winifred had insin-uated that Harry was working with the hippie living in her house—the hippie who was an *artist*.

Could it be? No. *No.*

This wasn't one of the bohemian's paintings, was it? How on earth could it be of such value? June was horrified to think that she had been so emotionally *moved* by something created by that . . . that . . . *woman*—the woman who knew June's husband and lived with Winifred.

Suddenly, the room was too hot, too loud. June's anger flared again, scorching her chest.

"I'm so sorry, will you excuse me?" June asked. "I need to use the powder room."

Yvette patted June's arm. "Of course, dear. Congratulations on this impressive event."

June smiled tightly—it was the best she could do—and then scurried away.

Why on *earth* would Winifred donate something when she hadn't even planned to come? June doubted the painting had been donated before Winifred quit—she would've noticed. In fact, June suspected that this had been a last-minute addition. She wondered who on the committee had dared to approve such a thing. This was Winifred's stab at revenge, an effort to haunt June without bothering to show up.

Between the painting and Harry's intrusion, June could barely walk upright as she sought the shelter of the empty women's restroom. Inside, she locked herself in a stall and released the breath she'd been holding. It came out as a soft wail, and she pinched her lips together, embarrassed by the sound. Tears threatened, but she blinked them back, not wanting to disturb her makeup.

June could hear the thumping music emanating from Winifred's house. It faintly shook the bathroom walls, like a faraway earthquake destined to roll through June's event and make it all crumble. Two opposing urges warred inside her: one, to rush back out there to protect the SPW, and the other, to hide in here forever, where neither Harry nor the lawyers nor anyone's disappointment could find her.

And people *would* be disappointed, wouldn't they? It seemed June was never quite enough—not for her mother, or Harry, or the SPW. Things were going swimmingly now, but it was only a matter of time before people started pointing their fingers at June and blaming her for whatever was sure to go wrong. She constantly had the feeling of being watched—and tonight, that had only intensified.

She sank to the toilet and cradled her head in her hands, panting. She couldn't seem to get a full breath; it felt as if she were buried under rubble, the weight of brick and stone pressing down, oxygen scarce, like breathing through a straw.

Just then, the door to the restroom swung open, and two sets of heels shuffled in.

"I don't understand," one voice whispered. "June? Drugs? That doesn't sound right."

"I'm telling you," the other voice said, low but forceful. "Things were . . . *implied*."

Rosie and Barbara.

June gave up on the breath she was trying to heave in and made herself still. Her skin tingled with the racing of her pulse.

"*Implied* doesn't mean *true*," Rosie argued.

"But think about it," Barbara said. "If she's an *addict*"—she whispered the word so faintly, it became merely syllables, a breath filled with disdain—"do we really want her running the SPW?"

June's heart stumbled, and she was taken right back to the night Bella had fallen into the pool, when Harry had implied the same thing. But June was just a housewife in pain. Her pain was the one thing she could *never* control. Was it so wrong for her to want relief? To *achieve* relief in the form of a prescription?

"It sounds like a nasty rumor," Rosie protested.

"But if there's even a *chance*," Barbara enunciated.

June couldn't see the women, but the pause that followed implied Rosie's consideration. The weight on June's chest pressed harder, and she wheezed a slow, unsatisfactory breath, resisting the panic that seemed to take up all the room inside her chest.

"June has been a fixture of this organization," Barbara said. "I don't blame Deanna for giving June the leading role, but even Deanna herself admitted to me—just the other day—that she regrets her decision."

"It just doesn't *sound* like June," Rosie insisted. "I feel like we don't have the full picture."

June didn't understand Rosie's kindness—she never had. Rosie had plenty of information to bury June in scandal. Why wasn't she?

June would not have guessed that at that moment, Rosie was *not* thinking about all the times June had been snide toward her, or the easy revenge at her fingertips. Rosie was thinking about the park, when June had been so cross eyed and clammy that she couldn't even stoop down to pick up her own daughter. Rosie was thinking about how June had seemed like a bird with a broken wing: exhausted, afraid, and desperate to hide. Naive as Rosie seemed on the outside, she had always seen June for who she truly was: a woman of power and pride, with an immense pressure hidden behind her smooth facade.

Of course Rosie would defend June. June might have belittled and lashed out at Rosie at times, but her actions didn't make Rosie vengeful—they made her sympathetic. Rosie's heart went out to June—not just for her physical pain but for the strain she put on herself to be perfect. Eugene was always warning her of the ruthlessness of the women in this community, but the way Rosie saw it, it was society that was ruthless. And that was all the more reason to extend June some kindness.

"June has always been well meaning," Rosie stated. "I think we owe her the benefit of the doubt."

"Even so," Barbara said, clearly feigning concern, "do we really want the fate of the SPW to rest on the benefit of the doubt?"

"What are you proposing?" Rosie asked.

Both Rosie, as she stared into Barbara's opportunistic eyes, and June, listening to the fervor in Barbara's voice as it echoed through the ornate bathroom, sensed Barbara's diabolical intentions. When Barbara spoke next, their suspicions were confirmed.

"I'm going to make a statement—tonight," Barbara said, walking toward the door. "It's time this organization recognize what a mess June is—and elect someone more *suited* to the role."

June should've known that *this*—a power grab—had been Barbara's reason for not spreading rumors about June's divorce sooner. Barbara wanted to shock people. Barbara—June's best friend—wanted to disgrace her.

68

By eight o'clock, some four hundred people had wedged in through Winifred's front door. Cars swarmed her driveway, lined the grass along the street, and overflowed into the parking lot of the church down the road. A handful of Volkswagens and even one decommissioned school bus—painted with murals of flowers and clouds—had brought in a jumble of college students from Brown and Johnson & Wales. It seemed the students who'd summered in Wave Watch with their parents were back at school for the fall and had told their friends about Winifred's summer shindigs; she was stunned that they'd consider her end-of-summer party a worthy trip.

As Winifred wove through her house with a bottle of champagne, all around her, young waiters, artists, activists, musicians, students, and budding professionals were imbibing and connecting. A sense of belonging buzzed through the veins of everyone in attendance. There was no small talk or etiquette or awkwardness—everyone was a friend here, simply because they were *here*.

The community vibe thrilled Winifred, but it was the moments that she happened upon Marie or Irene in the crowd that she felt the happiest. There had always been something missing at her parties—some small part of Winifred that still felt lonely, no matter how many friendly people she hosted—but when Winifred saw her friends, that lonely feeling vanished. She'd experienced the same thing with Bruce—tense as their society parties had been, Winifred had always felt comforted to round a corner and find Bruce there, lighting up with a smile just for her.

Marie was starting to get that way again. It had been a long month of endless, blurry parties, with Winifred trying to drag Marie's mood out of the well it'd fallen into. But now, as Winifred stepped out onto the porch and spotted her friend, Marie's face brightened as Bruce's used to, and Winifred's heart swelled until it pressed on the walls of her chest, stealing her breath. Joy. Of all the people dancing and conversing and smoking on Winifred's property right now, Marie was the only one whose mere smile could bring Winifred that much *joy*.

Marie raised her glass in Winifred's direction. Winifred walked carefully down the porch steps, her heels sinking into the grass when she reached the lawn. She abandoned her shoes at the edge of the grass, wriggling free and leaving them behind, askew and embedded in the soft soil. The grass was surprisingly cool and soft on her toes, the best type of carpeting.

When Winifred reached Marie, she poured a fizz of champagne into her empty glass.

"And that is why I don't wear heels," Marie said, gesturing at Winifred's shoes. They looked like two little sunken ships, tipped sideways in a sea of green.

"You're a curmudgeon, you know that?" Winifred said.

Marie rolled her eyes, and Winifred pivoted, standing shoulder to shoulder with her to watch Giselle hanging from her aerial silks above the lawn. Her ankles were even with her ears in an impossible split. Winifred's eyes went wide. With the eyeliner, Marie thought the expression made her look like an Egyptian relief, a part of some pictographic story of war. It didn't hurt that her minidress made Winifred glitter like a queen.

"My crotch hurts just looking at her," Winifred commented, her gaze still fixed on Giselle.

"I don't think that's the intention behind her performance," Marie commented.

Winifred smirked, giving her a sidelong glance.

"Did you catch the first band?" Marie asked. "The guitar player kept watching her and playing the wrong chords."

Winifred chuckled. "I thought something sounded off."

The first band had played rock, with a few ballads for people to slow dance to. Now, as the sky faded into the pastels of sunset, the second band was playing a soulful folksy melody that made Marie's stomach twist. Half of her heart was still up in her studio, standing before the easel feeling fifty pounds lighter. The other half was shattered over losing her shot at Hurley Downs. The music tugged on the emotions she'd already been feeling; she wished they'd play something a little more . . . *fun*. But all around, people were grooving to the mellower sound.

"I can't believe it's the end of summer," Winifred said, and she was thinking about Bruce, and how last year's end-of-summer soiree seemed both too recent and too long ago.

"Me neither," Marie said, sipping her champagne. One song faded, and another more lively one began, much to her relief.

As if on cue, the nude, gold-painted actors filtered out of the house, dancing in slow motion, their metallic body paint reflecting off the pool. Giselle slid down her silks, bare tiptoes gracefully coming to rest on the ground. The drummer missed a beat when she landed but recovered much more gracefully than the guitar player had earlier. The transition was smooth: Giselle wandering into the house, her body covered in a sheen of sweat and crisscrossed with red lines; the actors pantomiming, holding the crowd's attention as effortlessly as Giselle had; the band matching the mood of the performers.

"Look who spotted us," Winifred said in a singsong tone, elbowing Marie in the ribs.

Marie knew before she saw him, just by the teasing lilt in Winifred's voice. She tried not to blush as Lawrence walked over, long limbs swinging in a smooth, amiable stride. He'd cut his hair since the last time she saw him but grown out his beard. He wore dark-lens shades and his signature op art shirt; this one was a dizzying tangle of black-and-white lines, punctuated with the occasional orange circle.

"Hey," Marie said.

"Hey, yourself," he replied.

Marie had slept with Lawrence a few times now, usually when they were high. Weed took the edge off her shyness, and she and Lawrence had had many late-night, pre- and postcoital existential conversations. But Marie wasn't high now—not even tipsy—and she felt too aware and inhibited. She'd grown to really like Lawrence over the summer, and it made her self-conscious.

"I dig your shirt," Lawrence said, reaching out with delicate fingers to pinch the sleeve. His knuckles grazed her arm in the process, sending a shiver down her spine.

"Thanks." Marie had found the geometrically pattered blouse in a consignment shop with Winifred last week; today, she'd tucked it into one of Winifred's miniskirts. She had to admit, she liked the outfit; it complemented her legs.

But Lawrence wasn't looking at her legs; he was staring at her face. She could see her own blush in the reflection of his shades.

"Lawrence, Marie, can I get you both a drink?" Winifred asked, even though she was holding a champagne bottle and had just filled Marie's glass. "There are pitchers of piña coladas in the kitchen."

Lawrence nodded without taking his stare off Marie.

Winifred pinched Marie's arm, then sashayed off, past her abandoned shoes and into the house. Winifred had no intention of returning.

When Marie swiveled back to Lawrence, he was still staring, a faint smile tugging at the corners of his lips. The folksy band had picked up their tempo, and through the previous band's amps, the music all but swallowed up the conversations happening around them.

Marie cleared her throat. "I didn't see you at the last party."

The banjo player was now strumming in a frenzy, and Lawrence tapped his ear. "What?"

Marie stepped closer and repeated herself.

"I was working," Lawrence explained in her ear. "Miss me?"

Marie shrugged, glancing down at her sandals.

"You're blushing," Lawrence teased, so close to her ear that his voice didn't need to rise above a murmur.

Marie leaned back to bring his face into focus again, the hairs of his beard grazing her cheek. She reached up and removed his shades so she could see his eyes. "Seems like *you* missed *me*," she said, and *oh*, she sounded so silly trying to flirt. Where was Winifred with that drink?

But Lawrence smiled. "I did," he purred and leaned in again, this time to kiss her neck.

Marie's eyelids fluttered closed, and she flexed her shy fingers. She wanted to grasp his biceps or touch his face, but her arms remained at her sides. She didn't understand *why* Lawrence had missed her. Why *her*? She wasn't smooth or brave enough to ask.

Meanwhile, the sonic chaos of the band had reached a fever pitch. Someone dancing nearby on the lawn bumped into Marie's back, jostling her out of her self-deprecating thoughts. She pitched forward into Lawrence's arms. Considering how they'd met, it seemed Marie was always stumbling into him. Thankfully, this time, she didn't have a plate full of food in her hands. He wrapped his arms around her, chuckling, and Marie spotted gold out of the corner of her eye. The person who'd bumped her was one of the gold-painted actors, buck naked and glittery. He pantomimed an apology, tracing a tear down his cheek with a melodramatic grimace and then pressing both palms to his hairy chest before bounding off.

Lawrence laughed and said something she couldn't hear.

"What?" she asked.

His arms tightened around her lower back, and he bent down, lips grazing the shell of her ear. "Want to go somewhere a little more . . . quiet?"

Marie swept her gaze across the crowded lawn. "You mean Connecticut?"

He grasped her hand. "Let's try upstairs, first."

69

Lawrence led Marie through the yard and into the house. She felt like a pinball, the way other people's shoulders bounced her this way and that. The kitchen, the parlor, the hall—everywhere was an absolute *press* of people. In a summer filled with parties, Marie had never seen Winifred's house so full.

But Lawrence wove confidently through the humid hordes. When they reached the staircase—climbing past a couple necking on the steps—Lawrence and Marie were finally able to walk side by side. His hand rested on her waist, right where her T-shirt was tucked into the back of her skirt. When they reached the top of the stairs, he halted abruptly, his arm hooking her around. One second, she was walking toward her room, and the next, she was flush against Lawrence's chest. The move made her yelp, and he chuckled as he leaned down to cover her mouth with his.

Marie sank into the kiss, letting her awkwardness dissipate with his touch. His hands splayed on her back, one of them trailing over her shoulder, up her neck, and into her hair. She loved the taste of him, the *solidness* of him, his long body folding to envelop her in strong arms, sheltered inside the concavity of his chest.

"Admit it," Lawrence whispered against her, "you missed me."

Marie nodded, just a little, and a smug smile quirked Lawrence's lips.

Marie glanced down the hall at her closed bedroom door and stiffened. She wanted him—she was certain of that—but without anything in her system, she felt . . . shy.

"Do you have any weed?" Marie asked.

Lawrence kept her body pressed to his but leaned his head back to regard her. "Why?"

"I don't know," Marie mumbled, "to take the edge off?"

"Sometimes the edge is fun," Lawrence said, kissing her again.

When he released her, he grasped her hand, continuing down the hall. At Marie's bedroom, Lawrence reached for the knob and said, "I want to be sober this time. Is that all right?"

He had an earnest expression on his face, and Marie found herself nodding without even thinking, so touched by the sentiment.

Lawrence opened her bedroom door, and at first Marie didn't see what was inside, because she was still staring at his profile. But then his eyes widened, and Marie shifted her attention to the tangle of limbs and bodies on her bed. A high-pitched "*No! Why? Sorry!*" tumbled from Marie, her cheeks ablaze. Marie reached for the doorknob—still clutched in Lawrence's hand—folded her fingers over his, and yanked the door closed.

Lawrence snorted with laughter.

"It's not funny," Marie protested. "That was *my bed*."

Her words only made Lawrence laugh harder, wheezing, his amusement so stark that it elicited a small, relenting chuckle from Marie too.

"My *bed*," she repeated, but now her chest was convulsing with the laugh she was trying to smother. "*I* wanted to use it."

Lawrence kissed her firmly. "Is there somewhere else we can go?"

Marie led Lawrence back down the hall, past the locked door of her studio—she wouldn't dare take him in there—and was dismayed to find the other guest rooms occupied. They even heard moaning coming from the towel closet.

Back downstairs in the sweaty, jam-packed air, they surveyed all the side rooms they could, finding each one filled with people talking, playing card games, touching up body paint, and more.

Marie and Lawrence paused in a downstairs hallway, a comparatively quiet part of the house, though there were enough people that they had to shrink into a corner, their bodies pressed together to take up as little space as possible.

"There are a thousand rooms in this house," Lawrence said somewhat breathlessly. "*One* of them has to be empty."

"You sure you don't want to just go back outside for a smoke?"

Lawrence smoothed her hair, his full-body sigh pushing into her chest. "I want to do what you want to do," he said. "I just want to be clearheaded. Sometimes it's better that way, is it not?"

"Don't you get self-conscious?"

One eyebrow lifted. "Is that why you smoke?"

Marie glanced away.

"And what do *you* have to feel self-conscious about?" he asked, touching her cheek, bringing her gaze back to his. But he went on before she could reply. "You know what, no. Don't even try to come up with something. We both know it won't be true."

"You're a flirt," Marie accused.

"Doesn't mean I'm wrong," he said.

Marie tried to stifle her smile, but her lips still twisted, eyes crinkling.

"So, what do *you* want to do?" he asked.

Marie tipped her chin down, fixing him with a heavy gaze.

His knowing laugh came out as a deep rumble, a vibration she felt in her ribs.

Her lips quirked. "Clearheaded, you say?"

Lawrence nodded.

Emboldened by his compliments, Marie arched her back, rising up on her tiptoes to reach his mouth. As she twined her arms around his neck, the kiss deepened, and she felt the tug of his mouth all the way down into her core. His groan thundered through both of them.

Marie slid back down to her normal height, releasing him. "Come this way; I have an idea."

She zigzagged down the hall, moving with the flow of dancers. Lawrence somehow kept up with her all the way to the kitchen. He hovered over her shoulder as she rifled through the drawer underneath the kitchen phone. There was one off-limits room in the house, one that had remained locked since the day Marie moved in: Bruce's study. Marie suspected Winifred kept it locked to dissuade theft during parties; she couldn't possibly mind it if Marie used it for an hour of privacy.

When she found the ring of keys, she held them up triumphantly.

"Where are you taking me?" Lawrence asked, but Marie was already making her way back through the parlor and down the hall, wedging herself between clusters of partygoers.

At the door, Marie fiddled with the keys, her frantic fingers slowing when Lawrence came up behind her and kissed her neck. Maybe he was right about being sober—she felt intoxicated just from his touch.

The lock released, and a pang of nervous anticipation shot through her belly. She removed the key from the slot and swung the door open. The inside was cool and dark, smelling of stale tobacco and leather. Marie closed the door behind them and locked them in, so no one could follow.

Alone, *finally*, they both reached for each other, colliding in a frenzied kiss. Marie's lips became raw from the firmness of his mouth and scrape of his beard. Lawrence walked her backward until she was pinned against the door, his body flattening her into the hard wood behind her back. His hand cupped the back of her head, pillowing it as his mouth devoured hers. A soft sound escaped her—she wasn't sure exactly what it was—a moan and a laugh and something else too. Crushed against the door and Lawrence's body, the air just sort of whooshed out of her.

He must've liked that sound, because his kiss slowed, wet lips sliding over hers, sucking at her bottom lip. Then he was bowing his head, tracing a slick line down the column of her throat to her collarbone. His hands slid down her body, under her skirt. Lawrence hoisted Marie up with a quick, strong jerk, surprising her; instinctually, she wrapped her legs around his waist.

Lawrence carried her toward a leather couch, setting her down gently. "Still need that smoke?" he asked, and she almost said yes, just to get that smug smile off his face.

But her lips were tingly from his rough kisses. Her heart was trilling. And she was so . . . *achy* for more. She shook her head *no*, and he grinned, *beamed*. It was the most delighted expression she'd ever seen, boyish and mischievous in one, and her whole body warmed to think that *she* had made him look like that. Marie had had plenty of flings over the years, but Lawrence was the first man she genuinely liked to see smiling because of something she did.

Marie lifted out of her supine position, propping herself up on weak elbows. The leather squeaked under their weight, and the party raged beyond the door, but it was all just background noise to the pounding of her heart and the steadiness of his breaths.

He bent down and kissed her again, sliding his hand up her inner thigh, under her skirt. Her body jerked at the deliciously sensitive contact, and she yanked at his shirt buttons, his belt, the hem of her shirt—everything in their way. Lawrence's fingers were somehow more assured than hers, and he helped them both undress: their shirts, his pants, her underwear.

Finally mostly naked, Lawrence knelt on the couch with one of his knees resting between her legs, his body hovering over hers. The light rimming the closed blinds illuminated the hairs on his chest, the wide planes of his pectorals, the armor-like power of his shoulders. His lips were parted, swollen as Marie's felt.

It was in this moment that Marie fully understood why he'd wanted to remain sober. The thrill of anticipation and the way her body buzzed with the promise of pleasure was unlike anything she'd ever experienced while drunk or high. She was far more self-conscious but also far more *aware*. And it made her hot.

Marie reached for Lawrence. But as she stretched upward, her attention flicked past him to the painting on the wall. Even in the darkness, it was . . .

Familiar.

She blinked, not fully believing what she was seeing at first, but as the girl in the meadow came into focus, all the heat drained from Marie's body. Her eyes widened, and Lawrence paused in his slow descent toward her lips.

"What is it?" he asked, tipping his head sideways.

Marie sat up completely, pushing past him. To say she couldn't believe it wouldn't be quite right—she *could* believe it; she just didn't want it to be true.

That was *Wildflower* on the wall. The most valuable thing she'd ever painted. The centerpiece of her famed collection. Here. Hanging in Winifred's home.

70

After Barbara and Rosie had left, June emerged from the stall, her ankles quivering as if they might twist and buckle with each step. Her rear was numb from sitting on the toilet so long, and her diamond bracelet rattled on her shaking wrist.

Barbara was planning a coup. June should've seen it coming. Barbara might've been a gossip and a lush, but she was also cunning. June had been a fool to put her hope and trust in her. She'd been navigating social land mines for years—she should've known better than to trust anyone who would benefit from her downfall. Even a friend.

When June was twelve, her mother had stopped her from befriending a girl from school, because the girl's mother had once worked as a maid. *She'll use you to climb the social ladder,* her mother had said. No matter that the girl—Suzie was her name—had gotten into the school on a scholarship. No matter that Suzie went on to study at Harvard Law. Sometimes June wondered what might've happened had she not shunned Suzie. Would June be getting divorced? Would June be hiding in the bathroom at a charity event?

June should've expected Barbara to betray her—but what June couldn't fully make sense of was Rosie's defense. Rosie didn't have to give June the benefit of the doubt. Rosie didn't have to be nice to June at all. A mean, sour part of June—the part who'd shunned Suzie at her mother's request—wanted to look down on Rosie for her unnecessary kindness.

But instead, it empowered June.

June washed her hands in the bathroom sink, chilling her sweaty palms with cold water. She patted her wet hands on the back of her neck. Defeat seemed to be around every corner, but there was no way she'd accept it without a fight. Barbara had been selected to get on stage and announce the auction results—a part of the night's program that would be starting soon. June could select someone else for the job, undermining Barbara's role, but she didn't think Barbara would allow herself to be foiled so easily.

No. June would have to stop Barbara herself. If she didn't, then Barbara would tell the entire auditorium that June was addicted to drugs and unfit to run the SPW. After such an announcement, June would be well and truly ruined, unable to get back into anyone's good graces. She would lose custody of her daughter, be removed from her role as head organizer of the SPW, and be exiled from her social group.

In short: she would lose everything.

Rolling her shoulders back, June exited the bathroom, holding her head high as she stalked back into the event hall. Barbara was already making her way toward the front of the room—toward the stage—with her stack of auction papers. Rosie was close on Barbara's heels, following in her wake.

June hurried after them, smiling politely as she breezed past clusters of people she recognized—people she knew from *years* of SPW events. Mrs. Adams, who used to attend meetings at June's mother's house and would scold June when she made too much ruckus with her dollies in the next room. Mrs. Thornton, who'd sneaked June candies until June's mother found out and claimed that the sweets would make her fat. Mrs. Applebaum, Dr. Applebaum's wife, who had birthed six sons, all of whom were tall, confident, but dull; any of whom she should've married instead of fun-loving Harry.

June wove through a sea of women who'd shaped her—women who'd eroded June into the person she was today. At past SPW events, knowing these women had made June feel like she was a part of their legacy—like one day, she'd carry their torch. But now, as she rushed through the crowd, June wondered if she'd ever earn a place among their ranks.

All her life, June had looked up to women like this. Women with style, and influence, and grace. Charitable women. Proud mothers. Expert homemakers. Their husbands and fathers might've run industries, but these women ran the men's *lives*. Without them, their men would have nothing. Among them, June felt a sense of power, influence, and sisterhood.

Tonight was supposed to be her crowning moment. As the new head of the SPW, after tonight's success, she would *become* one of the women she'd always yearned to be.

But now the opportunity was slipping away. Years' worth of hard work, threatened by Barbara's wicked intentions. Because of course, *of course* June was not the only woman vying for such an honor.

June fixed her stare on the back of Barbara's head, the perfectly styled shoulder-length hair. She quickened her pace, nearly knocking into a waiter's serving tray, which was held high and cluttered with champagne glasses—she had to duck under the waiter's arm to narrowly avoid disaster.

But then Barbara was taking the stage, and a part of June wished she *had* crashed into the waiter—the shattering of glasses would've served as a beautiful distraction from the even-worse disaster about to unfold. Barbara tapped the mic as Rosie came up beside her, hovering awkwardly.

"May I help you?" Barbara asked Rosie, the mic picking up her words and carrying them through the hall.

Many people in the crowd looked up, sharing amiable remarks as little cliques swiveled their attention toward the stage.

Rosie covered the mic with her hand and whispered forcefully to Barbara—as if she was trying to stop Barbara from what she was about to do.

June was utterly confounded by Rosie's disinterest in decorum, her willingness to interrupt Barbara onstage on June's behalf; in all other instances, June had looked down on Rosie for possessing such a quality, but now—well, right at this moment, June was reluctantly touched.

But Barbara would not be derailed so easily. She was slick as an eel, easily evading Rosie's protestations. She wrenched Rosie's palm off the mic, somehow managing to make it look playful.

"Everyone," Barbara said slowly, sweetly, "this is Rosie, one of the newest members of the SPW. Rosie, will you be a dear and find me a glass of champagne? Let's make a toast!"

Rosie had no choice but to smile at the crowd and exit the stage, where another waiter was already approaching with a tray of glasses.

June continued pushing her way toward the front, narrowly avoiding shoulders and gesturing arms as she slunk past her esteemed guests.

Barbara bent down to receive her glass of champagne, and then she was tapping the delicate flute with a long fingernail. The sound plinked through the microphone and through the event room, and the remaining chatter died off. In the silence, the thumping sound of Winifred's party rumbled from down the block, thunder in the distance.

Rosie loitered at the foot of the stage, glancing between Barbara and the crowd, clearly flustered.

June was almost there—

"Are you all ready to hear the auction results?" Barbara's amplified voice surrounded June, filling the hall.

People cheered, tapped glasses, clapped.

"Me too," Barbara drawled. "But first, I think we need to thank the woman of the hour, Ms. June Duxbury."

June was not foolish enough to miss the insult of Barbara calling her *Ms.* instead of Mrs.

Barbara continued, "Without June, none of this would've been possible."

The room erupted with a second round of applause, albeit a little more sparse.

This was supposed to be June's moment—the night she finally achieved everything her mother and grandmother had wanted for her. But as she watched the chandelier light glittering off the slight sheen of Barbara's forehead, watched her friend's red lips move, June felt her world quaking. Barbara's actions, paired with Harry's insinuation that he and Evelyn intended to give Bella a sibling, shook something loose in June. She felt it in her bones as sure as she felt the reverberations of bass coming from down the road.

June would not let this be the end. She was determined to fight for her dignity. She shoved her way toward the stage. As she neared, a hand landed on her arm. June spun, a viper ready to strike, but it was only Rosie, wide eyed with a panicked grimace.

"June, you have to stop Barbara," Rosie said, and her concern—it softened June's edge, just a little. "She's going to tell everyone you're—"

"Let's raise a glass!" Barbara said into the mic, halting Rosie midsentence. "To June! The powerhouse. A woman who has achieved so much with this stunning event." Barbara found June in the crowd and held her gaze. She stared straight into June's eyes as she said, "I'm amazed that despite your divorce, you've been able to pull this off. Even with the pills and the drinking, June has managed to keep it all together for the SP—"

A chorus of surprised gasps swept through the crowd as the power went out, and the room went dark.

71

"What's wrong?" Lawrence appeared genuinely concerned. "Marie?"

"That's my painting," she said, untangling her legs from his.

She stood and approached the painting. She hadn't seen it in years, and she'd forgotten how disarming it was. She could smell the rot of the Susquehanna and Dottie's rosemary shampoo. A ribbon of inspiration slipped between her ribs, silken and hard to grasp. She couldn't feel her toes or her tongue in her mouth, just the absence of a brush in her fingers and the solemn, cold ache of grief in her chest.

Marie both hated and loved this painting. Feared and revered it.

"*You* painted *that?*" Lawrence asked, coming up beside her. His finger traced her bare spine with a sensual slowness that reminded Marie where she was, what she was doing, who she was with.

She glanced down at her naked breasts and the crooked waistline of Winifred's skirt still cinched around her waist. She wore nothing else. Beside her, Lawrence was completely nude, save for his socks. Marie might've made fun of his socks if it weren't for the leaden dread pooling in her stomach.

"It's incredible, Marie," Lawrence went on, bending down to kiss her shoulder. "It's—"

"Diabolical," Marie interrupted, realization permeating.

"What are you talking about?"

Marie turned away from *Wildflower* and met Lawrence's eyes. "Winifred didn't tell me she had this," Marie explained. "She didn't tell me she knew . . . who I am." She pointed at the painting, straight armed. "Who I was."

"And who were you?" Lawrence asked gently. He didn't sound confused, angry, or accusatory—just curious.

"I painted a semifamous collection, years ago."

His brow creased. "Should I recognize it?"

"Not unless you're an art collector."

His expression softened. "Ah. So Winifred is an art collector?"

Marie bent down to retrieve her shirt. She yanked it over her head and forced her arms through the sleeves. "She's been lying to me."

"I'm not sure I'm following," Lawrence said, but Marie was already storming toward the door. Her heart was a hurricane in her chest, roaring.

When she reached the doorknob, she turned abruptly; Lawrence had been close on her heels, and she placed a quivering hand on his bare chest. "I like you. Like this," she said, gesturing between them, too distracted by her anger toward Winifred to feel shy about what she was saying. "I like it a lot."

He tucked a springy strand of her hair behind her ear. "Yeah, we got a good thing going."

"I have to go, but I want to see you again," she said. "Sober."

"Whatever you want," he said, like it was a promise. "But Marie, what's—"

She kissed him firmly, and then she was out the door, down the hall, on a collision course toward wherever Winifred was hiding.

All those outings to buy paint. All those instances when Winifred had encouraged Marie to spend time at her easel. All the effort she put into creating a studio for Marie. If not for friendship, why had Winifred invested so much in Marie's art? Had Winifred wanted to capitalize on Marie's new work? Was their arrangement some sort of attempt at ownership over Marie's future success?

Her skin felt cold, clammy, violated by the thought.

It would explain why Winifred had discouraged Marie's illustration job, had pushed her to keep painting—but it didn't seem right for this to have been some sort of long con. Marie had thought they were friends. She didn't want to believe that Winifred would fake an entire friendship just for . . . what, exactly? Profit? Status?

Betrayal swirled in Marie's chest like storm bands, whipping up old feelings of fear, loss, and vulnerability. She should've never befriended Winifred. She should've never entered into this arrangement, no matter how advantageous it'd seemed at the time.

Marie ran into Irene in the kitchen, helping caterers shift tiny meatballs from a greasy baking pan onto three separate serving platters.

"Where's Winifred?" Marie demanded.

"Outside, I think," Irene said, her face scrunching. "Is something wrong?"

Marie was already out the patio door, storming across the lawn. There was a new band playing, horns wailing. The sun was setting, and the sky was a riot of orange. Marie spotted Winifred's sequin dress, glittering like gold fire as it reflected the colors of the sky. Winifred was talking to someone, laughing amiably. Marie grabbed her shoulder and jerked her around. Winifred stumbled on her still-bare feet.

"How long have you known?" Marie began. "How long have you been . . . *conning* me?"

A few nearby partygoers side-eyed Marie, but most were too inebriated to care. The band was so loud that Marie's voice was all but swallowed up.

Winifred's perfectly shaped eyebrows tipped upward. "What are you talking about?"

Just then, Lawrence arrived by Marie's side. She saw him out of the corner of her eye, but her furious gaze remained fixed on the woman whom she thought was her friend.

"*Wildflower*," Marie said.

The single word hit Winifred like a gut punch. It explained Marie's disheveled state, her angry eyes and quivering mouth. Winifred tried to keep her expression neutral, to smother her urge to blanche, but it didn't work. She felt her cheeks quake and her mouth part.

"You went into Bruce's study?" Winifred asked calmly, not sure what else to say. Judging by Marie's and Lawrence's rumpled appearances, they'd sought out the empty room for a reason unrelated to snooping.

"Don't pretend to be angry," Marie spat.

"I wasn't, I—" Winifred's voice cracked as she realized what was happening.

Marie knew that Winifred knew who Marie was. Marie knew that Winifred owned her most famous painting—and after giving her a studio and buying her paints, that made Winifred seem suspicious. There was no way out of this. None that Winifred could identify in her tipsy state. Damn the champagne. Damn her dishonesty.

"I didn't know at first," Winifred explained. "I didn't know until I saw you sign that painting of me."

Marie opened her mouth to speak but shut it again, shaking her head. Her cheeks were an outrageous shade of pink. Winifred was no artist, but she'd call the color a flustered fuchsia.

"I know I should've told you right then and there, but—"

"You lied to me."

"I didn't think it mattered," Winifred said, but they both knew that wasn't true.

"All this time," Marie said, "you were trying to milk a new collection out of me. Was inviting me to live with you some kind of ploy to—"

"I already told you. I didn't know until—"

"Oh my God," Marie said, and Winifred startled as realization flashed across Marie's face. "If you bought *Wildflower*, you must know Petra, at the Iris Gallery. You must—"

Winifred grabbed Marie's arm. "Excuse us," she said to a baffled-looking Lawrence and pulled Marie across the lawn, toward the beach. Better to do this away from the party, away from the noise and onlookers.

Once they'd cleared the crowd, Marie wrenched her arm from Winifred's hold, following freely as Winifred's feet pounded the sand path. The clouds had transitioned from orange to a traumatic plum and indigo, proud as the skin around a wound. Lanterns flickered in the sea wind, throwing long grass-blade shadows across the dunes.

Winifred's panic was so overt that she transcended its effects, her heart slowing instead of racing, her mind clearing instead of clamoring. She grew quiet on the inside—a quiet that was bone-deep and hollow and lonesome. Because she knew what was coming, and she was powerless to how Marie would react. She only knew that it would be bad.

Still, a small, punishing part of Winifred reveled in this calm terror of being caught. Because Winifred deserved it. Not just for what she'd done to Marie, but because of who she fundamentally was. Winifred's mother had seen it first: that when it came to other women—family, friends, and the certain solidarity felt between sisters of the heart—Winifred was unworthy.

She always had been.

Now was the time to fess up and prove it.

Winifred halted beyond the crest of the path, just past the rock on which she and Marie had sat, sharing breakfast on their first morning together. Out here, Winifred heard the roar of the party and the sea in equal measure.

Marie stared up at her, eyes red-rimmed and puffy. The hurt on Marie's face made Winifred's throat close up, and she swallowed, trying to drain the flood of emotion that threatened to drown her words. When she finally spoke, her voice came out watery, but she pushed past it.

"The first painting of yours I ever saw was *Junebug*," Winifred began. "I was in Providence for the day, looking for a birthday gift for Bruce, and I saw it hanging in the window of the Iris Gallery."

Winifred waited for the recognition to flash across Marie's face, but her friend's features—shadowed and shifting from the lantern light—remained hard.

"*Junebug* had already sold," Winifred went on, "but I just *had* to own something by this brilliant new artist." Her lips turned upward at the memory. "I was the only customer there, so Petra introduced herself and gave me a tour. With *Wildflower*, it was love at first sight. The perfect gift for Bruce. He had it appraised, and, well, soon after that I bought *Coneflower Cradle* and *Broken Ladder*."

Up until a few days ago—when she'd donated *Coneflower Cradle* to the SPW as a peace offering to June—those other two paintings had been in storage with a dozen other works she'd had to clear out of their New York home after Bruce died.

"It wasn't long after I bought those initial pieces that the collection exploded, and I knew I had to . . . support you, somehow."

Winifred drew in a ragged, lung-burning breath. She balled her fists, knowing that what she said next would change everything—but certain in her resolve to come clean. After spending weeks drowning in guilt, Winifred felt liberated by the truth, like she was breathing fresh air. And Marie deserved to know, even if that meant losing her forever. Marie deserved better than Winifred, anyhow.

"I was your first patron," Winifred said, and those words *did* crack through Marie's hard expression; her brow twitched, and her mouth slanted. "I supported many artists over the years through the Eckart Art Foundation, but you were my catalyst. In a way, your work was responsible for the creation of hundreds of paintings—not just yours but the roster of twenty female artists I still fund."

Realization was dawning on Marie's face, rippling her features. A tear fell, and that tear sealed Winifred's fate. "I was your first patron," she repeated, "and I was your last."

A second tear fell, streaking down Marie's cheek and glittering gold in the light from the lanterns. A gust of wind ruffled her hair. The swirling sand stung Winifred's bare feet.

"I'm the reason you lost the opportunity to buy the track," Winifred admitted. "I pulled my funding to wake you up to the insanity of that goal. I did it to keep you here—selfishly, because I've come to love your company—but also to force you to *paint*. I wanted to foster a breakthrough—a new collection—and you *did*—but—"

"You were wrong," Marie said, her voice throaty and thick. "Is that what you were about to say? That you were wrong?"

Winifred nodded, her nose stuffing up with tears.

"So let me get this straight." As she stared up at Winifred, Marie appeared shaken but mighty. "You invited me into your home because you were lonely after the death of your husband and wanted a charity case to keep you busy." She paused, allowing Winifred the chance to protest, but Winifred remained silent.

"Then you found out who I was, and rather than come clean, you groomed me to pump out another lucrative collection," Marie said. "When I seemingly lost focus, you cut my funding, effectively *trapping me here* with you. And—what?—you planned to take ownership of my breakthrough? Profit from it?"

"*No*," Winifred said. "God, no, I would never—"

"So you *do* have a line you won't cross?"

"Marie, I care about you." Winifred took a step closer, but Marie evaded.

"I thought you were my friend," Marie said, "but it turns out you were my puppet master."

"Marie—" Winifred reached out.

"I never want to see you again." Marie's feet sank into the sand, slowing her pace but not her resolve as she marched away.

"Marie, wait," Winifred said, rushing after her.

Marie spun. "You know what your problem is, Winifred? You're terrified of being alone, and that's the exact thing standing in your way of having even just one single meaningful relationship. You *trapped me*, for fuck's sake. You weren't my friend; you were manipulative, calculating. No better than June and all the other fake, bored women in this neighborhood, thinking you're better than those of us who have real problems, who have to work tirelessly just to earn a place in this world. I don't care if you're sorry about what you did—you betrayed me. And I'll never forgive you."

Winifred reached out. "Marie—"

"Don't follow me," Marie said, stomping back toward the party.

72

Marie didn't bother to take many of her possessions.

There were still people in her bedroom, so she left her personal effects behind; she figured she could ruin new sets of clothes with paint.

The contents of her studio proved a tougher decision. She'd leave the paints and blank canvases—anything Winifred bought. She wouldn't be able to look at them without feeling sick to her stomach; the shiny new paint tubes and pristine white canvases were now tainted by her betrayal. She did retrieve her charcoals and sketchbook, which she'd purchased before her arrangement with Winifred; the spiral binding still had a handful of blank pages left. Her travel easel—which had been tucked into the large bottom drawer of the cabinet—would also come with her.

The completed pieces were the hardest choice. The Thoroughbred paintings—three of them, now—rested against the wall in a neat row. Spectacular but also disturbing. The memories they had brought forth were things Marie had long since buried, and painting them had dug up emotions she'd rather have kept in the ground. Whenever Marie looked at them, she felt a pang deep inside, like an echo in a cave, a hole in her heart that should've been solid rock. She didn't want to take them. She knew she should—knew they could be the bones of a new collection, a new life—but it hurt too much to look at them. Every time she did, they threatened to quake through the caverns of her chest and cave her in.

But what was the alternative? If she left them here, Winifred could sell them. Marie didn't want to give Winifred the satisfaction. Should she destroy them, then? Marie could find a knife downstairs and slash the faces of each Thoroughbred, but that didn't feel right either. After tonight's revelations, nothing felt right.

Marie opted to leave them. Let Winifred sell them if she wanted to. Marie couldn't imagine Winifred doing that behind her back, but an hour ago, Marie would've never expected Winifred to have cut her funding and killed her dream either.

God, it sickened her to think of that day when Marie had crumpled into Winifred's arms at the news. Winifred had consoled and comforted Marie—all the while knowing that Marie's pain was her fault.

What kind of person would do that? The thought left Marie feeling violated, shaken.

Marie turned her back on the Thoroughbreds. Her final decision remained with the incomplete painting on her easel. The paint from this morning was still soft and tacky. It wouldn't be easy to travel with, but when her eyes landed on the ethereal shape of Dottie's ghost shoulder to shoulder with her own solid figure, the thought of leaving the piece unfinished made Marie's lungs seize.

Unlike the Thoroughbred paintings, whose completion had seemed to dispel the recollections that had haunted her, this painting's memory hadn't fully cleared from her mind. Which meant that Marie *had* to finish it.

In the end, the painting was the only thing of real importance that Marie took from her studio in Winifred's house. With her sketchbook tucked under her arm and the painting held above her head to avoid smudging the partially wet paint, along with her clumsy travel easel and palette, Marie made a steady path through the sweaty, raging party and out the front door into the evening's chill.

She did not look back.

73

Winifred hadn't waited long before following Marie off the beach, but she lost her friend in the swelling sea of partygoers. Things were getting out of hand: rowdy sons and daughters of the elite were skeet shooting her dinner plates with a BB gun over the dunes; women were letting the actors paint their breasts with the remaining metallic paint; the three bands had devolved into many musicians all jamming at once; couples were fooling around in the pool; smoke wafted through the open windows like the house was on fire; and nowhere did Winifred see Marie.

She was probably already gone.

Winifred stumbled through the patio door, into the kitchen. The clock on the wall read a quarter till nine, but the party's strange turn and her weariness made it feel much later. Someone had unplugged her phone again—her neighbors were probably fuming—and the cord was coiled on the counter.

Winifred looked around for Lawrence, hoping he might know where Marie had gone, but she didn't see him. She didn't see anybody she knew. Her home was a blur of wild faces, red-cheeked with dilated pupils, shouting and distorted in their rampant glee.

Winifred's earlier feelings of belonging and solidarity were disbursed by the chaos; weeks ago, Winifred would've fed off the insanity but not now. Without someone she loved to share in the merriment, the mayhem was suddenly . . . meaningless. These people weren't her friends—they were strangers. They didn't know who owned this house, who had paid the caterers, who had hired a decorator.

They weren't here for her; they were just here for the good time.

Just like every one of her parties.

Winifred had spent her whole life seeking the company of others. From her backbending attempts at popularity in high school, to winning over her male classmates in college, to the parties she threw with Bruce—all of these efforts had been an attempt to manufacture camaraderie and feel some semblance of relief from the gaping wound her mother had left behind.

Her father had been right. Loneliness *was* a rot. It had eaten away at Winifred's confidence until she stank of desperation. Until she did unforgivable things. June and the other women here might've shunned Winifred, but what about the women before? In school, in life before Bruce, Winifred had been just as clutching, smothering, intense—willing to shape herself into the woman she thought other people wanted her to be. The irony was that in doing so, she had alienated herself.

Losing Bruce had only plunged her deeper into such ill-fated aspirations, but with Marie's exit, Winifred saw clearer. It wasn't the world that had done this to Winifred—it was Winifred who had done this to herself. She used to think that the more people she could pack around her, the less isolated she'd feel, but now, surrounded by hundreds of destructive strangers having the time of their lives, Winifred felt lonelier than ever.

Now, as Winifred pressed farther into the kitchen, her ears ringing from the jumble of amplified music and gunshots outside, she thought back to times she *hadn't* felt lonely: visiting her father on the university campus, or on her wedding day with Bruce, and most recently, when she was shopping with Marie, or—hell—just having coffee with her, hungover at the breakfast table.

Such instances all had one thing in common: she hadn't been trying.

Winifred had felt most supported and loved not when she was surrounded by happy people, not when she felt as if she was successfully *fitting in*, but when she was her most authentic.

The revelation was heavy on Winifred's shoulders; she became unsteady on her dirty bare feet and leaned against the countertop, breathing deeply with the strain of hindsight and regret.

"Is everything all right?"

Winifred looked up to find Irene standing there, her brows creased. Winifred's chest warmed at the sight of her, the only other familiar face in a house of hundreds.

"I saw Marie leaving in tears," Irene said. "She took a painting with her."

Winifred blinked back her own threatening tears. "Just one?"

"And a few art supplies, it looked like."

Winifred pressed her fingers against her mouth, blocking the small cry that tried to clamber out.

"What happened, Winifred? Is Marie all right?"

"I messed up," Winifred said. "I drove her away."

"Is there a quiet place we can talk?" Irene asked. She appeared haggard.

"Irene, you've been working yourself to the bone, haven't you?"

Irene waved her away. "I like to feel useful. It's my weakness."

Winifred knew the feeling.

"Is there somewhere we can talk?"

Winifred nodded, leading a serpentine path through the jungle of people. She found Bruce's office door unlocked and cracked open; inside, a foursome was divvying up dried mushrooms on his mahogany desk.

"This room is off-limits," Winifred said.

A young man, stooped above the piles, straightened. "C'mon, lady, we found this room first."

"But I *own* the room." Winifred folded her arms. "And I said it's off-limits."

The girl standing next to the young man tapped her wrist against his arm. "Let's go, Pat."

Pat bent, scooping up the mushrooms, and stood again. "Fine."

Winifred stepped aside as the four kids filed out, then closed the door behind them. For months, this room had been a tomb of her husband; to see people treating it like *just another room*—to be sullied and enjoyed as they saw fit—should've filled Winifred's bones with lead. Instead, these walls felt a little . . . meaningless, now. A room Bruce had once occupied, but he had graced many rooms, many places. The most important of which wasn't a tangible place at all, but Winifred's heart—and his place there could never be sullied.

"This party is getting out of hand," Winifred said, locking herself and Irene inside.

To Winifred, the kind, older woman's presence seemed so incongruous with the drugs and blaring music. It saddened Winifred to see Irene here, so late at night, witnessing the carelessness of the young. Irene had weathered many of Winifred's parties by now, but it never changed Winifred's inkling that Irene ought to be home with a book and a cup of tea. But who was Winifred to judge Irene's choices and whereabouts? She of all people knew the lonesomeness of widowhood.

Winifred walked to the leather couch and sat, Irene following suit. Only a single side-table lamp was on, and the white lampshade cast a conical glow toward the ceiling. The house rumbled around them, thumping so resonantly it felt like the earth was moving.

The scent of Bruce's office sent a wave of grief rolling through Winifred, white-capped and turbulent. She could feel *Wildflower* looming on the wall, staring at her, taunting her. She refused to look at it.

Her eyes settled on Irene, her *sorrow sister*, as Irene had called them way back when. The memory made her smile wistfully at the older woman, before her face crumpled into utter pain.

"Oh, Winifred, dear," Irene said, scooting closer on the couch to wrap an arm around Winifred's shaking shoulders.

A high-pitched hiccup of air rattled Winifred's throat, and then she was sobbing in Irene's arms, her chest convulsing with ugly, involuntary wails.

"Winifred, dear, what happened?"

"I am a terrible person," Winifred said through heaving breaths. "A terrible, terrible person."

"Now, what makes you say that?"

Winifred explained the whole story of how she'd betrayed Marie. Every last deed. Hearing it all told in one breath, Winifred determined that she was, in fact, the villain in everyone's story.

When Winifred was done, Irene sat back under the glow of the lamp beside her. Angelic. To Winifred, she seemed to be pondering what she had just heard, weighing the details against her own sense of wrong and right.

But what Irene was actually doing was trying to formulate her next words in a way that would wake Winifred up. Because clearly this woman needed a reality check.

"Do you regret what you did?" Irene finally asked.

They weren't the damning words Winifred had expected. She fiddled with the lay of sequins along the lap of her dress, considering Irene's question. "I don't regret inviting Marie to live with me," Winifred said slowly. "But I do regret hurting her. Of *course* I do."

"Do you regret trapping her here?"

The word *trap* tore through Winifred's heart like one of the BBs still being fired outside Bruce's office window. Marie had said it, too, and as much as Winifred hated it, it was the truest word Irene could've chosen.

"I'm not sure," Winifred admitted, and it felt like her heart was bleeding out from the puncture wounds of the word. *Trap, trap, trap.* "I don't regret the time we spent together, or the creative breakthrough my actions facilitated, but I never meant to—"

"Hurt her?" Irene supplied. "It seems you *did* mean to hurt her, though. You knew that foiling Marie's plans would hurt her."

"Temporarily," Winifred defended, but then she deflated, falling back against the couch cushions. She closed her eyes, pinched the bridge of her nose, trying to hold her shame and anger inside, where Irene couldn't see it.

But Irene saw it. And she wanted to force Winifred to see it too.

"You can't control people, Winifred," Irene said. "That's not what friendship is about."

"But how else can I guarantee they'll never leave?" The words escaped her mouth before she could rein them in, and suddenly her vision was flooded with tears again, and she couldn't suck in enough breath around the ballooning emotion in her sternum.

"Winifred, dear, you can't," Irene said softly, pityingly. "You can never guarantee that the people you love won't leave in one way or another—haven't you learned that by now?"

Winifred *had* learned that. From her mother, from Bruce, and now from Marie. She just didn't want to accept it.

"Besides," Irene said, "when you take away free will, it's not love anymore."

Irene placed her soft hands on either side of Winifred's red-blotched, tear-slick face. Irene wanted Winifred to hear her words all the way into her cells and bones. Irene wanted Winifred to understand.

"What your mother did to you was not your fault," she said. "What happened to Bruce was not your fault."

Winifred shook her head, her mouth pulling wide in an agonized grimace.

"But Marie leaving tonight—*that* was your fault. You can pretend that what you did was solely about Marie's painting career, but you'd be lying to yourself."

"But what do I do *now*, Irene? How do I show Marie that . . ." She hiccuped. "That I . . . ?"

"Be a friend," Irene said, letting go of Winifred's face. "Be unwavering and unconditional. Let go of your expectations and desire for control. Just *be there* for her."

Winifred shook her head at first, her thoughts cloudy with uncertainty. But when she stared into Irene's kind eyes, truly considering her words, Winifred suddenly knew what she should do.

Winifred stood, circling Bruce's desk. She opened the drawer in which Bruce had kept his contact book and flipped to a name: *Gene Chaney, Realtor*. Her fingers had only just grazed the edge of the page when the single lamp by the couch flickered off, the music outside cut out, and the screams of four hundred partygoers shook the walls of the Seacastle.

74

"What just happened?" June asked Rosie as the voices in the room devolved into questions and startled shrieks. "Did someone cut the power?"

"I don't know," Rosie said, her soft voice swallowed up by the rising panic.

June looked around but could barely see the outlines of tables and guests; her vision was spotty and depthless, not having yet adjusted to the dark. And unlike before, she couldn't hear Winifred's party anymore.

June looked back to Rosie, who was no more than a shadowy shape. "I think this outage goes beyond the Shore House," June said, leading Rosie toward the patio doors, which were faintly illuminated by the starry night sky.

Shore House employees were ushering guests through the doors, too, trying to assuage irritation and calm the frantic.

June was trying not to panic, either, but not because of the darkness. When before she could've rushed the stage to defend herself or discredit Barbara's words, now there was nothing June could do. She was powerless. Barbara had succeeded in disgracing her.

Desperate to escape the crowd, June circled the Shore House with Rosie in tow, cutting through the manicured yard. Her heart was pounding in her throat, and she swallowed hard, trying to get a hold of herself. But her alarm only rose. What would happen when the lights came back on? What would happen tomorrow or next week?

Barbara's glib comments onstage wouldn't just have June removed from the SPW—Harry would use them against June in court. And then June's entire life purpose would crumble. People would forever see her as an alcoholic, drug-addicted, terrible mother. She'd lose the daughter she had gone through so much to conceive, her baby girl, the most important thing in June's life. She could do without Harry and, after tonight, even her insincere friends at the SPW—but what would June do without Bella?

When she reached the parking lot on the opposite side of the Shore House, she halted. All the neighboring homes were also dark, which meant that the power outage extended beyond just this block—perhaps the whole neighborhood.

"How did this happen?" June wailed.

Rosie was looking around, seeming to get her bearings. "I wonder if a transformer blew?"

"What does that mean?" June demanded. "Could someone at the fundraiser have done this?" She wanted to know if Barbara had planned this, too, somehow—to ensure that June couldn't stop her public ruin.

But Rosie shook her head. "No, I don't think so. It must've been something else—perhaps a nearby car accident or a power surge of some kind."

June squinted at Rosie.

"My brother was an electrical engineer in the army," she explained sheepishly.

June began walking toward the Shore House entrance; she wanted to see the road, see how many houses were out. Could it really be the whole neighborhood? Everything was eerily quiet, and June—

She spun around. "Could Winifred's party have done this?"

Rosie shrugged and glanced around, as if looking for evidence. "Possibly? But it's just as likely that something else—"

June continued walking briskly toward the road, relieved to have someone to blame. When she reached the curb, she peered down the long street lined with rock walls and privacy hedges. From here to the end of June's vision was overcome by shadow, and that darkness lit an internal fire inside June's belly that blazed and spit.

June started down the gentle hill toward Winifred's house.

Rosie was close behind her, heels click-clacking on the pavement. "Are you all right, June?" she asked, clearly struggling to keep up with June's quick, determined pace. "What Barbara said . . . she couldn't possibly mean . . ."

"I heard you in the restroom," June said.

"I—I don't know what to say."

"There's nothing to say." June pumped her arms, the balls of her feet aching as she pushed herself to walk faster.

"I'm sorry this is happening to you," Rosie said.

June's gait faltered but only for a second. "None of it's true," she said, eyes fixed on the black road ahead of her. "I am a good mother. A good *person*. Do you know how many years I've put into the SPW? My mother, and my grandmother before her. Now *this*. It's not right."

Who would she be, without her place here? The legacy of all the women in her family's orbit had come to rest on her shoulders. June's entire existence—her purpose, her self-worth, *everything*—had been irreversibly woven into this community, like a thin gold thread in a massive tapestry. At the end of the day, the tapestry could do without her small contribution—but to pull her from the weave would be to pull her from her whole world, everything that brought June's life structure and meaning.

"Of course you're a good mother," Rosie replied, and whether or not June heard the sincerity in Rosie's voice, she meant it. She'd seen June in that park, doing everything she could to be there for her daughter, in spite of the pain she'd clearly been experiencing. A bad mother wouldn't have bothered trying.

But June wasn't thinking about modest virtues. She was falling apart, her resolve unspooling and fraying. Suddenly, June didn't care if she sounded weak, or angry, or *emotional*. At least not in front of Rosie.

She spun around. "Am I?" she asked, voice straining. "A good mother? My daughter is about to be taken away from me. That wouldn't happen to a good mother." A fire flared inside her—one that consumed all her soft, well-meaning, spineless instincts. What was left was molten fury. "I've allowed my marriage to fall apart. I'm often unable to even pick up my own child—you saw it, you know—and I think I'm incapable of having another baby." The last word cracked. "Perhaps I *don't* deserve to keep Bella. Perhaps I don't deserve to be a part of the SPW or this neighborhood. A good mother—a good *woman*—would've never allowed herself to be disgraced like this."

June started walking again, feeling her anger grow white hot inside her chest. It reminded her of the fury she'd felt when she got in that accident with Winifred; only this time, it was all-consuming. It burned through every last platitude, every last drop of shame June had experienced in her thirty-five years. It ignited all the *shoulds* and *have tos* that had been forced upon her over her life. June had done so much to be perfect—contorting herself into impossible shapes, breaking bones, twisting her neck, just to be what she was *supposed* to be.

And all that effort, agony, sorrow, tongue-holding, tolerating, and faking had been for nothing. It all became moot the moment Winifred's party blew a fuse and stole away June's chance to defend herself against Barbara's claims. Why was Winifred allowed to be who she was, without any consequences? June's resentment toward Winifred—for everything Winifred represented: her free will, her freedom from the expectations of this neighborhood, her ability to be no one but *herself*—stoked the fire inside June until it blazed so hot it melted the cage in which she had kept herself.

She quickened her pace. It wasn't fair; it didn't make sense, but in that moment, with her feet pounding the pavement on the shadow-shrouded residential street, June blamed Winifred for all of it. It was easier to blame Winifred. Simpler. Better. Because if June didn't blame Winifred, she'd self-destruct.

Rosie had stopped following June; she worried for June, but she also didn't know how to help her; she thought that she should let June walk down the road alone to cool off, and maybe tomorrow, it would all be better.

But Rosie had a tendency to assume the best in people—it was part of her charm, her weakness, her virtue.

June wasn't cooling off the farther she walked—she was heating up.

When June made it to Winifred's house, a box on a nearby power line was indeed smoking. People were in the yard laughing, running around, twirling, smoking, drinking, and who knows what else. Had no one called the police? Or had the police simply given up?

She stormed up the drive, unsure of what she was doing here, only certain that she needed to find Winifred—to tell her off, perhaps. June didn't know. She couldn't picture herself being violent with Winifred, but perhaps screaming at the woman would make June feel better. She'd just have to find Winifred and see what happened.

But June was still June; she'd rather die than enter that godforsaken cottage ever again.

Rather than climb the steps toward the front door—which was currently ajar, with funny-smelling smoke pouring out—June took the side yard, following a narrow pathway toward the back of the house. Overgrown hedges snagged at the skirt of her dress; uneven pavers and snarled weeds made her stumble. Paper lanterns lit her way, candles flickering ominously. When she reached the backyard, she stopped in the shadows, appalled by what she saw.

Musicians were playing instruments in a horrible acoustic jumble. Men were dumping champagne into the mouths of ladies in the pool. Gold-painted individuals were dancing obscenely. More were simply making a racket: howling at the stars, yodeling, whooping, giggling. June heard moans of ecstasy from inside the gardening shed to her right. No one seemed to notice or care that the power was out—in fact, they seemed enlivened by the night.

It sickened her that this sort of disgusting merriment had been the cause of *her* ruin.

Whatever envy June had held for Winifred's freedom from the expectations of this neighborhood vanished. She didn't envy this—she *despised* it. And June was now determined to put a stop to it.

She walked forward, unsure of how to break up such chaos. Her eyes were fixed on the drunk people in the pool when she tripped over a paper lantern, landing hard on her hands and knees. The candle caught flame on the paper dome, transforming it into ash before shrinking down to a mere spark and extinguishing completely.

June swiveled so she was sitting on her hip, her knees curled. She examined the scrapes on her skin, already beading with blood. Not ten feet away, a couple stumbled out of the gardening shed, holding hands. The man accidentally kicked a metal can just inside the door; it toppled, spilling gasoline into the grass. The couple ran off, oblivious.

Pushing herself up off the ground, June walked over to the can and set it upright. The harsh scent of gasoline burned her nostrils. Her gaze trailed from the spill to a nearby candlelit orb to the house looming above.

She was always fixing things. Always setting them right. Always doing what a good woman would do. In her fog of hurt and anger, she wondered what would happen if she did the opposite: if she poured out the rest of the gasoline on the lantern.

Some things could be so easy. Too easy. Destruction right at her fingertips. She had the potential to stop a fire or start one—or walk away and let fate decide.

The thought frightened June; it also made her feel powerful. She'd never wielded so much agency than in this moment, standing at the base of Winifred's house next to a can of gasoline and an already-lit flame.

75

Marie compressed the gas pedal and clutch, thrusting her Plymouth into a higher gear. Tears blurred the dark shapes of the trees framing the road; at this strange hour, few other cars existed. The emptiness of the neighborhood made her drive even faster, as if she could outrun Winifred's betrayal.

But she couldn't. It sat in the passenger seat, as real as a person, repeating Winifred's explanation as clearly as if Winifred herself were sitting there: *I was your first patron, and I was your last.*

Marie sniffled and rubbed her damp nose with the back of her wrist. She thought of all the instances Winifred had been kind to her and wondered which had strings attached. She felt like an animal being used for profit, a horse sent round and round a track. Every time Marie stumbled, Winifred had been there to encourage her, to convince her that she could run faster; to think that Winifred's actions had been driven not by friendship, but profit, made Marie want to cry, or scream, or—perhaps most disturbingly—paint.

Her gaze flicked to the rearview mirror and the painting in her back seat. It faced forward, like a child. It might as well have been Dottie's ten-year-old figure back there; the painting went beyond inanimate. Between Winifred's betrayal in the front and Dottie in the back, the car felt oddly *full*. Crowded.

Marie stared at the painting in the mirror for far too long before blinking back to the road—but even then, she only half saw what was ahead of her. As it went with any work in progress, she couldn't help but think about her next move. Adding highlights to the forest in the background, perhaps, or better defining James's shoulders. Come to think of it, Dottie's gown appeared a little off, too; she'd imagined it as a nightgown, but now she wondered if it ought to be a hospital gown.

Her breath caught, and she tapped the brakes, even though nothing was there. To paint a hospital gown would be to acknowledge what'd happened, and Marie had never done that. *Never.* Even *Coneflower Cradle* had been fictitious enough to sidestep reality—a nightmare painted as if it were a dream.

But a hospital gown . . . that was different. That was *real.* Before, she hadn't been able to face it. Now, she wondered if she should.

It wasn't long after their adventure in the Thoroughbred stable that Dottie had grown pale, complaining about her tummy. Her father had accused her of dramatics, putting off her mother's pleas to call a doctor. But after just two days, she became so lethargic that even her father grew concerned, and her parents admitted her to the local hospital.

Marie could still remember the afternoon that Dottie's mother called their house with news that Dottie was worryingly sick. Marie's own mother had been in the middle of baking bread, and when she heard their ring code and hurriedly answered the phone, her flour-covered hands had left a white, dusty residue on the receiver. Marie had been sitting on the kitchen floor with a pencil and paper, drawing a horse, of all things. But at the sound of her mother's concern, she'd pushed up off the hardwood and walked closer.

"No, not at all, Marie has been just fine, haven't you dear?" Marie's mother said, pivoting to look down at her daughter. "Have you had an upset tummy? Do you feel unwell?"

Marie shook her head.

"She feels fine," her mother repeated into the phone, her voice too high, too concerned.

"Mama," Marie said, tugging on the ties of her mother's apron. The bow loosened, and the apron came undone. "What's wrong?"

"Yes, all right," her mother said, ignoring her. "Of course, I'll have Jim pick up your boys now. I'll bring—" A pause. "Goodness, no, it's no trouble. Marie and I will be there shortly."

Marie didn't know exactly what was going on, but the tone of her mother's voice had made her chest grow cold, like the slow seep of icy creek water spreading from her heart out into her extremities.

When her mother hung up, she slung her apron off her neck and crouched down to Marie's level, her housedress dusting the floor. "You're sure you feel all right, dear?"

Marie nodded.

"Okay," she said and drew Marie into a quick hug. When she pulled back, she kept her hands on Marie's shoulders. "Sweetheart, that was Dottie's mother. Dottie is in the hospital, and she's very sick. We're going to pay her a visit, all right?"

Marie nodded again, clutching her pencil to her chest.

Marie had never seen the inside of a hospital before, and when they arrived, the otherworldliness of it scared her. The nursemaids all wore funny caps, and the doctors wore long coats, and everything was a disturbing starch white or steel gray. Her mother had asked Marie to clip a bouquet of garden flowers, and Marie clutched the bundle of coneflowers and lavender in one hand, holding her mother's with the other.

They were shown to a room, and Marie's mother paused outside it and crouched down to her level again. "Marie, dear," she said, and her voice had an odd note to it—both melodic and low. "Now, Dottie is very sick, so it's important we use our whisper voices. Can you do that?"

It seemed all Marie could do since her mother had gotten the call was nod, so that's what she did.

"Good." Her mother straightened the bib of Marie's dress, her warm fingers brushing Marie's neck. Her voice was watery when she added, "You chose the prettiest flowers, dear."

And then her mother stood and ushered Marie inside.

The room smelled of sickness—that's the first thing Marie noticed. Sour, cloying, wrong—so far beyond the freshness of the forest and fields in which Dottie and Marie often frolicked. The room was also too hot. She tugged at the collar of her dress, overcome by the awful smell and the stuffy air.

The next thing Marie noticed were Dottie's parents. They had sunken blue shadows under their eyes, mouths and foreheads twisted. It was Dottie's father's expression that disturbed Marie the most. She'd never seen a man look troubled; she was used to men looking strong, confident, self-assured. Uneasiness cut deep lines on her friend's father's cheek, and that cold feeling returned to Marie's chest, spreading.

Marie's mother ushered her farther into the room. "Bill, Laura," she said. "Marie picked flowers."

"Oh, how thoughtful. Thank you, dear," Mrs. Evers said to Marie. "Dottie is so glad you could pay her a visit. She's very poorly, but I'm sure you being here will lift her spirits."

It took Marie a moment to loosen her grasp on the flowers, but then Mrs. Evers had them and passed them to Mr. Evers, who clutched them awkwardly but tenderly in his huge calloused hand, the hand he used to hold a bottle and discipline his boys, the hand that now shook.

"I'll find a vase for those," Marie's mother said, and then the flowers were passed along once again.

Marie didn't understand why the adults were so fixated on her stupid bundle of yard flowers. But then her gaze rose to the big hospital bed, and suddenly she understood how bad it was.

Dottie was swaddled in stiff sheets and appeared so small that the pillows seemed to swallow her up. Her skin was yellow, her lips cracked and pale, her hair oily and pressed flat against her scalp. As Marie crept closer, she noticed the bed was surrounded by scary-looking metal machines. It dawned on her that something was, in fact, very, *very* wrong.

The hot air pressed down on Marie's forehead, making her skin clammy.

"Look, Dottie, Marie is here. She came to see you," Mrs. Evers said, brushing past Marie to place a gentle hand on her daughter's colorless forehead.

A hand pressed into Marie's back, urging her forward. Marie was afraid to get closer: both afraid of catching whatever sickness had made Dottie look so frail and afraid of accidentally hurting Dottie's delicate body with her perfectly healthy one. But then Dottie smiled weakly and raised her arm, and Marie was inexplicably drawn to her friend, just as she always had been, a sunflower swiveling toward the sun.

She grasped her friend's hand, noticing the surprising heat of Dottie's skin. A fever. Marie had had one of those before, but it'd passed.

"Hi," Marie said.

Dottie only squeezed her hand, her cracked lips pursing. She let go of Marie's hand and reached for her stuffed doggie, Patches, whom she tugged close.

"Would you like some water, dear?" Mrs. Evers asked her daughter, offering up a cup.

Dottie turned away, clutching Patches even closer.

"What's . . . ?" Marie's mother asked weakly.

"The doctor says it's a bacterial infection," Dottie's father said gruffly. "It's gotten severe. They're worried about her kidneys."

Marie didn't understand the words, and that lack of understanding made the situation all the more frightening—to not even know her friend's sickness made it feel huge, monstrous.

"How could this happen?" Marie's mother asked.

"Who knows? The most likely cause is manure, but by the way the doctor described it, she could've picked it up anywhere."

Marie wanted to climb into bed with Dottie, but her fear made her back away, instead. Tears welled and fell, and she shook all over. Not long after that, Marie's mother took her home.

Looking back on it now, Marie always saw that moment—her body shaking and leaking liquid sorrow—as the moment she realized her friend was going to die. It was a fear not unlike the one she'd experienced in the horse stable, when she thought Dottie would get kicked by the Thoroughbred. Down among the hay and horse piss, Marie had been certain that the Thoroughbred was about to kill Dottie—and ultimately, Marie might've been right. She just hadn't expected it to drag out as long as it did.

Marie gripped the steering wheel harder, the road shimmering from her blurred vision. She tapped the brakes and pulled over, shaking just as hard as she had in that hospital room when she was ten years old.

She glanced over her shoulder at the painting in the back seat. Come to think of it, Dottie's ethereal gown *did* look like the one she'd worn in the hospital. Marie considered unpacking her paints right here, fixing the lines while inside her car. But instead, she faced forward again and bowed her head against the steering wheel.

Dottie had been Marie's first love. Grief and paint had become the only ways Marie could still feel her near. To move on, to let go, would mean to lose Dottie forever.

Hurley Downs deserved to be razed to the ground for what it had done to Dottie. And Marie—maybe Marie deserved her misery too. Because had Marie not lived on a racetrack, had she not allowed Dottie to explore the horse stable, Dottie might still be alive.

For so long, Marie had believed that isolation was an adequate punishment for what happened. It had first come to fruition as elective mutism. Then social anxiety in school. After her parents died, it meant moving away, to the city, living alone, existing alone. It wasn't until Winifred had come along that Marie allowed herself to unfurl again, just a little, just enough to feel exposed to the warm possibility of friendship and feel her cold heart thawing.

Marie didn't want to lose another friend, but here she was, leaving, probably to never see Winifred again. It didn't seem fair. It didn't seem *right*. Marie had tried to paint it out of her, but she realized now, as she pressed her head into the wheel, that she'd been painting around the pain, not through it. This past summer had been the first time she'd felt like painting *dispelled* the pain in a real way—and now she was driving away again, instead of facing the pain head-on.

Marie lifted her gaze to the windshield and out at the night beyond. The sky was ink black and speckled crystalline. A single car neared, headlights blinding. Her vision blurred again, but this time, she saw the concepts of paintings flash across the windshield, one after another, like a slideshow of a whole new collection. Paintings of Thoroughbreds and Hurley Downs, schoolyard sandwiches and her brother's boots. She saw the hospital gown and the hearse and the graveyard. She saw the paint set her mother bought and Dottie's stuffed dog, which Marie hoped Dottie's parents still had in a box somewhere safe. She saw many fixtures of her childhood, and Dottie's childhood, and their brief time together. The colors weren't that of reality but a pastel world: Easter pinks, sky blue, and sweet peach. Happy colors. Sunrise colors.

Marie blinked, her heart welling with an inspiration so strong and surging it threatened to drown her in warmth. She needed to paint—now. She needed to find a place to set up her easel and get it out.

Marie shifted her car into first gear and glanced in the rearview mirror for anyone else on the road. The long neighborhood road stretched behind her, empty. Above, the sky beyond was . . . gray. Gray with a black cloud. Except . . . no, it wasn't a cloud. It was a plume of smoke, rising above the rooftops to blot out the stars.

The smoke was coming from Winifred's house.

76

At first, Winifred thought the smoke in the hallway was innocent. Her house had been filled with it since the first busload of college students had arrived, and in the wake of the partygoers' thrill toward the power going out, the debauchery outside Bruce's study had only increased.

But as she and Irene exited the solitude of the empty office, she noticed—belatedly—that the smoke clouding throughout the house was dark, and the scent was all wrong. They heard screaming next—not high-pitched glee this time but genuine fear.

That's when Winifred put two and two together: her house was on fire.

It seemed that the worst of the smoke was coming from the library, which was on the western side, farther down the hall from Bruce's study. Winifred couldn't guess how the fire had started—a stray cigarette? an overturned lantern on the pathway just outside?—but she knew that all those old books of Bruce's would go up fast.

Winifred called out into the chaos, urging people to exit the cottage. She ushered Irene away from the library, toward the parlor. The smoke was thick in the hall, choking them. Irene held the collar of her shirt over her mouth, ducking her head as Winifred pressed her forward through the panicking crowd. Caught up in a stampede, they soon found themselves pushing through the patio doors and outside, where folks spilled gratefully onto the lawn and the smoke billowed up into the night.

But for Winifred, the relief of the fresh evening air was brief.

Marie had left practically everything behind, and Winifred couldn't stand to think that all those magnificent pieces of art—paintings that could one day lead Marie back into the light of the recognition she so deserved—would be lost in flame. So she ran back into her burning house before Irene or anyone else could stop her.

That's how she found herself in Marie's studio—blinded by smoke, coughing and sweating in the immense crackling heat—trying to decide which paintings to save. People were still escaping, Good Samaritans sweeping the dark corners of the house for lovers or introverts, yelling *fire* at the tops of their coughing lungs all through the upstairs corridor. Their voices and the smoke distracted Winifred's thoughts, but she pushed through the panic, trying to focus.

Marie's studio was filled with paintings—more than Winifred had originally thought. She'd tried hard to respect Marie's privacy, so aside from a couple of glimpses, she hadn't looked around when she was last here. Now, she was overwhelmed by Marie's prolific and somewhat chaotic system: finished paintings leaning together in one upright stack against the far wall, unfinished (or abandoned?) paintings leaning in their own stack, and fresh canvases in a third. Not to mention the endless supplies: new and partially used tubes of paint, brushes with stained bristles, paper, and Marie's large easel by the window.

Winifred would have to make multiple trips, she realized. She'd rescue the finished paintings first, then the unfinished canvases next; the blank canvases and paints were replaceable. Marie's original artwork was not.

Winifred grabbed as much of the first stack as she could, gripping four wooden frames and squeezing them together. The canvases were large—at least a couple of feet on each side—and they were unwieldy to carry. By the time she made it into the hall, her fingers were already burning with the strain, the canvases slipping as the muscles in her palms cramped.

Winifred dumped the paintings on the floor, choking on the smoke. She could *hear* the fire now, a terrifying, snapping roar. She couldn't see farther than a few feet ahead, but she knew this house; she could do this.

She decided to adjust the paintings to two in each hand, carrying them at her sides like odd briefcases. That was better. With a sturdier grip, she ran down the stairs and out the closest door: the front.

When she hit the clean outdoor air, she gasped, sputtering and coughing out the smoke that had already begun to choke her lungs, making her dizzy. She deposited the paintings in the grass, huffing and puffing.

From her front yard, she could clearly see that most of the smoke was rising from the right side of her house, back by the toolshed— exactly what she'd suspected. People were still helping each other escape, arms and shoulders clutched as they guided one another out of the burning house and into the grass.

A man nearby had removed his shirt, holding the cloth over his mouth. Winifred approached him.

"Can I have that?" she asked. "This is my house, and I need to go back inside."

The man regarded her, dilated pupils flicking from her face to the house and back. "It's not safe," he rasped.

"I know," she said, reaching for the shirt clutched in his fist.

He handed it over. "Good luck, lady."

She tied the shirt around the lower half of her face—over her nose and mouth—and ran back into the house without another word.

Inside, things were beginning to fall apart. The velvet drapes on the opposite end of the huge foyer were singed, their hems flickering with flame. The hall that led to the library—just past the staircase—was illuminated with a frighteningly loud blaze. All those books had surely stoked the fire beyond containment, and it would be dangerous for her to travel back upstairs to Marie's studio.

She thought about what else was up there—what needed saving. Then it occurred to her: *Wildflower* in Bruce's study.

Winifred diverted her path toward the illuminated hallway. Bruce's door was the second one on the left—she could make it, she could—

When she rounded the bend, she halted. The air was thick and unbearably hot, the flames roaring in a way she'd never experienced in her life. The end of the hall looked like the depths of hell, a black maw with flames licking out of it. Every instinct inside her body told her to run, *escape*, but she was so close.

Winifred pushed forward, moving slowly through the heat. She hunched low, watching each barefooted step, careful not to tread on melted bits of carpet, embers, or broken glass. The shirt around her face helped shield a bit of the smoke, but she still tried to duck under the worst of it, plumes pooling along the ceiling like the blackest thundercloud.

When she reached Bruce's door, she pushed it inward, only it stopped partway. Something inside had toppled and now blocked the door from opening beyond a few inches. Winifred threw herself at the open space, using her body weight to wedge through. When she finally broke into the room, the sight was horrifying: the wall Bruce's study shared with the library had caved in, scattering timber and drywall and drapery across the floor. The bar cart had fallen, too, glass everywhere; flames had followed the spilled alcohol across the floor, igniting the wooden beams and pooled curtains.

Winifred raced to the wall on which *Wildflower* hung and lifted the painting off its hook. It was a large piece: three feet tall and five feet wide. Winifred carried it over her head; if worse came to worst, and the ceiling fell, perhaps the painting would shield her a little.

But she resisted thoughts of fear and possibility. She'd be fine; she just had to—

Winifred stifled a shriek as she stepped on a shard of broken glass. She lifted her foot to inspect the damage, but she couldn't see much detail beyond the dark blood covering her sole. Setting the painting on the ground beside her, she reached down, feeling along the wound.

When her fingers met hard glass, she tugged on the edge, pulling the shard out with a soft cry of pain.

Her body was beginning to shake uncontrollably, not just from the slice across her foot but from the approaching blaze, the heat, the choke of smoke. She was growing dizzy, sweating profusely, and the lack of control over her quivering limbs made her shake even harder. She had to get out of this room.

A large crash made her scramble backward; the ceiling was starting to cave, crossbeams cracking. She looked around, considering climbing out the window, but it was blocked by flaming drapery. She'd have to go out the way she'd come in: through the hall.

With one foot in front of the other, Winifred crept slowly along, wincing with each step on her bleeding foot. She had to hurry, so she pushed through the pain, carrying the painting upright in one hand like a makeshift walking stick. It was a toppled lamp that had blocked the door; its broken glass shade created more obstacles. With care, Winifred navigated around it and wrenched the door farther open.

She had imagined that reaching the door would be her salvation, but her hope now turned to ash.

The hall was black with an opaque darkness, save for the wall of shimmering heat emanating ever closer. At this pace, she'd never make it; she was growing faint. The T-shirt covering her mouth had grown damp from her breath, and it smelled like smoke, and maybe it was suffocating her. She had to pick up the pace. *Now.*

Screaming through the pain in her foot, Winifred ran. Bits of ash stung her eyes, sparks swept through her hair, and rubble hurt her feet, but instinct told her not to slow. When she broke free of the hall, the visibility improved slightly; she fixed her gaze upon her open front door, a faint rectangle of lighter gray in the charcoal haze. Winifred shifted *Wildflower* over her head again and pushed through her panic and pain toward the promise of safety.

77

Parked cars clogged the shoulder of Winifred's street all the way to the Shore House, so Marie abandoned her Plymouth in someone else's driveway.

Then she ran.

The pavement jolted up through her knees, and her thighs cramped. She only ran harder, pumping her arms and hauling cool sea-breezy air into her lungs until they burned with exertion.

When she reached Winifred's lawn, she asked coughing, confused partygoers if they'd seen the tall woman in the sequin dress. No one knew who she was talking about, and a cold and familiar fear seeped into her chest, spreading outward.

The house had gone up in an immense blaze, flames licking out of upstairs windows, smoke billowing high into the night sky. Marie made her way toward the front steps, asking every person she could if they'd seen Winifred. Perhaps she was just around back, perhaps Marie should—

"The redheaded woman?" a shirtless man asked, having overheard her frantic questioning.

Marie grasped his sweaty arms in relief. "Yes! Yes, have you seen her?"

He nodded, but his face didn't pull into the hopeful expression that Marie expected. He frowned. "She went inside."

"She *what?*"

"She was trying to save those . . . paintings," he said, sounding dumbfounded as he gestured at a jumbled stack of canvases resting in the grass.

Marie knew they were hers without looking. Still, her gaze slid to the Thoroughbred staring up at her from the pile.

Why would Winifred risk her life for Marie's half-finished art? Was Winifred trying to save an investment? The thought incensed Marie, but it didn't seem right. Winifred had plenty of money. She also had an impressive collection of far more valuable works by far more important painters. Why risk her life for Marie's paltry attempts?

Stooping, Marie looked through the canvases. All her recently finished paintings were here. Three Thoroughbreds and the painting of Winifred, which they'd never gotten around to hanging.

She faced the man again. "Did she say what else she was trying to save?"

He shook his head.

If he'd been wearing a shirt, Marie would've grasped his collar and rattled him. "She didn't say *anything*?"

He shook his head again. "Sorry."

Marie turned away from him, facing the blaze. The cold, seeping dread was beginning to freeze Marie's blood. She couldn't lose another friend. She *wouldn't*.

Marie ran toward the front steps, her icy heart in her throat.

It was exactly then that Winifred tumbled out of the front door, sputtering and hacking. Her red hair was dusted gray with soot, as was the shirt wrapped around the bottom half of her face. Her arms were slick with sweat and smudged with ash and were quivering even as she clutched a painting by its wooden frame.

Marie's pulse fluttered with reluctant relief. When she reached Winifred's side, she grasped her friend's arm, helping her down the porch steps. One of Winifred's feet was covered in blood, leaving a trail of it on the stone pathway.

"Are you insane?" Marie said to her over the roar of the snapping, humming, *burning.*

Winifred pulled the shirt off her neck and collapsed in the grass, one hand still clutching the painting she'd risked her life to rescue. *Wildflower.* Emotion welled in Marie's chest faster than a flash flood; she let out a watery sob and threw her arms around Winifred's neck, pulling her close. For a moment, they held each other, shaking with shock and relief and regret and gratitude.

Then Marie pulled back and grasped Winifred's shoulders, the emotion in her chest beginning to simmer and steam. "What were you thinking Winifred? You could've died in there."

Winifred's lips twisted into a small smile. She looked ridiculous, the top of her face a raccoon mask of ash, and the bottom half still pale and clean.

"Why are you smiling?" Marie asked, wiping the tears off her face. "That was incredibly stupid and dangerous."

"You came back," Winifred said.

Marie's anger faltered but only slightly. "Of course I did."

Winifred's eyes brimmed again, and Marie glanced away. All around them, folks were huddled in the grass, wide eyed, and watching the hot wreckage of Winifred's home. But all of that seemed meaningless compared to the woman sitting beside her.

"I don't get it," Marie said. "Why my paintings?"

Winifred leaned back on her hands, stretching out her sooty legs in a wide *V.* To Marie, she appeared both exhausted and in shock as her home burned before her. The adrenaline was probably keeping her true hysteria at bay.

"I didn't really think about it," Winifred said slowly. "I just felt like—of all the things in my house—the paintings were the most important."

Marie swallowed the hard lump in her throat and diverted her attention to Winifred's bloody foot. She reached for the discarded T-shirt, rolled it, and then wrapped it tightly around the nasty gash.

Without looking up, she whispered, "But why? What about Bruce's things?"

Winifred was quiet for a long moment, long enough for Marie to regard her face again; she was watching the fire.

"Bruce was never his stuff, to me," Winifred finally said, and she was thinking about her house and what it meant to lose it, this place that she and Bruce had shared, this place filled with happy memories and memories she wouldn't mind forgetting. She knew she was in shock; later, she would mourn their cottage by the sea. But Winifred had already *been* mourning, and nothing would ever amount to the pain of losing Bruce.

The pain of losing Marie had come close, though. Not in the same way—because, as Irene had said, Marie leaving was Winifred's doing—but it was similar. Losing someone you loved—whether through abandonment, death, or a falling-out—it all hurt. But that, she realized now, couldn't be solved by holding on at all costs.

She turned to Marie. "I am so sorry for what I did," she said. "I should've told you about the patronage as soon as I realized who you were. Hell, I probably should've asked who you were before I invited you to move in with me." A pause. "But I never should've used my money to control you. It was ugly, awful, despicable of me."

Marie's dark eyebrows pinched together. "Then why go to such lengths?"

Winifred slumped. "Because I believe in you, Marie. And that's the truth. You're too talented to toil in obscurity." Her lips pressed together. "And because . . . well, I already lost Bruce. I didn't want to lose you too." She pivoted to face Marie, tucking her knees up under herself. "But that was wrong. I allowed my fear of being alone to overtake my reason. I was controlling, and calculating, and bullheaded, and just a terrible friend. And I'm so sorry."

Marie stared into Winifred's eyes, digesting her words. The eyeliner that Marie had painted on hours ago had long since smudged off, leaving odd black streaks amid the smears of ash on her cheeks and forehead. She looked wild—and maybe she was—but as Marie regarded her, she began to wonder if she didn't love Winifred's particular brand of wildness.

Marie had once thought that security and freedom were mutually exclusive, but she'd been wrong. There was one thing in the world that supplied both: love. She'd learned it way back when, with Dottie; now she was relearning it with Winifred. Love could make a person feel secure and protected and safe, and yet simultaneously empowered and enlivened and free. Unlike romantic love, with its heady angst, or familial love, with its obligation, the love between two friends seemed to Marie to be the most pure.

At least, that was its potential. And here, among the many folks sitting in the grass as if they were at an outdoor concert and not an active tragedy, Marie saw that potential in Winifred.

Marie cleared her throat. "I lost a friend," she said softly. "Her name was Dottie, and as kids, we were inseparable. She was a free spirit—always pushing me to do things I was too timid to try on my own, taking me on adventures in the woods behind the racetrack, making me laugh . . . making me *better*.

"We were playing in the track stables one day—a place we shouldn't've been—and we ducked into a horse's stall to avoid being seen by some barn staff. I don't know if it was the manure, or the horse licking Dottie's face, or what, but she . . . she got sick from it. And she died. And I was the one who took her there in the first place."

"The girl," Winifred said softly. "D for . . . Dottie."

Hot tears streamed down Marie's face, and she swiped them away with her fingertips, nodded. "For months after her death, I couldn't speak. All I could do was draw. That's how it began. The entire collection was built upon that grief . . . and regret. But it didn't dispel the memories. With each new piece, it felt like the paintings might eat me alive—they were corrosive. Obsessive." Marie paused, trying to rein in her tears. "The work got stale. That's the only way I can explain it. I felt like one of those Thoroughbreds, racing round and round the same track, over and over again. Never fast enough. Never *winning*."

Winifred glanced toward the Thoroughbred paintings, mirroring the direction of Marie's thoughts.

"Then you came along," Marie said. "You reminded me of Dottie: funny, outgoing, encouraging. You both made me better. But I didn't want to grow close to another . . . I tried to resist . . ." Marie attempted a smirk. "It didn't work."

Winifred giggled, and it seemed so out of place for her to laugh on the lawn, surrounded by strangers, all of them watching her house burn down.

"A valve opened up in me," Marie went on. "And suddenly, all these memories I'd tried to forget came bubbling up to the surface. I started painting them, and this time, the paintings felt like they were dispelling the pain somehow—helping me to face it and then let it go." She pointed at the pile of new canvases. "Every single one of those is a memory I tried not to face, a source of grief I kept buried inside. And every single one of those made me feel better, despite my resistance." She smiled softly. "I thought that if I could buy the track and destroy it, that maybe I could be free from it—but you were right. The track was never my answer."

"Oh, Marie," Winifred said, tears cutting clear paths through dust on her cheeks.

"I don't think the paintings were my answer either," Marie said, watching Winifred closely. "I think becoming your friend—"

Her last word was cut off by the impact of Winifred's body. She threw her arms around Marie and squeezed her tight, tipping them over in the grass. They were sobbing and smiling, hearts bursting open like seeds in springtime, alive with the promise of a gentler season. With warm soil and sunshine.

Flashing red lights and loud, loud sirens interrupted their moment, and Winifred released Marie. "You're a genius, you know?" she asked matter-of-factly. "Those paintings—those bad memories—that grief—*Dottie*—they're going to make you famous one day."

Marie rolled her eyes and stood, offering Winifred a hand. "You should probably talk to the firefighters."

Winifred rose on one foot, hovering her injured, shirt-wrapped sole above the ground. "Yes, right. But first, I wanted to give you this." She fished a wrinkled piece of paper out of her bra.

It was a business card for a Realtor. Marie stared down at it, confused.

Winifred began hobbling down the sloped lawn toward the fire trucks parked in the middle of the street. After a moment, Marie caught up with her, snaking her arm around Winifred's waist, helping her along.

"Aren't you going to explain what this is about?" Marie asked.

"Isn't it obvious?" Winifred asked. "We're going to buy the track together."

78

June knelt in the mud on the back lawn of Winifred's house among a crowd of hippies, performers, and adolescents, watching the flames. The fire was spectacular and terrible and overwhelming: a monster of heat, sound, and destruction. It hissed, it banged, it crackled, and it roared. The crowd around her stared at it with horror and fascination in their bleary eyes.

Who's to say what started it? A paper lantern, a can of gasoline. A strong gust of wind, an act of will.

Like the snap of a rubber band against the tender skin of an inner wrist, June's whole body buzzed with the sting of this night. Tomorrow—in a few hours, perhaps—she'd hear from her lawyer that she didn't have a case. She would lose her daughter. She would lose her seat on the SPW, the first woman in an entire family lineage to fail. Harry would sign the divorce papers and marry his mistress, and June would be officially alone and disgraced. Tomorrow, she would lose all the things that made her, her. Then who would she be?

For now, she was just another onlooker of a tragedy. An anonymous spectator. But as sirens approached, it occurred to June that her mere presence would be incriminating—or at least highly suspicious. So she stood, attempting to wipe the mud from her dress, only to smudge it further. One more thing that couldn't be saved.

June wove through the mesmerized crowd and slunk around the left side of the house, far away from the flames, which had overtaken the right along with the gardening shed. Her heels sank into the land-scaping mulch as she brushed past overgrown bushes.

When she reached the front lawn—which was just as crowded as the back—she spotted the fire engines and a team of firefighters swarming underneath the flashing truck lights, the crew urging people backward and hauling a large hose toward the flames.

One of the firemen—dressed in a pristine yellow coat and reflective helmet—was chatting with a sooty woman in a shiny minidress, who sat on the back edge of an ambulance. One leg was crossed over the other, allowing a medic to inspect the bottom of her foot. Winifred.

June paused on the edge of the landscaping, unsure of what to do. She considered crouching underneath one of the bushes until she could slip away, but if someone found her like that, it would be even more questionable than if they'd spotted her out in the open. Her indecision immobilized her as she watched the firefighter tip his helmet at Winifred and walk away, calling orders to the assemblage of uniformed men.

The medic straightened; Winifred said something to him, and he laughed. The bright-white bandage around Winifred's foot changed colors with the flashing lights of the fire engine. She uncrossed her legs and gingerly hopped down. The medic waved over a young man who was cradling his wrist. Winifred turned toward a shorter woman—Marie, the artist—who helped Winifred walk a little ways off before plopping down in the grass.

They held hands, and it confounded June to see them both so calm. They appeared content simply to have each other, safe and well amid disaster. Seeing them like that caused June's heart to twist, clench, *ache*—a rag getting wrung. But it wasn't out of hatred or disgust or even resentment.

It was jealousy.

To her friends, June had justified her dislike of Winifred with the excuse of Winifred's mistake at the wedding—but the truth was, deep down, June disliked Winifred because Winifred was different. She didn't conform to others' expectations, as June had tried so hard to do. While June bent over backward in her pursuit of perfection, Winifred had blundered that tightrope walk and still managed to end up better off. And somehow, that had felt like a threat to June. An insult.

Because as much as Winifred seemed to crave attention and connection, she did it as *herself*. Imperfect and quirky and different. Sure, she'd tried to fit in with June's crowd, but ultimately, Winifred had found love and happiness without them. In fact, it seemed that Winifred had found love and happiness *despite* them. Even after Bruce's death, Winifred had managed to secure friendship and joy amid her calamity, seemingly not caring what other people thought.

Because what did it matter what other people thought, if you had a house full of happy guests and a friend to lean on when life became too much? June's life on the outside might've been shiny and smooth, but it was hollow; Winifred's life was imperfect but full.

June saw it plainly as she watched Winifred playfully elbow her friend from their place in the grass. Winifred had eschewed all that June strived for in lieu of what June now recognized as more important: a marriage built on bliss instead of status, delicious (if improper) food, laughter over propriety, and an unconventional friend who wasn't a strategic connection but rather someone who was simply *there for her*.

June thought about Barbara, her so-called best friend, who'd betrayed her tonight. Barbara had always been judgmental; June had just never been on the receiving end of it. She'd thought she'd been safe from Barbara's wrath, but she was wrong. Barbara was only loyal to Barbara.

Rosie, on the other hand, had defended June—even when it would've benefited her to look the other way. From the park to tonight's blackout, Rosie had stood by June and been a helper, a friend. Naive, but no hidden intentions. She was just . . . *good*. And June had been cruel to her. She'd never deserved Rosie's kindness, and yet Rosie had continued to offer it.

What had June's conformity done, besides make June miserable and lead to the loss of her daughter? Pride, social expectations, and her own self-hatred had only harmed Bella. Just as June's parents had unknowingly harmed her with those same qualities.

The twinge in June's chest screwed tighter; she had to get out of here.

She crept forward, watching Winifred and Marie as she tried to stealthily make her way toward the street. Edging along the bushes, she aimed for a cluster of onlookers standing near the pileup of emergency trucks. She was so close—almost to cover and safety. No one would ever know she was here. She would go home, take a shower, and wait in solitude for her life to fall apart tomorrow.

Except Winifred had noticed June from her spot in the grass. She squeezed Marie's hand twice, cutting off their conversation. Marie quieted, brow creased, and Winifred subtly jerked her head toward the bushes. Marie stole a glance, eyes widening.

She spun back toward Winifred. "What is *she* doing here?" Marie whispered.

Winifred narrowed her eyes. "I'm not sure."

After all that had happened tonight, Winifred felt spent—physically and emotionally. Her body ached, and a dull melancholy had settled at the base of her sternum. She mourned the loss of her beloved cottage, even as she entertained a small nugget of relief from being free of it and this neighborhood and the memories of Bruce tucked into every room and restaurant and street corner.

She didn't want a confrontation with June Duxbury tonight—but her curiosity and suspicion got the better of her.

"June!" Winifred raised her hand and waved, beckoning the woman over.

June flinched and froze, her shoulders hunched. She'd clearly wanted to escape without being seen, and the pure fear on her face gave Winifred pause. Why *was* she here?

June's hesitation lasted only a few seconds, and then she schooled her pretty features into a comically indifferent mask. She approached with confident steps—as if the uneven grass and her high heels were no matter—and stopped in front of them with her hands on her hips.

"Ah, there you are," she said haughtily, a mask all three of them could see right through. "Your party caused a blackout that shut down the entire SPW fundraiser. Happy?"

Winifred smothered her urge to laugh at June's frustration. She wanted to tell June to look around—at the ambulances and the fire trucks and the roaring flames of her destroyed cottage—but a breeze picked up behind June and past her, ruffling Winifred's hair. The scent of ash, perfume, and gasoline met Winifred's nostrils.

She glanced at Marie, who had apparently scented the same thing. June's dress was covered in mud and filth, and strands of her hair had been pulled loose, perhaps from . . . shrubbery, judging by the twig poking out of June's French twist. Like the backdrop of an impossibly realistic play, the firefighters behind June had gotten the fire under control, wood hissing and steaming as water doused the flames.

Winifred and Marie quietly took in the evidence on June's person and realized simultaneously what it might mean: Could June have lit this fire?

There were many alternative possibilities, plenty of ways the fire could've been started that had nothing to do with June Duxbury. After all, a transformer had blown. The yard had been filled with little lit candles in paper lanterns. People had been smoking cigarettes and spilling alcohol all over the house.

Marie doubted that this uptight housewife could've done such a thing, but Winifred was certain, because Winifred saw June better than anyone else. June was a long line of dominoes, each one more capable of this fire than the last. The judgmental June who Bruce had first introduced to Winifred had long since toppled, as had the cruel and catty June that had attended Winifred's party last summer. Even the June that had hit Winifred's car couldn't have done *this*, but all these versions had gotten her closer to the June who stood before them now. This June was the only domino left standing.

This June was *real*.

And in this particular moment, the real June appeared defeated. Raw. Lost. Winifred could see a June like that doing damage like this, because a disgraced June was a June without anything left to lose.

Somehow, it was this June that Winifred found the most likable. Endearing, even. Because Winifred knew what it was like to contort herself into something she was not. Such efforts could drive any woman mad.

"I'm sorry about the fundraiser," Winifred said to her, and June's neutral face quaked.

She recovered quickly, though—practiced as she was. "You should be," she said, but the words were halfhearted.

Winifred *was* sorry, even though it wasn't her fault. The SPW meant a lot to June—as did her image, which was already unstable, what with her impending divorce. For June to have committed arson, something terrible must've happened. A public shaming, perhaps? Something with June's daughter?

Winifred felt Marie's stare on her; she practically heard Marie's silent question: *What are you going to do?*

The one thing about June's face that June couldn't control was her eyes, and when Winifred looked into them, she saw an agony there so deep and intense that it spurred Winifred to do something that surprised all three of them.

She patted the grass. "You look tired. Why don't you sit?"

79

Winifred's offer seemed loaded, but June couldn't deduce how or why. She saw only compassion on Winifred's face, and though she didn't completely trust her—this woman June had scorned so relentlessly— her kindness was enough to melt the last of June's resolve.

June bent her knees and arranged herself on the ground. The damp cold of the grass seeped through her dress, chilling her bottom, but Winifred felt warm beside her. The relief of rest spread through her tense muscles.

For a minute, the three women wordlessly watched the smoldering house by the sea.

The wind picked up again, and June scented the gasoline on her hands and shoes. She stiffened, pressing her lips together.

"There are many ways the fire could've started," Winifred said, still staring at the firefighters and the blackened carcass of her home.

June's pulse rocketed, accelerating so quickly she thought she might pass out.

"Did you see the paper lanterns in the yard when you were looking for me, just now?"

She nodded slowly, knowing she was caught in a trap.

"The power surge from my party caused a transformer to blow," Winifred continued. "People were smoking, drinking, spilling things. I heard people fooling around in my gardening shed, perhaps they knocked over a can of gasoline." Winifred turned toward June, fixing her with an even stare. "Perhaps you tripped and fell in that spilled gasoline, judging by the state of your dress and the twig in your hair and smell of it all over you."

June lifted her hand to her hair, feeling for the twig. She pulled it from the strands and fiddled with it in her lap, afraid to look directly at Winifred for fear that Winifred would see the truth in her eyes. Panic swept through her as easily as flame had swept through Winifred's house. When she finally opened her mouth to defend herself, Winifred cut her off.

"Who can say? As far as I can tell, the fire could've started in any number of ways."

June's eyes flicked up to Winifred's, and she saw the cunning and understanding there. The recognition.

Winifred turned toward her friend. "Isn't that right, Marie?"

Marie nodded, clearly confused.

Winifred turned back to June. "You're having a bad night, aren't you?"

And it was that question—that damning, accusatory, compassionate question—that finally broke through the final layer of June's strength. Her facade crumbled, and she buried her face in her hands, tears flooding her vision.

"I don't understand," she said into her cupped palms. "Why are you . . . ? Why are you not . . . ?" She couldn't complete the questions. To ask them in full would be to incriminate herself.

Winifred touched June's shoulder, her warm palm a surprising comfort. June looked up into the eyes of the woman she'd bullied and belittled and scoffed at, knowing that in this moment, her future was in Winifred's hands.

"Because, June," Winifred shared a small smile with Marie, then squeezed June's shoulder, her grin widening warmly, "everyone deserves a chance to start over. Even you."

80

Rosie squeezed June's hand reassuringly. "I promise you, she's the best gynecologist around," she said. "My friend said Dr. Chen saved her life."

June smoothed the flimsy johnny gown that the nurse had asked her to don. Her legs hung off the side of the examination table, and she nervously swung her white-socked feet back and forth. At one time, June would've braved this appointment alone, but she'd given up on propriety—or at least, she'd loosened her grip on it. Today, Rosie's hand in hers provided solace in this cold, hard-edged room; it heated and softened her nerves.

In the aftermath of June's fallout with the SPW and her divorce from Harry, Rosie had been the only friend to stick around. The two of them had a lot in common, right down to their overbearing mothers and their learned self-hatred. Only Rosie had found a way to rise above it—in part thanks to what she'd read in *The Feminine Mystique*—and now she was helping June do the same. And on the days when June had Bella, she used what she was learning from Rosie to raise her daughter to be strong, opinionated, and self-confident. To live outside the rigid definitions of womanhood that had benefited Harry but had kept June small. Bella deserved no less.

But this appointment was about what June deserved, and that was *answers*.

A month ago, June had made plans to have lunch with Rosie, but her pains had forced her to cancel. The old June would've been vague about her reasoning, but Winifred's words on the last night of summer—*everyone deserves a chance to start over*—had been rattling around June's mind ever since, and she'd decided to take a risk and be honest with Rosie about why she couldn't make it.

For Rosie, June's admission had made perfect sense, and it spurred a realization that had led to this appointment. A friend of Rosie's had struggled with the same ailment, and after nearly ten years of not being taken seriously by various doctors, Dr. Chen had suggested the rare diagnosis. As soon as Rosie had gotten off the phone with June that day, mind whirring, she'd called her friend to get the referral.

So now here June was, sitting on the examination table, hopeful that this doctor—a *woman*—could solve something that had plagued June's life since she was a pubescent girl. She didn't want to get her hopes up, but she couldn't help it.

June and Rosie waited in silence for another few minutes, and then the door clicked open, and they both sat a little straighter as a petite woman in a white coat walked in.

"Hi, Ms. Clearmont," Dr. Chen said, using June's maiden name, which she'd put on the form. "How are you feeling today? Nervous?"

June nodded, thankful that Dr. Chen said the word for her.

Dr. Chen's gaze flicked down to June and Rosie's still-clasped hands. "Would you like your friend to stay with you throughout the exam?"

June looked to Rosie, not wanting to force her into staying if she didn't want to but hoping beyond hope that she would.

Thankfully, Rosie answered for her. "I'll stay," she said, positioning herself up by June's head. "For moral support."

Dr. Chen smiled. "All right, then. June, if you could put your feet in the stirrups now."

June did as Dr. Chen requested, expecting the discomfort that Dr. Applebaum had always given her. But Dr. Chen's hands were warm, gentle. The examination didn't last long before she was removing her gloves.

"And you've been experiencing these pains for how long?"

"My whole life," June said, removing her feet from the stirrups to sit upright. Rosie patted June's back.

"And they diminished when you were pregnant with Bella?"

"Yes, for about two years," June said. "Although it was"—she pushed through the embarrassment—"it was very hard to get pregnant."

Dr. Chen nodded slowly. She still sat on her doctor's stool, and her hands were resting on her knees, eyes fixed on June, giving June her full attention. "Can you describe the pain for me? Cramping, aching, radiating?"

"All of those," June said, and for some reason, her voice choked up as she continued. "Especially the radiating pain. It travels up into my rib cage, and often into my hips, down one or both of my legs. And the pain in my back is excruciating. It's . . . it often makes me dizzy or ill."

Dr. Chen nodded again, eyebrows tipping upward in a soft expression, as if she believed June. As if she sympathized.

Suddenly, June had tears running down her cheeks, and she wasn't sure exactly why. Rosie reached for a box of tissues on the countertop and handed it to her.

Dr. Chen stood and walked up beside June, opposite Rosie. She clasped June's free hand and gazed squarely at her. "There is emerging research into a rare condition called endometriosis. It's a disorder in which tissue similar to your uterine lining—called your endometrium—grows outside your uterus. It can cause cysts, scarring, and very painful adhesions." She frowned slightly, as if imagining it herself. "Infertility too. It's hard to confidently diagnose, but the severity of your symptoms points in that direction."

"So . . . it's not . . ." June broke off, sniffled, regathered herself. "It's not all in my head?" Her voice was thin and distorted by tears.

"No, June. In fact, it horrifies me that you've been suffering in silence for so long."

June's lips pressed together, and she shook her head, tears raining on her gown.

"What about treatment?" Rosie asked helpfully.

"We'll want to take some X-rays and ultrasounds, first, but there are things we can do to lessen the pain." A pause. "There is no surefire cure," Dr. Chen said gently. "But we can work together to make you more comfortable, June."

For a moment, June sat with this news, letting it permeate every cell in her center. And then she was sobbing, big, heaving sobs, right there in the examination room. Rosie rubbed her back, telling her it was okay, she would be okay.

But June wasn't crying because of looming X-rays and ultrasounds and the rare incurability of her condition, or the fact that something was *wrong*.

She was crying with relief.

Pure, profound, overwhelming relief. It was as if June had been trapped in a dark room all her life, fumbling around all by herself, and Dr. Chen had just switched on the lights.

Even before menstruation, June had been acutely aware of her womanhood. When she screamed with glee in the yard, she was told her actions were unladylike. But what that really implied was that ladies were meant to be meek and polite, as if such qualities were the ultimate signs of femininity and virtue.

Over time, June had watched her mother fret over her own body: the scale, the measuring tape, the skipped breakfasts and refusals of dessert. Pulling and pinching and primping in the mirror. These were the habits of womanhood. The methods of maintaining marriages and status. Sometimes, women even did these things together, to bond.

When June was a teenager, that awareness of her body had quickly turned to self-consciousness, then—with her pain—self-hatred. She'd become detached and resentful of her body and the excruciating discomforts she endured. She had done her best to hide how she was different, because if she wanted a family of her own one day, then her future depended on how flawlessly she mastered her womanhood.

When she married, she'd despised the difficulty with which her body navigated the most basic of womanly roles: motherhood. It seemed her body had always been incapable of doing the things expected of it, and no amount of self-mastery had ever solved the failure of her biology.

So, yes, June had lamented and resented and *hated* her body. And that hatred had permeated her marriage, her parenting, her happiness.

But June's body hadn't been the villain—it was her self-reproach.

Now, in the light of Dr. Chen's words, her hatred softened into pity. And then that pity morphed into compassion. Because, even with great difficulty, her body had created the greatest love of June's life: Bella. Her body had shivered in the breeze off the ocean, been kissed by the warmth of the sun. It'd twirled to music and convulsed with laughter. It had loved and made love and tasted and sweated and smiled. Even through the pain, it had done so much for her over the years.

June had been cruel to many but never so cruel as she had been to herself.

The road to feeling better was long, complicated, and without a cure—but to know that it wasn't just in her head, that there was a *reason*, and to know that she was not *alone*, was the greatest gift June had ever been given. The second chance that all women, she now believed, deserved.

She wrapped her arm around Rosie, pulling her into a half hug. Rosie's arms folded around June, squeezing tightly. When they finished their embrace, June lifted her tearful gaze to Dr. Chen.

"Thank you," she said. "Thank you."

81

March 1967

As the sun rose over the eastern field behind Hurley Downs Racetrack, it zinged across the gentle slope, igniting the spring-green grasses. Mist rose from the valley, and the Susquehanna sang sweetly from inside the budding forest. A gentle, crisp morning breeze disturbed the fog that had collected overnight.

Winifred and Marie stood on the rise, looking out across the untouched land, the sagging barbed wire fences and overgrown slopes. Aside from the river and the trilling birds, the morning was quiet, peaceful.

It smelled like Marie remembered it, the bright tang of orchard grass mixed with forest decay and fertile loam. To Winifred, it smelled like possibilities.

They had pooled their money in an even split to buy the racetrack and surrounding land. Marie had become co-owner not to destroy this place but to make amends with it. Winifred had become co-owner because she'd had an idea.

Most of the abandoned buildings of Hurley Downs were still in good shape. There were long stables and high-ceilinged hay barns, old farmhouses and supply sheds. Winifred had come to Marie with her seedling of a proposition: transform the buildings into bunkhouses and studios, and host artist residencies on the property. It was a blend of

Winifred's foundation—a sound investment, she assured Marie—and Marie's talents in painting. Winifred could host parties and help artists make connections, and Marie could help them overcome their creative blocks and create collections worth selling.

It would take a while to get things up and running, they knew. Winifred was determined to convince Irene to move to Pennsylvania to act as head chef and eventually retire. Marie was determined to convince Lawrence to help them run the nonprofit once he finished his degree in economics at Howard. She still had yet to paint him, and she intended now to paint all the scenes and people in her life that made her blush with joy.

The possibilities of this place were still as fresh and new as the buds on the trees, the germinating wildflower seeds, the thawing ground. But though there was a long road ahead, it was Winifred and Marie's solidarity that gave them power and purpose.

On the night Winifred's house had burned down, her words to June had been true. It seemed that life was all about starting over. Just like the rise and fall of Hurley Downs, just like the drought and surge of the Susquehanna River, just like the changing of the seasons. Births and deaths, joys and sorrows. Blank canvases and canvases filled with color. Winifred and Marie couldn't control the summers and winters of their lives, but they could keep each other warm when the world was cold, and dance under the harvest moon when life was plentiful.

The important thing—the only thing—was that they enjoyed it all while it lasted.

Author's Note

Inspiration is hard to pinpoint.

It can come from music, books, films, experiences, emotions, observations, and so much more. One of the sparks of inspiration for this book came from Rebekah Harkness, brought to present-day fame by Taylor Swift's "The Last Great American Dynasty." I found myself enamored by the what-ifs written between the lines of the Harkness story. (To be honest: being enamored by what-ifs is what sparks *every* book I write—but I digress).

That said, I did not set out to tell a story *about* Harkness. I took inspiration from her house parties, the neighborhood disruption, and her charitable work—and then set out to write about someone new and unique, with her own set of quirks, problems, backstory, and opinions. (In early stages, I also sometimes thought of Winifred as a female Jay Gatsby, not obsessed with a romantic interest but the hope of friendship; in this sense, Winifred—like all fictional characters—is a patchwork of many converging ideas.)

Harkness is also how I landed on setting this story in Rhode Island. Countless authors, artists, and vacationers have long been captivated by the Rhode Island coastline, and I found myself quickly joining that list. Even with my fictional town of Wave Watch, I hope I did the area justice. I visited beaches from Watch Hill to Newport, spoke with locals, and peppered friends who grew up there with as many questions as I could. I also spent a crippling amount of time terrified that I'd get something wrong (let's be real: I'm still terrified), so apologies if any fictionalizations rang false or if you noticed something out of place. I tried my best. That's all any of us can do, right?

While huge house parties in the sixties couldn't be further from my introverted, millennial existence, Marie's backstory holds a lot more familiarity. My father grew up in rural Pennsylvania. His mother—my grandmother—was named Dorothy Hurley, and she was one of the kindest women I've ever known. While Hurley Downs plays a somewhat villainous role in Marie's story, the splendor of the horses, the fields, Dottie's warmth, and the general nostalgia of rural Pennsylvania are all for my grammy, whom I miss dearly.

Dottie's journey was another overlap with my life: when I was a child, a friend was hospitalized with *E. coli*. Thankfully, she pulled through—but I remember her illness as one of the first times I truly faced the delicacy of life.

June's endometriosis also hits close to home. I have numerous friends who are among the one in ten women of reproductive age (that's 190 million women worldwide, according to the World Health Organization) who suffer from this chronic, incurable condition. Additionally, I know what it's like for pain to interfere with daily life, to talk down to my body, and for my concerns to be dismissed by health professionals. I also know what it's like to find a doctor like Dr. Chen. Special thanks to *my* doctor for hearing me, helping me, and taking the time to answer all my questions about June's condition too.

Of course, endometriosis was barely a whisper in the medical field in the 1960s, but a select few were paving the way for better understanding. Nowadays, increased awareness and research into endometriosis are offering many more people clarity and help. For anyone experiencing pain like June's: I see you, and I'm cheering you on.

As I said: inspiration is hard to pinpoint. It's a series of flint strikes, sparks, candles, and gasoline. Sometimes I feel like a firefighter trying to contain it. Sometimes I feed it kindling. Much of the time—like Winifred, Marie, and June sitting in the grass—I simply stare up at it in awe.

Acknowledgments

With *Polite Calamities*, I wanted to write a story about female friendships in all their various shades of color. It seems only fitting to acknowledge some of the many women in my life who uplift my career as a writer.

To my editor, Alicia, and my agent, Michelle: your belief in me empowers me to write fearlessly. Thank you for trusting me and championing my books. Thanks, also, to Mary G., Rachel, and Alicia L. for the attention to detail during various stages of editing.

Sara, thank you for Del's Lemonade, stuffies, coffee milk, and many other Rhode Island details you brought to my attention! Marla, I'm still embarrassed that I forgot your name in *Halfway to You*, so I'm thanking you here for being the very best beta reader—and brunch maker.

Emily, thank you for all the cocktail dates and coffee coworks. I did a lot of editing with you sitting across from me, making me laugh between track changes. Thank you for being one of my biggest cheerleaders through all the ups and downs of my career. (I mean, if I *have* to have a meltdown in someone's back seat, I'm glad it's yours.) I can't wait for all our bookish adventures to come.

To Samantha at the Imprint Bookstore, thank you for sharing my books at launch events and on the shelves at your lovely store—but more than that, thank you for hugs, laughs, and swims.

Nhatt, whether we're bonding over creative ventures, grief, or vegan ice cream, I am so grateful to have you in my corner. Your encouragement and understanding have held me up on numerous occasions. Thank you for making me feel seen and heard.

Thank you to my reader, Michele, who won the naming contest for Dottie in my newsletter; suggesting my grandma Dorothy's name was the perfect sort of kismet!

Nani, your enthusiasm and support bring me so much joy. Thank you for cheering me on and sharing your love of fiction.

Sue, I couldn't've asked for a more loving and supportive mother-in-law. Thank you for championing my books far and wide.

To Goldie, my very best childhood friend: thank you for your toughness, your kindness, and for looking after me.

To Violet, my sweet pea, I thanked you in the dedication, so all I'll say here is: I miss you.

I wanted to focus on women in my acknowledgments this time around, but I'd be remiss if I didn't mention my dad and my husband. Dad: I'm so grateful we share a passion for writing; so much of my success I owe to you (and readers, check out his books! terrypersun.com). Joe: thank you for believing in me when my belief in myself flags. I'm so happy to spend all my big and small moments with you.

And finally: Mom. You're strong, you're compassionate, and you're incredibly generous. I'm lucky to be your daughter, and I'm grateful to be your friend.

Book Club Questions

1. One of the major themes in the book is belonging. What do you think the difference is between fitting in and true belonging?

2. Have you ever had a friend like Dottie? Have you ever had a friend like Rosie? Have you ever had a friend like Barbara?

3. Many of June's struggles are tied to her efforts to uphold societal expectations of womanhood. How have societal expectations related to your gender impacted you?

4. Winifred's father speaks to the importance of mutual respect in friendships. To you, what qualities or values make someone a good friend?

5. If you could paint one memory from your childhood, what would it be, and what colors would you use?

6. Who do you think gained the most from Winifred's parties—Winifred, Marie, or Irene, and why?

7. We never truly learn what June did with the gasoline. Do you think she actively started the fire? Or do you think she let fate decide?

8. What is the most fun party you ever attended? What made it so enjoyable? Was there a specific occasion or reason to celebrate?

9. What's your party style? Do you enjoy hosting, attending, sticking to the sidelines, or staying home?

About the Author

Photo © 2019 Pinto Portrait

Jennifer Gold writes discussable book club fiction about love, second chances, and self-discovery. She's the multiaward-winning author of *The Ingredients of Us, Keep Me Afloat,* and *Halfway to You.*

When she's not writing, Gold can be found traveling, enjoying the outdoors, or curled up with a book. She lives in the Pacific Northwest with her husband and two cats.

To hear first about Jenni's upcoming novels, receive bonus content and sneak peeks, and chat with her directly, join her monthly newsletter at jennifergoldauthor.com/newsletter. You can also connect with Jenni on Instagram: @jennifergoldauthor.